THE FIRST POLKA

Horst Bienek
The First Polka

Translated by Ralph R. Read

Fjord Press
San Francisco
1984

Title of German edition: *Die erste Polka*
Published by Carl Hanser Verlag, München
Copyright © 1975 Carl Hanser Verlag München Wien

Published and distributed by:
Fjord Press
P.O. Box 615
Corte Madera, California 94925

Editors: Steven T. Murray and Susan Doran
Book design & typography: Accent & Alphabet
Front cover design & illustration: Tom Cervenak
Back cover drawing: David Hockney; used with the kind permission of the artist

Library of Congress Cataloging in Publication Data

Bienek, Horst, 1930–
    The first polka.

    Revised translation of: Die erste Polka.
    I. Title.
PT2662.I39E713   1984   833´.914   84-1513
ISBN 0-940242-08-7
ISBN 0-940242-07-9 (pbk.)

Printed in the United States of America
Second printing, May 1984

Was, said the weeds,
Gone, said the sky,
Dead, said the woods . . .

Truman Capote

The characters and events in this book are fictitious
— or perhaps not.

I

VALESKA PIONTEK WOKE at the hour when morning light gently moves the curtains and sketches violet shadows on the windows. The floor was still a pallid, smoky white in which one would sink, but objects were already emerging from their shadows, coming closer and then withdrawing again as the light shifted until their contours grew more plastic and their corners and edges sharper; a little more light and the yellow roses would be cascading from the walls.

Valeska listened in the direction of the next room: silence, ticking in the walls.

The August sky had cast out the first doves; their shadows spun into the room and shattered the light. The beating of their wings brought Valeska memories of the evening before . . . but she would rather be reminded of the duties of the coming day, which were more important to her. There were so many she was bound to forget a few of them: the visit to Archpriest Pattas, the sale of the abandoned brickyard in Ziegeleistrasse, the transfer of title to the Dressler old people's quarters, the marriage of her daughter by the judge, invitations to be gotten out for the wedding reception at the Hotel Upper Silesia — so, for today at least, she had canceled all her piano lessons. Without saying an Our Father, she would hardly be armed for all that, and probably a couple of Hailmaryfullofgraces wouldn't hurt either. She looked over in the corner at the little domestic altar with the Black Madonna in the middle which she had gotten on her pilgrimage to Częstochowa, and her confidence in the new day began to grow. How would it be if she knelt down before the altar and with her lips touched the rosary she had bought in Albendorf and had had Cardinal Bertram bless in Breslau?

The silence ticked louder until it was broken by coughing in the next room.

Valeska sat up. She shook her head, and it was as if she were casting off the anxieties of the night and all her dreams and even the realities. Except for that one, there she didn't succeed: her husband in there, shut up in his room with his asthma and his coughing, with his sticks of incense whose smell penetrated all the doors, all the halls, all the rooms, the whole house—Leo Maria Piontek, the photographer, refusing to die. The coughing did not stop, and Valeska knew that she had to get up now. The curtains had been restored to their daytime green, the wallpaper displayed its faded roses, the floor became as black and steady as the floor of a solid, middle-class house in Silesia can be.

Valeska got up and went to the wardrobe. It was quite a distance away. A second bed had once stood in between, one meter wide and two meters long; it had been high, much higher than hers, at least at the pillow end. For even then he had loved to sleep with his head high; he could breathe more freely like that, he said, and dream better—but perhaps the pillows were only piled up high because he liked to look out over the world when he woke early in the morning, even if it was only the narrow, close world of the bedroom. For more than twenty years his bed had stood there, and for as long as she could remember his breath had been labored and loud. Later he began to gasp, then the coughing began, and then he spat blood. At that point, she had his bed moved into the next room, which had been empty since her father's death.

Rising early trapped her in an old habit. She took a long step, as if she needed to climb across his bed.

As she passed the house altar, she touched two fingers to the gilded frame of the picture of the Madonna and then brought them to her lips; then she made the sign of the cross from left to right and began to recite an Our Father silently. She had no time to kneel before the altar today; she would get through her quota while washing and dressing, praying on the side, as she called it.

Valeska went downstairs. In the stairwell it was still dark; the windows let no light in because blackout paper had been pasted over them. Josel had done that; he found it practical. During the day the windows could simply be left open, then it would be light.

And surely the blackout wouldn't last until winter anyway. Valeska opened a window to let in some light.

She washed herself at the basin. With both hands she splashed cold water over her face, over her flaccid breasts; she soaped the hair of her armpits. But she avoided looking in the mirror. This was easy enough, it had become a habit years ago. She coiled the braid which hung over her shoulder and down her back into a bun and fastened it with long black hairpins. Only now did she bend closer to the mirror and press a wave into her hair above both temples. Then she dipped the comb into the water and reshaped the waves. She simply let the soapy foam beneath her arms dry, so that she wouldn't sweat so easily.

Valeska wondered for a moment whether she shouldn't go to the hairdresser and have her braid cut off. Irma's wedding reception today would serve as the occasion. All her friends and acquaintances had permanent waves now, and she imagined that Leo Maria would like it if she surprised him one day with short hair, but naturally she hadn't spoken to him about it. She had been wanting to have the braid cut off for some time, but something always kept her from doing so. And besides, she really couldn't go around the corner to the hairdresser in Breslaustrasse. No, she would have to go to Hindenburg or Richtersdorf where no one knew her. Somehow it embarrassed her simply to say: Please cut off my braid and give me one of those permanent waves that are supposed to last so long; I've heard they last half a year, and even a whole year, if you have the right kind of hair. Rosa Willimczyk, who as a bookseller got around much more than she did, had told her that. Valeska was only partly aware that she constantly invented excuses for herself because she simply wasn't determined enough, and while pushing the bun of hair into place she thus put off the decision once again.

She had finished her prayers. To be sure, she had been thinking of things other than God, but she didn't notice this until the ritual closing tumbled over her lips. She resolved to repeat the prayers later, but it would be better done upstairs, kneeling before the altar.

It was quiet in the house: Leo Maria had stopped coughing. Valeska stood still on the stairs and listened. There were no sounds from the kitchen either, so today she must have risen before Halina. That didn't happen very often, and it reassured her. She decided to make breakfast herself.

She pushed the hangers in the wardrobe aside, and considered which dress to put on. It was Irma's wedding day, a festive day for Irma even if she were being married by a judge and not in church, and perhaps a half-festive day for her, too, now that she had reconciled herself to the marriage — though naturally not to Irma's adamant refusal to be married in church. She would never be able to reconcile herself to that, for marriage is a sacrament and can be administered only by the Church; it would be a sin to live with a man without being wedded before God, even today. Valeska was convinced of this, and she had by no means given up trying to convince Irma and Heiko of it too. She intended to concentrate more on Heiko, since Irma refused to discuss the matter and avoided her whenever she could. Valeska was sure she would be successful if she were equally adamant, and perhaps, although she didn't want to admit it to herself, the celebration she had prepared for the wedding couple in the ballroom of the largest hotel in town this evening would advance her plan a step. She had arranged for them to be married on Sunday by Archpriest Pattas just in case.

From the wardrobe Valeska took the clothes bag in which she stored her winter things and those she wore only rarely. She unfastened it at the side, and the pungent smell of mothballs went up her nose and made her cough. She tried to stop so as not to wake Leo Maria, who had perhaps fallen asleep again, but that only made it worse. Her head grew hot, and the fist she was holding in front of her mouth quivered. She finally took out a dress and swung it through the air a few times before the window. It was the dark blue Cossack dress, decorated with two hundred tiny black beads sewn on the bosom and shoulders, which she had bought for the wedding of her brother, Willi Wondraczek, but then had never worn, as the wedding had been canceled two days before the date. Today she would wear it for the first time, but she didn't know whether she should be glad. She held the dress up just to see herself in it quickly, but she had only a hand mirror in the room, and so tried to make do with a windowpane. She saw a black shadow and glitter, that was the beads: the black on black pleased her especially. Valeska hung the dress on the door handle in the hallway. The smell of mothballs emanating from it made her feel queasy. Later she would ask Halina to hang it out in the garden, so that it would be well aired by evening.

During the day she would wear the light brown dress with the dark brown braid and quilted cuffs, and liven it up with a white lace collar. She looked in the clothes chest, but couldn't find the right collar. She tried on others in front of the window; she dug out still others, and as she did so a little ship carved out of bark fell into her hands. She tried to remember where she had gotten it and how it had come to be in the clothes chest. The recollection came slowly and from the distant past, a tale that made her giggle and even blush as she continued to search through the dressers and to try on more and more collars in front of the windowpane. Then she reached quickly for the little ship and hid it way at the back of a drawer, beneath a pile of napkins and towels. Erich Stroheim had given her the ship, and it would remain their secret. She liked having secrets as much as wearing white collars, but she liked forgetting them just as much, and that's why the drawers and wardrobes, the chests and dressers were full of white collars and secrets: here a red ribbon, there the stump of a burnt-out pilgrim's candle, an old silver kopeck, an envelope with an Italian stamp on it, a dried adder's skin, an iridescent gold marble, a little carved boat. And when someone asked her about them (Leo Maria: This revolting *pierunnisch* adder, how long is it going to stay on the cabinet?), she would not reply, but instead would assume an ambiguous smile, remaining silent with gleaming eyes, her mouth half open and her arms hanging down as if the dreams and secrets themselves might leave her because they had been asked about too loudly. That was the signal for the others to abandon their curiosity.

Valeska had found a suitable collar, a white one of openwork lace embroidered also in white, which made it look especially simple and expensive. She went into the kitchen, put on an apron over her dress, ignited the gas, and put a kettle of water on the flame. She did this unthinkingly, quite mechanically, as if repeating an action she always performed, that of putting the kettle on and waiting for the water to sing.

There was a sound. Josel came down the stairs in his nightshirt, his motions slow, circular, and hesitant, as if he were moving through water. Valeska pressed him to her without speaking, and Josel endured this although he was already fifteen.

But today he didn't smell her hair. When he got up early in the morning, or when he went to bed late in the evening, he loved to take leave of Mamuscha when her hair was down. Then her long braid smelled of summer and of wilted lilies, or so it seemed to him, from the cologne she splashed on sometimes, and a faint odor of sweat was there as well, which he had discovered on himself, too, ever since the hair had begun to grow under his arms and around his *pullok*. He liked the smell, and caught himself wiping under his right arm with his left hand and then bringing the hand to his nose to take in the odor directly. He also rubbed his *pullok* and then sniffed at his fingers, and there was the sharp smell of urine too, which some days he detected on Mamuscha, but not very often.

Today she had already put up her hair. Rubbing the sleep and the light from his face with one hand, he said: "You're up early, Mamuscha!"

Valeska wanted to say something else, but then she saw that he was standing barefoot on the tile kitchen floor and said: "You've forgotten your slippers again!" She didn't care if the children ran around outside barefoot the whole summer long, but they could catch cold quickly on the tiles in the hall or the kitchen, although not now, in August. She immediately regretted her nagging and added: "Let's drink a cup of tea together, and then you go back to bed and sleep in for a while; after all, you don't have to go to school." Just to make sure, she tacked on: "Or do you?"

Josel shook his head. As long as the soldiers are here, there won't be any school. Sooner or later they'll have to leave, either back to where they came from or over into Poland. But he didn't say that, he just thought it: he didn't want to get involved in a discussion right now; it was too early for that. He might discuss things with a friend at this hour — with Andreas, for example, who was still sleeping — but never with his own mother.

Valeska found nothing odd about her son sitting on a stool in the kitchen this morning, watching her every move and saying nothing; she never found anything odd about people as long as they didn't announce out of the blue that they were going to get married and no one in the world could stop them, and that if anyone tried, even their own mother, they would leave home, enter the Labor Service, become an NS nurse, or join the Party. She thought she had already gotten around that, but she knew it wasn't so. She said, "What will this new day bring us?" The sigh that followed showed this was not a question but rather a declaration. And, turning to Josel, she said, "Have you thought of something for this evening? I mean for the cabaret part?" She poured the hot water into the teapot and watched the steam rise in thin white clouds. It reminded her of something, she would remember what in a minute.

"I don't know if I'll be there on time," Josel said. He drew up his knees and pulled his nightshirt down over them.

"Do you have to go to the HY even on the day your only sister gets married?" She didn't like it that he had been coming home so late in the evening recently and was always at the Hitler Youth. They would take her son away from her, just as they had already taken her daughter.

"Andreas'll be there," said Josel listlessly. The whole cabaret bored him except for Uncle Willi as Zarah Leander, but he had already seen that act a few times. "Andreas really gets excited about that kind of thing," he said. "Maybe he'll come up with something."

Valeska had left the organizing of the cabaret to her brother Willi; he was good at it. She wanted to contribute two *tableaux vivants* as a climax, as that was her specialty: *The Angelus* after Millet and *The Volga Boatmen* after Repin. Reproductions of both pictures had long been hanging in the music room. "I could use Andreas for the Volga boatmen," she said.

She stirred her tea with a long spoon, then let it steep. "Yes," she said, "please tell him to be here this afternoon, I'm rehearsing the Volga boatmen. Erich Pfeiffer and Willi Konsalek have to be replaced, they've already been called up."

Mama's *tableaux vivants* bored Josel. But they delighted her; she put them on every time any kind of family celebration was held, and they seemed actually to please people; they really clapped for them, like at a theatrical performance. To be sure, Josel suspected his mother of arranging the applause as well.

"Maybe I'll get today off," he said.

That meant he would probably have to close his shed. But after all, his sister Irma would only be getting married once, and he would have his fun too at the Hotel Upper Silesia. "Well," he said, "I could sing my favorite song, with Andreas and Ulla. You know the one: 'Airman, greet the sun for me.' Ulla could accompany us on the piano."

"But you'll have to rehearse it in advance," she said. In fact, the only part of the cabaret program that interested her was her *tableaux vivants*. "Are you always at the . . . HY in the evenings now?"

Josel thought it better to get a cup of tea now than to answer her. And he was already reaching for it.

"What time did you get home last night?" she asked. She pulled a chair out from the table.

"Not very late," Josel said. He sat down on the chair and pulled his leg up under him.

Valeska did remember that he had been there the night before at midnight, when everyone gathered in the music room to listen to the latest news broadcast, but when she had been looking for him only shortly before that he was nowhere to be found. For a fifteen-year-old that was pretty late. She didn't want to reproach him for it; the HY was to blame. If it went on this way much longer, though, she would have to pay a visit to the HY. The boy was already getting circles under his eyes.

"What they want," she said, sitting down herself, "is to make soldiers out of you children too."

Josel considered going back to bed now after all, or visiting his sick father, teacup in hand, sitting down on his bed and finishing his tea with him in silence, or talking with him again about the international soccer match at Pressburg last Sunday, which they had lost to Slovakia 2–0. He had told Mamuscha enough about the HY; that is, fibbed enough about it in the hope of having some peace from her questioning. She kept on asking the same questions; it was not so much curiosity as a demonstrative avowal of her sympathy.

"Are they already making you handle guns?" Valeska reached out for her cup. She put sugar in her tea and stirred it, then laid her spoon on the table with a clatter. She did this rather energetically on purpose, for she wanted answers to her questions.

"But I've already told you, Mama, that's not the way it is. As a matter of fact, they use us wherever they can; but naturally we don't have anything to do with weapons. We drill . . . drill with sort of medics' equipment, you know . . ."

That should satisfy her. Mamuscha was against the war, he had already worked that out, although he could not quite grasp why, now that it looked as if they were going to win the war; you're only against war, aren't you, if to all appearances you're going to lose one, that's obvious. And people like that are always for the Red Cross and medics and stuff like that, so let her go ahead and think that.

"You know," he said, "just air raid drills and first aid, that's all." After all, he couldn't tell her about the shed. He put two spoonfuls of sugar into his tea, stirred it, and blew over the rim of the cup.

"I would really be worried, Josel," Valeska said, in a really worried voice. You couldn't even run your own children's lives these days; those organizations and the Party were much more powerful. Today a child not yet twenty-one was marrying a soldier whom she had known for exactly one week, and the other child, aged fifteen, was possibly already learning how to shoot other people. Besides, the compromise worked out by the Church was deteriorating. Two hours of the Don Bosco League and two hours of the HY — after all, the Don Bosco League existed before the HY — that was what they had all agreed on originally. Any more than that, besides school, would have made too great demands on the children. But hardly had school closed when those in the organization increased the hours. Perhaps she should discuss this too with the Archpriest today; they could make the Don Bosco hours twice a week now, she would prefer that. Valeska looked at the begonia on the window ledge; its leaves hung down to the table, and the sunbeams were reflected in their rich, gleaming green. The last day of August promised to be hot.

Josel really would have liked to ask his mother a question, one that he'd long been wanting to ask her, but so far he'd been unable to muster the courage. Perhaps it would soon be too late to ask it, so he ought to begin now, as a matter of fact. Was what Ulla had told him true, that if you wanted to become a famous pianist, you had to go to the Church of the Cross in Warsaw to pray to the heart of Chopin and kiss the stone where it is buried? He framed the question in his mind, but couldn't get it out. Ulla might call him a traitor, Mama would make fun of him, and—what he feared more than anything else—she might begin giving him piano lessons again. So instead he asked something that didn't seem so fantastic:

"Is it true that you received instructions not to play Chopin in your lessons any more?"

Valeska was surprised. It seemed strange that Josel was interested. He could only have heard that from Ulla Ossadnik, who was just learning the second Scherzo in B flat minor, Op. 31, and nothing could make her give it up, not even an order from Beuthen, even if it came from the Reich Bureau of Music. She smiled, or perhaps it only looked as if she did because the sun was shining directly in her face.

"Well, a bulletin was sent to all piano teachers from the Bureau of Music. German piano teachers are supposed to concentrate more on the German keyboard heritage, as a German duty . . ."

Suddenly Valeska felt more strength to carry on, for this was something she liked to talk about: "You know, even today children still practice études by Mendelssohn, and for that they can take away your permission to teach in the Reich. As long as any pianist in Germany still plays Chopin in a German concert hall, I will teach my pupils Chopin, and that's that."

She would have liked to go upstairs right then and play the Scherzo. It was true, she hadn't played Chopin herself for a long time, but only because Ulla Ossadnik, that child, already played the Scherzo No. 2 so brilliantly that she felt like a bumbler by comparison.

Besides, the bulletin wasn't an official directive, and the name of Chopin had not been expressly mentioned. And anyway, no one was checking up on her. As for the Gmyrek child, whose father was in the Party, she would just take care in the future that the girl had no tales to tell at home.

"Is the tea all right?" Valeska asked.

"Yes, fine," said Josel politely. He knew his mother expected this answer from him, at least early in the morning. But a cup of cocoa would have been better.

Josel let her pour him a second cup. So what Ulla had told him ˙ was true. He was glad his mother hadn't let herself be intimidated by it. He followed the sunbeams as they moved through the room and flashed in Mamuscha's hair as she was putting back a hairpin. He had long since noticed that she no longer wore her wedding ring. He could think of no reason for this, except that her hands were more beautiful without rings. He probably couldn't ask her about that either. But he could ask her about something else, even if this was not the right time, for who knew when he would have his mother to himself again? When school started up again, and her piano lessons, then at best he only saw her alone on Sundays. So it was better to ask now. He ran his tongue along his upper teeth, his mouth already half open, which made it easier for him to ask: "Mama, don't you think Papusch is getting near the end?"

Valeska, who was just about to bend toward the begonia leaves, jerked back as if someone had hit her. What do you mean? What kind of a question is that? Such nonsense! What makes you think that? You don't say things like that! Who told you that? — she wanted to ask. But she could tell those were reactions rather than answers; at least not answers of the kind that her fifteen-year-old son Josef Leo demanded from her at six in the morning.

"I think the incense Uncle Willi got for him helps." She fell silent. She saw that this wasn't what he wanted to hear from her.

He moved his foot from beneath him because he was afraid it would fall asleep in that position.

She said: "You're right." She wanted her husband to die in this house, perhaps even in her arms — if he had to die. If there were a hospital anywhere that could make him well again, she would even carry him there on her back, but she no longer believed there was. He had already been in the hospital twice, and neither time had he returned home healthier — just lonelier.

She said: "The hospitals are overcrowded now with the soldiers. I did speak with the head doctor on the phone . . . I could do so again, if you think . . ." She was resigned. No ordinary doctor could help him now.

She had finished her tea. She didn't have the strength to pour herself more. Nor did she have the strength to answer any more questions from Josel. She no longer had any strength at all, because ever since Leo Maria had gone to bed and not gotten up again, he had managed in some strange way to suck the strength from her. All at once in the begonia leaves she saw not the green, but the network of brown veins.

Josel hadn't considered a hospital, although it would be reassuring for everyone to know his father was in one, where doctors or nurses would constantly be around him. On the other hand, what about him dead in a strange whitewashed room, in a hospital with long corridors, and behind all the doors patients who soon would die: he didn't want to imagine that either. It had also struck him that the fits of coughing had increased during the past few days, and that his father, when he visited him, lay exhausted on the pillows and spoke very little; sometimes his voice was so faint between his loud, rattling breaths that you had to bend down to understand him.

Some undissolved sugar remained at the bottom of his cup, and he scraped it out. The sounds reminded him of other things. He would have liked Mamuscha to do something or other, too, to make some sound so he could tell that she was still there and alive.

She tore off two begonia leaves that were withered. Josel was right. She was upset about the fits of coughing, which had grown worse, and what worried her most was that Leo Maria was now spitting blood again, though she had concealed her anxiety from him. She hoped that in time the new medication would relieve the coughing spasms. She had already thought of sending for the doctor, but Leo Maria wouldn't hear of it, and so she didn't dare; for every time she sent for a doctor against his will, his coughing fits started up and he accused her of expecting him to die . . . She was afraid of scenes like that. But she would send the doctor a sample of what he was coughing up; yes, she could do that.

The events of the last few days, which had excited him and left him susceptible, must be to blame. Not Irma's marriage, though, which seemed hardly to interest him; he had even declined to urge Irma to have a church wedding, although Valeska, in tears, had begged him to; it was the political events. She didn't know what to do now. Leo Maria lay upstairs coughing, and the two of them were sitting here at the table thinking of nothing — yes, nothing — but his death.

She crumbled the withered leaves with her fingers and smelled them. They smelled of cardamom and the briefness of life.

She had nothing left to hold on to. By his way of sitting, of stretching his legs and drawing them up, by the way he scraped the sugar out of his cup and asked questions, Josel had taken the ground from under her feet.

Josel, by comparison, had a few consolations: Andreas, for example, with whom he was going to ride through town on his bike later, and Ulla Ossadnik, who was going to dress up like Martha Eggerth for the wedding tonight; he had the smoky potato fires, he had the harvest time which would begin again soon, when they hurled glowing coals into the night in punctured tin cans; above all he had his shed on the Wild Klodnitz, which kept him so busy that he could forget everything else. He pressed his cheek with a finger; he was ashamed deep down inside, none-theless, of all he had already forgotten about because of that.

Josel slid down from his stool. By now he had decided not to go to his shed that evening; his mother was capable of asking ques-tions until she found out that he had only been twice this week to the HY, and both times in the afternoon. That would only cause trouble. For him it meant losing five to ten marks, but that was the price he had to pay. Maybe by evening he could talk Andreas into taking turns with him on the lookout; then their absence would not be so noticeable. They'd work that out together. Until now, he hadn't found the courage to talk to him about the shed, but he felt he had grown a lot closer to Andreas in the few hours that he had been here.

"I'm not going to the HY today."

Valeska took note, but more or less as if she had expected this. Just as it was characteristic of her to resist new things initially, so, if they became facts, they also became matter-of-fact for her. "More tea?" she asked. She reached for the teapot and was glad to have something solid to hold in her hand.

Josel didn't want any more tea. He preferred hot chocolate anyway. To Mama tea was a treat she allowed herself only on special occasions, a kind of luxury, almost like champagne. Josel thought maybe you had to be completely grown up to get used to the taste; for the time being, at any rate, he had to have two spoonfuls of sugar to make the tea taste good.

Josel wanted to go upstairs to see whether Andreas was awake yet. Later he would show him the town on his bike. They'd be back by three o'clock; maybe then they could help with the wedding preparations.

Valeska was amazed by the lightness with which the boy moved as he left. How beautiful and harmonious his movements were, like a dancer's, she thought, or was it because he moved through stripes of light and shadow on his way to the stairs, and she had never seen him like this before? Spots of yellow light danced on the table; Valeska rubbed them slowly with her fingers and a gentle feeling of happiness came over her, because the wood was real wood and grew hot under her fingers.

2

Josel STOOD STILL on the stairs; a strange sound had caused him to stop, and to him strange sounds were like intruders. He listened. He knew all the sounds in this house. Every new sound that arose was first registered by him, located and identified before it was added to the familiar sounds in his subconscious. Too many new sounds at once could thoroughly confuse him, like recently when the soldiers came to the house to be quartered, and it had taken him a few hours to learn to tell them apart by the sounds they made. When he thought of the Sergeant the first things that occurred to him were his sounds (which he made while walking, eating, driving a car); he could have described them more precisely than the features of his face. The noise just now had sounded like someone pulling the cork out of an empty bottle, only much louder. Josel waited for the sound to be repeated, but it wasn't. There weren't many sounds in the house at this time, but plenty of new habits. Last night, when he was in the bathroom, he had seen Heiko coming out of Irma's room, and he wouldn't be surprised if behind one of the brown doors someone was opening a bottle of schnapps at this very moment. Josel continued up the stairs even more softly than before.

He hardly noticed the sound of suppressed coughing, for that was one of the most familiar sounds. But a faint metallic clink accompanied it, and as the door was open a crack, Josel slipped in, into the room of his sick father. His father was lying there propped up in bed; his right arm hung down, and with one finger he was stirring in the wash basin, which he had drawn toward him on a footstool. Whenever his ring finger bumped the side of the basin it produced a metallic sound.

When he saw Josel, he gestured him forward with his eyes; the gray skin of his face gleamed. Perhaps a smile had even appeared between his cheeks and his nose.

In the wash basin floated colorful Japanese paper flowers — a yellow narcissus, a violet lily, a silver rose, and a few other exotic-looking flowers that Josel had never seen before. He knelt down, and before his eyes the flowers described their circles, and their colors blended together and merged. Leo Maria took a small white paper ball from a drawer and handed it to Josel, who waited a bit until the water was calm and the flowers had stopped moving; then he tossed it into the right-hand side of the basin. Leo Maria tossed a ball in too, to the left.

They both looked away; you had to count to twenty-five and then look down: by then the flowers had blossomed! To watch how the paper softened and the petals unfolded and extended would rob the secret of its magic, and bring bad luck. Everyone knew the rules, for the paper flowers from Japan had been a fad for some time, and it was not just children who were charmed by the wildly colored, fantastic flowers that grew in seconds from homely white clumps of paper. Some grownups could predict the future from them.

They both turned their heads now and looked into the wash basin.

"*Paddum*," said Leo Maria.

"*Fantastichnek*," said Josel.

To the left floated a bright pink orchid twining upward, artfully folded in upon itself; to the right, on Josel's side, a simple blue star flower which hadn't fully opened: he helped it along with a light snap of the finger. The blue star jiggled on the water.

"Water Milka brought them," said Leo Maria.

"You can buy them everywhere now," said Josel. "A whole bag of them costs ten pfennigs. But Ulla Ossadnik says you shouldn't buy them, you should only get them as a gift, then they bring good luck. Or you can trade old rags or bones for them at Podmanitzki the rag-picker's."

His father lifted the pale pink orchid and the blue star out of the water and placed them on the nightstand. "Put the others away," he said to his son. "When Mamuscha comes, she might laugh at us."

Josel fished the others out and placed them on the windowsill.

He was happy that they had a secret from the women, even if it was such a silly one, for they hadn't had many secrets together for some time now. And father and son should always have a few secrets in common. His friends did. At least that's the way they talked. For example, he would have liked to tell his father the secret of the construction shed on the Wild Klodnitz, and three or four years ago he would have done so without a second thought. But now he didn't dare, for secrets grow with age, and this one was already too powerful for a man who no longer left his room. Secrets were not for lonely people. You could carry them around alone for a while, but not for too long . . . That was his opinion, at any rate. And so he hoped he could entrust the secret of the shed to the newly arrived Andreas.

He said: "Mamuscha is in the kitchen already, she's so excited she can't sleep."

"Yes, all this about Irma's wedding happened too fast for her. But you know, I couldn't do anything, your sister Irma is old enough." He pursued a thought: "I think Mamuscha prayed that *wojna* would prevent it all, but the war has been slow in coming."

"Mamuscha worries about too many things at once," Josel said. "She always wants to do everything herself." That was a hidden reproach for involving him too little in the wedding preparations. He moved around the bed and sat down on the edge. Now he was closer to the paper flowers. To his blue star, too. What did a blue star signify? He would give Ulla a paper flower today and wait until it blossomed in the water.

"Tonight when you come back from the reception, things will look better for Mamuscha. But right now nothing can help her. And tomorrow you'll come and tell me about the reception, right?" Leo Maria settled back deeper into the pillows.

Josel thought: I wonder whether my flower and Ulla's will go together.

His father slipped even deeper into the pillows. He was breathing heavily and with a soft whistle, as if he had overstrained himself. But that was the way he'd been breathing for a long time. And Josel asked himself secretly how long that could go on.

Josel visited his sick father once every day—at least once a day.

Usually more often. He tried to manage it in the morning or when he came home from school, sometimes even before he left for school. Or in the early evening, before darkness transformed his father's room, making it seem a bit creepy, even during the day sometimes when Mama lit the incense, and the green smoke formed faces and masks if you stared at it long enough. He loved his father best in the light; sometimes when he came into the sickroom, he set the casement window so that the pane reflected the sunlight onto him and made his gray scaly skin gleam like silver. A black silhouette against a white background: that's the way he liked to remember him from the times when he had been permitted to go photographing with him, outside by the towers, when his father, buttoned up in his Sunday suit, measured distances with long expansive movements of his arm, set up and took down his equipment, constantly searching out new angles, and Josel would patiently bring him this or that: the tripod, a plate, a piece of wood, sometimes just his joy at being allowed to be there.

Josel had also loved these outings with his father because they took him farther away from this house, which he had hated for some time because of its sounds, most of all the jangling of the piano that pursued you everywhere, even into your sleep. Neither he nor his sister Irma had inherited any of their mother's talent, but Mamuscha began their piano exercises early, before either of them could copy or read a note. After Irma had rejected the torture of the lessons (and thus her mother) by holding her hands in scalding water and then going around the house almost triumphantly for weeks with thick white bandages on her hands, the mother had set her hopes on Josel, and had once slammed the piano lid on his hands in anger and, weeping, claimed that it had accidentally fallen shut. He had not touched a piano key since then. And it was Ulla Ossadnik who first managed to impart to him a new, reluctant pleasure in piano music. She could play the record of the four Chopin Nocturnes a dozen times in a row on her phonograph without saying a word, listening with closed eyes and whispering the name "Gieseking" like that of Saint Anne.

At that time he was often with his father in his *kabinetchik,* as he called it — Mamuscha called it "Papusch's atelier" — helping with simple tasks. He liked best to squat next to the rectangular tray and swish the white paper in a clear, transparent liquid which his father had mixed earlier from water and various chemicals. He watched the white surfaces in suspense to see how, without anyone doing anything, the first gray contours appeared, then dark points, shadows, and surfaces, which gradually merged to form faces, uniforms, trees, hats, towers, and walls. It had been the only time in his life that he had had no secrets from one person, and that was his father.

But his father had not wanted to reveal *his* secret, the one big secret: why one day, not so long ago, he had gone to bed, his breath whistling, the towels wet from his coughing. He would not ask him about it, either. But ever since, something had been destroyed between them, and Josel now approached his father as other children do their stern fathers, softly, shyly, with reverence.

"Maybe we should put you in your wheelchair," Josel said softly, "and take you to the Hotel Upper Silesia for two or three hours—at least for the cabaret program, with Uncle Willi as Zarah Leander." Josel would have loved to burst out laughing, if it hadn't been so early. He could tell it was by the light coming, bright and obtrusive, through the window. He felt it in the sounds.

Leo Maria shook his head. "I've already told Maminka, it would kill me. No, no, just leave me here alone. Enjoy yourselves and don't worry about your sick father, no, no." He slipped even deeper into his bed and pulled the covers higher; only his face jutted white from the white pillows. It was as if he wanted to hide.

"All right, Papusch," Josel said, somewhat startled. He was afraid his father might withdraw so far that he couldn't be brought back. So he brought him back right away. Josel said, "They only lost at Pressburg because they didn't send in Schaletzki."

Under the covers Leo Maria wriggled closer. "Yes, it was Schaletzki who in the earlier international match—that was at Reval, wasn't it?—who kicked the winning goal against Estonia."

Schaletzki was Father's favorite. Josel was more a fan of Schön, the tall goal kicker. He had saved cards from R6 cigarettes and had the one with Schön's picture tacked on the wall of his room. But that was a while ago. He felt too grown up for that now.

Papusch, ever since he had become interested in soccer, under-lined with an indelible pencil the names of the players from Upper Silesia in the newspaper reports of the international games played by the German national team. When he came to Schaletzki he moistened the pencil on his lips so often that his mouth turned purple, and Mamuscha was afraid that he would poison himself one day with the lead. If he had had his way he would have had a national team composed of Schaletzki and Tibulski, Kuzorra and Bialas, Kaburek and Dzur, Durek and Zolanowski, Kobierski and Willimowski, with Lachmann, who had the sporting goods store in Bahnhofstrasse, as the goalie. Leo Maria had never been to a soccer match, not even to a local game. He hadn't begun to get interested in soccer until he was bedridden and started to read what the newspapers had to say.

"Will you give me another paper flower?" asked Josel so softly that his father, without even interrupting his train of thought, absentmindedly reached into the drawer and took out a little white paper ball and pressed it into Josel's hand.

"I tell you," he said to Josel, "if they don't use Schaletzki in the next match against Budapest, they'll lose that one too." He said it as if he already knew that they wouldn't use Schaletzki again.

Outside two birds flew past the window so close that Josel thought he could hear the sound of their outstretched, flapping wings. Yesterday evening the starlings had flown so low around the house, they had almost brushed against the old County Magis-trate who was sitting hidden at the back of the garden. Mamuscha had seen him from another window. "The weather's going to turn soon," she had said. Perhaps she had just wanted to say something out of embarrassment, because she felt herself being watched by Josel, just as she was watching the County Magistrate. Yet the County Magistrate had only been sitting on a little bench among the bushes, with newspapers under his arm, waiting for the night to fall. Nothing else.

From the hall came the sounds of the living. Josel got up. "You know that Andreas would really like to come to see you sometime too. When can I bring him up here?"

Leo Maria trailed the washcloth through the water. "After the wedding, that would be better. Today so many people are going to come." He slapped the wet cloth on his face as if the cold water soothed him. Maybe it was the sound as well.

"Yes, tomorrow morning," he said. "You are taking Andreas along to the wedding, aren't you?"

"Of course," said Josel. He still hadn't seen much of his cousin Andreas, but that he should be one of the wedding guests was natural. "Tomorrow morning, then," Josel repeated.

He measured his steps slowly. He left the tomb slowly. "I'll tell you later about the wedding, Papusch." He was glad he could say that.

3

By decree of *Mościci, the President of the Polish State, from 1 July 1930 the Sejm was dissolved and that of Silesia adjourned indefinitely. (The latter was dissolved on 26 September.) New elections were scheduled. On 10 September 1930, practically all the parliamentary leaders of the opposition parties, 88 in number, were arrested en masse. Among them was Wojciech Korfanty, head of the Christian Democratic Party.* (According to another source it was on 26 September; he would have to verify that. He put a question mark in red ink in the margin.) *Commissar Ryczkowski, chief of public security in Kattowitz, arrested him at about eight o'clock in the morning in his villa in Kattowitz. Accompanied by the military policeman Chomerański, they drove in a closed automobile through Kattowitz, Bogutschütz, Rozdzien, Sosnowitz (all scenes of his past triumphs) to the fortress of Brest-Litovsk.*

There he was brought before the commanding officer, Colonel Kostek-Biernacki. The interrogation was limited to personal data. All valuables, including his suspenders and shoelaces, were taken from him. He was given a tin dish and was locked in a private cell. Thus Poland treated its "second greatest son," thus it thanked him for the acquisition of Upper Silesia! But more was to follow . . .

During the exercise period he found good company in Brest. Former President Witos was there, in whose cabinet he had served as vice president; the deputy Adam Pragier, who had sat on the tribunal in the Korfanty case; the most famous lawyer in Warsaw, the Socialist Dr. Libermann; Professor Baricki, vice president of the PPG; former Minister of the Interior Kiernik; Aleksander Dąbski of the right-wing opposition; and others as well.

Only now did Korfanty learn how well he had been treated in transit. Not a single time had he been torn from the car, not a single time beaten with rifle butts or pistol-whipped, whereas Dr. Libermann, for example, had come away with twenty bleeding wounds on his head and his entire body, as was later ascertained by the Sejm's Judicial Committee. (He had a newspaper article on that which he would look up.) *In the fortress itself Korfanty fared no better than the rest. Like the others, he had to scrub the casemates and clean the officers' latrines.*

Poland was not wholly ungrateful to Korfanty. He was still treated better than many of his fellow sufferers; to be sure, they did beat him, but not till he was half dead like the deputy Popiel, and they did not subject him to a mock execution, as they did Libermann and Popiel. On the infamous night of the mock executions, 10 November 1930, he was led down to the windowless cells, where he was forced to strip and was horribly beaten by the guards.

Montag pondered the last sentence and could find no continuation for it. He crossed out the last half of the sentence and wrote instead, . . . *he is said to have been taken to the windowless cells and there beaten.* He had no proof of it except for the statement of an eyewitness, a co-worker on *Polonia* who wished to remain anonymous. And the *Polonia* people were too partisan for him. *The majority of his companions in adversity were accused of conspiring to overthrow the government by violent means and convicted. Korfanty was freed after a petition for his release sponsored by the Christian Democrats was passed as the first order of business by the new Silesian Sejm. The German Party too had voted in his favor.* (He couldn't resist adding three exclamation points here.)

He thought it over and then struck out *his fellow sufferers* and wrote above it: *the arrested members of the opposition.*

He wasn't quite sure, but somehow he felt that his sentences were acquiring a more and more sentimental tone, ever since he had begun to concern himself in this chapter with K's persecution, his arrest, and his humiliation. He decided to go through it again and compare this part with the beginning. So much time had passed since he wrote that, and especially in the last few months his views had not changed altogether, but had shifted a bit; only a few days ago he had begun to consider reworking the entire chapter on the plebiscite struggles, and maybe even rewriting it. He should have quoted more Polish accounts here instead of relying mainly on German records and testimony.

He was still holding his pen above the paper when he noticed that the ink had long since dried. He put down his pen and screwed the cap onto the ink bottle; that was enough for today. He leaned back in his chair. It had been affecting him this way for some time; the further and deeper he drifted into Wojciech K's biography, the more it confused him. K's scintillating personality certainly had something to do with it, as did the (sometimes surprising) shifts in his political position—but he himself lacked the resoluteness with which he had judged and analyzed K's actions in the beginning. And again he was filled with doubts, as so often in the past weeks and months, as to why he had undertaken this project at all. He could probably not have given a reason, even to himself, for becoming involved three or four years before with the figure of Wojciech K, but he had been making notes about him, sketches, drafts, for quite a while before he had begun to write up this data. He had met K only once, and that was almost thirty years ago, and during the time of the plebiscite when his name became a household word, a hated or idolized symbol, a legend, K had not even been in Upper Silesia. For a long time his opinion of K was not much different from that of most people in this region, to whom he was something like the devil incarnate, a *djobok*. They sang derisive verses about him, reviled him, and held him up as a bogeyman to frighten the children on long winter evenings. ("You'd better say another Our Father, or Korfanty will get you!") Sometimes after three or four glasses of homemade schnapps they even ridiculed him. At any rate, no one spoke dispassionately about him. Women crossed themselves when they heard his name, and if they had to utter it, crossed themselves thrice, and the men spat on the ground.

His specific interest in the personality of K was first aroused when he started to read vigorous attacks on him in the Polish newspapers, when he was arrested and finally driven into exile— the man who, after he had acquired the eastern portion of Upper Silesia for Poland, had been celebrated in the Polish press as "Poland's second greatest son," right after Pilsudski, and compared to George Washington, the father of the North American republic. (He had those quotations.) At that time he began to

collect material about him, not systematically but at random, as
things turned up: reports from German newspapers, from Polish
ones, which he cut out and saved, pamphlets, handouts, manifes-
tos from the time of the plebiscite. He subscribed to *Polonia*,
found back issues in a secondhand bookshop in Kattowitz, and in
the municipal library he read newspapers and magazines in which
K had been published before the World War. He had also spoken
with a few people in Polish Upper Silesia who had seen and
known K, and with K's last secretary during his Kattowitz period,
but they all reacted so suspiciously to his questions that he gave
up. In German Upper Silesia he had not even dared to ask. He did
not want anyone to find out about his interest, about his work,
and apart from Valeska Piontek he had told no one.

Initially he had intended nothing more than to describe K from
a German viewpoint, after all the Polish attempts to praise, celebrate, or damn him; to grant him objectivity, or perhaps even
justice. He had cleared the kitchen table and made a desk of it,
bought paper and a box of dip pens, as well as red, green, and
black ink which he planned to use to differentiate between text,
quotations, and notes. And now from this mass of material ("a
slag heap of opinions, defamations, deifications, or falsified,
twisted, perverted history") he was attempting to distill the facts:
birth, childhood, school, university, manhood.

He began with simple sentences: *Adalbert (Wojciech) Korfanty
was born in Zawadze (meaning "barrier"), a suburb of Laurahütte,
which lies close to the Russian border, on 20 April 1873, the son of a
cottager and miner. He came from a family of German sympathizers.
His father's brother, from Przelaika, always wore the medals he had
won in the Prussian wars when he went to church or to a court of
law. Until the age of fourteen, he attended the grammar school in
Laurahütte.*

He had opened to the first page and was reading the beginning.
He no longer liked it. He knew other sentences were needed to
make K's childhood clear.

*The Catholic Church always has a sharp eye for bright boys from the
lower classes; thus Korfanty, clever and quick as he was, attracted the
attention of a curate in Laurahütte, who gave him private tutoring,*

and on Easter of 1888 he was admitted to the municipal secondary school in Kattowitz. The elder Korfanty was unable to pay for lodgings in Kattowitz, and so the boy had to make the two-hour trek between Kattowitz and Zawadze twice on schooldays. It was not a pretty path, as in some parts of Germany, winding through picturesque woods and across meadows. Korfanty's way to school led across a bleak marshland, past the chimneys of Laurahütte and the Hohenlohe works on an open road which afforded no protection from the raw Russian winds of winter or the hot sun of summer. The dreariness of such a journey would have caused many children to leave school. Korfanty stuck it out, already showing in this the perseverance and will power that led to his later successes.

All at once such sentences seemed to him too simple, too straightforward; they remained superficial. Would he write today a sentence like this one: *His family were German sympathizers?* He had read in Skowroński what an important part Piotr Skarga's book, *Żywoty Świętych (Lives of the Saints)*, had played in young K's education, and how his mother taught him to read Polish from it. And hadn't he written in 1931, in his *Appeal to the People of Upper Silesia,* that he, who had attended only German schools, owed the awakening of his Polish nationalism to his Hakatist* high school teachers who scorned anything Polish?

Montag closed the folder. An explosion of sentences lay concealed behind this one sentence.

Perhaps he should have treated this in a more narrative vein. Now every sentence was an assertion, sharp and pointed as a knife. Atmosphere would make his sentences more amenable. He took a book from the shelf, opened it and leafed through; his eye was caught by a passage:

In the summer the boy had walked to school barefoot, in the winter he wore a pair of old shoes full of holes, and the cold snow packed in against his feet. How hard it was for the boy to get an education. Later it would be worthwile, but who could know that? Spring came, the snow dripped busily from the

* From HKT, initials of the founders of the Eastern Border Union, Hansemann, Kennemann, Tiedemann; thus "Hakatist" is a Polish term of abuse.

roofs, and the sparrows twittered and tumbled about in the wet; I was sitting on the doorstep rubbing the sleep out of my eyes; it felt so good in the warm sunshine. Just then Father came out of the house; he had been tinkering around in the mill since daybreak and, with his nightcap sitting crookedly on his head, he said to me: "You good-for-nothing! There you are, basking in the sun, stretching and loafing until you're tired, letting me do all the work myself. I can't feed you here any longer. Spring is on its way, go out into the world and earn your own living."

"Well," I said, "if I'm a good-for-nothing, that's fine with me, I'll go out into the world and seek my fortune." And it really was fine with me, for it had already occurred to me to do some traveling, since I heard the yellowhammer—which always sang sadly at our window in autumn and winter: Farmer hire me, farmer hire me!—now in the beautiful springtime proudly and merrily calling from a tree: Farmer, keep your work!

So I went back into the house and took down my fiddle, which I could play well, from the wall. My father gave me a few coins for the road, and I sauntered on out of the village. I felt a secret joy as I saw all my old friends and acquaintances going off to work, as they had done yesterday and the day before and would do forever, to dig and plow, while I strolled out into freedom. Proud and content, I called out my farewell to the poor souls on all sides, but none of them seemed to take much heed. To me it was like an eternal Sunday in my soul.

Montag clapped the book shut. That hadn't helped either, that was a world an Eichendorff had dreamed up, a world that had never existed in the industrial region of Upper Silesia, on the right bank of the Oder. Nobody there went out into the world with a fiddle; you were driven out, a burlap sack with a few belongings in it over your shoulder, maybe to the Ruhr or the Saar because here there were too many mouths to feed. These were rougher times.

It was not supposed to be a biography either; that was much too grand a label for this attempt, for these fragments, for nothing more than a few insights into a person who all at once had come to fascinate him; after all, he was no historian. Rather, he wanted to follow the trail that history had left, which both sides were trying to erase, and he had to begin it now, for later on he would be given only official, sanctioned, orthodox views. Weren't historians people who only became interested in a person after he was dead, preferably for quite some time, maybe ten, fifty, a hundred years?

Montag stretched his back, looking at the white wooden ceiling from which a tattered dusty cobweb hung; it moved gently, sending him secret signals.

He stood up from the table where he had been sitting now for almost seven hours, except for the usual interruptions when he went into the pantry to spread himself a slice of bread and drippings, to the bathroom to piss, or when he sat down on the sofa, put on the headphones and tuned the crystal set to the news from Breslau, from Kattowitz, from Paris. He stood up and wiped his eyes and his glasses. He was never sure what made his eyesight hazy and uncertain, even in the daytime—was it his eyes or the fogged lenses? He switched off the desk lamp, went to the window, and pulled back the edge of the curtain a little, just a crack: a customary, almost rehearsed gesture. Now he could look out without being seen.

The light struck him and drew a bright stripe across his face. He had arranged the curtains in this way—it had been some time ago—after the teacher, Skowronnek, had spoken to him in the street one day: "Ah, I see your light burning late at night, at midnight or one o'clock when I'm coming home from Party meetings." (He did not suspect that Montag read or wrote by the desk lamp, usually until three or four o'clock, sometimes even until five.) "What are you up to?"

And he had answered without hesitating, for he had devised a response to such a question: "When my heart's giving me trouble" (although he had all sorts of ailments, there was nothing wrong with his heart) "I always leave a light on." And then he had added: "Sometimes I also write letters, to my daughter; she lives abroad."

But immediately afterwards he had the old curtains removed

and replaced by new ones made of heavy green velvet, so that no light could escape to the outside. He would much rather have installed shades that pulled down.

He looked out now upon light and shadow that were about to part company and become distinct, spreading themselves over specific objects. The Piontek's house was still a foggy gray, but it was slowly regaining that full yellow which set it off from all the other houses on the street. The path leading to it was still a murky, smoky gray-black. He was glad he did not have to walk it now; the path needed more light to become a reality, and his face, reflected in the windowpane as a gray oval, needed more light for him to be able to recognize himself. Perhaps.

The birds that had perched in the black trees for the night spread their wings and flew up, slowly at first, then fluttering faster and faster, drawing black dashes in the sky. They were screeching in a frightful way, as if they were dying or being born, but it was only the beginning of a new day. They turned a light pink and then as gray as the sky, and when they were far overhead, a shimmering, shining white swallowed them up. At this hour the first miners were on their way to the early shift.

Georg Montag closed the curtains again, absentmindedly undressed down to his undershirt and drawers, and went back into the kitchen, where he turned on the water, filled his cupped hand and drank from it. He urinated into the sink, as he always did before going to bed.

He had grown accustomed to working late at night, perhaps because there were too many sounds around him in the day, perhaps also—and this he never would have admitted to himself— because he was working on a manuscript which in these times seemed to belong more to the night than to the day.

Now he drew the blanket up to his chin, that made him feel secure; he rested his head high on the pillows, to retain his clarity; he laid his arms on top of the covers and interlaced his fingers, he had seen that done somewhere. Georg Montag stared into the darkness and at islands of vibrating light; he was preparing to fall asleep and go a little farther down the path that everyone must travel.

He pondered why he pored over old newspaper clippings, yellowed handbills, over tattered pamphlets which he translated laboriously from the Polish (for his proficiency in Polish was not great), why he ordered books from the libraries and copied out page after page of quotations by hand, why he sent out letters with questions and counter-questions, with corrections and confirmations. Perhaps he did all this in order to sit there, to read and write, to experience another life, to share in another person's existence, at least fragmentarily.

No matter how many topics to be dealt with had accumulated at the beginning, all at once that was no longer important, not now, he had forgotten them, repressed them, and constantly thought up new topics. But in the end only his own person remained, sitting at the table with his hands in the cone of light beneath the lamp, in front of them a sheet of paper, a pen, a few pages of scribbled notes.

And the other time. His own time.

4

THE IMAGES HOPPED about in Andreas's head, and it was some time before they merged into another, larger image, and he comprehended where he was. Above him hung a white bell-shaped lamp, which began to move to the right and to the left in the dim light, and he waited for the first peal of the bell. The white eiderdown towered up massively in front of him, and when he pressed it down with both hands, it puffed itself up again — he couldn't see over it. Somewhere beyond it someone else must be sleeping. Josel, his cousin Josel, in another bed — he listened, and the calm, deep breathing in the bare and still strange room told him that Josel was still asleep.

They had gone to bed late, long after midnight. Josel had been gone the entire evening and didn't return home until the late news broadcast in the music room, where, as Andreas learned, they had all been assembling at midnight for the past few days to discuss the political situation. This was the first time he had joined them. He sat down next to Valeska and listened to the voice coming from the brown box, talking a lot about border provocations but not about war, which, he knew, was the word they were waiting for. And afterward they had all talked at once, again about nothing except the war, which was coming or was not coming. He had listened to them without daring to ask questions, although there was much he didn't understand, for they used words that were unfamiliar to him, for example — it now occurred to him — the word *wojna*. Later, when they are all awake, I'll ask Josel or Aunt Valeska about it, Andreas thought.

The talk about war seemed different to him here than it had back home. When he left Breslau, the mobilization had indeed been under way, and at the stations and in the trains he had encountered more and more soldiers, but he had felt, first of all, that it was the grownups' business, and second, that it was far, far away. But here it was quite close. "It could break out at any time," Aunt Valeska had said, "we're only six kilometers from the border." These sentences burrowed into his memory, and the longer he stared at the white lamp, the more clearly and coherently the images of the preceding day came together. It had ended with Josel singing a song that must have had something or other to do with what they had been talking about before. He could recall no more than the first line, which Josel had repeated a few times: *Korfanty came a-riding upon a billy goat.* The others had fallen silent and listened, probably out of embarrassment, then suddenly they grumbled and hissed until finally Aunt Valeska came and hurried the two boys out of the room and off to bed.

Andreas heard a coughing that seemed to come from all the walls at once.

His father had taken him to the station in Breslau, and while they were waiting for the train to depart, Andreas had talked constantly about school, about the new gymnasium, about the air-raid drills—only to keep from talking about leaving. Into the tiny pauses Andreas left him, his father fitted sentences about the fine traits of his Aunt Valeska in Gleiwitz, and Andreas, who had last seen her five years before at the funeral of his mother, her sister, in Breslau and could no longer remember what she looked like, could have repeated the laudatory but unchanging sentences, like a poem learned by heart, long after the train had left the station. But then he had started to cry after all, and he was glad his father could no longer see him. He knew his father would send for him as soon as he had found a place for them to live in the new town, Lebenstedt, which was still so small it was not even shown on most maps—they had looked it up in his Diercke atlas: it was supposed to be somewhere between Hannover and Braunschweig, that was where they had sent his father "on assignment," as they put it.

But now the train was taking him farther and farther from his city with every click of the rails, away from the familiar streets and houses, from his river and its bridges, from his teachers and the classroom that always smelled like damp moss, and from the rowan trees along the road to school that would be bearing their bright red fruit now. And he had stared out at the yellow fields of grain speeding past, some of them already half harvested, which alternated with green potato and turnip fields and later, more and more, with endless black forests. In Oppeln he changed trains for the first time and in Heydebreck for the second, and each time he had trouble with his suitcase and with the trains. Finally there were only soldiers with him in the compartment, and one of them had asked him whether he had ever . . . done anything with a girl.

Andreas pushed the eiderdown aside a little; he was too warm under it.

"Is this really the right train for Gleiwitz?" he had asked the soldiers for the third time now. They had put a rucksack on their knees to play cards on, and where they slapped down the cards the nap was worn bare and smooth. "Hell's bells!" yelled a soldier. He jumped up, stretching out an arm, the card between his fingers higher still; it touched the ceiling before he flung it down triumphantly, like a lightning bolt. Thunder came from the rucksack.

Andreas had sat by the window and for a long time had seen nothing but trees and trees and trees, an endless forest etching itself on his sight. When the train stopped he heard names of stations which seemed strange and foreign, and he wondered whether he really was on the right train. But then he succumbed to the monotonous clicking of the rails and to a journey in which time and distance were obliterated so that he did not know how long it would last, maybe all the way into Poland, into another day, another language, into a dream.

Opposite him sat a soldier who was not playing cards with the others, but like him was simply looking out at the endless black expanse of forest. From time to time he puffed out his cheeks and scratched his crotch, and, to judge by his face, he was somewhere other than in a train going from Heydebreck to Gleiwitz: "Yes, it's the right train, I think we'll be there in half an hour, youngster."

He didn't like being called a youngster, he had even said so out loud earlier, when they had all gotten into the compartment together and were busy stowing their baggage: rucksacks beneath the seats, rifles into the luggage nets where they hung heavily and swayed threateningly. Because he wanted to say something friendly, to thank them for helping him, he had said, "This thing with the war, it won't last long." And a soldier who was already shuffling cards had rejoined, "What would you know about it, youngster, have you even laid hands on a gun yet?"

He had hesitated with his answer at first. In the *Jungvolk* they had practiced with a .38-caliber which, admittedly, was positioned in a sand pit, and you only had to adjust it a little for the target. Not one of them could hold the thing in his hands unsupported and take aim, it was too heavy; they would have to be bigger and stronger, like the men in the Labor Service, before they were able to practice that way. At any rate, he had tried to hold the weapon by himself once, when the patrol leader was somewhere else, but the barrel immediately tipped down so that he would have shot himself in the foot if he had fired. The soldier said, as Andreas still hesitated with his answer: "Then you don't know a thing about war, youngster."

And now he hurried to answer: "I do, I do, we practiced in the sand pit with one, but it was only what they call simulated. I'm almost old enough for the HY, they give you training with real weapons there."

"How old are you, then?"

"Fifteen," Andreas said, adding a year for good measure.

"So they're already into the kids now," said another soldier. "Like I've said all along, no good'll come of this."

"At any rate, someone who can handle a gun is not a youngster any more." Andreas was proud that he had managed his speech without stammering. He felt hugely courageous. But his heart had been pounding.

The others laughed. Still, he hoped they would stop calling him "youngster" now.

"So what are you going to do in Gleiwitz?" Andreas asked the soldiers. Somehow the question seemed daring to him, now that there was so much talk about spies in school and on the radio— Watch out, the enemy is listening!—but that must mean foreigners, whom you could recognize immediately by their accents, and besides, the soldier wouldn't suspect a fourteen-year-old schoolboy of being a spy. Nevertheless, he added precociously: "Naturally you don't have to answer that if it's classified information."

The soldier turned to face him now. He laughed at the words "classified information" and casually scratched his crotch. "Did you hear anything about border provocations, youngst—?" He caught himself. "That's why we're in transit, we're being posted from Osnabrück to Gleiwitz, all of us, see, to some barracks, Katzer or Katzler, where we'll probably roast for a few weeks at some damned outpost on the border, already half in Poland . . ."

One of the cardplayers yelled out: "That'll cost you a schnapps, you better believe it."

And in another corner of the compartment, one of them began to sing:

> Life is a game of dice,
> We roll them every day . . .

"I've never been in this region either," Andreas said, "but I'm looking forward to it. My aunt lives in Gleiwitz, she'll meet me at the station, my Aunt Valeska." Andreas felt a vague anxiety, so he continued to talk about his aunt: "My Aunt Valeska is going to be wearing a green dress at the station so we won't miss each other, that's what she wrote to my father, they've got a big house there, all to themselves, with lots of rooms and a piano. My Aunt Valeska is a piano teacher, you see, and my father told me that she even gives lessons to the families of counts and princes."

The soldier continued to cup his fly, indifferent, and Andreas wasn't sure whether he was even listening to him. He wondered whether he should tell the soldier why he was on his way to Gleiwitz. He had taken a sort of liking to him, although they hadn't spoken much up to now; by watching him for so long, he had become familiar with his face and with his gestures, too, especially the way he puffed out his cheeks and constantly scratched at his crotch. He would have liked to show his understanding somehow or other, perhaps by acting like the soldier. So he slouched down in his seat, puffed out his cheeks and expelled the air, and he even scratched between his legs—although he shielded himself with his other hand, even though no one was watching, since he was self-conscious.

> What fate brings some of us is nice,
> Though others it dismay . . .

"So, all I can say is that this place is the asshole of the world," said the soldier. "I don't know what brings you here, but at your age you belong somewhere other than in this sooty foundry belt. Do you think any of us would come here by choice? There's nothing here but mines and smelters; we heard about it in advance, and besides that, the forests, huge, lonely, frightening forests and nothing else, just Poland surrounding you, brrrrrr . . ."

That reminded Andreas of what his father had stressed to him, at home and again at the station, while they were waiting for the train: "Be sure that you change to the right train; the Polish border won't be far off, and if you wind up in Poland, you'll be stuck there for good . . ."

Just as long as this train is headed for Gleiwitz, was what passed through his mind. I absolutely have to get to Gleiwitz . . . to Gleiwitz. And for him the name Gleiwitz held an almost magic ring.

The train moved slowly and stopped suddenly with a jerk. He looked out but couldn't see a station sign, and he had neither seen the conductor nor heard him call out a station because the soldiers in the compartment were too noisy. They kept on roaring out the same words: "Eighteen, twenty, twentytwofourseven, thirty withtwoinplaythree hearts against"—words he didn't comprehend. And when the train started up again, a soldier on the other side of the compartment began a new song:

> The mi-highty eagle of the storm is the powerful king
>   of the a-a-a-ir.
> And the birds quake when they hear
> The beat of his wings' rushing pa-a-a-ir . . .

Andreas pressed his face against the windowpane, but still nothing could be seen outside except the black forests speeding

by. All at once, though, he saw big letters, black letters on white
boards secured to poles. "Look at that," he said excitedly to the
soldier, and tried to fit the letters together to mean something . . .
F-F-G-O-T-S-C-H-A-F-F-G-O-T-S-C-H, but then came a fence,
and the letters began all over again. "Do you see that? It's a
name!" And since the train was now moving faster, the name
spelled itself more quickly and clearly: SCHAFFGOTSCH SCHAFF-
GOTSCH SCHAFFGOTSCH. "Haven't the slightest," the soldier had
only grumbled.

> And if in the desert the lion roars,
> The other beasts shake in their la-a-a-ir,

the singer blasted out again; the others, in contrast, just blasted
their cards.

"That's my null ouvert!" yelled one of them who had kept silent
till now. "This game is mine, you guys are fucked, it's all over, I've
got four sevens and a *Fahne,* you guys." He jumped up excitedly
and pranced around the compartment, which was itself dancing
along the tracks. His triumph was smothered by the song, which
they all must have known, for they roared it as one man:

> We are the masters of the world,
> The kings upon the sea.
> Tirallala-tirallala, tirallala-tirallala.

"Schaffgotsch, what can that mean?" asked Andreas.

The soldier was still plucking at his trousers. But he was also
looking out the window now, following the big letters. "Schaffgotsch," he suddenly shouted into the compartment. "Schaffgotsch, does anybody know what that means? Schaffgotsch is
written all over the place, and it's been like that for a while now,
hasn't it? Nothing but Schaffgotsch."

From the next compartment a muffled song could be heard. For
a moment no one spoke and the rhythm of the cardplayers
matched the rhythm of the train. Then one of the players called
out: "Schaffgotsch! Of course. Don't you know who that is?

That's one of the richest families in Silesia, they own everything: coal, iron, casting works, forests, paper, wood, real estate, even banks, they own everything — wherever you spit."

"The trick is mine!" And then the hard, dry sound again when a card is slapped down.

For some time the letters continued to flow together into the name SCHAFFGOTSCH as they passed by Andreas. Then fields could be seen, houses, streets. He resolved not to forget the name Schaffgotsch; he intended to ask his aunt about it. Aunt Valeska would be able to explain it better than the soldier there.

"That should be Gleiwitz," the soldier across from him said. He gazed out the window, meanwhile scratching routinely at his crotch, then he stood up and tugged his things from the baggage net. The train started to brake, quite slowly; you could hear it by the sound and see it in the posture of the soldiers, whose bodies inclined automatically in the direction they were traveling. Slowly the soldiers put away their cards, got up from their seats, collected their baggage. They were hardly talking at all now, and Andreas felt as if he were in a different compartment.

No one had said anything about Gleiwitz or getting off; it was as if they were in silent agreement that the next station had to be *the* town, Central Station Gleiwitz OS. The strange accord of the grownups lay like an ebbing noise in the compartment, so clear that no one wanted to question it, not even Andreas, although he did not quite understand it. He tugged his suitcase from beneath the seat and watched the soldiers fishing their rifles from the baggage net, shouldering them, and crowding toward the exit.

His soldier was standing next to him now. He was holding on to a metal bar overhead, his rucksack wedged between his boots. "What are you doing here in town?"

And Andreas, who for two hours had been expecting this question from one person or another, hastily dug out of his memory what he had pasted together earlier: "Oh, that's simple, I'm going to live here in town, for one thing, at my Aunt Valeska Piontek's, who is a piano teacher at Strachwitzstrasse, No. 12, and for another, I'll be going to school here. My mother died a while back, you see, and my father said I needed a real home, because he's been sent on assignment to the Hermann Göring Works in Leben-stedt, that's why I'm on my way to Aunt Valeska's. She's going to meet me at the station along with my cousin Josel Piontek, that's her son, that's what she wrote me at least, she'll be wearing a green hat and . . ."

The train had reached the station. The brakes began to screech so loudly that no one could hear anything. He looked out the window, but he didn't see his Aunt Valeska's green dress; only uniforms, gray garrison caps, and here and there the visored hat of an officer. The soldier scratched his trousers again, as if in leave-taking, and in so doing, his hand brushed against Andreas's crotch too, as if by chance, and for an instant it even rested there. Andreas burned and shut his eyes, even liking it in a certain way, and then he heard the soldier say suddenly: "Be good now, son."

"Well, *salut,* then," he said, as he did to his classmates at the Eichendorff secondary school since they had been learning French. And with the greeting *salut,* he wanted to show the soldier that he counted him among his friends.

The soldier puffed out his cheeks once again, put his rucksack down on the floor for a moment, then climbed down onto the platform and tugged his pack after him. "Take care that you never get mixed up in this, youngster," he said, then turned around and disappeared. Andreas didn't have time to answer the soldier, for Aunt Valeska had come up wearing a green dress and a green hat just as she had written, but to him it was all a single, flowing green into which he practically leaped from the step.

Aunt Valeska planted a wet kiss on both his cheeks and then from behind her back she produced a boy who was somewhat taller than Andreas but quite thin, and whom embarrassment seemed to be making even thinner. "This is your cousin Josel." And to Josel she said: "This is your cousin Andreas."

The cousin advanced with one hand out, and his eyes wandered back and forth, up and down, over him. "Well, let's see that suit-case, An-dre-as," said the cousin, Josel, and you could tell he was not exactly familiar with the name. He took the suitcase and dragged it across the station platform ahead of Andreas and Aunt Valeska, his body bent like a comma.

"Nice that you've come," his aunt said, and twisted his head so that he would have to look at her for a while and so that she could look at him too. Andreas burst into a laugh, but deep down in this laugh embarrassment and fear were hiding.

"You must be really tired from the journey, but you won't get a chance to rest, since tomorrow, well, you didn't know it and neither did your father, tomorrow your cousin Irma is getting married, yes, even for us it's a surprise, and there will be a big celebration. A big celebration," she said, and her voice expressed the opposite of what she was saying.

In the concourse a military band began playing a march, perhaps as a welcome for an arriving company, perhaps as a goodbye to a departing one. At any rate, the music was so loud that you couldn't hear yourself speak.

Josel had stopped to switch hands dragging the suitcase. Andreas and his aunt had caught up with him by now, so Andreas jumped to the other side, and together they towed the suitcase outside.

The square in front of the train station was empty. Only a few army trucks were parked there. And a tank with its cannon aimed at the building.

"The war is here already, as you can see," his aunt had said.

Josel mumbled something.

"Beg pardon?" said Andreas, and he felt immensely genteel.

"Oh, nothing," replied Josel. "They just put that panzer there because the Poles want to ambush us."

Valeska waved and a car came driving up. "As a matter of fact, there are no taxis at all any more," Josel said. And his aunt said: "We've got men quartered in our house, a sergeant, he's got an official car."

"Our school is closed," Josel said. "Everything's full here, all the school buildings, all the barracks, even the squares, all full of soldiers."

And he was being introduced to a real live sergeant right away: "So that's him, our nephew from the big city!" The car took off with a roar. And he, wedged in between the suitcase and Josel, was looking straight at the Sergeant's shoulder straps with the silver star on them, and he had the tingling feeling that more was happening in this little town than at home. Gratified, he had pressed his hands between his legs and groped for his *pullok* through his baggy trousers.

Andreas was too hot. He threw back the comforter.

Slow, muffled steps came from the room above him. He opened his eyes and looked up; there was a shadowy light in the room, and although the curtains were still closed, he could see the bell-shaped lamp clearly which now, it seemed to him, was beginning to grow and expand, getting bigger and bigger and more powerful, and starting to sink down, like a mighty bell that would suck him up and use his body as a clapper—the pealing of the bell was already ringing in his ears.

Then the drive in the car. Obviously the Sergeant had been drunk, since he scraped against the sidewalk while taking the corners, and once he stopped at the last instant, almost hitting a tree. They had got out and pushed the car backwards, for the befuddled Sergeant could not find the reverse gear and none of the others knew anything about cars, nothing as complicated as that, anyway. When they finally reached the gleaming yellow house in Strachwitzstrasse, the others were already standing in the hall and on the steps to greet them. Andreas went past them as if on parade, and they all touched him, as if they could not otherwise comprehend that he was here, among them, the boy from the big city. They would lay a hand upon his hair or his shoulder, or touch a cheek or his forehead or his chin, and they even hugged him: it was like a ceremony, and after he had gone through this ceremony the others around him laughed and all talked at once, and it was as if he had been taken into their circle, with everything he had brought with him, not just what was in his suitcase.

Then the maid, Halina, came up and asked him in a brittle voice: "Where you have suitcase?" He had to look around for it, and finally found it next to the stairs where he had left it, and she took it and towed it effortlessly up the stairs, as if it were empty: "Come! I show you your bed. You sleep by your cousin in one room, because no place, you have seen, we have soldiers in house." She giggled to herself, holding a white embroidered hankie to her mouth.

And Josel had come to him: "Tomorrow morning I'll show you the town and some of the countryside, maybe the Gleiwitz mine or our river, the tired old Klodka, and Lake Beuthen; maybe we'll ride all the way to the border too, you can see the Polish soldiers with their square caps, *fantastichnek,* I tell you," Josel had said.

And now Andreas was lying here in a strange bed in which he had spent his first night buried under an oversized white eiderdown. He thought of the soldier in the train, his friend, and he groped beneath the quilt and felt his member was hard.

It was quiet in the room; only a distant coughing came through the walls. Not even Josel's breathing could be heard. Andreas sat up and looked across at the other bed. The bed was empty. Josel must have got up quite a while before him, and it was his own breathing he had been listening to earlier in this bare strange room.

5

VALESKA HAD GONE to the Archpriest at the time agreed upon, but had found no opportunity to speak to him about the sale of the fields next to the cemetery. She had met him only briefly, and he had conducted himself very strangely. The door was ajar, so she saw him as she entered the church grounds. He was on his way to the sacristy, accompanied by two men dressed entirely in black, but who obviously were not priests, at least not Catholics; she could tell this by their collars. The Archpriest skipped along nervously between the two of them, and sometimes he looked up at them with wide eyes, as if he could gain better and more precise information from their faces than from what they were saying, and the curate, Mikas, walked along next to them with head bowed, almost stooping.

Valeska had come a few steps closer, and they all seemed to have noticed her except the Archpriest, and she did not know whether it would be better simply to leave or somehow call attention to herself. She decided on the latter and adjusted her hat, which she had already adjusted in front of the rectory, snapped open her purse, and took out a pair of black net gloves she had buried there like an old secret. Since she did not know what to do, she drew on the gloves meticulously. While doing so she avoided looking at the group until she heard the voice of the Archpriest who was walking toward her with short steps. (She would have described them as mincing, without intending to make him seem ridiculous.)

"Praised be Christ Jesus," she said, when he was near enough. It did not seem that he was particularly pleased to see her; rather he seemed to be taking advantage of her presence to get away from the others, at least for a moment. He took her by the arm and steered her a few steps farther away from the others.

"You've come on account of the fields, dear Frau Valeska, yes, I know . . . Now and forever, amen." It was as if he only now had remembered to act like a priest.

"Am I intruding, Father?"

The Archpriest cast a glance at the others, who had stopped, and decided to continue a few paces farther.

"You'll come this evening, won't you?" she inquired in a cautious voice. An all too cautious voice, as she herself was forced to admit.

"Oh, yes." He touched her hand. "Thank you very much for the invitation to the wedding reception. At the Hotel Upper Silesia, dear Frau Valeska! You'll bankrupt yourself for your daughter!"

But all at once he withdrew his hand and his voice grew stern, for now he had remembered: "I will be unable to come! To a wedding reception without a church ceremony!"

Valeska assumed an expression as if she were kneeling at the confessional. "But Your Reverence knows that it's not my fault. I've been trying everything for days, I've talked, I've shouted, I've prayed, I've begged, and I've shed tears. It's pure spite, my daughter's acting out of pure spite . . . But I'll manage it somehow, I wrote you that."

"How would it be if you were just to send the bridal pair to see me?"

"I'd like to, Father, I'd like to, but young people these days, Father, you know, they simply refuse." She thought of crying, or at least pretending to. And she began digging in her purse for a handkerchief that was still presentable.

"I think I can talk them into it. My son-in-law" (she didn't want it to, but her voice cracked on the word) "is very easygoing, so by Sunday . . . yes, schedule the marriage for Sunday at 2 P.M. in St. Peter and Paul's Church."

"Then you should hold the reception on Sunday as well!" The Archpriest had to force his voice; he did not like treating his flock sternly, and besides, he would rather have returned to the others, who, it seemed, were looking over at him suspiciously.

Valeska emitted a sob as a last resort.

The Archpriest thought of how many of his flock had left the Church in the last few months, and he paused to consider that Valeska Piontek, as far as he could recall, had not missed a single Sunday mass or rosary devotion in the month of October.

"I'll send Curate Mikas tonight," he said, almost friendly now.

"Your Reverence," Valeska said, and she took his hand and drew it to her lips, "it will be a special honor for us . . . you know, it's all for my daughter . . . Personally I would be especially happy, of course, if you too, Your Reverence, would come and would just say a few words to Irma . . ."

It was hopeless, she could tell. She had counted on him to accept in spite of everything.

"You're right, Frau Valeska," the Archpriest said, and withdrew his hand. She did not know whether kissing his hand in public had embarrassed him, or whether he was angry with her because of the wedding reception. "It looks as if a time of trial lies ahead of us," the Archpriest said. But she sensed that he was thinking of something quite different.

"Perhaps you'll come after all, maybe for just an hour, maybe for my *tableaux vivants,* we're doing *The Angelus* after Millet this time . . . It will please you . . ." Valeska was trying words again. She did not dare kiss his hand again, not here.

"Those are visiting dignitaries"—the Archpriest was trying to change the subject—"from Oppeln, a government commission, very important." He looked over at them again, somewhat restless now.

Valeska pulled herself together; she had no choice, her daughter's happiness was at stake. "On Sunday Irma will be married by you, and you'll come this evening around nine o'clock, won't you?" She said it as if she were simply reconfirming what they had agreed upon. "And you can have the fields next to the cemetery even cheaper," she added, though with a bad conscience.

At any other time he would have thanked Valeska for this, but it seemed as if it did not concern him now. The other disaster was greater.

"They want the church bells!" The Archpriest could not hold back the sentence any longer; it burst out of him, along with all the bitterness that had collected in him.

Valeska's jaw dropped. It happened so unmistakably that it would have disturbed her to see it. The Archpriest did see it.

"No, not yet," he added quickly, and walked a few steps more with her. "For the time being, they only want a pledge that we, the German clergy, are prepared to sacrifice the church bells for our country . . . if the time should come . . ."

"But the war hasn't even begun yet!" Valeska said.

If this was a ploy of the Archpriest to distract her from the subject of the reception, it succeeded masterfully, Valeska thought, for only now did she remember what she had asked of him. "You shouldn't sign!" she whispered.

To be sure, the others were rather far off, but she considered them her enemies and did not want to take any chances.

"I have no idea how to react to it," the Archpriest said, half to himself.

That was ambiguous, but Valeska took advantage of it at once. "Just come for half an hour! You could lead them back to the path of the Lord . . ."

The Archpriest nodded. He was playing for time; he wanted first to discuss the matter with his curates. He was thinking more of the commission and the church bells. He looked around and waved to the others, who were waiting by the church door. "How is your husband?" He shook her hand in parting, and quite clearly he did it less for Valeska than for the others.

"Thank you, Your Reverence." She believed she had won him over for the wedding reception now. She flicked a little bit of cobweb from his shoulder. She did have her gloves on. Naturally, you don't touch an archpriest with your bare hands.

"The same as always," she answered. "Won't you drop in again sometime? I just have to prepare Leo Maria for it, you know, otherwise when you appear he always thinks his time has come . . ."

She looked at the priest and wished she could discover something else on his coat that she could flick away — a long hair, or a shred of paper, or a bit of licorice stuck on by those Don Bosco boys, but she found nothing else. "Praised be Christ Jesus."

Thus they parted, both with the feeling of having been thrust into a terrible secret and a frightful betrayal, and each suffered under the heavy burden of the secret and the heavier burden of the betrayal.

Outside an idea came to her: she could talk to him about the fields this evening at the reception, or on Sunday, after the ceremony. She didn't want to sell for less than 4 marks per square meter under any circumstances; three years ago she had paid 50 pfennigs, and 3.70 marks would be the absolute limit. Otherwise she would rather sell them to Count Tiele-Winckler; he was a Lutheran, and would top the parish by 2 marks.

"Now and forever, amen."

In the street open trucks were driving toward the border filled with armed soldiers in uniform. Many of them had camouflage netting on their helmets, some had bouquets in the muzzles of their rifles. Their faces were impassive; not cheerful, at any rate. They were singing songs. The one about the Westerwald she already knew. Josel sang that one with the HY. All she could catch of one song was: "We were lying off Madagascar and had the plague on board, in the kettles the water was boiling and suddenly . . ."—then they had disappeared around a bend. Too bad, she would have liked to find out what happened then so *suddenly*.

In Blücherstrasse she boarded the No. 4 streetcar. It would take her as far as Germaniaplatz, then she could change and ride two stops farther to Bismarckplatz, and from there it was only a five-minute walk to her brother Willi's. These days she wouldn't be able to get a taxi anyway.

The streetcar was overcrowded. For days it had seemed as if no one would work again, as if the whole town were on the move. The streets and squares were fuller than usual, the cafés, bars, and restaurants crowded; nowadays nobody wanted to be alone, everyone looked for solace from others. Some people had put radios in their windows, and when it was time for the news, clusters of people formed who listened silently to the broadcast. And they broke up silently afterwards. The people were not depressed or apprehensive, they were—how were they, actually? Valeska looked around in the streetcar. She looked into tired, serious, extinguished faces . . . they looked quite different than, for example, in 1914. Valeska could still remember the days before the outbreak of war, that had been a jubilant time for everyone, as if they were headed to a wedding, not to death.

Valeska ran her eyes over the advertising slogans without really noticing them:

> *Your shoes are always looking fine*
> *If you don't forget that Egü shine*

Between them, in thick black letters:

ONLY GERMAN SPOKEN HERE

She looked at a few old women in white headscarves, whose faces the Upper Silesian land had furrowed and turned to stone, their lips thin and pressed shut so that not a word could slip out. Sometimes they nodded or looked at each other, and one of them even pointed out of the window. At home they spoke a language that was forbidden here. Here they were mute. Valeska could have said: *Jak wam idzie?* how do you do? to them, but she did not have the nerve to speak Polish aloud either, in this situation. At the next stop she started toward the door, as she had to get off soon.

Her brother Willi Wondraczek had his law practice in one of the best neighborhoods in Gleiwitz, he specialized in claims for compensation arising from the formerly Prussian areas which were now Polish-Silesian. He spoke Polish as fluently as German and was thoroughly acquainted with Polish law as well; his clientele ranged from Counts Tiele-Winckler and Poremba down to small landowners and simple peasants. Besides that he counseled his sister Valeska Piontek, who for some time had been speculating in real estate. More precisely, she organized all those business deals which a respectable lawyer of the community could not permit himself to be involved in. But no one, and a smile stole over Valeska's face as she thought of it, seemed that interested in finding out. For a time rumors had circulated that Herr Wondraczek had forged evidence authenticating a collection of paintings owned by Prince Pless which had been taken over by the Poles, and thereby won millions for the Pless family. And when the rumors refused to die down, he requested that his character be investigated before a court of honor of his own profession—he had been cleared on all counts, and ever since had been much sought after as a lawyer for compensation claims. Recently he had become Attorney Willy Wondrak.

Valeska got off the streetcar. For the second time now she was on her way to sign a contract of sale with the widow Kupka, whose old people's quarters in Lilienthalweg had attached to them five acres of land near the airstrip. The first time, the widow Kupka had not opened up because she had suddenly felt herself besieged by everyone; she had locked herself in, nailed the doors and windows shut, and had only come out weeks later when her stock of groceries ran out. She was supposed to have gone to the neighbors one morning with a white tablecloth in her hand and surrendered. At the last minute, Willi was able to prevent her being taken to the insane asylum at Tost for a compulsory examination; the neighbors had already reported her. (Yet it was a good contract for the widow Kupka, she could continue to live in her little cottage until her death, and she would start receiving money right away.) Earlier, Valeska had acquired the rest of the surrounding real estate; she lacked only the land belonging to the widow Kupka, then almost all the property surrounding the airstrip would be in her possession. The new central airport for the towns of Gleiwitz, Hindenburg, and Beuthen was now planned for a site to the north, to be sure, but Valeska counted on the acquisition of land in the north to present so many difficulties that it would be easier to expand the Gleiwitz airport; she herself could offer all the land needed from a single holding. That would be the business deal of her life.

The first thing she would do would be to stop teaching piano . . . then she would take Leo Maria to Davos in Switzerland, to one of the miraculous sanatoriums . . . then she'd travel to Italy, to Capri, they say it's always summer there . . . then she would send Josel to the capital to study, to Berlin . . . then she would . . . she didn't want to finish the thought.

In the gardens, roses and dahlias were blossoming in the sun. Their fragrance wafted over the fences into the street, dizzying Valeska; in the gardens she saw fields of roses, walls, hedges, benches of roses, fences of roses . . . sometimes she stopped and inhaled the heavy, sweetish, sun-drenched scent and thought, this could make her forget herself.

At the garden's edge she saw a woman in a blue dress who was senselessly jabbing at the rosebushes with flashing shears and snapping the blades, roses in bloom and even buds fell to the ground. Valeska stood leaning against the wire fence and watched, and the even, rhythmic clicking of the shears began to excite her in a strange way. She watched the woman bend down and begin to gather the roses; she picked them up with her right hand and stacked them in her left arm, and she could see the thorns scratching a red pattern on the white skin, but finally everything was engulfed by the green of the leaves, and the roses in it were only colorful splotches, no hands, no arms, no face left. The woman had come closer and closer, now she was looking at her through the abundance of green. Then she turned around abruptly and dashed into the house, as if caught in a forbidden act.

Suddenly Valeska was ashamed of herself for having stopped to watch. She walked on quickly. But her step was no longer so sure. Once she twisted her ankle. It wasn't only the stone that had caught her heel.

She could have done the same in her own garden, it's true there were only a few rosebushes growing between her house and the cottage of the County Magistrate, but she had dahlias and stocks in bloom, asters, larkspur, and sunflowers. And she wasn't certain whether a situation wouldn't arise for her too one day, when she would go down into the garden and behead all the flowers with the green shears. Yes, maybe she would do it, yes. When the soldiers started shooting. Or when the end came for Leo Maria. Sweet Jesus.

On the other side of the road the Wild Monk was tightrope-walking along the curb. Valeska recognized him from far off, with his unusually long hair, his full beard, his broad cassock, and his flailing arms. When he spotted Valeska, he opened his long arms like wings; in one hand he was carrying a glass jar that flashed in the sun. Valeska waved across at him, waving him back at the same time, for she knew that he would cross the road immediately without looking to the left or right. She ran across the street to him and let the monk hug her, and the bitter-wet-rotten smell of his cassock hit her. For a fraction of a second she even thought she would be unable to free herself.

The Wild Monk held the fruit jar up high, in front of her face; tiny fish were swimming in it, they looked like colored stripes flitting back and forth.

"Aren't they pretty," laughed the Wild Monk, "these fish, like drops of color in the sea, aren't they?" His face gleamed beside the glass, which reflected the sun, and it seemed as if he would never be able to tear his eyes away from it, he was gazing at it so enchantedly. His face, with its coarse pores and the redness near the bridge of the nose, seemed gentle and smoother to her today. "Dr. Wittek gave them to me," he said. "I'm going to raise tropical fish!" Valeska couldn't imagine where the Wild Monk intended to raise the fish. They were always after him, every year he had to move somewhere else, and once they had even put him in a detention camp. For some time now he had been living in a broken-down bus near the Laband Woods, where she had visited him twice. "Those are probably very rare fish," she said, for she couldn't imagine why else the Wild Monk would be carrying a few tiny fish through the streets in a fruit jar.

"Yes," the monk said, "these are expensive fish. This blue one here costs seventy-five pfennigs in Reute's pet shop on Germania-platz, and that one there, with the tail like a golden veil, even costs three marks, and that green one, with the hammer head, just look how it sparkles, costs seven marks, Dr. Wittek told me so. There are two of every kind. All I need now is a few more fruit jars. Could I get some from you?"

"Of course," Valeska said. "You can have those big two-liter jars." She was quite surprised; she had thought that except for God, he was interested only in his still, which he had been able to rescue after having it confiscated several times—at least parts of it.

"There are fish," the Wild Monk said, "that cost a hundred or even two hundred marks, did you know that?" The Wild Monk seemed to be constantly talking himself into his astonishment at the prices. He held the jar in the sun, and now the fish really did sparkle in the water.

"Do you know how to . . . how to raise fish, I mean, feed them and take care of them?"

"Yes," the monk said, pressing the jar into her hands. "I've got the full picture." He took a tattered pamphlet from inside his cassock: Benedek, *How to Raise Tropical Fish,* and his whole face beamed. His voice climbed higher, and as he did not seem to be drunk, Valeska had to assume that he was beginning a new life. She did not know whether to encourage him in that. He would end up involved in such repulsive things as fish breeding, and you wouldn't be able to go visit him any more to find out something about the future. She gave him back the jar.

What did she care about the fish? There were so many things she did care about, more immediate things. "My daughter's getting married this evening," Valeska said, "to a soldier—an officer candidate, which means he'll soon be an officer." And as the Wild Monk didn't understand this, she added: "I don't understand it either. But do come to the wedding reception tonight at the Hotel Upper Silesia, at seven o'clock in the Mint Room. You're invited!"

She thought: If the Archpriest doesn't want to come because my daughter is getting married today by the judge and the church ceremony isn't until Sunday, then at least the Wild Monk, the outcast, should be there. Thus she would punish the Church in her own way.

"Should I really come?" the Wild Monk asked, and now his voice was normal again.

"Of course," Valeska reassured him. "I'll make sure that they let you in." The thought struck her as she glanced down at his shabby cassock: the Church too should be able to tolerate rebels. But she was also imagining how the Archpriest would squirm.

"Fine, I'll come," the monk said. "Thank you."

"Do you have money for the streetcar?" Valeska cradled her handbag, about to open it and take out her coin purse.

"Don't bother," the monk said patronizingly. "I'm working at the old people's home. I have to prove I'm working, or else they'll lock me up again. The Lord be with you!" And inconspicuously he made the sign of the cross with his right hand. From left to right.

Valeska did not venture to kiss the monk's hand. But after he had gone, she brought the fingers that had touched his cassock pensively to her lips.

He had gone away with the jar of fish in his hands. If the invitation made him happy, he did not show it. Perhaps he had expended too much happiness on the fish. She wondered why he was called the Wild Monk. Shouldn't he have been called the mild monk instead? Nevertheless, she was not quite certain whether it had been right to invite him. Just to make sure, she said silently: "And with you as well!"

Then the bells began to peal. They must be striking noon. Valeska wondered how far Archpriest Pattas had gotten by now with the commission from Oppeln. And whether he had signed. She did not want to imagine now what his face would look like at the reception that evening, in case he did come after all. Valeska quickened her pace and straightened her hat, which had slipped to one side. She had grown older. She did not need a mirror to tell her that, she felt it when she ran her hand across her face; it had grown rougher, more brittle. She was aware of the bells tolling noon, and that there was still time for a whole series of defeats before the day was over.

When she entered the office of lawyer Wondrak, she saw that the widow Kupka was already sitting there, the documents were laid out, and all they had to do was sign. Widow Kupka's hand was trembling so badly that Valeska had to guide it with her own. The lawyer nodded as she did so, and he hastened to blot the wet ink and lock the documents in a drawer. Valeska decided to invite the widow Kupka to the reception; the Flabinskis had declined, so there were still two places to be filled. Widow Kupka thanked her with her eyes, in which something moist glistened. But she did not utter a word.

Lawyer Willi Wondrak brought in three glasses on a tray: "We must drink to that!" And Valeska took a glass and drank it down.

Doesn't anyone, she thought, doesn't anyone hear the bells tolling?

6

MONTAG WAS AWAKENED by the noise of voices outside. The children had found a dead bird and were burying it next to the wall of the garden cottage, almost beneath Montag's window. They were playing bird funeral. Just as they had played butterfly birth earlier, or june bug wedding, or doll communion, or cricket execution. Montag knew all this.

He opened the drawer of the nightstand and groped for the pocket watch he had put there. (There were nights when even the ticking of the watch disturbed him, so then he put it in the drawer or covered it with a handkerchief.) He took it out and held it right before his eyes. It was shortly after twelve o'clock.

"So I bless thee, thou poor black bird, and give thee back to the black earth, earth thou art, wast and evermore shalt be . . ."

Montag could clearly distinguish Josel's voice, which outdid even the incantations of Archpriest Pattas. Ulla Ossadnik's pathos-filled litany now followed: "Oh, my poor heart breaks in two when I see that thou, black bird, art leaving us and that thou willst rot here in the Pionteks' garden and nourish the old pear tree." Then Josel again: "Oh dust are we all, dust of this earth . . ." And the other children giggled or went boo-hoo-hoo in the pauses, or repeated the simple, resounding words that had lodged in their brains, and Montag, surprised, wondered where they had learned all that.

Montag's ancestors had come from far to the east; each generation had moved farther west, always following the sun. Thus he came into the world in Myslowitz, which at the time was Prussian; his father was a cloth merchant there. He could still remember the small, steep-gabled house in the Horse Market, in the middle of town, which still stank of horse piss although no horse auction had been held there for years; he could remember a little park with chestnut trees and carousels and swings for children, and girls in white fluttering dresses and boys in black unpressed suits, their knees white, with rattles in their hands or paper trumpets at their mouths with which they made funny noises.

I was shut out from that, Montag thought.

He remembered excursions on the narrow-gauge railway in the summer, to the green birch forests that seemed to go on forever and probably did. Sometimes they would get off, at some little station where there wasn't even a stationmaster's cabin, and walk into the great green luminous forest, over paths carpeted with soft moss, he ahead of his parents, his mother in a wide yellow straw hat with two blue ribbons hanging down behind, his father in a black jacket as always, which he would take off and carry over his arm. The only time he ever heard his mother laugh was on these walks. Then she would take off her shoes, dance across the moss, hide behind trees and imitate birdcalls. When a cuckoo called, she would ask aloud: "Cuckoo, how long will I live?" and add the number of calls to her age; if the cuckoo answered many times, she would run barefoot in a circle, laughing, pulling his father along, but if there were too few for her, she would put her shoes back on, take his father by the hand, and walk the rest of the way quietly at his side.

Once one of the paths had led them near a castle in whose windows chandeliers were already burning in the afternoon. He had run a little ahead of his parents and had climbed a tree, and then had crawled along a thick branch toward an open window, perhaps to discover a secret he could tell his father. When he was close enough he saw elegantly dressed ladies and gentlemen standing around talking, holding tapered glasses in their hands, and others sitting at a large oval table laying down cards, while gold and silver coins were being pushed back and forth across the tabletop in a manner mysterious to him.

Just then someone spotted him, a man with a bushy black mustache who stretched his hand out the window and tried to grab him but couldn't reach him. And he uttered that word which Montag would be long in forgetting: "*Schiddok,* Jew-brat, get the hell out of here."

But best of all he remembered his grandfather, who must have been very old at the time. He liked to sit on a tall chair by the window, with a mirror wedged in the sash; that way he could silently observe the street and the people passing by. From time to time he would heave a sigh and spread the fingers of one hand before his eyes and gaze through them into a vague distance. At any rate, it was not the marketplace, paved with cobblestones, that he saw, and not the dirty-red clinker houses across the street or the new post office; he was seeing another street, other people, another town—indeed another time. And then he would talk to the boy about God in dark, glowing riddles; he would talk of the robber chieftain Mendel Krik and his sons Benja and Lwow, who threatened the landowner Propitschin that they would slay his favorite horse, the black mare Sonja, if he refused to give his beautiful daughter Ljubka in marriage to the gimpy Lwow, along with a handsome dowry. And he told of Moldawanka, where he had been a peddler, going from door to door through the neighborhoods of Odessa with a satchel full of yarn (in all colors and all thicknesses; he carried buttons and elastic and needles too), and every evening he had brought home a few kopecks and the latest exploits of Krik's robber band.

When his father was there he warned the old man not to confuse the child, and he said to the boy, "You shouldn't believe all your grandfather's stories; they're inventions, and besides, that was over a hundred years ago."

I myself believed everything Grandfather said, and one day I set out for Odessa to join Benja Krik's band of robbers, but I only got as far as Schoppinitz, down the road and across the river; the police picked me up there and brought me back home.

And then there was something else, more than a memory: those dark corners of the house in the Horse Market, where there were whispers and murmurs and groans in the evenings. Sometimes there was nothing there, nothing at all, just the fright when he reached his hand into the darkness and emptiness; sometimes there was someone lying there, a bundle that moved, a body that groaned, or there were only sounds, like a watery litany, and only later did he comprehend that someone had come from Odessa or Lemberg, fleeing a pogrom, and had spent two nights here in murmured conversation with his grandfather and then set out again for the west . . .

Perhaps that was the reason he now kept lamps burning throughout the cottage, in the hall too, even in his room; he was still afraid of dark, poorly lighted corners.

He had been either four or five years old when his grandfather died, he could no longer remember which. Hardly had the Kaddish sung by the old Jews faded away when his father converted to the Catholic faith; then they cut off his own sidelocks and he was baptized a Catholic. His mother wanted it that way; she read him the story of Genevieve of Brabant, and sometimes she called him my son *Schmerzensreich,* while she stroked his face with her hand.

Soon after that they moved still further west. In the capital of the province his father rented a shop in Oppelnstrasse, not far from St. Agnes's Church, which was twice the size of the one in Myslowitz. And now he had customers who spoke only German and who sometimes brought a maid along to carry the material away in her arms or even had a driver outside, who urged on two emaciated horses with a thin whip and a coarse voice. The boy, Georg Montag, entered a Catholic school, the St. Matthew Gymnasium in Breslau; his mother took him there herself, and she made sure that he did not say "Good day" as a greeting, but rather "Praised be Christ Jesus."

And if I said "*kokolores*" there, I got a stroke of the cane across my hands, and if I said "*meschugge*" at home, my father gave me a rap on the head.

One day the lad stood for a long time in front of the spire of St. Vincent's Church, gazing up. He had never seen such a slender spire before, it seemed to him as if the peak were tearing a wound in the sky, which now, in this evening light, was pouring its blood over the city. It was Good Friday, and he went with the others into the church where all the crosses were draped with violet cloths, except at the front where, on the steps to the altar, lay a mighty wooden crucifix whose wounds glowed red. He watched the others kneel down, clamber up the steps on their knees, he watched them bend over the crucifix and kiss the stigmata — children, old women, even an old man with only one leg who had laid

aside his crutch. And then it was his turn; he was afraid of doing
it, but others were waiting behind him, so he knelt down and
touched the five red stigmata with his lips. An altar boy knelt
beside him and wiped off the places with a gray cloth, but no
matter how often he wiped his lips, they kept on burning long
after. In the meantime, a wind had suddenly arisen outside which
pushed gray and black clouds closer, piling them up, and knocked
them together with a first clap of thunder. He waited for the
storm, he waited for blood to rain from the sky, and when the first
drops fell onto his outstretched hand, he was surprised that it was
only rain, just as on any other day. For him much had changed
since then.

When he was at home for the holidays, he had said to his father,
"I don't understand it, at school every evening we pray together
to Jesus Christ our Lord, who was nailed to the cross by the Jews,
but Grandfather told me once that Yahweh, the God of the Jews,
is your God too." And his father answered him gravely: "It is
time for you, my son, to forget what it was like back there in the
east. You are Catholic, and you can only remain under the
Church's protection if you believe in the crucified Jesus Christ, so
believe in him."

At the University of Breslau, where the rector was the historian
Felix Dahn, he studied law and wrote his dissertation on "Land
Law in Silesia under the Piast Duke, Władysław II." Then he
married Fräulein Erika Weinreich, the daughter of a railway
inspector, who had acquired a simple but solid education at a
school of home economics. They were married in the Catholic
church of St. Vincent in Breslau. It had been a long time since
Georg had seen his father as happy as he was on this evening, and
when the waiters in the Hotel Black Eagle served French champagne at midnight, his father embraced him, tears streaming
down his face: "You have a great career before you, my son," he
said, and kissed him on both cheeks. "Nobody will be able to
stand in your way." He turned away and whispered in quite a
different voice, a strange one: "Forgive me, Father, it had to be
this way, it's the right thing."

And Georg Montag remembered his grandfather in Myslowitz,

who was not allowed out of the house in the last years of his life because he looked too Jewish to his son who had married a Catholic. And then he too believed that it had to be this way and that it was the right thing. Besides, he loved his wife. Only at night did he still dream of Mendel Krik and his sons, and he did not know whether he had read or had heard about them.

A few years later he again encountered that word that should no longer have applied to him: a colleague with whom he was on good if not exactly friendly terms had aspirations of becoming county magistrate in Gleiwitz, but then he, Montag, had been appointed, and when he was taking leave of his colleagues, this man hissed at him: "Jew!" And said: "This country's run by Jews, but one day it'll all be different, we'll get rid of you all."

"I'm no Jew," Georg Montag had answered, insulted. He could have proved it, but he said no more. He swept the word aside, and thanked his colleagues for the bouquet of tiger lilies they had presented to him. He became magistrate of the County Court in Gleiwitz, and later a member of the board of directors of the Good Hope foundry, member of the board of directors of the Concordia mine, member of the board of directors of the Upper Silesian Electrical Works, member of the editorial board of the *Journal of Legal History,* and member of the parish council of St. Peter and Paul's Church.

His wife Erika bore him a daughter whom she wanted to name Ruth, but he insisted that she be given the name of a Catholic saint: in memory of his Breslau years, she was baptized Agnes Elisabeth. His wife died giving birth to their second child, a son, who did not survive. The most beautiful wreath on her grave came from the Cecilia Association, of which she had been treasurer.

From now on Georg Montag devoted himself wholly to bringing up Elisabeth. He had no interest in anything which lay outside his profession. Gradually he resigned his offices. He sent his daughter to Switzerland, to a Catholic boarding school in Olten.

Georg Montag had forgotten that his father was named Benjamin Montag and had owned a small drygoods shop in Myslowitz, that his grandfather was named Moischele Ponedjelnik, and had gone from house to house in Odessa selling yarn. He, Georg

Montag, magistrate of the County Court in Gleiwitz, Upper Silesia, believed in Jesus Christ, the Son of God, begotten by the Holy Ghost and born of the Virgin Mary, and at mass, which he attended regularly every Sunday, he made the sign of the cross from left to right.

The decree of April 1933 reinstating German civil servants did not apply to him; he had been a civil servant before 1914, and besides, he had fought for the German Reich in the World War and had been decorated with the Iron Cross second class on the Isonzo front. In 1937, when the legal protection of minorities in Upper Silesia was annulled and the second decree on the civil service was issued, they demanded proof from him of his Aryan descent.

Georg Montag went to his priest for advice. "Why am I caught up in this mess?" he asked. "I don't think like Jews do, I'm different. I feel sorry for them, but I have nothing to do with them."

The Archpriest promised him the protection of the Catholic Church and his personal protection as well, and as he was leaving, the priest blessed him at the door.

But there was the word again: Jew, which they had dug out of an old file and from a deeper, long-buried level of his consciousness. He was no Jew; his mother came from a Catholic family of artisans in Liegnitz, he had been baptized with the names of St. George and St. Paul; he had been educated at the Catholic St. Matthew Gymnasium in Breslau, he recited the Lord's Prayer and the Apostles' Creed, and he attended high mass every Sunday at St. Peter and Paul's.

But he did not want to justify himself to them. He had only three years to go until his retirement, so he retired early. He moved out of the house in Pruskestrasse, which they now had renamed Schlageterstrasse, he sold his furniture and rented Valeska Piontek's garden cottage in Strachwitzstrasse for fifty marks a month. He went to Paris once again to see his daughter, who was now a teacher of German at the Lycée Ste-Veronique.

After the *Kristallnacht,* he had not been ordered to go to the police station, they did not stamp a "J" after his name in his passport, or insert an "Israel" in parentheses after Georg and Paul.

And nobody came to register his possessions, as they had now done, he learned, with the Jews in the town. In the newspapers he read about the introduction of residence restrictions on Jews, but no official had come to him about this matter either. For a time he had stood behind the curtain watching the street, waiting for someone in uniform to walk up the path toward him. But no one had come.

So it did not affect him. It did not concern him. They did not have him in mind.

He observed himself more frequently in the mirror, he tried to ascertain whether he had any of the characteristics which they ascribed to Jews. He paid attention to his hands while speaking. He listened to less music now. He examined his feet. He observed his walk and his posture. He loved the forest and long walks in the woods, he especially loved the birch forests near Zernik. He could read Hermann Stehr and Knut Hamsun, endlessly. He did not like eating garlic. He spoke German very precisely.

When he thought about all this now, he burst out laughing.

7

THE HOTEL UPPER SILESIA, symbol of the new era and the new architecture, had been placed in the center of town, where its ugliness was perhaps somewhat less offensive: a massive, dull gray-black pile flanked on the right by the Klodnitz, here tamed between concrete banks, which flowed during the summer with deceptive peacefulness, and bordered on the Wilhelmstrasse side by a few scanty flower beds covered with coal dust, with a fountain in front on whose rim three life-sized lascivious fauns were dancing, gleaming with verdigris. On warm summer evenings, as the water jetted and fell in front of the huge concrete structure, they told stories about the old Polish water spirits, and anyone in the neighborhood with time and leisure—there were not many, to be sure—would sit on the terrace of the café and listen to them. People came from everywhere to have a look at the colossal building, the highest for miles around. The townspeople and those from the immediate environs came with a mixture of pride and fear, and after they had walked back and forth in front of it three times, they mustered enough courage at least to sit downstairs in the café and order a cup of coffee and a piece of Silesian Streuselkuchen or (imitation) Sachertorte or Prasselkuchen. They gaped at the white-coated waiters who moved like mimes, they stared in wonder at the little black polished-marble tables, at the muslin drapes which muffled the light and the sounds coming from outside, and made everything inside unreal. And when the headwaiter, dressed in black, brought the check, they dug into their coin purses, pale and composed, not cursing the prices as outrageous highway robbery until they were outside on the street: *Pierruna,* they certainly charge enough for that Italian marble . . .

The people from Schönwald or Ratibor or Cosel or Brzezinka or Pilchowitz or Schakanau, who came to town on the narrow-gauge railway or in horse-drawn wagons, crossed themselves three times (from left to right) before the hotel and said, "*O muj Bosche,* that is perdition, that is America!" Great-aunt Lucie (Lanolin), who had come on a visit from Kalinowitz, near Gross-Strehlitz, with her blind son, said, "He who builds so high, up to the heavens, will be plunged down one day. Holy Mother of God!"

To Josel the Hotel Upper Silesia was a great mystery. He had gone past it often, but sitting on the terrace of the café once with Mamuscha was as far as he had yet penetrated into the mystery. For instance, he had not yet been through that funny round door they called a windbreaker (whatastupidname). He had been up to the very top floor once with Uncle Wondrak, in the offices, and while his uncle was haranguing someone who sank deeper and deeper into his chair until he finally disappeared completely be- hind his desk, Josel looked out the window at the town. The view was nothing short of *fantastichnek,* but it made little impression on him: since they had come up in the elevator, he felt he had been cheated out of the adventure of finally penetrating into the heart of this house of stone.

"Well, here you see the Hotel Upper Silesia," Josel called to Andreas; he gave a ring on his bicycle bell, for a little girl wearing a red cap had almost run into him. He turned into Markgrafen- strasse and rode quite slowly: "Take a look at that," he said, almost proud of the concrete pile. "That's about the biggest and classiest thing around here, and that, of all places, is where Mamuscha is going to marry off my sister this evening . . ." Josel let out a little whoop.

"Very nice," said Andreas, but he meant the three naked green figures on the fountain. The building itself was nothing more than a gray box to him.

Josel braked sharply and got off his bike. "Go ahead and say it: In Breslau we've got one like that on every corner . . ."

Andreas was so surprised by Josel's voice that he could only stop his girl's bike with difficulty. Earlier, when they had passed the old parish church and Josel had pointed to the tower, from which in good weather you could see Poland and Moravia, Andreas had said only, "You should see our St. Elisabeth's, the tower is at least three times as high as this one, and I'm not exaggerating. It takes half an hour to climb the steps all the way to the top, and on the way down you get dizzy from going around in circles, and even when you're back on the street, for a while you keep going round and round and round and round." He laughed.

"Yes, I know, where you come from everything is much bigger, prettier, and better," Josel had said grudgingly. "Heiko, my sister's fiancé, says so too, he saw Cologne Cathedral once, and you can't even look down from its tower, you'd get dizzy and fall off, it's so high . . ." And Andreas had not been sure whether that was a reproach or maybe just amazement. Now, as he stood next to Josel, confused, he said only, "Well, I don't know what's eating you. I told you I think this is all very nice, the fountain there for instance, with the three naked men."

"On Sunday evening the fountain is even illuminated, want to come here then?"

Andreas hastened to say, "Of course, we'll go to Breslau together sometime too, isn't that right, Josel, and I'll show you everything there."

Josel watched an elegantly dressed lady in a big green hat disappear through the revolving door of the hotel. "You know what's so beautiful in Breslau," Andreas said, "is that the Oder is everywhere, around the cathedral, along the streets and the old houses, the river is everywhere."

Josel pushed his bike on slowly, and Andreas followed him. "You really should see our tired old Klodka after the snow melts, farther out of town, that is. It floods the roads and the pastures and the fields, it's like an ocean. Yes, that little river you saw a while ago." Josel's voice grew quite emphatic. "It claims a few children early every spring, did you know that?" Both had stopped directly in front of the entrance to the hotel. They were holding on firmly to their bicycles and looking over at the revolving door, which did not move; a red awning hung above it like a bell.

"Early every spring a few kids who've been playing too near the banks or who break through the ice drown there. Aunt Milka said they are the offerings we have to give to the river to calm it down . . . Yes, really, a day or two after we read in the newspaper that a child was drowned, the flooding stops."

Andreas could not believe that. He laughed and looked Josel in the face, expecting to find him smiling too. But Josel was quite serious. Andreas said, "What'll we do now? Want to go inside?" He gestured with his head toward the hotel entrance.

"No, no, they won't let us in there, inside they've got thick carpets all over, your shoes have to be spick-and-span . . . that's only for rich people."

To Andreas the Hotel Upper Silesia was just an ugly gray concrete box with a simple, sober hotel entrance. "Couldn't we go in and have them show us the room where the reception will be? You could tell them Frau Piontek sent us . . ."

To Josel the Hotel Upper Silesia was a building of stone in which a thousand secrets were hidden, and it was clear to him that only gradually would he discover a few of them; Andreas's suggestion was almost shocking to him. Josel bent over his handlebars and said softly:

"You know, sometimes I imagine the counts and countesses staying here who come from the big estates, the rich people who own the coal mines and the ironworks in our region, the barons, dukes and princes, and all the von Whoevers. I imagine them filling the big ballroom, music and candles, the girls in white and the men in black, and then they line up in long rows for a dance, a polka or a polonaise. I saw that in a film once called *A Thrilling Night at the Ball*. Uncle Wondrak took me along and told the cashier, 'The boy is eighteen, you can let him in,' so there I sat, and that's how it was."

Andreas was astonished at how much his cousin Josel knew, and that he had always gotten it from some film or other. He himself had not been to the movies very often, and when he went, it was mostly to children's films, which didn't teach you anything. But he had been to the theater a few times, and surely Josel never had; he would tell him that at the next opportunity, not now. He would like to find out more about that film. "Would you take me to the movies sometime? I could treat you, I've got a little money left."

"*Otusch.*" Josel bent even lower over his handlebars and rocked the pedals with one foot. "You know, my dear cousin and good friend, I only go to films for those over eighteen. I've got no use for children's pictures and stuff like that . . . Wonder if they'd let you in, too?" He looked Andreas over from head to toe, as if assessing his age. "I'll take you along to the Arena, that's the fleapit near us, they know me there; on Mondays they always let me in, there's not much going on then, as a matter of fact. And of course you'll be *my* guest, that's settled . . . You know what puzzles me," he added in quite a different tone of voice, "all the time we've been standing here, not a single person has come out of the hotel."

Josel pushed his bike a bit closer to the hotel entrance. Andreas followed him, and now they were only a few meters from the revolving door; through the glass you could see lights inside.

Behind the door a boy could be seen in a high-collared uniform and a bellhop's cap on his head. Then the door began to revolve, and suddenly it spat out an elderly gentleman dressed in black who put on a green hat as soon as he was outside; Josel immediately thought of mourning attire and a funeral—but the green hat was out of place. That woman, earlier, didn't she put on a bright green hat too? In the hot August sun, now climbing to the center of the sky, that looked funny.

Josel stared after the man, who hurried by without taking notice of them. Behind him he could hear the sound of the revolving door slowly ebbing away.

"Those epic films from Italy are playing now. We can go, if you want." Josel looked back at the hotel entrance and saw again the face of the boy as he leaned against the glass, staring out at them. For an instant Josel thought that their glances had met, and that a small, invisible spark had been struck; at any rate he had felt a response, without a doubt. The boy could be my age, thought Josel, looking acutely at him, and surely he already knows all the secrets of this great house of stone. And if the glass had not been between them, slightly milky, separating them, he would have gone over and asked him about them. Surely what held him back even more was the serious, almost sad expression of the face, motionless, which seemed as though it were suspended behind the door, almost like a mask. He thought perhaps he perceived

something like yearning in the boy's face — yearning for the outdoors, for a bicycle that he could ride around town and along the
Klodnitz. Or was it all just the mirror image of his own yearning?

"How about some ice cream?" Andreas asked.

From Andreas's tone of voice, Josel could tell that he had
grasped nothing of this. Maybe he had not seen the boy in the
bellhop's uniform at all. "Later," he said. It seemed to him as if
this loudly spoken word, like a spell, had made the face behind the
glass vanish. Slowly he turned his bike around in the other direction. "Come on, let's ride some more." Two officers passed,
headed directly for the hotel entrance. Josel rose on his pedals.
"Let's ride off to the left," he called to Andreas. As he turned into
Wilhelmstrasse, he was just able to see the two officers disappear
into the hotel. "Keep really close behind me," he yelled to Andreas. "Watch out, here comes a streetcar! Jesus!"

Even after riding around town with Andreas for almost two
hours, Josel still wasn't sure whether he had found a new friend.
He had planned this bicycle tour less to show Andreas the sights
of the town than to have an excuse for being alone with him, and
perhaps even to test him. He had shown him:

    the Christ the King Church
    the Church of the Holy Cross
    the railroad station and Germaniaplatz
    Kaiser-Wilhelmstrasse
    the Hotel Upper Silesia
    Weichmann's silk shop
    the Klodnitz, the Wild Klodnitz, the Klodnitz canal, and all
        three bridges across it
    the municipal theater and the Victoria baths
    Niederwallstrasse, Oberwallstrasse, the Ring, and the old City
        Hall
    and from afar the Gleiwitz mine

He had not shown him the construction shed in the park by the
Wild Klodnitz! Yet he had arranged all this, as a matter of fact, in

order to entrust him with the secret of the shed. For, after having opened and closed the shed five evenings in a row and taken in thirty marks (he had hidden ten at the bottom of a flowerpot and buried twenty next to the garden cottage), he had a stronge urge to confide in someone. He had ridden through the park with Andreas and stopped in front of the shed at 11:30 that morning, when, admittedly, it gave the impression of being only an ordinary, somewhat dilapidated construction shed, which did not even hint of its secret in the intense sharpness of the midday light, let alone betray it, and if he began to tell Andreas about it now, he wouldn't believe him. Not now, at any rate; perhaps in the evening, when it grows dark, and the groaning wood reveals a few of its features. So he rode past the shed without slowing down. In his pocket he felt the cold key; with it he could unlock the padlock on the shed and the secret for Andreas too — but he did not.

During the conversation along the way, which was so often broken off and then begun anew, he had found time for the following questions:

Do you believe in God?
What do you think of Chopin?
Would you have the guts to run away from home?
How fast can you run the hundred-meter dash?
How far can you piss? (They even tried it out, and Andreas won!)
How often do you do it in a week?
Do you do it alone?

When Andreas didn't catch on right away, Josel immediately added another question:

"Have you ever done anything with a girl? I mean, really? I mean, have you ever kissed a girl, actually, on the mouth?"

Andreas had answered all his questions guilelessly. Only when the talk turned to girls was he flustered; after stammering, he finally answered Josel affirmatively, but he was not willing to say anything about it beyond this meager "Yes."

And Josel did not press the point, for all at once he did not

know how to go from there to the matter of the shed, and the
shed was his main concern. How long, he thought, will I be able
to live with this thing about the shed without telling somebody
about it? He had thought of confiding in the old County Magistrate, of explaining everything to him, but that probably would
not do until it was all over—only who could say when it would be
over?

When he heard that Andreas was coming to visit, he was ob-
sessed by the thought that he could confess to no one but Andreas. For it never would have occurred to him really to confess
this matter, that is, into the ear of Curate Mikas. Every four weeks
you spread out before Curate Mikas all those venial sins which at
communion classes it had been agreed you were prone to; not a
single one had been added since then. That might change some
day, when he was grown up, but not now, at any rate.

"Have you ever watched anybody else . . ." He paused. They
were in the park for the second time and had reached the construction shed. Josel leaned his bicycle against a tree and sat down
on a thick clump of grass. He remembered that there was one
more cigarette hidden in his saddlebag and fished it out. "You feel
like a smoke?" he asked Andreas.

He did not want to. "It makes me feel, well, sick. I tried it a few
times, but I can't seem to."

"No, no," Josel objected, "you're doing it wrong. You mustn't
inhale the smoke, not at all; you just hold it in your mouth a while
and then let it out slowly, and nothing will happen to you." Josel
struck a match on his sandal.

"Well, at the school where I go they say you have to draw it
right down into your lungs, otherwise it's like the way little kids
smoke."

"They say, they say," said Josel and drew the smoke in. He
looked at Andreas unwaveringly and then slowly blew the smoke
into his eyes. "It just has to look real . . . Here, try it."

Andreas took the cigarette and sucked on it, but his mouth had
scarcely filled up with smoke before it began to tickle the back of
his throat, he began to cough, and the smoke came out of his
mouth in puffs; it must have looked ridiculous. Tears welled up in

his eyes. Andreas felt like a fool. And he coughed even more, although the tickling had stopped. "Excuse me," he said. "I told you so." He lay in the grass looking up into the green crown of a tree that turned paler and paler.

Josel sucked contentedly on the damp tip of the cigarette and gazed at the construction shed over in the trees. "Have you ever watched two people when they're in love, two grownups . . . when they're actually doing it?" He puffed on his cigarette.

"You mean . . ."

"Right, I mean really *duppen*."

"*Duppen,* what's that?"

"Jesus Christ, you don't know what *duppen* is? Well, what do you call it?

"Well what?"

"Oh, I mean, like what makes babies afterward."

"But the girl doesn't always get pregnant, not if you're careful."

Now it was Josel who coughed out the smoke. He suspected that Andreas had known from the very start what was on his mind. And he, Josel, puff, had fallen for it, puff puff.

"So, have you ever watched?"

"So *duppen* is what you call it? We call it *pudern!*"

"I don't care what they call it in Breslau, Andreas. I want to know if you've ever watched." Josel was getting annoyed. Clearly he couldn't reveal the secret of the shed to Andreas, not now at any rate.

Andreas shook his head. "No, no. Besides, I wouldn't look at them, I'd be afraid they'd try to kill me, the man, I mean, if he found out somebody had been watching him do it . . ." Andreas's throat constricted, so that Josel did not catch the final words.

Josel stubbed out the cigarette butt in the grass and exhaled the rest of the smoke. "Look at them without their knowing. That's it. Would that excite you?"

Andreas said nothing. He would have liked to ride back to Strachwitzstrasse, to Aunt Valeska's. He'd had enough of the town for now. He was hungry too. He wanted to write a letter to his father, he wanted to tell him that he had arrived safely, and that the people here always gathered around the radio for the news broadcasts and talked about *wojna.* He wanted to tell him that everything here was different than in Breslau, but he would get used to it all right. He wanted to go see Aunt Milka, so she could tell him more about the Klodnitz, which he didn't know much about except that it was a narrow, dirty, sluggishly flowing river and had to be memorized in school as one of the tributaries to the right of the Oder: Olsa Ruda Birawka Klodnitz Malapane . . . With a shove Andreas set his rear wheel spinning.

Josel watched him closely. He had gotten a bit closer to Andreas. Maybe, just maybe he might take him along to the shed this evening after all. Or tomorrow. He would think it over.

"If you want," Josel said to Andreas, "I'll take you over to see my girl later on."

Andreas had to cough once again in surprise.

They hurried to get back home in time for dinner. Of course they were not hungry any more, because first one had treated the other to ice cream, and then the other had treated the first, and the first had bought another round. And when they had passed by the Kaiser Park, where the concession stand at the little fair was already open, Josel bought two grab-bags, which apart from some colored paper, tinfoil medals, and a decal, contained a little tube of love-drops, which they gulped down, laughing and sputtering. Then Josel insisted that Andreas try a Polish waffle, but he refused; he had burped up the sweetish ice cream twice already. Maybe it was because of the cigarette.

"They don't open until three," Josel said. "Why don't we come back then, and ride the merry-go-round?"

Andreas saw his savings melting away. If he were really going to take Josel to the movies on Monday as he had promised, then he'd better stop spending money. Josel seemed to understand his hesitation. He ate the Polish waffle himself, then he said, "Well, that doesn't cost a thing, nothing at all. Hey, I know, let's go to the merry-go-round owner and help push, then he'll let us ride for free." He led Andreas to a merry-go-round with white horses in front of black coaches.

"Here, this belongs to old Konjetzny, he's always looking for older kids to push that thing from inside, he doesn't have much money, you know, not nearly enough to afford a helper."

Josel swung himself up onto the merry-go-round and sprang

around among the horses as if he were at home here. "We can't get in now," he called to Andreas. "The old man has covered everything with canvas and tied it down."

Andreas had stopped in front of a horse that was rearing up, its forelegs in the air; an iron rod bored through the horse from below and came out above on its back—the rider could hold on to it. The horse was white and made of wood with rough-hewn legs; but its head was carefully carved and its nostrils were painted red, a fiery red. Suddenly Andreas saw his mother before him; she was riding a horse, and all at once the horse stumbled to its knees, and she tumbled off and lay motionless on the ground . . . Andreas hooked his hand into the horse's ropy mane and clutched it firmly.

"What you doing there?" From behind the canvas-covered bandstand appeared a man with whitish-blond hair and big doughy hands rowing through the air. Andreas jumped, but before he could say anything at all, Josel answered casually: "Oh, I've always helped out with the pushing, every year. I just wanted to see if Herr Konjetzny can use me again."

"Nix, nix, we no need nobody," said the big man with the whitish-blond hair, who loomed like a giant among the little wooden horses. "Get out of here, scramscramscram. Nix Konjetzny." And his heavy hands swung back and forth.

"Oh, is old Herr Konjetzny dead or something?" asked Josel with wary friendliness. "Herr Konjetzny," and he emphasized the *Herr*, "always let us ride for free, no matter what . . . Where is the old man anyway?"

"Nix Konjetzny," the giant said. "That be my merry-go-round, my merry-go-round, I no need bad kids, scram, scram, get lost!" And his big hands rowed closer and closer.

Josel was already on the ground and pulled Andreas down after him. That deep, excited voice promised no good for the two of them. "Let's beat it!" And when they had reached the safety of their bikes, Josel yelled out "*Heilhitler*" as a kind of protest.

Maybe as a kind of defeat too, Andreas thought. He pedaled along after his cousin without looking back a single time.

They arrived home drenched with sweat. It was too late for dinner. In the garden they met the Sergeant, who was holding a dirty
rag in one hand and a wrench in the other. Since the Sergeant had
been quartered there, Josel had seen him lying under the car so
often that he would not have been surprised if he were going out
to the parked car now to take his afternoon nap underneath it.
"Hi," Josel said. Andreas mumbled something. The Sergeant said
nothing, he didn't even look up. Maybe he was loaded again.

They met Halina in the hall, she was emptying a bucket.
"*Obiadu nie ma. Każdy bierze z komory co się da, tak pani kazała.*"
(No dinner today. Everybody helps himself in the pantry, Ma-
dame's orders.) "*Verstehen?* Madame in church . . ."

"Oh, Madame in church?" Josel asked, imitating Halina.

"In church," Halina repeated. "*Dziś nie będzie brzdąkaniny.*"
(No piano lessons today.)

Josel went into the kitchen with Andreas and spread a slice of
bread and drippings for each of them. He scraped up some cracklings from the bottom of the jar and sprinkled salt on liberally. He
did not want to say so in front of Andreas, but he preferred the
bread and drippings to a formal meal with three courses. Tomorrow someone was sure to carp about who had fished out the
cracklings, but he didn't give a damn, as a matter of fact. To
Andreas he said apologetically, "The banquet tonight'll make up
for it—roast goose, I think." He bit into the bread. Andreas
nodded.

He didn't talk much, this cousin from Breslau. Before, on the
merry-go-round, he had wished that Andreas would say something to back him up, but he had simply clutched at the mane of a
wooden horse, his eyes bulging. The two of them could have
taken care of that crude blond fellow all right. Oh well, as the
Gleiwitz saying goes: A crab cuts with shears that don't squeak. It
occurred to Josel that he needed someone for his shed enterprise
who could keep his mouth shut—just like Andreas.

"Everything's in a mess, *muj Bosche,* it'll be a disaster," Aunt
Lucie (Widera) called out as she came rustling down the stairs.
"Oh, there you are," she said as she passed Josel and Andreas. She
said it as if she had been searching for them the whole day and had

finally found them. She took hold of both of them as if this were the only way to assure herself of their presence, and a strong smell of starch remained behind where she touched them.

"The seamstress is here, but not the bride," she lamented. "Miss Bride-to-be is gone, along with the groom."

Aunt Lucie (Widera) had wrapped a white shawl about her head to make a turban, as was currently the fashion, and had fastened the end of the cloth with a diamond hatpin so big and flashy it must have been fake.

"And your mother went to see Father Pattas, what could she want with Father Pattas? . . . And guests are here already, go on into the music room, Josel, there are already guests there, from all over." Aunt Lucie (Widera) disappeared into the next room; she was really excited.

This was not the same Aunt Lucie Josel knew, and he knew her pretty well.

Andreas waited to see what Josel would say, but Josel said nothing at all; he bit heartily into his bread, as if the whole thing didn't concern him. "Well, I don't exactly have the feeling that a wedding's going on here. How about you? Come on, let's go have a look at who's here already."

Andreas chewed in embarrassment. "I'm too new here, how can I tell? I only know about a wedding we had in Breslau once, it began in the morning, with music and children singing, and the doorbell never stopped ringing, and people came and brought presents . . ."

"Oh, sure, that's the way it is here too, but this time it's really a rush wedding." Josel laughed. "I don't know if you noticed how red-eyed Mamuscha looked last night. She's been trying to stop the wedding, that's why she keeps running back to Father Pattas, but my sister Irma is bound and determined . . . if only to spite Mamuscha and, yes, to punish her too."

"I have to admit, you have a funny sister," Andreas said. "I ask her something, she looks at me and doesn't answer. She's sitting in her room, the door is open, she's staring at the wall. I come by again an hour later, she's still sitting that way."

Josel grinned. "That Heiko—I mean, what kind of a name is

that, how can anybody be named Heiko, there's no such name around here—well, this Heiko, who is becoming my brother-in-law tonight... What am I saying?" he interrupted himself and looked at the clock. "He's marrying my sister right now in front of the judge in Niederwallstrasse!"

Upstairs a door banged. Aunt Lucie (Widera) screeched downstairs: "And the guests for the bachelor party are going to come this evening too, as soon as it gets dark. One of them has already been here, to let us know. Somehow or other they must have found out about the wedding. I told them they were too late, but the man said, 'You can't cheat us out of the bachelor party.'"

In the hall, Josel hopped around on one leg giggling: "The reception and the bachelor party at the same time, that ought to bring good luck." And to Andreas: "Isn't this a crazy wedding?"

The diamond hatpin flashed, and Aunt Lucie (Widera) zoomed past them. "You can send the seamstress home," Josel called after her. "Fräulein Irma Piontek, as a matter of fact, is getting married in precisely"—he stuck his head into the kitchen—"precisely eight minutes by the judge in Niederwallstrasse to Private and Officer Candidate Heiko Birkner. (Now where is he from? Not from our cold homeland, at any rate... *wszystko jedno*, too.) Well, they're getting married, anyway, and Mamuscha couldn't stop them." He raised his voice at the end, as if he were happy about it.

"*Djobok!*" Aunt Lucie (Widera) said. "And the gown? What was she wearing, then?" She sat down on a step. "*Muj Bosche, muj Bosche!*" she said. The second time her voice trembled with indignation. In that instant she remembered that it was Irma's mother, not she, who had to bear the sorrow. "Poor Valeska," she said, "poor Valeska."

All at once it was quiet in the house. Behind the door to the music room voices buzzed; in the wild grapevines outside by the open window a cricket began to chirp; far away the sounds of coughing could be heard, surging and receding like surf. Aunt Lucie (Widera) thought: Tomorrow morning, when it's all over, I'll go to the river, to Water Milka, and ask her what the future has in store for me.

Josel thought: Maybe I'll be lucky and the war won't start for a few days more, and I'll make enough money to go with Ulla to Warsaw, to the Church of the Holy Cross, to Chopin's heart.

Andreas was thinking of his letter: Since I've been here, this is the quietest it's been. More happens here in a day than in Breslau in a year, but still, I'd rather be with you, Father.

They remained silent, and their silence dusted them as if with snow, leaving them motionless.

Josel was the first to shake off the spell. "I'm going upstairs to see Papusch. Aunt Lucie-in-parentheses-Widera, you can take Andreas into the parlor" (sometimes, ironically, he called the music room the parlor). "And if Ulla comes" — he winked at Andreas — "then have her play something for him until I get there." Josel ran up the stairs. "Something classical!"

8

Montag noted down for later: "Perhaps insert a separate chapter on the role of publicity." That had only become clear to him recently. No politician of that era (at the very beginning of the century!), not even one from the capital, had enlisted the press so knowingly and consistently for his own purposes. Not in Germany, in any case. The first thing K did when he decided to run for the Prussian Landtag was to create a broad platform for himself with the help of the press. He bought and sold newspapers and put his own people on their editorial staffs; he himself was often the editor of as many as three newspapers (or magazines) at the same time. At one time or another he owned the *Polak*, the *Kurier Śląski*, the *Katolik*, the *Dziennik Śląski*. The newspaper *Górnoślązak* (the *Upper Silesian*) he built up into his fighting voice in the postwar and plebiscite years. During this period he founded German-language newspapers such as the *Upper Silesian Border News*, the *Catholic People's News*, the *Upper Silesian Post* in Gleiwitz, and the *Oder Sentry*. Satirical magazines that were published under his aegis were *What You Look Like* in German and *Kocynder* in Polish. He was so successful with these among the common people that the Germans felt themselves compelled to distribute a similar periodical, the *Pjerun*. The *White Eagle* made K bilingual for the bilingual inhabitants of Upper Silesia. The magazine *Polonia* appeared in Kattowitz until his death; he continued to edit it from exile. By the end, however, the issues were said to be selling only 1280 copies.

In a letter to Tadeusz Nowicki he wrote in 1903: "For me, politics and newspapers are one and the same. I do not understand why politicians have made so little use of the press up to now. It seems to me to be the best means of influencing the masses in countries where illiteracy has been wiped out. If a politician succeeds in getting the Church and the press behind him, then his rise can no longer be prevented. . . ."

Perhaps there ought to be a chapter on its own summarizing K's efforts to achieve autonomy. At least three times, with the evidence at his disposal (sometimes amounting to no more than a fragmentary eyewitness account, a passage in a letter, or even mere speculation), K threatened the central government in Warsaw with the secession of Upper Silesia. The first time facing the military commander Nowina-Doliwa during the third uprising. The second time in 1922 when the Sejm in Warsaw refused to let him form a new government. The third time when Piłsudski appointed the Galician Michael Grażyński *wojewoda* of Upper Silesia and shortly thereafter declared void the Upper Silesians' claims to autonomy. After the eastern part of Upper Silesia was ceded to the Polish republic, K embarked on a process of reconciliation between the two parts of Upper Silesia — the German and the Polish — across linguistic barriers, certainly not across religious ones. But the third time it was nothing but the rattling of an empty scabbard. For with the help of a group of rebels, Grażyński had already placed his people everywhere and driven out Korfanty's followers.

There is no proof that K had been playing with the idea of an independent state before the referendum of March 1921. Through an emissary from diplomatic circles in Berlin, he learned that Matthias Erzberger, whom K had known during the war years, had been making a thrust in that direction. The local elections on 28 November 1919 had been a catastrophe; a large majority of the rural population of Upper Silesia had voted for Polish candidates. It was a nightmare for Berlin: in a plebiscite the whole of Upper Silesia with its rich deposits of coal and ore could be lost. To meet the threat, Erzberger suggested sending a delegation to K to sound him out on whether he would agree to a Free State of Upper Silesia, along the lines of Danzig, if he were given a high position in the government. This suggestion of Erzberger's was rejected by the Reich authorities.

He must write to Sopicki about this.

9

VALESKA HAD GROWN UP in a little river town where Polish was spoken on the east bank, while across the river, on the west bank where her home was, the language was principally German. That broad German which rolls the consonants and draws the lips down, sprinkled with Polish words but following German syntax, was something of which her family was especially proud, for most of the people in the area teetered back and forth between German and Polish constructions. Her family felt a certain superiority to them, but it was one they did not care to flaunt — for her father, as a drygoods merchant, was dependent on them as customers — or only occasionally, in official conversations with a bureaucrat or on Sedan Day or when a visitor from the Reich was there. Then they would purse their lips, constantly moistening them out of nervousness but also to make the hard rolled *r*'s more supple, and in general spoke only when spoken to. Later they would send the children to Breslau or Berlin, where they would lose their poor accents.

In school the instruction was carried on in German, but if a pupil answered a teacher's question in Polish, nobody made a fuss; the teachers were as familiar with one language as with the other, and the head teacher, Grabowski, always said: "I don't give a *wszystko jedno* whether you read a *polska książka* or a German book, children, all that matters is that you read." But after 1900 things changed; stricter regulations came from Berlin, and when the use of Polish was forbidden, even in religious instruction, there were pupils' strikes in Posen, and even in their town children of purely Polish parents were kept out of school for weeks. In church more Polish was spoken than German; that depended also on the composition of the congregation, which the priest, Father Starczewski, could tell at a glance when he stepped from his sacristy into his little church, and make allowances for. Directed by the officials to preach in German he did so; but if, for example, he announced a Requiem Mass for the deceased Franziska Kandrzyn, who had left seven children behind her and also a drunkard who claimed to be the father of the seven poor urchins, but whom she had thrown out of the house a few years before, he rattled it off first in German, as the upper bodies of the worshippers swayed back and forth in their pews tired and exhausted from the heavy labor of their day in the fields or the coal mines; if, however, he recited it more slowly and in Polish, they straightened up and listened more closely. "*Święta Maria,*" they sighed and looked at one another, "it's already a year since Franziska left us."

And when in March or April, during the Stations of the Cross, the congregation crawled on its knees from one station to the next, and Father Starczewski, filling the whole church with his fine bass, sang before the ninth station: "And then Jesus for the third time fell beneath the weight of the cross," the women murmured in prayer: "We beseech thee, hear us O Lord," some in German, some in Polish, it did not matter, it did not even affect the speech rhythm. Those who could not speak Polish were mostly officials who had been posted there from the Reich; they were Protestants anyway, and there in the Lutheran church they were among their own kind . . . So it came about that Valeska Wondraczek first learned the alphabet in German and the Lord's Prayer in Polish, and even today the Hail Mary passed her lips more easily in Polish, and her supplications to God she could not imagine in any other language: *mój ty Boże kochany. . . .*

Until the end of the war, both segments of the population had lived together in relative peace; tensions occasionally arose, after the Prussian regulations about religious instruction, for example, or after election rallies for Korfanty, or after demonstrations by the Hakatists, but there was little hostility. Even though Valeska's father's drygoods shop was on the west bank, people did come from across the river to buy special things—English tweed or French silk, Belgian lace or Czech worsted yarns, velours, chenilles, chintzes, cretonnes, gauze curtains or voiles. In his shop he spoke Polish as readily as German; indeed, if several customers were there, he could switch quickly from one language to the other in mid-sentence. Valeska had always admired him for the way he handled his customers, particularly the ladies, and she sometimes went with her brother to visit him; they would sit on a little bench next to the big oval mirror and would not move, not because their father had forbidden them to (which he had), but because it was so exciting when people came in and fished around in the drawers, rolled the bolts of fabric about and dug into the cartons and crates, meanwhile not forgetting to sway their bodies in front of the mirrors now and then, at least the ladies, and pouring cascades of words over everything, until sometimes they disappeared out the door without buying anything. Then the children, along with a silent father who did not betray his feelings, would spend the next half hour restoring order in the shop.

No one had ever been disturbed by their father counting out money in Polish, *raz, dwa, trzy, cztery,* or in German, even if he said it to a *wschodniok* in German and to an *Ostler* in Polish. Actually, it was rather hard to work out which of his customers were Germans and which Poles, and after the plebiscite and the third uprising, when the town became part of the new Polish territory, families in which "Water Polish" was spoken exclusively emigrated with the Wondraczeks, and only the younger ones could manage some broken German in the refugee huts in Gleiwitz.

To all those who would stay and had voted for Poland, Korfanty had promised a cow and crop land, and in Sosnowitz he had already had livestock distributed to peasants and miners; many families had remained for that reason, but after the plebiscite the Polish aristocracy took over the estates of the German aristocracy, and land reform became as far-fetched as it had been earlier under the Prussians. So the upshot of it all was that the poor cottagers, if they got anything at all, received only a goat, which in Upper Silesia was dubbed a "Korfanty cow."

It was the river which both divided the little town and held it together, which accompanied Valeska on her way to school, to the drygoods shop, and to church, bright and soft and streaming, a narrow river which in summer was more of a brook that you could wade across. But in early spring when the snows melted, it was unpredictable, it swelled, gushed across the pastures, over the crop land, it stomped, tore, and stormed, it rose up beneath the bridges and made them quake. And in the spring of '15, she would never forget it, she was on the way to her father's shop, twilight already descending, when from the bridge she saw a massive slab of ice with a child on it, drifting downriver, bobbing on the foaming waves like a cork. The block of ice had just disappeared under the bridge. She had run over to the other side, bent far over the railing and looked for it, yes, there, her eyes had not deceived her, a child three or four years old was lying there like a caterpillar with its hands clutching the ice. All at once, the block disappeared in the raging torrent and when it surfaced again, the child was gone; she saw the block rise from the waters twice more before it was lost in distance and dusk.

She could not have said how long she remained on the bridge, leaning against the railing, staring at the foamy peaks on the river. At the time she believed she could never rid herself of the experience. She had gone home when it was dark and had locked herself in her room. She was unable to tell anyone a thing about it. Not even her father.

She had hated the river ever since. Perhaps it had made her departure from the little town easier.

10

Montag walked out to the garden gate, where the mailbox was. Ever since he had acquired the habit of working far into the night, of reading, listening to the radio, or simply sitting there awake and registering the sounds from outside and inside, he had gotten up late, sometimes not until almost noon. His first move, after he had washed, dressed, and put on the teakettle, was to go to the mailbox.

He followed the path beneath the fruit trees. The midday light blinded him so much that he shaded his eyes with his hands. August light, vibrating through the silver-green leaves of the trees. He pulled from the box the newspapers he subscribed to, the *Silesian Daily News,* the *Völkischer Beobachter,* the *Frankfurter Zeitung.* The only Polish newspaper, the *Kurjer Poranny,* was missing again; it had stopped coming two weeks ago. At the very bottom he found a letter with Polish stamps, he spotted those right away. He turned the envelope over: *Stanisław Sopicki, Katowice.* This was the letter he had been waiting for. Only a few days ago, on the 20th or 21st of August, if he remembered correctly, he had found a brief notice of the death of Korfanty in the *Voice of Upper Silesia.* He did not find it in the other papers, not even in those from the capitals, and had almost overlooked it in the *Voice,* for it was only three lines long. It merely stated that Adalbert Korfanty, the Polish Plebiscite Commissioner in Upper Silesia, had died in a Warsaw hospital at the age of sixty-six. Nothing more, no commentary, no polemics, not even a sentence by way of explanation. He had read in the *Kurjer Poranny* that Korfanty had returned to Poland from exile in France, some time in the early spring, and had promptly been arrested by Polish officials. The same day, he had written to Stanisław Sopicki, whom he had met twice in Kattowitz in the early 1930s, and who, as he learned only later, had been a friend of Korfanty and, in the years before his exile, his last secretary. Of course he no longer had an address for him, so he simply wrote in care of the editors of *Polonia*.

Montag walked back to the garden cottage. He wondered why the Pionteks' house was so quiet. Perhaps they were already on their way to the judge, yes, this was Irma's wedding day, Frau Piontek had invited him to a big wedding feast this evening at the Hotel Upper Silesia. Only the Sergeant seemed to be there, he could hear his whistling through the open window on the second floor.

Montag scanned the headlines of the newspapers while his tea steeped. In the *V.B.*, underlined in red: POLAND LIGHTS THE FUSE. TOTAL WAR MOBILIZATION IN POLAND. FORMATION OF MINISTRY FOR DEFENSE OF THE REICH.

In the edition of the *Frankfurter Zeitung* from the Reich: POLISH TERRORISM CONTINUES. More important was the little notice at the very top: SIR NEVILLE HENDERSON VISITS THE FÜHRER. In the *Voice of Upper Silesia*: POLAND RESORTS TO ACTS OF DESPERATION. TOTAL MOBILIZATION IN PANIC.

But he was really more concerned with the letter from Sopicki, with the Piłsudski stamps that caught his eye. After all, the headlines of the papers from the capitals were already a day old. He slit open the envelope with a kitchen knife, being careful not to damage the stamps, then unfolded the letter. There were three pages, completely filled by a rather nervous hand, with wide gaps between the lines.

It was the hour when people living well-ordered lives were ladling soup from the tureen at the dinner table while listening to the midday concert on the radio, the *Poet and Peasant* overture. Montag went to the pantry for the bowl of clabber, he sprinkled some cinnamon on it and a bit more sugar and ate it along with a piece of dry bread as he read the letter:

Dear Dr. Montag,

I am writing to you while still under the influence of recent events, nevertheless I will try to be as objective as possible and answer your questions. And please pardon my somewhat inadequate written German.

(It occurred to him that no date was given. He picked up the
envelope and, trying to decipher the postmark, could make out 25
Aug with some certainty. So the letter had taken almost a week to
go from Kattowitz to Gleiwitz although it was no more than 30
kilometers. Still, he was glad that any mail at all was getting across
the Polish border, since the censors for whatever reasons were
already stopping Polish newspapers.)

You ask about Korfanty's last years. I'll give you a few bare
facts. Such as: Wojciech Korfanty, the most famous Polish politician of Upper Silesia, spent the years 1935–39 in Czechoslovakia. When Hitler ordered the occupation of the remnant of
Czechoslovakia on 15 March 1939, Korfanty succeeded in fleeing.
He traveled in the automobile of a French diplomat. For only a
few weeks in France was he able to study the tense international
situation. For him it was quite clear that Poland's turn had
come and that his place was in his threatened fatherland.

Toward the end of April of that same year, he returned to
Poland by ship. Before reaching Gdingen, he heard on the radio
Hitler's speech listing his demands of Poland. The next day he
was back in his beloved work place, the editorial office of
Polonia in Kattowitz.

But the very next day a police car came to arrest him. They
took him to Warsaw and threw him in prison. The public prosecutor, Herr Michalowski — I set down his name so that one day
shame and misfortune may befall him — naturally had no real
grounds for his arrest. Confiscated articles? Unpaid personal
taxes? All these matters had long since been settled, and there
was absolutely no cause for arrest. But the energetic public
prosecutor declared: "It doesn't matter, one way or another I'll
find a clause that will keep you in prison."

"Yes," replied Korfanty, "I know that you are capable of
bringing about such a thing, but tell me, what has that to do
with the law" [the word "law" crossed out] "with justice?"

Herr Korfanty told me that later, otherwise I would not
quote him literally here.

The "disobedient" prisoner was put in a cell. A few weeks

later, when his condition was deteriorating rapidly, he was set free. He died in Warsaw, in a little hospital in Emilia-Plater-strasse, at about 4 A.M. on the 17th of August; his family was with him. He had no visible injuries. On the 24th of August he was buried at the central cemetery, the prettiest one in Katto-witz, in Francuskastrasse. About 30,000 people (some said 80,000) attended, from Kattowitz and the surrounding area, so many wreaths were delivered that they could not be counted, and three bands took turns playing. I saw many simple people: miners, railway workers, peasants too, who were weeping. Lots of the clergy were there, including Chaplain General Gawlina. We all realized that with Korfanty a great chapter in the history of Upper Silesia had ended.

Thus at this critical moment Poland lost a gifted politician and leader of the Polish masses, who understood the psychology of the German nationalists better than any other Polish statesman.

Born in 1873, he lived until 1935 in this beautiful and rich country that he loved so much and where his family also lived.

Many Germans believed he was a "German-hater." This view, however, was very superficial. To be sure, he fought strongly against the Germans in the decade before the World War, and he led the Polish masses at the time of the plebiscite (1921) and during the three uprisings, but he knew that the two peoples should live peacefully together in this small but important region and he expressed this opinion in public statements, for example, in welcoming the Polish occupation troops and offi-cials (in June of 1922) or at the opening of the Upper Silesian Landtag in Kattowitz. He declared specifically that the Polish republic must be fair not only to Poles but also to non-Poles, and that all citizens, all minorities must be protected by the White Eagle. For a time he even attempted to make Upper Silesia a free province, somewhat like the free city of Danzig, but only very briefly, because as a realistic politician he soon saw that neither the Poles, the Germans, nor the Allies would consent to this. But he had kept on trying to win a certain autonomy for Upper Silesia, such as exemption from service in the Polish army for Upper Silesian men, which Field Marshal Piłsudski simply abolished. Since Piłsudski did not understand the mentality of the Upper Silesians, he could not grasp the consequences this would have. Many mistakes were made in that respect, on both sides, in Warsaw and in Berlin.

Shortly after what was to be (as it turned out) my last conversation with Korfanty, on 26 July, when he also talked of writing a book about his Polish imprisonment, I decided to take a few days' vacation to rest a little. I traveled to the southeast of Poland, toward the Romanian border, to stay for a few days in the mild climate. I was convinced that the remaining days of August would be critical for Germany and Poland. The year before, the second half of September had seen the decisive phase in the contest for the Sudetenland. Since Poland is situated further to the north than Czechoslovakia, it is only to be expected that some decisive move toward war or peace will come earlier—not in September, but in August. It seems, though, that sufficient reason prevails in Europe that the statesmen will still somehow reach an agreement.

In any case, when I approached the Romanian border, I saw in the papers the sad news that Korfanty had died. I traveled to Kattowitz at once in order to attend the funeral. Though people and politicians quarreled over Korfanty when he was alive, now after his death they were unanimous about his greatness as a political leader; that was expressed in all the speeches, most handsomely in that of Chaplain Gawlina, for in all that he did Korfanty remained a good Catholic.

In great sorrow!

Stanisław Sopicki

Montag also found a slip of paper enclosed, obviously written in the same hand, but faster and more carelessly, so that the loops leaned strongly to the right. He read:

Rumors are circulating here that Korfanty's cell in the Mokotow prison (that is a section of Warsaw) was redecorated with a paint that gave off a toxic vapor which he inhaled, and which is probably why he died so rapidly. The government in Warsaw got rid of him, for they would never have been able to convict him. If that is true

Montag was surprised by this communication. He read the note again. He compared the handwriting; no doubt about it, the two were identical even if written in different states of excitement. The paper too was different, thicker. He pinned the note firmly to the wall above the table. *If that is true*—followed by no punctuation; no period, no question or exclamation mark. He wondered whether he should pursue the matter.

There were three pages, written on both sides, and on the back of the third there would certainly have been enough room for the note. Why did Sopicki write this on a different piece of paper? And was that not an unusual, indeed, almost absurd speculation? A rumor that could only have arisen in Kattowitz where, like everywhere else in Upper Silesia, both sides enjoyed having martyrs? It was a rumor, nothing more. Sopicki had written that himself, but he had taken it seriously enough to want to communicate it to him, a stranger.

Montag poured himself a cup of tea, which had grown cold in the meantime. He took a sheet of paper and a pencil, he wanted to write something down, but he did not know what—anything that might make the answers to such a question easier. But when he looked at the paper after a brief, absentminded pause, he could only decipher a few confused scribbles and strokes. He wanted to forget the note, and the foolish rumor as well, which at this very moment would be circulating in the streets of Kattowitz. It had no bearing on him, on his work. But he did not take the note down from the wall.

I should go back to an earlier period, he thought, one I know better and more precisely. Besides, he could write Sopicki another letter and ask him for further details. He would like to know whether anyone from the German Party or the German Democratic bloc had spoken at the funeral. He had read that in recent years more than 7,000 people had emigrated from German to Polish Upper Silesia. The language was not that different. They could understand one another. The towns, the landscape, the coal mines, the rivers around them—one could not tell them apart. And the land was the same land. Others, not counting on an eventual return, went farther, to America or to Chile, like the Passwegs.

Perhaps he should return again to the beginning. It was clear to him that he would find the key to K's political biography only in his childhood. Everything he had written up till now—was it not all reciting, cataloguing, illustrating, depicting events? Did it not all depend on K's decision in favor of Poland, which he must have made some time or other? And what facts, motives, and causes, what sort of syndrome lay behind this decision? Or was it not a decision at all? Was it family, education, history? Was it the Polish songs his grandmother sang to him, the stories the peasants told around the potato fires on autumn evenings, the little red booklets giving the *Historia Polski* in 25 pictures, the *Żywoty Świętych* by Piotr Skarga, with which, according to Skowroński, his mother had taught him to read Polish?

In an article in the *Kurjer Poranny* he had read: "Even as a child Korfanty enjoyed reading the patriotic Polish poets, and later on he confounded his German teachers by reciting stanzas from Mickiewicz from memory."

Montag was inclined to class this, with so much, as slanted information, propaganda. In school K had written his themes in German, as he did his seminar papers at the University. But his first piece of professional journalism, a newspaper article for which he was paid, was composed in Polish, and appeared in the *Katolik* in Beuthen. In his *Appeal to the People of Upper Silesia* (Kattowitz, 1931) K mentions that he first really learned to write and think in Polish, apart from school, in an illegal Polish student organization. His German teacher's intolerance of everything Polish and his own enthusiasm for the greatness of the Polish past had finally turned him into a Polish nationalist. That did not convince Montag, it was too rationally thought out for a boy of twelve or fourteen years. But these sentences could be taken more seriously: "Even as a Catholic one was already disadvantaged, only the poor were Catholic. The teachers and officials came from Prussia and were Protestants."

K had grown up during the years of *Kulturkampf* and this had

molded him. It was the undoing of Prussian policies in Upper
Silesia that they had been formulated, in Breslau as well as in
Berlin, by Lutherans, who never comprehended what strong
roots Catholicism had put down in Upper Silesia. (For instance,
the dogma of the Virgin Birth.) Language was not the issue here.
K grew up bilingual. His education, however, was shaped wholly
by the German language; he could have been influential in German politics, as Rosa Luxemburg was. In the beginning K was as
much Polish as he was German. Or the other way around. There
was no doubt of that. No one who was not born in this region or
had not lived here for a considerable time would be able to understand what it means: to speak Polish and be a German. Or the
other way around: to speak German and be a Pole (which admittedly was much rarer).

Among his materials there was a note he had taken from Scholtis: "It is the tragedy of the Upper Silesian that he is neither a
German nor a Pole, but simply an Upper Silesian, and that injus-
tice will be done to him in either case, whether he be claimed by
Germany or by Poland."

Montag thought through various possibilities. He paced back
and forth in the room. He resolved to read more about the history
of Ireland, of Lithuania, of the Basques, of the Ukraine. Montag
stopped pacing.

K was a Pole because he wanted to be a Pole.

It was as simple as that. He did not want to believe it at first, he
sought for some other formulation. But again and again he returned to this lapidary sentence. He was someone who was seek-
ing his identity, who had been set down between Poland and
Germany and had opted for one side. Because he wanted to! That
would explain many of the contradictions in K's behavior. His
fanaticism, too. He would have to investigate this more closely.

He sat down and put that much on paper. He understood K
better now. And himself too.

II

ANDREAS LOOKED UP at Aunt Lucie (Widera). Only now did
he notice that she had green polish on her fingernails. He stared at
them, he hadn't seen that before. "Come," she said, and laid her
hand on his shoulder like a crocodile's claw. Her dress was black,
the turban white. She was so close to Andreas now that he
breathed in the smell of laundry starch and glue. "You've walked
in on some exciting times," she said, pushing the boy along before
her. "But how does that nice Gleiwitz saying go? Learn from
life! — So, and now I'll show you your relatives, the whole lot of
them, whoever's arrived by now."

Aunt Lucie (Widera), he had learned from Josel, was not a real
aunt, but an old friend of Valeska's from her girlhood, who was so
much a part of the family now that everyone called her Aunt. She
lived in Hindenburg-Mathesdorf, but since the illness of Leo
Maria Piontek, she had come to visit more and more frequently
and more and more often had stayed on. She and Halina ran the
household, she worked in the garden and helped do the shopping.
She was quite different from the genuine great-aunt, Lucie
(Lanolin), who lived with her blind son in Kalinowitz, near
Gross-Strehlitz, and came twice a year to visit her niece Valeska in
Strachwitzstrasse. She would show up unannounced and spend
the whole day leafing through newspapers and magazines, reading
to her son, devouring double helpings at mealtimes, and after two
weeks would finally disappear, to carry out the same routine at
some other relative's in some other town.

When Andreas and Lucie (Widera) entered the music room, the
voices of those present died down and their movements slowed
too until they were frozen in a particular gesture. Andreas was
confronted by silence and this picture: two women sitting on the
sofa opposite him with their heads close together; next to them,
the Sergeant leaning against the wall in the shadow of the half-open

veranda door, motionless; in a wicker chair by the window a
woman reading an illustrated magazine, holding it very close to
her eyes, as if she were nearsighted, and next to her a plump blind
man in dark glasses, no longer young. In the middle of the room a
boy and a girl, both of them younger than he, holding each other
firmly around the waist and obviously, from their position, in the
act of practicing some dance step. On the round black stool in
front of the piano sat a girl with dark hair cut in a severe page-boy
style; she was holding one finger threateningly above a piano key,
as if waiting for a signal to pound it down like a hammer.

Aunt Lucie (Widera) gestured broadly with her arm as if she
were presenting him: "This is little Andreas," she said. "Valeska's
sister's boy. She" (now she spoke softly and only to the others)
"was killed in an accident a few years ago, a runaway horse . . ."
Then louder again: "He's from the Reich, from Breslau."

She let go of Andreas and sat down on the sofa with the two
women. Suddenly Andreas felt as alone and as wavering as an
acrobat on the tightrope. Someone clapped his hands, it must
have been the blind man by the window, and the two women on
the sofa turned their faces sharply toward Andreas. Aunt Lucie
(Lanolin), if it was she, and judging by Josel's description it had
to be, turned a page in her magazine and read on. The girl at the
piano banged down her finger and sounded a staccato note on a
single key, and the pair of young dancers went through some
grotesque contortions suggesting a Negro dance step which had
once been the fashion.

Andreas let his arms hang down loosely. It was not just the
words "little Andreas" which had thrown him into an almost
paralyzing embarrassment, for he had long since felt himself to be
"grown up" (at school he had even had teachers who addressed
him with the formal "Sie"). Rather it was the situation which
divided him from the others, he alone on the one side, as if on a
stage, and they, the spectators, on the other—whereas he would
have much preferred to have been in their midst. But to do the
simplest thing, such as to walk straight over to the Sergeant,
whom he had already met, or to Aunt Lucie (Widera), also
seemed the hardest thing to do just now. He summoned all his

dancing-class deportment and steered for the girl with the page-boy. That was probably Ulla, whom Josel had spoken of as "my girl," and she, when she saw the strange boy coming up to her, forgot in her surprise to keep on banging the key. Andreas, who still felt himself to be in a very unreal situation, came closer and closer; he took the girl's hand, which was still up in the air, and pressed it to his lips just as he had seen the other grownups do the evening before.

Later, thinking back on the scene, Andreas felt quite dizzy, and could not imagine how he had mustered the audacity.

He had a feeling that he should say something now, so, without thinking, he said to the page-boy haircut something he had read somewhere: "The piano, yes, the piano is a royal instrument, isn't it, I admire anyone who has mastered the instrument . . ." He was about to kiss Ulla's fingertips again, but she quickly withdrew her hand and tossed him a look that conveyed more of complicity than a rebuff.

Ulla took a long look around the room, somewhat embarrassed. The boy, still frozen in the dance pose, called to her: "*Zagraj, poćwiczmy jeszcze!*" (Go on, play, let's try it again!) And with his little sister he executed a few dance steps, which reminded Andreas of the midgets he had once seen with his father at the Busch Circus in Luisenplatz.

Ulla glanced at Andreas as if needing his consent; he gave her an encouraging nod, and, as if she had only been waiting for his signal, she played a few runs which not only galvanized the child-like dancers into a few wild steps but also attracted the attention of the others. Andreas stepped back a bit and from there observed her hands flying over the keys. Ulla looked first at the children and then at Andreas as she played, and in her face was reflected what Andreas had himself felt when he kissed her fingers: bravado.

From the women on the sofa came gurgles of delight, but more at the clumsy movements of the children than at Ulla's piano playing. Aunt Lucie (Lanolin) lowered her magazine and looked over its edge at the dancers through thick reflecting spectacles.

Almost imperceptibly the tempo slackened, the rhythm gave way to lustrous phrases from which a melancholy, languorous melody then arose which thrilled everyone's ears. Even the dancing children stopped, it was hard to tell whether it was because they had missed the beat or were simply listening to the music. Andreas held on to the piano with one hand and shut his eyes; he had seen a teacher do that once in a concert at school.

Then the girl abruptly interrupted her playing and hammered away at one key again with her index finger, loudly and obtrusively, as she had done before. But what earlier might have been taken as practicing, was now shocking, indeed tormenting, as if someone were beating them all with a whip. Andreas felt the constant high pitch climbing higher and higher in his head, until it reached a point at which he reacted first with perplexity, then with astonishment, then with anger, and finally with a stab of pain. But then the plunking noise broke off. The girl slammed the piano lid shut with a bang. Obviously she had kept her foot on the pedal, for a muffled tone reverberated for a while in the suddenly silent room, keeping those present under its spell, even long after it had died away.

The girl began to turn the piano stool, she spun around once, twice, three times, then finally she jumped off and fell in an arc to the floor in the middle of the room and burst out laughing. But nobody else laughed with her. They all stared down at her as at something alien.

Andreas did not know whether he should go over to the girl and help her up; it all came as such a surprise to him, and the emotions which the music had expressed in such rapid alternation had confused even him. Then Aunt Lucie (Widera) got up from the sofa and waddled over to the girl, and that gave Andreas the courage to approach her too. "This, dear Andreas," said Aunt Lucie (Widera), "is Ulla Ossadnik, she plays the piano like the young Clara Schumann—at least that's what your Aunt Valeska claims, and after all, she should know . . ."

Andreas took Ulla's hand and raised her from the floor; he could feel the warmth of her hand in his long after, even after Aunt Lucie (Widera) had prodded him over to the others to shake hands; the two women on the sofa even kissed him on the forehead. One of these women, whose name he did not catch, the one with the thickly woven hairnet, came from Sosnowitz, in the Polish part of Upper Silesia. She and her children had been on vacation at her brother's in Leobschütz, and just as they were about to return home rumors of war broke out; she wanted to stay here for the time being and await further developments. The other was Fräulein Bombonnek, whose brother was being sought by the police, for a reason nobody wanted to talk about, and who therefore had fled to Kattowitz.

"What a big boy he is! Fifteen years old and so tall already, I must say, young people do shoot up these days," said one of the women, mostly to herself. And the one with the hairnet: "*Tak, tak, biedna Rita, czemu nie poszła za kogoś z naszych stron, tylko z Rajchu.*" (Yes, yes, poor Rita, why did she have to marry someone who wasn't from our region, but from the Reich?) Hardly had he turned away from them when the two women fell into a language that was foreign to him. It was Polish, he could distinguish the word *wojna*, at least, which he did know.

Now that he had greeted them all he had no further need of them. Except Ulla. What he wanted most was to run down into the garden and pick her a handful of flowers. He wanted to tell her at least how beautifully she had played and that one day (in his mind he could see it now) she would be a great pianist. Yet he did not even know what to call her. She was just at that age, fourteen or fifteen, when young girls attach a particular importance to being addressed as Fräulein, he knew that from school in Breslau, but if he addressed her as "Honored Fräulein Ulla," wouldn't he be making a fool of himself? . . . and such phrases were more for grownups anyhow. He wondered whether he should simply say, "Great playing!" or maybe better, "Really great playing!"

Then the round mouth beneath the page-boy haircut said, "Bet you're Josel's new friend."

Andreas would have liked to say: "Bet you're Josel's girl." But he only managed what he had put together before: "Really great playing!"

"That stuff before"—Ulla charmed a wrinkle onto the bridge of her nose—"that was only a joke. *Tadek,*" she yelled at the little boy who was playing horsie with his sister under the table, "*Zofja, dosyć tej bijatki, bo was porwie policaj.*" (Tadek, Zofja, stop that roughhousing, or the cops'll get you.) The boy really did stop, and both of them came out from under the table, all out of breath, and straightened their rumpled clothes.

"*Świnia,*" the girl said.

"*Luntrus,*" the boy said.

"Stop that!" Ulla scolded, serious now. And in German.

"Was that Polish you were speaking to them before?" marveled Andreas.

"Yes," Ulla said, "they understand it better."

"And where did you learn it?"

"Oh, everybody around here can speak it." Ulla was almost embarrassed.

"I'd like to learn it too, now that I'm here." He was determined to be like the people here. But he knew perfectly well that it would be very hard. To begin with, scoldings and curses were expressed in Polish. God, strangely enough, must dwell in a Polish heaven, for He was always appealed to in Polish, as far as he could tell— and what was more, the people believed in mountain and water spirits as well as in St. Anthony, who was abroad in the flesh in the streets of Gleiwitz to restore to the pious the possessions they had recently lost.

"You're taking on more than you can manage, *bien sûr.*" All at once it seemed to Andreas that she was patronizing him. "Didn't you want to learn to play the piano, too?"

"Yes, yes," Andreas answered hastily. Nevertheless, he was astonished; how had she known that? He hadn't spoken to her about it. Josel must have given him away.

"Naturally, I'll never be able to play as well as you do," he gushed. "I've never yet had the time to learn to play an instrument, you know . . . But I thought since Aunt Valeska's a piano teacher, maybe she'd be able to teach me, I mean, if she has the time."

Andreas noticed that he wasn't getting through to Ulla, at least not with anything that might impress her, and he wanted so much to impress her! He remembered that Josel had told him how much Ulla loved the music of Chopin. So with some courage he added: "I l-o-o-ve Chopin."

"Nonsense," Ulla countered soberingly, "*elemele dudki!* Anybody can bang around on the piano, but talent is what it takes. Do you have any talent?"

The question confused Andreas. He knew what a genius was (Schiller was a genius, his teacher Hayduk always said), and to be talented was to be somewhat less than a genius, therefore a minor genius. To be sure, he never would have thought of himself as a minor genius. When he thought it over, it startled him.

"Well, do you know that all those people who come to Frau Piontek to learn the piano are completely hopeless; they're only doing finger calisthenics, that's all." And Ulla laughed at the unusual expression "finger calisthenics," which she must have picked up somewhere, laughed so loudly that she covered her mouth with her hand so the others wouldn't notice.

"Well, you can't do without talent," she said. "Chopin has enough people to l-o-o-ve him," she was mocking Andreas. "You have to be able to play him! Play him so that people jump out of their seats, you've got to thunder him out until houses come crashing down, the keys have got to whisper him, caress him, breathe him until people begin to weep . . . *bien sûr!*"

"What, for example" — Ulla grew stern again — "do you think of the Scherzo No. 2 in B minor, Opus 31, how would you play it?" And with her lips she indicated the rhythm of the beginning.

Surprised by Ulla's passion, Andreas at first remained silent. His face showed that he hadn't the faintest notion of the Scherzo No. 2 in B minor by Chopin. He could not think of any evasive answer to her question, either. He did something now which he had done a few times at school but more often at home, which always elicited the strongest reaction from the people around him: he simply sat down, tailor-fashion, on the floor. Ulla looked at him, astonished; she was confused for a moment, and asked him whether he was feeling all right. The others turned to him, surprised, and the woman in the hairnet uttered a little cry.

"Oh, please," Andreas said, without looking up, "play the

Chopin Scherzo for us now." And all at once Ulla knew that this
was the position in which one could best concentrate on music.
He did come from Breslau, and he ought to know.

"Shhh," Andreas admonished the others. For that silence had
not yet descended which an artist needs when about to exhibit a
masterpiece. Aunt Lucie (Lanolin) was just turning another page
of her magazine, it must have been the last page to judge by the
noisy way she flipped it, and the children were busy at the end of
the room pulling the music books off the bottom shelves of the
bookcase and hurling them at each other. "Shhh," Andreas went
again. And to Ulla: "Please! Or do you want to wait until Josel
gets here?" He said it warily.

Ulla had not for an instant thought of performing the Scherzo
in B minor here, of all places, for the Polish relatives of the
Pionteks—the Scherzo she had been practicing for weeks with
Valeska Piontek and had indeed already brought to a certain per-
fection; but Andreas's half-hidden barb, that she would not want
to play until Josel was there, roused her to protest. Well, she
would just play then, not for Josel, not for the jabbering, sweating
gaggle of Polish relatives assembled here, not for the Sergeant,
not for Frau Lucie (Lanolin), not for Fräulein Lucie (Widera),
not for the Polish woman with the hairnet, not for Andreas or
Josel either, but simply for herself, for nobody but herself.

Ulla walked to the piano and sat down dreamily on the stool.
Even her appeal to the children to be quiet was more a chord than
an order. And perhaps that was just what quieted the children in
an instant. Ulla played the dramatic opening theme, and before
the repeat she took her hands from the keys, let the chords die
away, and through them, half turned to Andreas, she whispered:
"Will you come with me to the Church of the Holy Cross in
Warsaw, where Chopin's heart lies buried?"

"Yes, I'll go with you," said Andreas, who didn't know quite
how far it was to Warsaw, but knew he would go with her to the
end of the world to find Chopin's heart. His hands were hot, and
in his temples a vein throbbed that he had never felt before.

It was quiet in the room now. Then Ulla began the repeat of the
theme. Her hands were like two birds which fluttered up and

settled down again quickly, hopped over the keys and ascended . . .
This was music that would scale a mountain. Andreas listened and
began to float away, he rose up, higher and higher. And he knew
that the moment Josel walked in the door—which would be any
minute now—he would plummet, plummet deep down.

12

PARTY AND GOVERNMENT offices had been urging for some time now the Germanization of surnames of Slavic origin and Polish spelling. The block warden, Gregor (formerly Grzegorczyk), from Teuchertstrasse, went from house to house making suggestions for changes in surnames. The Strzelczyks, at No. 1 Strachwitzstrasse, who refused, found the word POLACK in large, crude letters one morning under the windows that faced busy Teuchertstrasse. They wiped it off. A few days later someone painted a yellow Star of David on their wall. That very day, Alfons Strzelczyk went to the courthouse and had their name changed to Strehler. He had to have the house repainted at his own expense.

The block warden had not come to the Pionteks.

Valeska recorded these name changes among acquaintances and relatives:

Wondraczek to Wondrak
Krsyczek to Kreis
Cempulik to Stempel
Przybillok to Pschibillok
Nieradczyk to Neuhaus
Gwosdz to Nagel
Wosniczek to Wons
Kaczmarczyk to Katzmarzik, also to Katz
Czempowski to Kempowski
Scholtyssek to Scholtis
Graszowski to Grass
Nowakowski to Nowak, also to Neumann
Lenczowski to Lenz
Koczulla to Kotulla
Kowalski to Koval
Schmittkowski to Schmidt

Koschniczek to Koschnik
Sczachniczek to Schachtner
Bieniekowski to Bienik
Strycharczyk to Strich
Lipiczynski to Lipinski
Sczodrok to Schodrok
Wittkowski to Wittek, also to Witte
Schymiczek to Schiemek
Pylaczek to Platschek
Lubosz to Lubos
Grochowiaczycz to Grochowiak
Frydricharczyk to Friedrich
Pollaczek to Pfeiler (The Pfeilers changed their name once
  more, to Pfister, in November last year, after the *Kristall-
  nacht*. That night their shop windows had been smashed in.
  Because the name PFEILER was hanging above the outside
  door in large letters.)

In the town of Gleiwitz the following streets and squares were
renamed:

Pruskestrasse to Schlageterstrasse
Ebertstrasse to Markgrafenstrasse
Lustigstrasse to Reinhold-Muchowstrasse
Zabrzer Strasse to Grosse Hindenburgerstrasse
Zuckerkandlstrasse to Jägerstrasse
Schalschaerstrasse to Schenkendorffstrasse
Platz der Republik to Platz der SA
Trynnek to Trinnek
Sosnitza to Öhringen
Przeschlebie to Sandwiesen
Zernik to Gröling

13

In a book by Otto Ulitz, a German Nationalist politician, Montag had read the following:

In Upper Silesia the law of non-inheritable serf property obtained: i.e., the peasant possessed no inheritable property, only the usufruct of the acreage farmed by him. The owner of the estate was at liberty to determine into whose hands that acreage would fall upon the demise of the peasant. The terms of the owner were hard. On the one hand we see the arbitrary apportionment of land, on the other, a deprived rural populace, wholly incapable of bettering itself. The result was indescribable poverty. In 1766 the peasants in the district of Rybnik revolted against the large landowners, and the uprising spread to the districts of Tost and Gleiwitz, so that it had to be crushed by the military. There were renewed peasant rebellions in 1799, 1811, and 1848. There was strong feeling in Prussia as to the necessity of solving the issue of land ownership. The reforms introduced by Frederick the Great had failed due to resistance on the part of the privileged class in the state, the nobility. Nor did the emancipation of the serfs in 1807 bring about any change in Upper Silesia on the right bank of the Oder, because there, by contrast with the rest of Silesia, the peasants owned no property and were therefore in no position to better themselves *vis-à-vis* the landowners. After emancipation many of the peasants' plots were in any case absorbed into the larger landholdings. Not until 1849, a hundred years after the seizure of Upper Silesia by Prussia, was a compromise reached between the interests of the peasants and the landowners, after crop failures had intensified the misery of the population and a terrible epidemic of typhus and dysentery in 1847 in the districts of Pless and Rybnik had attracted public attention to the region.

In the Pless district alone this epidemic claimed more than 7,000 victims among the rural population. The failure to resolve the issue of land ownership in Upper Silesia was one of Prussia's gravest errors. A free peasant class is the cornerstone of any state. By comparing the returns in the plebiscite of 1921 in the exclusively peasant district of Leobschütz with those in the districts of Gross-Strehlitz, Pless, Rybnik, and Tost-Gleiwitz, where large landholdings are offset by small peasant holdings, the profound effects of the absence of a healthy agrarian reform can be measured.

It was important to know this in order to understand K. Serfdom had continued overtly on the right bank of the Oder until 1850, covertly until 1918. This fact was also responsible for cultural differences on the two sides of the Oder. While Marx and Engels were drawing up the *Communist Manifesto* on behalf of the "League of the Just," the peasants on the right bank of the Oder were still living as serfs, the only ones remaining in Prussia. Would not that (and even more so, the Bismarckian *Kulturkampf*) have had to produce a K?

He considered how he could bring that into his work on K.

Montag had drawn the curtains only far enough to let in the light he needed. He did not want to look outside at the green, the trees stretching their leaves toward his window; nature, he could not think why, was suddenly repugnant to him. He wanted to hold fast to the old, constant, familiar objects which did not change: to the table that was a table—dumb, brown, immovable. It did not grow and sprout leaves, did not need light or water or sun. He ran his hand over the edge of the table with an almost caressing gesture. Perhaps that was how he would have liked to be himself. Or like this Bohemian vase on the windowsill, an example of perfect form. Or the rock crystal on the cabinet which he had brought back from a trip to the Beskids, whose metallic inclusions hinted at its origin in another epoch.

He sat down and went on working on a translation of an article by Korfanty, "Capitalism, Dictatorship, and Catholicism," from 1936. In the afternoons not many ideas came to him, so he

usually busied himself with his sources, with his research, or with
translating.

Whenever times become critical, the Catholics too speak up. It
is no wonder that they do, for every social and political question is, after all, at bottom of ethical and therefore of religious
significance.
The loyal populace has a clear and specific task to perform
today too. Never to be on the side of those who advocate capitalism and dictatorship. Anyone who believes in Christ, who
dedicated his gospel to the poor, who chose his apostles from
among simple people, who drove the greedy moneychangers
from the temple, who cursed the evil glitter of gold, who
preached absolute justice and love of one's fellow man as the
basis for the conduct of human affairs, who wanted to form
man in his, in a divine image, by bestowing laws and dignity
upon him—yes, whosoever believeth in this Christ cannot be
led astray, or be led politically astray. . . .

He wrote it down, but he was thinking of something else. After
the fire in the synagogue in Wilhelmsplatz he had passed by there
a few times; the windows were shattered, the walls and domed
metal roof smoke-blackened. They had thrown in torches to burn
up everything inside, and when the flames burst through to the
outside they had extinguished the fire to prevent the buildings
around it from going up in flames. The snow had fallen upon it,
the spring rain, the first summer sunshine, nothing had changed,
and it seemed as though the blackened walls were to stand as a
memorial. People passed by quickly and timidly, usually on the
other side of the street, as if coming near it would involve them in
a guilt which they wanted nothing to do with.
He knew that numerous Jewish families still lived in Niederwallstrasse, the building at No. 17 belonged to the Israelite congregation. A few apartments had been emptied by emigration, but
Jews from other neighborhoods had moved in. He had walked
along slowly and tried inconspicuously to cast a glance through
the windows into the ground-floor apartments, but he had been

able to see nothing behind the windowpanes except heavy curtains, and in only a few windows was there a light in the evening. The shades were pulled in all the ground-floor windows facing the street, even in the daytime, as if the house were vacant, or as if the inhabitants feared stones would be thrown through the windows. Montag had stationed himself in the entrance of a house across the street and waited until someone came out. It was usually some elderly person, but when it was children they were always in pairs or in groups, and they disappeared quickly into other streets, as if they knew they were being observed, and not just by him. Only once had he succeeded in getting close to an old man and peering into his face without his noticing, and he was surprised to find it much younger than the man's doddering gait had suggested. It occurred to him later that this was the only thing about the face he had taken in; he avoided asking himself what it was about it that had caught his attention in the first place. It could have been the face of Arthur Silbergleit, who was supposed at one time to have lived in that street, but he had probably emigrated; until a few years ago, poems by him could occasionally be found in the *Upper Silesian Wayfarer,* and once he had even bought a volume of his poetry, entitled *Old Town* or some such thing, but that was rather long ago; he remembered only that he had liked some of the poems in it.

The last time he had been there was in June. They were just carrying a coffin out of No. 17 and loading it onto a horse-drawn carriage. Twenty, perhaps twenty-five, old bent people were following the carriage and nobody could have told by looking at them that they were Jews. Montag had not thought of it either, until he was past them and suddenly heard teenagers yelling from the end of the street: "Jew! Jew! *Schiddok!*" It sounded like a curse, like the swear words he had heard in his childhood: *djobok* or *kurwa* or *świntuch.* And as he walked the streets in agitation, he asked himself how it had come about that the mere word "Jew" could become a curse, and how long before the word "Catholic" would become one too.

And that mattered more to him.

Shortly after that he received a picture book about Copenhagen from his cousin, who lived in Denmark, and whom he remembered only vaguely. He leafed through it very slowly. He liked the gracefully arched bridges, the streets with the narrow, high-gabled houses from which many little windows shone, castles climbing up from meadows and water, and ships moored between sky and sea, a great amusement park with a Ferris wheel and lots of merry-go-rounds, with swingboats and shooting galleries, jam-packed with people, who swung Chinese lanterns in the air. Perhaps he would travel to Copenhagen some day.

He never thought of visiting his daughter in Paris although she had often invited him. It had taken numerous letters from him to talk her out of coming to Gleiwitz. One day she informed him that she was going to marry a Parisian art dealer, who was twelve years older than she and had two children from a previous marriage. She did not intend to convert to the Mosaic faith, nor had her husband required her to do so, but she would try to bring up his children in that religion. She would have preferred to discuss all this with him personally, but since he had long discouraged her from making a trip to Silesia, he should at least come to Paris for the wedding.

He did not go.

Never before had Montag felt himself to be a Jew. According to the proof of Aryan descent which he had had to submit to the provincial court, he was half-Jewish, his daughter a quarter. She knew nothing of this, however; she had been baptized, confirmed, bore the names of two Catholic saints: Agnes and Elisabeth. But now something in him broke open, a little boil, and he scratched and rubbed and squeezed at it until it became a big sore, full of pus and bleeding, and it frightened him.

And underneath all the Catholic prayers, litanies, and credos he had learned, he now pieced together fragments of the Kaddish, which he had heard in his childhood through the wall of his grandfather's room . . . *yitgadal ve yitkadash shme rabba . . . be alma di vera chiruteh ve yamlich malchuteh* . . . That came from a still deeper level and moved his body and made it tremble. He glanced down at himself, looking at the hands he had shoved into the pockets of his dressing gown, and was puzzled; he repeated the sentence aloud and wondered why he was not gesturing with his hands. He looked in the mirror, studying his face in the hope of discovering a few lines or wrinkles or characteristics belonging only to Jews — but it was a face that did not differ from other faces in any special way. If he studied his face long enough, perhaps he would discover that his nose was indeed beakier than others, and when he had walked far enough he would find that he did have flat feet, and he could readily acquire the habit of moving his hands when he spoke.

That's how they wanted a Jew to be. He was ready to oblige. With a little play-acting, he might put it across.

And he said to himself: "Georg Montag, son of the drygoods dealer Benjamin Montag from Myslowitz, grandson of the itinerant yarn peddler Moischele Ponedjelnik from Odessa, you are a Jew, born of a Christian mother and baptized a Catholic, raised a Catholic, received your first communion, were confirmed by Cardinal Bertram—but you're still a Jew. Don't forget what your grandfather said to you when you were still a child, perhaps you didn't understand the sense of the words, but remember their melody, wasn't this how it went? *Shma yisrael adonai elohenu adonai echad. Yahweh,* the God of the Jews, is thy God too!"

And he cut a tallith from a piece of white silk, and phylacteries from a piece of black leather, and he placed the tallith about his shoulders, but he did not know how to tie the phylacteries around his arm and head.

14

VALESKA PIONTEK AND her brother Willi Wondrak had
arrived at the Hotel Upper Silesia an hour ago. She immediately
got busy putting out the placecards while Willi Wondrak saw to
the decorations for the cabaret program and the dressing rooms.
By the time the first guests arrived, he had everything organized,
while she was still fluttering around the tables, switching a placecard from one place to another or rearranging an entire row; she
played with the flowers, straightened the place settings she'd
straightened before, and tightened the bun of hair she'd tightened
so many times before. The only thing that afforded Valeska some
satisfaction at the moment was her idea of placing the Archpriest
and the Wild Monk at opposite ends of the table, but facing each
other. On the monk's placecard she had written only "B.F." (for
Brother Francis), so as not to betray his presence in advance.

Her brother was in a good mood. He joked with a waiter, gave
instructions to have two tables placed near the door for the guests
to leave their wedding presents on, all the while giving Valeska a
running account of the cabaret program and scattering cigarette
ashes everywhere—the only sign of his nervousness was that he, a
non-smoker, was lighting one cigarette after another that evening. The emptiness of the hall did not seem to disturb him, nor
did the whiteness of the tablecloths, or of the light, alarm him.
Valeska admired that in him; she sat down and powdered her nose
and cheeks for the third time, feeling the sweat and oil standing
on her face in fat, shiny globules. She dashed eau de Cologne on
her hands, before going to greet the first guest with affectedly
relaxed charm copied from Willi and an artificially fixed smile. Her
phrases were forced and the tone a little too shrill, obviously
belying her pose, but none of the guests noticed. They were too
confused by the ordeal they had gone through just to find the
Mint Room: the liveried doorman, the dim foyer that swallowed

up all light and sound, the stairway with its wine-red carpet and gleaming gold railings were only a start; other traps yawned ahead of them. What were they to do, for example, with the wedding gifts they had brought, since the bridal couple was nowhere to be seen. Perhaps they had arrived too early, which showed again how unsophisticated they were compared to the Pionteks. But then waiters came hurrying up and pressed on them one of those very shallow glasses which spill so easily if you're not careful. They contained a viscous, sticky liqueur that tasted like blackberries and was supposed to be something Silesian. Now they had both hands full and in the end they presented their gifts to Valeska Piontek; it was more important anyway that she know what they had brought, and just to make sure, they had each placed a card inside the package so that the bridal couple would find out the next day who the donor was. Maybe they were not all thinking that way, but Fräulein Willimczyk, the bookseller, did, and since there was time, she began to untie the package and explain to her friend Valeska Piontek about the books from the Neumann bookshop which she had brought for her daughter Irma.

"Here," she said, enumerating, "that's the new Scholtis, *The Ironworks,* and here, by Alexander Lernet-Holenia, *A Dream in Red,* and *The Great Janja* by Arnold Ulitz, set in Kattowitz" — she kept on talking, even when Valeska moved away to greet the Kabellas from Biskupitz, and she kept on talking, for now a few other guests were clustered around her, and she was happy just having an audience — " . . . and this one's in great demand, *The Death of Reval* by Bergengruen." And when Valeska came back, Fräulein Willimczyk started all over again with Scholtis. Valeska listened attentively, and in fact she had never felt such a lively interest in books as at that moment. She picked up one of them and began to browse through it, trying to hide behind the words, but only to forget the big hall with its emptiness and the echoing, evanescent voices.

The emptiness felt almost like a physical pain. It always affected her this way, a big, empty, silent hall, where every person who entered only made it emptier, and every word spoken only made the silence more silent. Perhaps it was simply the pale and blurred recurrence of a fear which had attacked her in childhood when she was up on stage sitting at the piano, while down below in the big hall four, five, six people from the examining committee were gathered, waiting for her to begin, and all at once she could not so much as lift her hands, they were paralyzed, as if grown fast to her thighs . . . Valeska waited for the hall to fill up, not this slowly, but faster, with people, voices, laughter, music, with sounds that would rebound from the walls and create new sounds.

The silence slowly oozing away was not overcome until Polensky and Michalek walked into the hall. They were dragging in a tin tub full of flowers, an artfully decorated wedding crown resting on green moss, flanked by colorful little bouquets of the flowers that grow on the meadows of Upper Silesia. It was the gift of Willi Wondrak, and it was cheered by Valeska and Polensky, but perhaps only because they alone knew that ten bottles of *schnapsik,* home-distilled schnapps, were concealed beneath the moss, and would be dispensed to the guests at an advanced hour. Upper Silesians simply like to get drunk, it makes no difference whether at the wedding of a peasant in the country or of a miner in a tenement or in the biggest, poshest hotel in town, indeed in the whole province; but Willi Wondrak did not see why his sister should spend her money on enough of the Hotel Upper Silesia's expensive schnapps to secure this unholy end for eighty guests.

With Polensky and Michalek, the new sounds that Valeska longed for had finally arrived. When she opened her handbag to find her compact, the click could no longer be heard, nor the pat of the powder puff on her moist face. Valeska shook the hands of the guests as they entered, racking her brains for each new name and connection, and declaring to each one how happy she was that he had come. Even when it was not true.

Actually, she only enjoyed parties when they were over, when the guests had left the rooms and the house, and when silence, sobriety, and coolness came back in. Then she loved to walk through the silent, empty, deserted rooms, to upend a chair here and there, ruffle an all-too-smooth tablecloth, push back a plate, perhaps knock over a vase full of half-wilted flowers so that water poured over the tablecloth and the flowers scattered but the vase did not break, or to crush underfoot a glass that had rolled beneath the table. She did all this gently and carefully and deliberately, simply to make the traces of the party more apparent. She loved the cold, expressionless yellow cones of lamplight above the tables, the sweaty prints on the glasses, some of them still half full of repulsive yellow liquid, the soiled plates and crumpled napkins, the wine spots on the tablecloth, the overflowing ashtrays, the puddles on the floor which gave off a sharp smell of stale beer and urine. She liked parties less than their coarse and sensual and dirty remains, their noisy exuberance of the moment less than the mute testimony, afterwards, to excesses committed there.

Then Water Milka entered. She paused for an instant at the door, as if to show herself to everyone before mingling with the crowd. She scanned the tables and the guests, obviously enjoying being gaped at by more and more of them. Valeska too looked over now, and was so surprised by Milka's appearance that she had to snap her purse open and shut quickly to suppress a certain embarrassment. Water Milka was much thinner than before, or so it seemed to Valeska. She had had her hair done in a blonde-rinsed bob, which gave her rather coarse face an unaccustomed pertness; but more surprising still, she was wearing trousers, men's glen plaid trousers with wide cuffs, and over them a snug-fitting dark-blue suit jacket—and most surprising of all was the NS Women's Corps badge on the lapel. Valeska looked across at Willi, who confirmed her impression with a wink; then she walked quickly up to Water Milka and, while still at a distance, stretched her arms out to her without betraying any of her amazement.

"How happy I am," she said, and embraced her sister-in-law, brushing her face over her hair, in which the heavy dull scent of cigars and a stuffy cupboard mingled with the sweet freshness of hair lotion. "We haven't seen each other for ages," Valeska said, and had the feeling she was not even lying, for the last time she had seen Water Milka she had been a different person. "We're all so happy that you've come."

"My present," Water Milka said, and handed Valeska a black

leather case which was not gift-wrapped. She was carrying another one like it under her arm, a gray one — or perhaps it was just somewhat scuffed.

"Thank you!" Valeska said, and accepted the case with a sweeping gesture. "Irma will be so happy!" And it was her own voice, her own words, her own movements which seemed artificial to her.

"Perhaps it's more for the groom," Water Milka said, "whom you've really surprised us with!" Her tone was friendly, without insinuation, and she drew Valeska to her to touch her cheek with her own. "You have good taste," she said, running her eyes over the tables. "It'll be a grand party!"

"Do you think so?" Valeska asked in a faint voice, as if she had doubted so until now.

"Of course," Water Milka said, walking a few steps further. "Word reached me all the way out on the Klodnitz."

Valeska was very glad. She would even get used to a Milka with a bob and men's trousers. She waved her brother over; he had been waiting for some signal.

Willi Wondrak began by complimenting her on her new hairdo, preferring not to mention her clothes — he had better check around and find out whether trousers might be coming into fashion now; but he could not take his eyes off the emblem of the NS Women's Corps. That Water Milka had joined the Corps would hardly have surprised him, but it disturbed him that she wore the badge on her suit jacket, and to a private celebration such as this wedding, and that she had appeared here in this unusual, to say the least, getup; he had a feeling it would turn out to mean even more. In time he himself had joined practically all the NS groups and organizations which had been established in the town since 1933, but always with the thought that it might spare him the worst, namely, joining the Party itself. He had even changed his name, Wondraczek, to Wondrak.

"You have to keep up with the times," Milka said, leaving it open whether she meant her new hairdo or her membership in the Women's Corps.

"We're happy that Milka has come to the wedding — Leo Maria

will be happy too," Valeska added more softly. "He feels too ill to come. But he wanted so much for you to be here."

Now she spoke so quietly that no one heard her. Besides, it was more her own wish that she was expressing. Valeska had the feeling that she and Milka were already reconciled. In token of their closeness, she touched her arm, and Milka did not draw it away. That made her more confident. She decided to run over to the table afterward and change her placecard. Milka could move up two seats; if she removed the badge, even three. Later she would make a proposal that she move into the house in Strachwitzstrasse.

Willi Wondrak saw it all much more soberly. "Come, I'd like to introduce you to my secretary, Fräulein Heiduczek."

The secretary had the information and was to discuss the contract with Milka later. He extended his cigarette case. "Do you smoke?" It was more a general question, to everyone.

"Thanks," Water Milka said, "I'll smoke my own brand." She took the leather case from under her arm and unfolded it. "Home-grown and home-cured!" she said with a note of triumph, and held out the case to the others. "Perhaps one of you?"

"Oh," Valeska said, motioning it away. She was insulted. That struck her almost as a relapse. Fräulein Willimczyk, who had just come up, would have liked just once to try a cigar, but she was afraid her boss would smell it the next day and reprimand her.

Willi Wondrak braced himself: she would be no easy job, he realized that, but he was confident. He said, "Thanks very much! Perhaps after dinner. Just now a cigar would be too strong for me." He tried to offer her a light, but Water Milka waved him away. There was a ritual to be observed before lighting a cigar, that was obvious. The others watched in silence as she rolled the cigar over the back of her hand, cut off the end with a tiny blade, sucked on the cigar several times, and then touched the tip of her tongue to her teeth. Not until the taste of the air and the tobacco were to her satisfaction did she lean forward to accept the light.

As Milka emitted the first puff of smoke, Valeska shuddered and felt a bitter taste rising in her throat; maybe she should keep her in her old place after all. Luckily she could leave the scene now, the president of the waterworks and his wife had arrived; he held a

bouquet of salmon-pink roses in his hand, and his wife was waving
the tissue paper with the shop's label on it so that everyone could
see they had bought them at Szupek's, the expensive flower shop
on Wilhelmstrasse.

Willi Wondrak looked on as Milka puffed away, he even put up
with her blowing a smoke ring onto the tip of his nose; he was
determined to do anything to win Emilie Piontek over to the new
firm.

"I'd like you to meet some guests you don't know yet," he said
to her, and gave her his arm. Water Milka slipped her arm in his
and walked with him as if she had spent her whole life crossing
ballrooms on the arm of a man. In any case, no one expressed
surprise at the cigar-smoking Milka; at most, an occasional astonished or mocking word about her clothes was softly uttered.

Frau Bohne, who had moved here from the Reich not too long
ago, said to the head librarian, Neumann: "Perhaps there's a new
directive from the Führer, that women are to smoke cigars
now . . . that wouldn't surprise me, they say he's also against
women using makeup." She pressed her thin lips even more
closely together.

It was exactly a quarter past seven (Valeska suspected her
brother of having organized that too) when the bridal couple
appeared, preceded by two children scattering flowers. Irma, in
her Labor Service uniform (and that gave Valeska another stab in
the heart), carried a bouquet of white roses, and Heiko wore his
soldier's uniform, with green myrtle pinned on the collar and
sleeves. Willi Wondrak attempted to rouse some of the guests
standing nearby to a chorus:

"Three cheers for the bride and groom!"

Valeska and Aunt Lucie (Widera) went up to the bridal pair,
embraced them, and kissed them three times on both cheeks.
Valeska had resolved to display the most radiant smile she was still
able to manage on such a day, but she did not know whether she
was successful.

The guests began to clap, and that confused her somewhat as
the applause continued, after all most of them were in a real hotel
for the first time in their lives, in a ballroom, and perhaps they

were expressing some of their uneasy feelings in their clumsy
clapping, responding to the occasion with gratitude for being
allowed in here, with surprise that the doorman to whom they
had carefully presented their elegantly printed invitation had not
just thrown them out, and with fear that it might all be an illusion, and that when they awoke they would be back in their old
humdrum lives.

For Valeska too it was a new experience. She did not forget that
this wedding banquet in the Hotel Upper Silesia was costing her a
lot of money. She had tried for a whole week to talk her daughter
out of this marriage, but when Irma locked herself in her room
and came out only to volunteer again for the Labor Service, she
abandoned her resistance. She gave her consent, indeed she even
promised Irma a celebration which everyone who took part in it
would remember for years afterward. Not a wedding reception in
a cleared-out living room with borrowed china and dancing to an
accordion in the hallway, no, she would offer her the best in town,
the ballroom at the Hotel Upper Silesia. She had sold two pieces
of property to pay for it, the abandoned brickyard in Ziegeleistrasse and the field next to the Zernik woods. But she was determined to get the money back, and tonight was not too soon to
begin. As she could see, her brother had done something to this
end: Count Poremba had come, the president of the waterworks,
the Polenskys from Polensky & Michalek, the chairman of the
savings and loan association, Water Milka, with whom she had a
deal in the works, the Neumanns from the municipal printing
plant, and perhaps even one of the Ballestrems would come too.

Now the guests began peering at the placecards, and there were
moments of cordial confusion until at last they had all found their
seats. While the soup was being served, Valeska ascertained that
neither Curate Mikas nor the Wild Monk had come. And the
chairs for Josel, Andreas, and Ulla Ossadnik likewise were empty.
That made her anxious.

Valeska raised the spoon to her lips, she dipped from her soup
plate. She listened to the voices of the others, sometimes the clink
of a glass came to her, a peal of laughter came from far off and
seemed to fade into even greater distance.

On her right sat the groom; he was speaking to the person on his other side and only rarely turned his face to her. She had to ask him something repeatedly, and he answered her curtly, anything. They looked at each other, and then each glanced away in the opposite direction.

The chair on her left remained empty, symbolically reserved for Leo Maria; she considered seating Josel there, if he came. Had he gone to the HY after all? Maybe they'd come to pick him up? She should have brought him along to begin with!

Valeska leaned over toward Countess Poremba, whom she was meeting today for only the second time. From her brother she had learned that the Porembas had been living in Bavaria at some distant cousin's, and from there had been attempting with her brother's help to get compensation for their property in eastern Upper Silesia; for the last four weeks they had been in Gleiwitz staying at the Hotel Upper Silesia, waiting for the outbreak of war to regain their holdings, for which Willi had in any case already reaped a tidy sum. To be sure, he had not told his sister that he had had to pay the hotel bill for the Porembas, who had no money left. The silver fox around the Countess's shoulders nearly hid her head. Valeska searched for a question which would be audible even over the fur: "How is the young lady these days?"

The Countess had no daughter, but she was so happy that Valeska had invited her to the reception that she quickly invented one. "Thank you, very well, she writes such charming letters from London," she wheezed into her fur.

"From London!" Valeska said. She left her spoon in her mouth for a moment as she pondered the name. A friend from her Kattowitz days had gone to London as a piano teacher, she had received two letters from her. In the first she had written that the city was so huge you could walk through the streets for days without reaching its edge; in some places the river was so broad that you had to use a telescope to see the other side; and in the second she enclosed an announcement of her marriage. Since then Valeska had read whatever she could find in the papers about London, for now she could imagine the city quite well.

"Isn't London too large and too dangerous for a young girl?" she said, putting her spoon back into her soup.

Countess Poremba had to lean far to her right to hear Valeska; she would have needed to be left-handed to go on eating. Besides, she had to be careful not to spill any soup on her fur. But to let the soup cool seemed just as risky as the invented daughter in London, so she said quickly, "At the moment our daughter is in Vienna, you see, things in London are rather . . ." She did not know how to put it (oh, if only she hadn't invented that daughter), she got muddled and said: *"comme çi comme ça."* But in tone it was meant to suggest danger.

"What will the Crown do if there's war with Poland?" Fräulein Willimczyk asked from her other side. She was proud that she did not say "England." Somewhere or other she had read that the English spoke of their country simply as "the Crown."

"The English will keep out of it, the English are cowards, just think of the Boer War!" Count Poremba spoke up emphatically. The Count had firm views on this subject. At one time he had contemplated emigrating to South Africa, and had therefore read many books on the Boer War. Since then he had always thought in this way, and when you watched him emptying his plate with such dedication, you knew that nothing would change in the near future.

"But the French? What about the French?" asked the president of the waterworks, across the table, seeming at the same time about to bite a chunk out of his wine glass.

Countess Poremba was starting to perspire. She undid the clasp of her fur and let the silver fox slide down her shoulders, then arranged it over the back of her chair so as not to sit on it later. Even for Valeska, who had observed the struggle of the little lady under the fur, this was a visible relief.

Valeska was worried about Andreas, who had gone to Zernik with Ulla Ossadnik to invite Tina Zoppas. They should have been back a long time ago. Tina Zoppas had not come either. She was keeping an eye on their chairs.

Not until the entrée did the Countess return to the subject.

"I tell you," she said, "the French won't budge, I know it, we are just taking back the little bit that belonged to us before; we are not being aggressive." Countess Poremba loved to put on a slight Austrian accent on occasion, in order to emphasize that this entire region had once belonged to Austria.

Valeska watched the Countess struggling with her meat and her words. She looked ugly when she was eating, it distorted her face grotesquely. "There'll be no war on account of Kattowitz and Poremba," her husband amplified, laughing, and he pushed a bit of dumpling into his open mouth.

Valeska leaned back. She dabbed at her lips with her napkin and hoped that she did not look like the Countess when she chewed.

The president of the waterworks, a robust black-and-white rectangle sitting opposite her, radiated a vibrant cheerfulness to left and right which made her feel quite uneasy. He somehow managed to scrape back and forth with his chair, make smacking noises through his teeth, and crack jokes which he laughed at himself. Now he even attacked a liqueur glass and passed the bitten glass around the table as proof of his talent. He jabbered unceasingly at Valeska, who only slowly grasped his curious sentences: "That's just it . . . as I say . . . your daughter, the bride, such a charming bride, and everything so modern without the white dress and white veil, simply, so simple, just as our modern times demand." His gaze swung between Valeska and Irma, he raised his glass high and waved it back and forth: "And the celebration in this beautiful room! To the health of the bride!"

He shoved his glass at others; sometimes they clinked, sometimes not, he paid no heed—he was inspired.

Valeska missed his glass, and besides there was only white wine in hers, though she had ordered an Italian red for herself. She looked over at her brother, who was engrossed in conversation with Milka and in cutting his meat.

Her ears were filled with a tissue of voices, into which on occasion Valeska wove a resonant thread, but she could not prevent a great wall of silence and mistrust from building up on her right where her daughter was sitting; when Valeska threw a few words at it, they bounced back, the wall grew higher and higher, for a

moment it seemed to Valeska as if they had all been whisked into a
fairy play, and Irma had just transformed herself into an old tower
because she was afraid that the Queen had designed such a pomp-
ous party only to plunge them at the end into some evil trance . . .

Valeska ripped this curtain in two. She saw quite clearly again;
she saw Irma, who was just turning to her soldier with a sharp
provocative laugh, she saw the others biting obscenely into the
brown meat on their plates, she saw her gray hands, flopping back
and forth between plate and tablecloth like old hens, saw the red,
sweating faces of the others continue to swell up, and the direct
question of Curate Mikas, who had arrived by now, jangled
against her ear over Archpriest Pattas' empty chair: "How did
you do it, how did you manage it, dear lady" (like all priests, he
could not keep track of names; or, like all priests, he avoided
addressing the faithful too often by name, were they not all the
same before God, all one?) "now, when rationing is already in
force? Well, war or peace, there should be limitations everywhere
as long as our missionary brethren in India and Africa are suffering hunger, they are fighting a war there every day against hunger
and misery, against sickness and the tsetse fly and against igno-
rance, which after all is much worse, don't you agree, dear lady?
Perhaps we could even, I mean at the end, when the Archpriest is
here, take up a little collection for our mission in Rawalpindi, you
understand . . . dear lady."

"Of course, of course," Valeska said, at the same time indicating
by gesture and an icy expression that she meant the very opposite.
They were sending in young priests from the Reich who could not
speak a word of Polish and who never set foot outside the town,
and yet they could find their India just as easily in the Huldschinsky housing project, in Bobrek and Peiskretscham and who
knows where. And from the other side of the table the president
of the waterworks was looking at her; the veins of his forehead
were so swollen that they twitched like little red snakes each time
he chewed. His diminutive wife, who could have been fitted
inside him four times over, said something in a soft voice which
could not be understood; for twenty years it had been her habit to
speak softly, in the hope of somehow modulating her husband, in

whom everything was fat, coarse, and loud, but it seemed to have been in vain. He translated her words immediately, and his voice was like a trumpet blast: "My wife says she's thrilled, everything with so much . . . good taste and culture, the wine of such . . . rare vintage, the meal of such . . . delicacy, my wife says that when our daughter is eligible for . . . marriage, then we too will have a . . . celebration like this, in these surroundings." The president of the waterworks made nouns of everything and pronounced them like foreign words, always with a little pause before them. Fräulein Willimczyk, who had been listening, giggled into her little bookseller's fist.

Valeska nodded. She longed for the sort of hat which had been fashionable a short time ago, one with a veil that could be pulled down over her face—or why not a magic cap that made her invisible? She had hoped to bid farewell to Irma that evening with the same embrace—perhaps insincere, perhaps sentimental, but still traditional and ceremonious—with which her mother had once bid farewell to her, and her grandmother likewise to her mother, an embrace which at the moment might seem rather strange, artificial, even ridiculous, but which she would remember for the rest of her life. In her own case it had been in the kitchen, between the windows facing the yard and the sink; the water faucet had dripped loudly, the wedding cake, baked the evening before, had wafted its heavy, numbing vapor of citron, almonds, and cardamom into her eyes, and then in a silent embrace, merging again with the body of her mother from which she had come, feeling again the other's breath in her breath, the other's warmth in her warmth, the other's smell in her smell, the other's heartbeat in her heartbeat . . . She saw Irma there, next to her yet at the same time far away, and slowly she realized, more painfully than ever before, that she had said farewell to Irma long ago. Perhaps even on the day she was born.

On the table before her the glasses and silver flashed, rings sparkled on hands which rose and fell like shovels, plates showed their golden rims, the heads of the dahlias decorating the table in a not quite discernible pattern distributed the stored-up sun of this last day of August in all directions, and light sprayed out from the massive chandelier above and tried to repeat itself over and over in everything that gleamed. Valeska gazed over the guests' heads at the wall opposite; it was a gray, drab, bare wall—and that seemed rather fitting to her mood.

Valeska would have liked to drop out of time. At least until they were finished with the meal, or until Josel was there, or until she stood face to face with Irma bidding her farewell and embracing her for the last time before she belonged entirely to that man, or until the band began to play, or a mine shaft collapsed or a storm broke out—that was what she was waiting for, and she hoped it would happen in that order. But she herself moved nothing except the fork on which she was piling meat, peas, and gravy, and that made her even more powerless.

It was the summer of the mullein, a dry summer of white dust and black slag heaps. No matter where you set your foot, the stems and runners whipped against your skin, and the smell of the yellow bellflowers worked itself into your clothes and was trapped there until the spring. In gardens the roses and dahlias were strangled by the rampant mullein, the gooseberry and red currant bushes bore only half as much fruit as in other years, and in the fields farther out there was a soundless battle every night between the wheat and the mullein. That year it even grew right up into the house, into the gaps in the stairs, the cracks in the walls, into the casements of the windows, it even blossomed on the slag heaps, which glowed so hotly that you could not walk on them barefoot. It was a dry summer, the summer of the mullein, the summer when Josel had not come home one evening.

It was almost midnight when Valeska left the house to report it to the police. However, they were not willing to send out a search party until the next morning, so she set out alone to look for him, with only her voice and a flashlight. Ulla Ossadnik thought she had last seen him at the Concordia mine, Frantek in the Laband Woods, and Janosch on the loose gravel along the Klodnitz. Valeska searched for him the whole night, she called his name until her voice gave out and shone the flashlight until the batteries were used up. Not until the gray of dawn did Valeska discover him, Josel, in the dry bed of the Klodnitz, which that summer was only a trickle, with the mullein growing in profusion above the banks, a forest of mullein. Josel had lost his way in the dark, become tired, and with the trustfulness of a child had lain down to sleep on a mattress which had been washed ashore.

Valeska looked at the child in the forest of mullein, knowing that here, at this spot, the flood waters raged by in early spring, whirling and swirling, and when the snow was melting, blocks of ice rushed by. She was still afraid of the river, and when her sister-in-law Milka returned and moved into the refugee barracks on the Klodnitz, she forbade her children to go there; only from a distance could they watch their aunt, whom they called Water Milka because she walked through the river and talked and joked with it, because she implored and defended it, questioned and listened to it, prayed to it and blessed it. When they told Valeska about this at home, she laughed at them. "Nobody can talk to a river or question it either." But she could not look at the children as she said this; then she went into the kitchen and said an Our Father to St. Nepomuk, never would she forget what she had seen from the bridge that time.

She had never crossed that bridge again.

15

THE SKY LOOKED like blue-gray paper that someone had crumpled up and then smoothed out and spread across the firmament; a few stars were hiding in it, and behind the Zernik Woods the moon was preparing her entrance. Ulla rode quickly down the road, as if each stroke of the pedals could push back a bit of the darkness like a stage set, and Andreas had trouble keeping up with her. They had been at Frau Zoppas's in the pensioners' settlement, to take her Valeska's invitation to the wedding reception at the Hotel Upper Silesia, but the still-young widow Zoppas was busy becoming engaged to one of the soldiers billeted with her. She had talked them into having some coffee, and they also drank a few small glasses of her homemade raspberry cordial, and set out for home much too late.

Ulla pressed the dynamo against her front wheel and rode without hesitation out onto the Linnéstrasse by the weak, trembling yellow light. She would never have admitted to Andreas that she was afraid of the long ride home in the dark, and perhaps afraid was too strong a word for a rather vague feeling of helplessness which she could best try to overcome by riding fast, hoping that the prickling sensation she felt at the back of her neck and the little white flashes behind her eyelids would go away.

Andreas would much rather have ridden more slowly, a half-hour more or less did not matter to him now, they were too late anyway for dinner at the Hotel Upper Silesia, and he would have liked to pedal quietly along beside her, by tossing sentences back and forth they could have made the gloom transparent, and perhaps later he could have put his arm on her shoulder and she might have done the same, and time and distance would have shrunk. But now he had to pedal after her frantically to keep from being left behind. His own dynamo was working so poorly that he needed her light to guide him. And he would have run into Ulla's rear wheel if he hadn't jerked his handlebars at the last moment, and nearly skidded. He had noticed too late that she had braked to turn into another road.

"Andreas!" Ulla motioned him forward. She slowed down and finally stopped. "Listen, we've still got twenty minutes to ride, maybe twenty-five in the dark. Are you afraid?"

Andreas shook his head. "No, no." He hadn't thought of being afraid. Maybe he would have been if he had thought about it. But he hadn't thought about it. With Ulla on a country road it wouldn't have occurred to him. "No, I'm really not," he insisted.

"There's a bus that goes along the Tarnowitz road into town. We could ride back and leave our bikes with Frau Zoppas and take the bus, what do you think?"

"Well," said Andreas, "I'll leave that to you. I don't really know my way around here yet. But I'm not afraid at all."

Ulla wished Andreas were afraid, at least a bit, even if he wouldn't admit it. That would make it easier for her to decide to take the bus home after all. She had not yet made up her mind.

"But we could ride through that little wood over there, it's a good shortcut and you come out by the new transmitter," she suggested.

Unless the moon were to come out from behind the paper clouds or the forest, this notion seemed very risky to her, and she was already regretting her suggestion. She hoped Andreas wouldn't even consider it, since he didn't know the way.

But to Andreas, who for quite some time had been wondering how to get closer to Ulla, close enough so that their hands, their arms, their shoulders, their skin would touch as if by chance, this course seemed rich in possibilities. That was his way of overcoming his fears.

"So, should we go back and then take the bus? And who knows whether there is a bus—if there isn't, we wouldn't get to the celebration until it's over!" He played with a pedal. He was ready to lead her through the woods.

Ulla looked up at the sky. Now she was hoping for the moon. "Of course there's a bus, I know it," she said firmly. And added less firmly: "But I think this late there's only one every hour, who knows how long we'd have to wait . . ." She made up her mind. "*Piernika,* let's ride! Keep behind me, I know the way pretty well."

And so they rode out of the darkness into the pitch black, and if they had known that the pitch dark is not only black but also oppressive and bumpy and robs you of your breath, sets off little explosions in your head and draws the sweat from your pores, perhaps they would have turned back. But by that time it was already too late.

The path grew more and more uneven, their front wheels would slip off to one side or the other, and Ulla had trouble keeping hold of the handlebars. She stopped. "The path is getting worse and worse," she complained, breathing heavily. She was no longer sure whether it was riding that was such a strain or if she might not be afraid after all.

"Should I go on ahead?" Andreas asked. "Come on, let me past!" The path was rather narrow here, he had to squeeze past Ulla, walking his bicycle. That's what he'd been waiting for, now he could touch her, perhaps even take hold of her, but then he panicked and pressed back against his own bike, so as not to come too close to Ulla, and he licked his lips, which all at once had gotten dry. Whenever he set out to do something, he felt inhibited. He was past her now. He decided not to think about it, maybe then it would happen by itself.

"I think, I mean . . . we can't be far from the transmitter," Ulla said, somewhat confused, revealing that she had been waiting for something.

"We can get through this way," Andreas said, pointing to a path that led back toward an open field.

"Yes, let's try that," Ulla said. "The Tarnowitz road must be right on the other side."

Raspberry runners caught at them from right and left, and it must have been raspberry pickers who had trampled down the path. The bumpy forest ground almost made them stumble, and twigs and long grass caught in the spokes of their wheels and made them twang. When they finally reached the dirt road through the field and could see the transmitter's antenna in the distance, they both discovered to their amazement that they'd been holding hands for some time, and here, where it was easier to push their bikes, Andreas even put his hand on Ulla's shoulder.

Neither of them said anything. They did not dare look at each other. It was enough for each to feel the skin and warmth of the other and to be enmeshed in the other's smell, and the closer they came to the highway the more slowly they walked. But perhaps it was only the bumpy ground, the ruts; they had to avoid piles of dirt because a new drainage line was being laid next to the road.

Andreas stopped. He tipped his bicycle over. He leaned against one of the brown sections of clay conduit lining the side of the road. "We made it," he said. He drew Ulla over to him. She was standing next to him now, but still holding on to her handlebars.

They were looking straight ahead across the road at the wire fence surrounding the transmitter yard; beyond it was the long, low operations building and off to the side, the antenna thrusting into the sky. The moon had emerged above the Zernik Woods and through a thin veil of clouds cast a sallow light.

"The moon is so beautiful," Andreas said. Actually he wanted to say something else, but maybe it was too soon for that. Talking about the moon was more neutral and didn't commit you. So he said it quickly. The rest, well that would come later.

Ulla stood there vacillating, she would have liked to ride on, she was thinking that the wedding banquet at the Hotel Upper Silesia would already have begun. She looked at the moon. "There's a halo around the moon. I wonder if there'll be a change in the weather."

"Let's catch our breath for a minute," Andreas said. He took Ulla's bike from her and laid it on the ground. The back wheel kept turning for a little while and made a humming sound. He moved over next to Ulla again; the clay pipe was pleasantly cool against his back.

"I read in a book," Ulla said, "that the moon looks like a gold coin worn smooth. Can you imagine that, Andreas? Poets are funny sometimes." She giggled softly. Maybe because secretly the description pleased her. Maybe too because Andreas had reached for her hand at that instant.

It was very quiet, only a high-pitched, monotonous buzz could be heard from the transmitter.

"That's well put," Andreas said. He wondered whether he should sit down with her in the grass now and kiss her. In spite of his fourteen years, he knew only too well that if he thought about it he'd never do it. That made him sad.

"Without the moon you couldn't see your hand in front of your face now. It's getting dark, *bien sûr,*" she said. She was annoyed that she always thought of the obvious, but she couldn't help it, it just came to her. At least she had said "*bien sûr,*" that should impress Andreas.

Andreas held her hand tighter and said, "The moon is like an egg yolk. The moon is like a flax blossom. The moon is like a boil. The moon is like a ripe yellow pear. The moon is like a Chinese gong. The moon is like the aura of a dying man."

At any other time Andreas would have been proud to have found such pretty expressions for the moon, but they did not satisfy him now. All at once everything seemed artificial to him. Besides, he thought, that's all out of books, and he was afraid Ulla might think he was trying to show off.

Ulla thought: Andreas finds strange and beautiful words for everything. Just let him keep on talking. Then I won't be afraid any more.

A frog hopped between her and Andreas in the grass. The light collected on its damp green skin and was reflected back, right into their eyes. They both closed their eyes. To their surprise, the frog did not change into either a prince or a princess. It hopped passed them and into another section of pipe. The antenna of the transmitter buzzed. In the distance the faint sound of a motor could be heard.

"We'll be too late for the reception," said Ulla. It occurred to her that the wedding reception of Josel's sister Irma didn't interest her in the least; she didn't have a new dress for it, and as she knew from her big sister Hedel, you simply had to have a new dress for a wedding. Besides, it wasn't a real wedding, strictly speaking, but only a celebration in a hotel from which children (and she was at the age where she felt herself to be a grownup, though the grownups still considered her a child) were sent home early. Being here, with Andreas, was probably better. But it still wasn't clear to her what "better" would mean. Maybe she should simply kiss him.

"Oh yes, the wedding," said Andreas. "You know, I'd almost forgotten about it, my cousin Irma's wedding. She's a strange one, she doesn't talk to anybody, not even her own mother, and always shuts herself up in her room. You're right, they'll be waiting for us."

The sound of the motor grew louder as it crept up the road toward them.

"Well, I can't say that I feel like celebrating, *bien sûr,*" Ulla said.

"I'd like to get inside the transmitter, just to see what it looks like in there." Andreas pointed at the building in front of them, across the road.

"We're going there with the school, the class ahead of us has already visited it," Ulla said. "They said there wasn't anything to see there, just technical stuff."

The sound of the motor grew louder and louder, and two black cars emerged one after the other from the trees along the road. Certainly there was nothing unusual about two black sedans driving in tandem along the Tarnowitz road at eight o'clock at night, nor that their headlights were switched off, after all, a blackout had been ordered in the border area a few days ago — and yet both Andreas and Ulla sensed that they were witnessing something unusual. Perhaps because the cars were moving so slowly, perhaps too because the driver of one raced the engine in neutral a few times, but perhaps it was only because Ulla and Andreas were so close together now, as close as they had both wanted to be for some time.

The two cars stopped. A man got out of one car and ran to the other, leaned down to the window, and then went back. Both cars started up and slowly approached.

Andreas took hold of Ulla's arm at once, crouched down, and crawled into the length of drainage pipe, pulling the girl after him. Ulla stumbled, she lost her footing and fell to her knees, the dirt was soft and sticky. For a time darkness surrounded them, intensified by the sudden braking of the cars outside; the sound blanketed all the other sounds around them, their breath, their steps, the rustling of their clothes.

Light reached them from the mouth of the pipe, and it gave them a view of a circular landscape: an empty road drifted over with moonlight, two black sedans in the middle, the radio station and behind it a portion of the conical antenna.

Andreas was crouched in the drainage pipe, he had his head tucked in and his right shoulder pressed against the top wall, Ulla was kneeling next to Andreas, supported by him, and the smell of mold and decay rose up to them from below.

Andreas looked out through the round hole. People were getting out of the cars, not soldiers as he had thought but civilians; they assembled in front of the first car and it seemed they were discussing what to do next. Andreas felt the vein in his forehead throbbing again. He tried to think what to say if they found them here in the pipe. Somehow he could not believe the cars had driven there, of all places, to flush the two of them, Andreas Pilgrim and Ulla Ossadnik, from their cover at this spot on the long Tarnowitz road.

Then he watched the men go over to the fence and open the gate, he could clearly see one, two, three, four, five men walking along the narrow paved path to the transmitter; two had remained behind with the cars.

Andreas wanted to move forward a bit in the pipe to enlarge his view. Ulla's whole weight was pulling on him. So he simply fell forward, Ulla fell with him, and they scrambled to the edge of the shadow. The bottom of the pipe was damp and slippery, and it revolted them.

Now that the view was larger, the two cars were off to the right, and precisely in the middle, as if in cross-hairs, Andreas saw the five men walking toward the radio station, he could make out clearly that they drew pistols as they walked and held them extended at hip level. A door opened and light spilled out, the five men went through the door, and from inside came the thuds of two or three muffled shots.

Only now did the heads of the two watchers move toward each

other for the first time. Andreas heard Ulla's breathing as well as his own, that calmed him, even though his heart was still pounding so hard he could feel it in his eyes. But perhaps that was only because he had been straining so hard to see. Their cheeks touched as if by chance and their lips met, and the lightning that struck them should have told them that they were charged with too much voltage.

They heard three crisp shots in succession from the building over there. One of the two men up ahead was fiddling with the hood of the second car. Andreas thought lights were being turned on and off in the top windows of the radio station. But it must have been an illusion, because in a radio transmitter they would have been especially strict about observing the blackout regulations.

The sound of another motor could be heard. Andreas stretched his head forward as far as he could. It was coming from the same direction as the other two cars. He was expecting it to race past so quickly that he would not even be able to signal to it. But the sound suddenly stopped, and a new car intruded into Andreas's view, also a black sedan, the same make as the other two. The car stopped. Two men jumped out and spoke with the others, then returned to their car and wrestled something out of it, but at first Andreas could not make out what. It was a person (a sick man? a dead man?). They dragged him by the shoulders and legs through the gate and along the walk to the radio station and left him lying there on the steps. One of the men pulled his gun and aimed it at the man they'd dropped there (Andreas quickly pressed Ulla's head to his shoulder); three shots cracked. Then the two men ran back, got into their car, and drove away.

Andreas was the first to say something. He whispered: "This is horrible, horrible . . . It's a raid."

And Ulla, who needed the relief of saying something, said only, "My God, my God, my God." For the moment that was all she could manage. All at once it seemed to her that the pipe in which they were crouching, in which they were trapped, had begun to whisper. But it was only a frog jumping about somewhere.

"How are we going to get out of here?" Andreas asked. "There's something fishy about this, the whole thing was planned."

"Couldn't we just take our bikes and head down the road?" whispered Ulla.

"And those two there?" Andreas asked. "Over by the cars? They'd gun us down, we wouldn't have a chance. Better for us to go back through the woods."

"No!" Ulla burst out so loudly that they both held their breath in fright. "I'd rather stay here until it gets light or until I . . . die . . . not through the woods again."

Andreas felt her trembling beneath his hands.

"What if we just went over to them and said we got lost on the way to Gleiwitz, what would they do? They couldn't just start shooting at us."

It was so peaceful out there now that it seemed to Andreas as though all that had happened was some kind of illusion. But the two cars were still there in the round sight. And he had counted eight shots.

"I wonder why nothing has come by," whispered Ulla, "no cars, no motorcycles, no bus."

"This really gives me the creeps," Andreas said. "But we've got to wait here until it's all over." He didn't reach for Ulla's hand or her shoulder or her head, he pressed her whole body to his. "I'm with you, Ulla—nothing can happen. And there won't be a war tonight, at any rate." He brushed her lips with his fingers. He remembered that afternoon. He kissed her hair, and she did not resist. "We'll travel to Warsaw together, to Chopin's heart. And wherever else you want to go." Andreas thought maybe they'd stay this way forever, in this pipe, hidden, intertwined. And he found nothing frightening about that.

The door to the radio station banged, the light announced a change. The men were coming back, Andreas counted five, the same number as had entered. The two up front on the road jumped into the cars, the engines roared to life, and the others, who came through the gate briskly but not hurriedly, climbed in too. The cars drove away.

Andreas listened to the sound of the motors, which quickly faded out and then was wholly swallowed up by the humming of the transmitter. He wanted to work his way still further forward in the pipe, but Ulla clung tightly to his body. Now that silence was restored, he could hear how she was trembling. She was tumbling into a dream, pulling him along, and far away in a different, more audible reality their bodies bored deeper and deeper into each other, they tortured and wounded themselves and finally merged into each other . . . and nothing remained of the dream but their short, rapid breathing, which grew more and more hostile, tore at their lips, and ended in a long silent scream of exhaustion with which they cast off their childhood once and for all.

Andreas crawled wearily from the pipe; he slapped the dirt from his clothes, which were damp in many places and gave off a smell of decay. A frog hopped past him. He stretched out his hands to Ulla, who was coming out of the pipe, but he did not look at her; it seemed to him that both of them, like the prince and the princess, had been under a spell for a long time.

"Let's get out of here, Ulla," he said in a voice that must have belonged to him once. He picked up her bicycle and pushed it toward her. "Ride in front, you know the way better."

"Right," Ulla said. "Away and *abtrimoo*."

The dynamo whirred, Ulla was pedaling so hard. The road rushed away behind them. Between the trees lining the road, far away, they discovered a blue light. Then two, three blue lights, flickering, swaying. The air was blue satin. Satin brushed their faces, a light wind arose, a blue breeze. (In a blue cloak, yes, inabluecloak the Blessed Virgin appeared above the town, inabluecloak.) Ulla felt the thin skin of fear that had enveloped her being peeled away and shredded by the air, by the wind, by the light. Beside her—she did not turn her head—was the whirring of Andreas's bicycle. She did not stop pedaling when the police siren began to howl and a car of the sabotage squad approached them and raced past with a blue, flickering light.

Only then did it occur to Andreas that this was the first vehicle they had encountered on the Tarnowitz road since they set out.

16

Since the night Montag tore apart the rosary, a change had taken place in him. He could not say precisely what it consisted of, indeed, when he thought about it, nothing was demonstrably changed, except that the darkness had assumed a different consistency. It now seemed heavier and more impenetrable, but perhaps that was only because of the thick curtains now hanging in front of his windows; and in spite of two desk lamps with forty-watt bulbs, it seemed to him the corners of the room were filled with a whispering blackness. Now when he sat for a long time at his table with his hand resting on the paper without writing anything, without thinking of anything at all (yes, now he could do that), he noticed that the fine, curled hairs on the back of his hand were growing redder from day to day while their tips turned white.

His work on the K biography was proceeding only very slowly, he had begun various chapters but could not finish any of them. He would delve into K's speeches campaigning for election to the German Reichstag in 1903, then into those days which were so decisive for K in July of 1922, when the central committee of the Sejm assigned him the task of forming a government and he failed, a fact which was seldom mentioned in Polish publications, then again into K's arrest in September 1930 by Piłsudski's colonels. Sometimes he sat there and stared at the blank paper, repeating the last sentence over and over in his mind without finding a transition to the next. Once he read everything available by or about Paderewski, after learning of K's encounter with the former Polish President in Morges, Switzerland, at which General Haller and the former prime minister Witos were present. Then again he would become absorbed in finding some historical date or in the search for a certain passage in a book, in which he then became so engrossed that he forgot K's story.

He discovered that one week he had written no more than a

single page. His excuse, he told himself, was that more and more he lacked source material. For a long time he had been unable to travel to Poland, in correspondence too he had to be more cautious now; a substitute mailman had already noticed that he received many letters with foreign stamps. One day the librarian at the municipal library told him he could no longer take out Polish books, that this was only permitted for scientific purposes, and for that he would need authorization. "Germans read German!" she had added sharply. But she had not been able to look him in the face.

Not only had this embarrassed Georg Montag, it had also worried him somewhat; he felt as if he had been caught committing an illegal act, and left the building quickly without saying anything. He had scarcely reached the street when he realized this could only have made him look suspicious, and besides, he had left his hat behind. He went back inside and ordered two books by Hans Christoph Kaergel which had at one time been praised in the Party newspaper *German Eastern Front*. The woman at the desk was so pacified and pleased by this that she would probably have given him the Polish books too, if he had asked for them.

He left the house less often now, went to church only on important religious holidays. He declined invitations from Valeska and other neighbors to go to concerts or to touring vaudeville shows, which he had once loved, at the New World. He used his poor state of health as an excuse, above all his persistent foot trouble. Almost the only place he would go was for a walk in the garden, usually in the morning when the children were at school and it was quiet outside, with only the monotonous piano exercises of some toiling pupil, with all their wrong notes, drifting out to him from the veranda window. Halina took care of his shopping, or Valeska. Sometimes he closed the curtains even in the early afternoon and switched on the electric light. He paced back and forth in his room. He leafed through the newspapers, became absorbed in the financial section after only glancing at the political news, as if he could learn something there which he had not found in the front pages. He would dip into this book or that. Books lay open everywhere, it was only the handwritten pages on K he concealed in folders and hid in the pantry—but perhaps "hid" was too portentous, he simply put them on a shelf there so they would not attract the attention of every visitor. Admittedly, in the last few months no one but Valeska Piontek had visited him. After the night the synagogue burned he had removed the door handle and since then had kept the door locked.

Valeska Piontek had come to him that night and had found him in bed, feverish. It was a cold, frosty night, and probably they had all stayed outside in the street too long. The flames and noise and the inexplicable urge to witness something had made people hurry from their homes, they streamed into Wilhelmstrasse from all directions to watch SA troops smash shop windows, break into stores, hurl merchandise into the street, and set fires. Montag too had gone and watched, and in this way learned which businesses belonged to Jews, which he had not known before: the Barrasch department store and the Weichmann silk shop, Wolf's shoes and Karpe's drygoods, the Bielschowski lingerie shop, Troplowitz's wine shop, and Markus's haberdashery—and Dr. Kapitzka arrived on his bicycle bringing the news that they had set fire to the synagogue, and that the chapel at the new Jewish cemetery in Leipzigerstrasse was burning like a torch.

Montag sometimes thought about what might have happened to him if Frau Valeska had not been with him that night. Yet it all had little to do with him. He had not been inside a synagogue a single time in his life, although several times he had intended to go out of curiosity. But since he was ignorant of how to conduct himself and was afraid of attracting attention, he refrained. His sorrow and his indignation might perhaps have been greater if the Church of the Holy Cross or the Peter and Paul's Church had burned that night instead of the synagogue. But why did he come down with such a fever on that particular night? The day before he had been well; now he lay in bed and was unable to speak, so violently were his teeth chattering. One minute a chill hit him, the next he would break out in a sweat, and Valeska put cold compresses on his forehead or heaped the blankets on him by turns. Montag heard the voice of his grandfather singing, and when Valeska wrung out the cold cloth he thought he heard him sighing.

He saw in his hallucination the old house in Myslowitz where his grandfather had hidden refugees from Odessa in dark corners, and then it seemed to him his grandfather had multiplied and was concealing himself in the dark corners of the garden cottage.

Valeska tried to comfort Montag, but nothing she could say was much consolation; she wound her rosary about his fingers.

Later she revealed to Montag something she had confided to no one, not even her husband: "Do you know, the first man I ever had in my life was a Jew, I didn't know it, I only found out about it later, when it was all over. After that I didn't want to marry a man who was like him, no, I wanted somebody entirely different, who didn't resemble him in the least, and who wouldn't let any thought of him creep in. So I settled on Piontek, whose lungs were already bad, I knew it."

"Frau Valeska," Montag said, addressing her for the first time by her Christian name, "I beg your pardon." He felt ashamed that he had caused this woman to make such a confession.

He asked for a glass of water, out of embarrassment, but also because he had sweated so much away, and it seemed to him as if he were asking someone else for a share of grace—and so he drank the water in little sips.

"I don't know," he said after a little while, "whether I ever loved my wife, certainly not at first, my father sort of allotted her to me. I don't know what had happened, but he wanted to get free of something that had to do with his childhood and his faith. He married a Catholic and stuck me into a Catholic school early on; later he chose a Catholic girl for me, it was as if he wanted to blot out everything he had ever experienced, in Odessa and elsewhere."

Both had exposed themselves in an unprecedented way to the other, but neither could cope with the situation. Montag tossed about on the bed, sweating and trying to rid himself of the covers, and Valeska tucked the blanket under his chin patiently and maternally. He perspired so heavily that night that she had to change the bed twice and put a fresh nightshirt on him. Once he called out "Benja," then screamed: "No, don't kill the horse, don't kill the child!" He did not say what he meant by the horse and the child, but he snapped the rosary then, and the beads rolled onto the white bed and onto the floor.

When the sirens outside announced the early shift, he began to relax. He rested his hands calmly and peacefully on the covers, breathed regularly and stared fixedly at the crucifix opposite him or perhaps only at the white wall, as if hoping for enlightenment or a sign he had secretly been awaiting for a long time but had then forgotten again.

Valeska told him stories from her childhood: about the little town on the river where she had grown up, about the coal mines all around it, the pithead towers, whose rhythmical clattering the wind carried to them, about the massive slag heaps that towered black against the sky and on which the red and blue fire spirits danced at night, about the occupation by Korfanty's people, and finally about how they had moved away in 1921, in borrowed farm wagons, always following the edge of the endless forests, singing the old songs together in the evenings:

> My wagon moves so quickly,
> And you're so far away,
> Wherever it may lead me,
> With you I'll always stay.

"Oh yes," Montag said, "I know that one, we sang it too, in Breslau, at school." He propped himself higher on his pillows and a gentle flush returned to his cheeks. He hummed along with the next verse:

> Hill and dale pass, flying,
> And larks aloft rejoice.
> The windblown woods pass, sighing,
> As though I heard your voice.

Did she know, Montag asked, that he had been educated at the St. Matthew Gymnasium and the St. Joseph boarding school in Breslau, both schools which Eichendorff had attended?

And did he know, Valeska asked, that her great-uncle had been steward on the Lubowitz estate, though by then it had long since ceased to be the property of the barons von Eichendorff?

Did she know, Montag asked, that his daughter Elisabeth had

written her dissertation on Eichendorff, German Romanticism, and a French poet called Gérard de Nerval, and that a half-hour excerpt from it had been read on the Silesian Radio Hour?

And did he know, Valeska asked, that she had taught the first song from Schumann's *Liederkreis,* Op. 39, "Far From Home," to one of her students, surely he had heard it on one of his walks outside in the garden?

Did she, Montag asked, know one of Eichendorff's most beautiful and mysterious poems, on the two wayfarers? "Sturdy wayfarers two set out from home anew, joyful into the ringing, singing waves of bright, full spring."

They chattered at each other, they anticipated each other's words, they laughed, their voices went along parallel to each other, merged into a single voice, then went their separate ways again; he made signs in the air with his hand, and she drummed with her fingers on the tabletop as if to call from the wood some imaginary music, never heard before, and so they both forgot what had brought them together that night: the fires outside.

She said: "I liked to sing 'Didst not hear the springs flowing' best, but only the first verse, they all started crying after that. I like that especially, I'll play it for you sometime . . . when you've recovered."

She was sitting on the chair beside Montag's bed, her hands in her lap, her shoulders sloping slightly forward, just as she sat every day beside Leo Maria's bed, and before her eyes the pale face on the pillows blurred into another face, the two faces dissolved, as in a film, merged and became one face . . .

> Didst not hear the springs flowing
> Far amidst flowers and stone
> Through the woods to still lakes going,
> Where the marble statues, showing
> Beauty in solitude, stand alone?
> Downhill softly its way making,
> Ancient songs in its path waking,
> Comes the night, its wondrous gleam
> From the vales reflection taking,
> As thou thoughtst it oft, a dream.

She sang it quite softly, more for herself than for him, and when she did not know a line, she simply hummed the melody.

"Yes," Montag said, "of course I know that one. 'Magic of Night.' Wait a moment, I'll recite the second verse."

> Dost thou know the flower growing
> Away down in the moonlit vale?
> From the bud but halfway showing,
> Youthful members sprouted, glowing,
> The mouth was red, the arms were pale,
> The nightingale's song was pounding,
> To lament it was redounding,
> For long-lost days resounding—
> Oh thou afflicted by love's bale,
> Come, oh come, to the quiet vale!

Valeska knew few poems by heart, mostly ones which had been set to music and which she had learned while studying the piano. More than any others, she loved those songs with words by Eichendorff.

" 'Afflicted by love's bale'," Valeska said, and jumped up from her chair, as if the words brought back some memory which kept her from sitting there quietly. "That was a time that shook us all," she said quietly, "turned us inside out . . . Afterwards you're . . . different. You know, I play this song on the piano sometimes, when I feel miserable and only when I'm alone . . . That's a song that wounds my soul."

She went to the window and drew aside the curtain. It had grown light outside by then, a dark pall of smoke hung over the town in the direction of Niederwallstrasse. Valeska sat down on the edge of the bed and placed her hands on his; she hoped that in this way his calm and quiet would flow into her. Montag could sense her hands trembling, her arms, her breasts, her shoulders, her entire body. Now neither of them said anything more. After a while they broke apart quickly, like two strangers whose intimacy was accidental. And a bit later, when Valeska had gone (shivering slightly on the way from the garden cottage to her bedroom), with only her scent left in the room, her warmth, and her crocheted shawl, Montag tried to forget all that. From this night he wanted to retain only a rather vague memory of fire, death, and Eichendorff. But he did not succeed. One night he took out his Bible, which he had not read for a long time. He opened to the Old Testament and read in the Book of Jonah and the Book of Isaiah. He read for a long time.

He knew now what had changed him so greatly.

17

THE WILD MONK had come. Valeska did not notice until he knelt down before the bride and presented her with a fruit jar containing a fish. Irma stood and drew the monk up to her, then seated him demonstratively in her place. As a child she and her friends had often visited the Wild Monk in his forest hut, and he had shown them how to weave reeds and how to plait wreaths from wildflowers, how to whittle millwheels and set them up in the brook, and how to mount butterflies and beetles, and in explaining this to the bridegroom she retreated a few paces into her childhood, which was closer than she had realized, indeed, she was surprised how quickly it happened: a few familiar syllables, a face and a cassock that still sheltered a few secrets, cornflowers, henbane, mullein, a little blue fish swimming in a zigzag and trailing a tiny shadow after itself.

It brought back to her all that she had pushed away from her during her year of Labor Service. She had not seen the monk for a long time and took it as a sign of good luck that he was there. (That Mamuscha had invited him without saying anything to her about it!) Plucking a white rose from her bouquet, she put it between the monk's fingers, and he pressed his hands together in embarrassment over the white-covered tables, the sparkling glasses, and the shining faces, all of which blurred into a single sea of light before him.

Valeska would have left him seated there, but she feared that if the Archpriest came, it would cause not just irritation but a serious conflict with the Church. So she signaled to her brother, and the two of them conducted the Wild Monk to the place already set for him. Valeska was glad to have something to do now. She turned up the monk's sleeves so he wouldn't get caught or knock anything over, she motioned to the waiter, fiddled with the setting again, she placed the white rose on the white tablecloth in front of him and rummaged in her memory for something which concerned only the two of them. She smiled; yes, there was something.

Some time ago, when his hut in the forest had burned down, she had gone to him with a pot of soup and a bag of provisions, and out of gratitude he wanted to show her something he had never shown to a soul. He led her by the hand through a fir thicket until they came to a clearing where a forest altar stood which the monk had built out of white birch logs, with a gigantic rough-hewn Cross of St. Andrew behind it, and in the center an immense golden monstrance woven of straw. She had knelt and prayed, and only later, when she was at home again, did it occur to her that she had prayed before an unconsecrated altar. Times had been different then, times had been different, and perhaps it was better not to think about them. Perhaps she had only invited the Wild Monk because wherever he went he always trailed something of those times along behind him.

She did not know that after being in the camp, the monk had forgotten everything that had gone before; that he scrubbed floors now in the old people's home in Rybnikerstrasse, and was raising tropical fish in a narrow room at the caretaker's where he lodged, that he roamed the fields in the evenings and brushed against the branches of the trees along the highway, waiting for the seasons to change, hoping that eventually they would run their course more quickly, that autumn would follow hard upon spring, without summer, until finally only winter would be left, a winter from which he did not intend to emerge.

She would not have believed him anyway.

The "wild," now so gentle monk was silent. He took a swallow of wine and then another. He spooned his soup. Who knows, after a few swallows more, he might think differently about the caretaker and the old people's home. Now he was silent. He was glad to listen as the woman next to him told the old stories, he had forgotten them all. He loved this strange, familiar voice, which was surrounded by so many other buzzing voices. He had heard only one voice for so long, his own.

It worried Valeska that Josel wasn't there yet. She wanted to telephone to find out whether he was at home, and to ask at the same time about Leo Maria, but she was afraid that Halina (as so often recently) would not answer the phone. The instrument had only been in the house a short time, and Halina was still afraid to touch it. She might also ring the HY, but she didn't know the number or whom to ask for.

Nor was her anxiety relieved by the monk, who took a crudely carved wooden cross from inside his cassock, pressed it to his lips, and then raised it to Valeska's mouth. She closed her eyes and felt the wood brush against her lips, imparting the smell and moisture of his skin. She thought of the forest altar and the straw monstrance. She had gone back a few times in secret later, but she could not find it again; only years later did she discover it when a right of way was being cleared for a new *Reichsautobahn*. The altar had been destroyed.

Valeska looked across the table and saw sweating, steaming, puffed-up white faces bent over their plates; they emitted grunting noises, juggled their knives in the air, and shoveled full forkloads into their mouths. It was as if each of them wanted to preserve this experience, this night, for that time when for one blue coupon he would receive a carefully weighed-out fifty grams of sausage at the butcher's; they already had their ration cards at home in a drawer.

Valeska almost began to laugh. They were all sitting there, everyone whom she hated, whom she despised, and, if that sounded exaggerated, well, they were people she didn't give a damn about, and they were stuffing their bellies with marinated and larded roast beef *à la polonaise,* and for this she had sold the old brickyard . . . And the tragic thing was that those she loved were not among them, not Leo Maria, not Josel, not Andreas, not Halina, no, not even Archpriest Pattas was there.

She watched the monk hurriedly spooning his soup. And as if he had just noticed the dirt on his hands, he slowly pulled back his left hand, which was lying outstretched on the white tablecloth, and hid it beneath the table; he clenched his right hand so that only a reddened fist was still visible. Valeska glanced away. All at once it bothered her that her hands were so white. She too hid her hands now.

Then she saw Andreas and Ulla coming in, and hurried over to them. Valeska received with iron calm the news that Tina Zoppas could not attend the wedding reception because she was celebrating her own engagement that same evening. She led the two to their places.

Ulla nudged Andreas. She would get a new lace handkerchief from him now, because he had bet her that Aunt Valeska would burst out laughing at the news.

Valeska did not even ask why they were so late in coming.

"Haven't you heard anything from Josel?" That was what she wanted to know. And they both understood now why she was so serious.

"What's the matter, has something happened?" Andreas asked, concerned.

"No, no, why should anything have happened? He's probably still at the HY . . ."

"There's lots going on outside, Wilhelmstrasse is full of people. The reason it took us so long is because we were there when the transmitter was raided," said Ulla.

Valeska thought about sending someone to the HY.

"Haven't heard about the raid on the transmitter?"

"About what?" Valeska asked, her voice almost as loud as the music. "A raid on the transmitter? What transmitter?"

"You know, the new radio transmitter, we had to go past it on our bikes on the way to Frau Zoppas's, and on the way back, well, that's when it happened," Ulla said.

Valeska called the waiter and ordered food for them. She shouldn't have asked. "All right," she said. "Go ahead and eat." And as she was leaving: "If Josel isn't back in time for the *tableaux vivants,* do you think Ulla might replace him in *The Volga Boatmen?*"

18

JOSEL WAS NOT afraid. Even when shadows detached themselves from the trees and came toward him and grew longer and longer—he was not scared. He began to whisper with the shadows; it was not long before they touched each other, and Josel opened the shed and let the shadows in.

Josel sat on a wooden bench next to the path in the park. He felt the coin in his hand which the soldier had given him, he warmed it in his fist. The soldier had been here before, at least three or four times, but he still could not describe his external appearance, his hair, eyes, face, he could not even say whether he was fat or thin, tall or short. He always materialized suddenly out of the darkness, it was only in the dark that Josel would be sure, anywhere, of knowing him: by his breathing, his voice, his smell, by the way he stretched out his hand, the sound that his uniform made with each movement. He had been the first one to give him money, it was with him that it all began.

It was more than a week ago that he had been riding his bike along the Wild Klodnitz and found the construction shed unlocked, just as Ripkens had told him at the last HY meeting. But it must have been ransacked already, there was nothing left that would have been worth taking. Two camp cots were still there, a washstand with a cracked marble top, broken-open wooden cupboards, a pile of rags in one corner: he had discovered them in the beam of his flashlight. He could take the rags to Podmanitzki the ragpicker, he wouldn't get much for them, maybe twenty pfennigs and a few cigarette cards of soccer players, or a few hatpins with colored heads, or Japanese paper flowers that he could give to Ulla. Josel was disappointed. Ripkens had told him they'd come away with shoes, books, bouillon cubes, and even full bottles of beer—well, he had gotten there too late.

As he was about to leave, Josel jammed the wedge into the door frame. Suddenly he saw someone coming directly toward him across the field, a soldier in uniform, and Josel did not know whether to run away or simply burst into tears, that's how frightened he was. But by then the soldier was standing quite close to him, and asked in a quiet, calm voice whether the shed was unlocked and whether it was all right to go in, and whether it was possible to be left undisturbed, for maybe half an hour, and whether Josel could "organize" it . . . it was worth one mark in silver to him, in fact. Josel, still rigid with fear, had nodded and stuttered: "Half an hour, yes, yes, maybe here in the shed, there's a camp cot, I'll keep watch . . ." And the soldier had disappeared suddenly, and had returned just as suddenly with a girl, and Josel had removed the wedge from the door again and the pair disappeared inside.

Josel did not know what to do except to remain standing in front of the shed, keeping watch. Somehow he felt exonerated. Even though the shed had been broken into by others, still he had felt a little like a thief, searching around inside with his flashlight. But nothing could happen to him now; a soldier, and if he had seen his shoulder-straps right in the dark, he was even a corporal, had asked him a favor, him of all people — Josel would have stood there in front of the shed until daybreak for him.

After half an hour (so he estimated), the soldier came out again with the girl and grinned at Josel: "Hey, first rate, I'll come back tomorrow and bring a few of my buddies." He had shaken Josel's hand, slipping him something hard and metallic. Josel felt immediately that it was money, which embarrassed him, but before he could say anything the soldier folded his hand into a fist: "You can earn that every day . . . till tomorrow, then." And he had put his arm around the girl and disappeared with her into the trees.

The next day Josel spent half the money on a padlock and mounted it on the door of the shed. Hardly had darkness fallen when the first pair of lovers appeared and headed straight for Josel; he removed the lock and let the soldier and his girl into the shed: for one mark. That evening two more couples came — the corporal must have been talking about it all over the camp. Josel might have made even more that evening, but he could not stay away from home any longer, it was already rather late when he rode back. He would make up some story about the HY meeting; Mamuscha would believe that. He calculated how many days he would have to stand watch in front of the shed to save enough money for two tickets to Warsaw.

Josel collected his fee in advance. He had been cheated by one of them, as it happened, on only the third day. The man came up with a chubby tart, spoke fast, hacking his words, always with pauses in between, and repeated everything twice, three times: could he go straight into the shed now, he didn't have much time because he had to be back at the camp by twelve, and the camp was somewhere outside town, and he had to take the streetcar part of the way, and as he spoke he averted his eyes as if he did not want anyone to look him directly in the face.

The two had not been in the shed for more than five minutes when the door was flung open, and Josel, who had moved away a bit, saw the soldier run out; before he could set out after him, the man had disappeared into the darkness and the underbrush. Josel went back to the shed, where the fat woman was stuffing her blouse into her skirt and combing her hair roughly with her fingers. When she saw Josel, she began to swear. "*Tako świnia,* filthy pig, I'll kill him, I'll kill him," she screamed. And Josel, who did not understand what was going on, simply said, "One mark, please. I charge one mark." But the tart shoved him aside and spat on the ground. "That swine, he wanted to do it from behind. From behind, am I a cow or something? . . . What a *świnia!*"

Josel tried to calm her down. He feared for his entire operation, for if this tart kept standing here screaming, it would attract people, and the whole secret of the shed would stop being one. He considered whether it might be better just to disappear for the time being. But the fat woman's curses were dying down, and then she trudged across the field down to the river.

From the shadows of the trees a soldier and his girl detached themselves, they must have been waiting there for some time. Josel let them into the shed without checking to see how it looked inside; he didn't give a damn. He was only astonished at how well the system was functioning.

He reflected that, in essence, he had the corporal to thank for his wealth. How all this would end, he would rather not think about. He would have let the corporal use the shed for nothing, but he always paid in advance, and always in the same discreet manner, by shaking his hand and slipping him the money. Except for the first time, Josel had scarcely spoken to him, though he would have enjoyed a conversation with him, for example about what he did otherwise, out of uniform, as a civilian. Or, which camp was he stationed at? And could he invite him to come meet his parents sometime? And did he think war was on the way? And who would win it, the war? Yes, Josel would have liked to ask him. He was a corporal, after all, and must know what was going on.

To be sure, at home everyone said the Germans would win this war, there could be no doubt of it. But Josel had secret doubts, for Uncle Wondrak said: "The Poles are weak, that is true, they are a small people, but the English will help them, and theirs is a rich and powerful country, one we can't compete with." And Josel believed Uncle Wondrak more than the others. But it was not quite clear to him how the English could help the Poles, for according to the map, England was somewhere far off, and there was a sea in between too.

But should he try to engage the corporal in conversation now, when he came out with the girl? Josel had learned from experience that when the soldiers arrived with their girls, they wanted only to go into the shed quickly and be left alone and undisturbed. And when they came out, they wanted to get away even faster, without pausing, without wasting a word, indeed it seemed to him that as soon as they were back on the park path, they did not want to be reminded that they had ever been in the shed. In this the corporal was the same. He had come with a different female each time, as far as Josel could make out in the dark, and Josel wondered where in the world he found all the girls. One evening he had even been there twice, and the second time had slipped him a two-mark piece, slapping him on the shoulder in recognition and friendship. Since that time the last remnant of fear weighing Josel down had dissolved.

A few times, Josel had pressed up against the shed and put his ear discreetly to the wood to catch some of the sounds. Once he had heard groaning, sobbing, and even cries which had excited him so much that he grew hot and could feel his head begin to glow and his breath come faster. Perhaps it was just the fear of being caught at it by someone.

Then the idea had also occurred to him of boring a hole in the wall. He could move the camp cot closer to the wall and then see everything! Josel was startled by his own thoughts, he tried to suppress them, but they would not go away. And remembering the sounds, which he recalled quite clearly, he fantasized bizarre scenes.

Now that Andreas was there, he thought of it more and more often. Maybe together they would do it. He thought of initiating Andreas into the secret this very evening; an opportunity might present itself to talk to him about it tonight during the wedding reception at the Hotel Upper Silesia. Maybe he could even persuade Andreas to come back here later on. Late at night, in the darkness, it would be easier to explain the secret of the shed. He had been trying to do so all day long, but he had not gotten beyond a few hints, even though he and Andreas had ridden past the shed twice that morning during the sightseeing tour.

The wooden door opened now and the corporal stepped out, the girl behind him, hesitantly putting one foot in front of the other, as if she could not see; Josel crossed the field toward them, feeling with his feet that the grass was already growing wet with dew. Josel mustered all his courage. "Sir," he said, "sir . . ." But the man went on past him, saying nothing. With an outstretched hand he guided the girl very carefully to the sand path, as if she really were blind.

"And the war, what about the war . . . what's your opinion, sir?" Josel walked a little way along with them. When they reached the park path, the sand crunched underfoot. The soldier put his arm around the girl and said to Josel, "Good night, youngster, and don't think about the war. It's on the way . . ."

Josel stopped. "Good night," he heard the soldier say again, a little farther off.

"Good night, sir," Josel said softly, almost to himself. He

waited until the two had disappeared around a curve, then slowly
he went back. He pursed his lips and imitated a jay's call twice. He
listened; a gurgling signal echoed from the top of a tree. Josel
went into the shed, straightened the covers on the camp bed,
dumped the water from the wash basin onto the grass, and poured
fresh water into it. Then he walked back and forth outside, waiting for customers. He wondered why no one else came, it wasn't
even nine yet. He wanted to admit one more couple, then it
would be time to appear at the reception at the Hotel Upper
Silesia. Ulla would be waiting for him, and Mamuscha, naturally.
He considered telling Ulla that evening that he had raised almost
enough money for them to be able to go to Warsaw together, to
the Church of the Holy Cross, where the heart of Chopin was
supposed to be buried inside a pillar. Since no one else came, Josel
took his bicycle out of the shed and padlocked the door. He
would shut up shop for today. Wedding receptions that he was
invited to did not come along every day—and besides, he had
resolved to do a little exploring inside the Hotel Upper Silesia.
He stuck the key in his pocket, swung himself onto his bike,
and rode without a light along the crunching sand path toward
Wilhelmstrasse.

19

JOSEL WAS NOT quite fifteen, true, but for five years he had been dreaming of entering the Hotel Upper Silesia through the front door. Even this afternoon he had only taken a long look through the glass, leaning on his handlebars. And now he was walking toward the building without faltering, he was pressing boldly against the revolving door with his left shoulder and spinning into the lobby.

The first thing that struck him was the many soldiers standing around in the lobby, and then, back in the hall in front of the bar, a big, broad sign that said, in thick letters: NO ADMISSION TO CIVILIANS; but he was puzzled only at the absence of bellboys. Uncle Wondrak had told him that in all the better hotels bellboys were like sand at the seashore, because they're not much more than children, who cost nothing, and now and then he had seen a bellboy on Wilhelmstrasse, in a smart uniform and with a round cap on his head—just this afternoon he had seen one through the windows of this hotel, and now there was not one to be seen, no matter how he craned his neck. If he didn't see a bellboy within the next hour Josel resolved to ask the desk clerk where he could find one, for he wouldn't have another such opportunity to talk with a real bellboy. Because secretly—no one knew about this, not even Ulla Ossadnik—he was still weighing the idea of leaving school to become a bellboy in some strange town in the west.

The clerk came out from behind the desk and asked Josel with routine politeness whether he could help the "young man." Admittedly, the term "young man" pleased Josel very much. He said, "I beg your pardon," because he knew that "I beg your pardon" sounded sophisticated and he wanted to be addressed as "young man" again. And the clerk actually did say it again, gently and politely: "What would the young man like?"

Josel let the question fade away in the air, carefully adjusted the

Byron collar of his shirt outside his jacket and said with studied nonchalance: "Well, you see, my sister is celebrating her wedding here at the Hotel Upper Silesia today . . ." He paused perceptibly. "And of course I'd like to join them, which I'm sure you'll understand, since I am as a matter of fact her brother . . ."

The clerk, who was about to interrupt him anyway, was somewhat less polite now: "Is that the Piontek reception?"

"Yes," Josel said softly, "right, that's it. Irma Piontek, the bride, is my dear sister."

"That's upstairs in the Mint Room," the clerk said, impatiently now, even sternly. (Earlier they were making such a racket up there that I had to go up and ask them to quiet down, after all, I have a hotel full of officers . . .)

Josel looked around; there was still no bellboy in sight, just the uniforms of the soldiers in the lobby. There were soldiers everywhere in Gleiwitz these days; the barracks were overcrowded, the schools were occupied, and soldiers were quartered in private homes. They had even set up a tent camp outside town on the training grounds of the barracks near the town woods, with anti-aircraft guns and spotlights and "goulash cannons," or field kitchens. But here in the hotel, Josel could tell by their uniforms, they were mainly officers. One of them was just going up the stairs, past Josel, and the red stripes on his trousers caught his eye. "Good evening, General," he said. The general smiled and looked at him without seeing him. He seemed preoccupied with something far away, for as he walked on he almost tripped on the carpet. Josel remembered having learned somewhere, probably at a *Jungvolk* meeting, that officers belonging to the General Staff had red stripes on their trousers regardless of their rank, as well as on their shoulder straps and even on their collar patches. Perhaps the General Staff was staying here at the hotel? Josel resolved to reconnoiter this evening and find out.

"A general?" Josel asked softly.

"That way to the Mint Room," the clerk said, curtly by this time, and motioned Josel in the other direction.

The room was draped in a curtain of smoke, sweaty air, and noisy music. Josel stood in the doorway and glanced along the table of the wedding party until he discovered the bride — and next to her, Mamuscha. Most of the guests did not even notice him; they were looking straight ahead at the little platform where the musicians were sitting and playing a foxtrot. Valeska kept looking at the door as if she were expecting someone, so she was the first to see Josel, and waved him over to the table. She pressed him close to her, drew his head down, and breathed a kiss on his hair.

Josel had already prepared an answer to the question which would now inevitably come (why he had gotten here so late, and where he had been for so long) — but no, his mother didn't ask, she seemed simply to be happy that he was there. She said, "Surely you haven't had any supper yet, yes, come, sit down" (she looked around to see where there was an empty chair; there was none) "next to Andreas and Ulla. I'll have them serve you something right away." She motioned to a waiter.

"To celebrate the occasion you could have put on your blue suit today," she said, "and your tassels as well, the red-and-white ones, they look so good on you."

It occurred to Valeska that she had had Josel's uniform washed last week and then had hidden it. Ever since the soldiers had been in town and with everyone waiting for the war, it was better for Josel not to show himself on the street in that HY uniform. You never can tell.

"Oh, here's Josel." Irma turned toward him. "What a great honor you're paying your little sister on her wedding day . . . Our Rumpelstiltskin is here."

Josel looked at Irma in her Labor Service uniform with the sprigs of myrtle on the collar and bosom. Her face glowed. Maybe she had already drunk too much too.

"After all, I was busy serving the Fatherland," Josel said with ironic pathos. "HY duty."

The groom bent forward across the table. "Did you just come from outside, Josel?"

"What do you mean, from outside?"

"How do things look in town?" Heiko asked.

"I came on my bike from Wilhelmstrasse. A real commotion, as if it were Saturday night." He did not intend to say anything about how quiet it had been by the Wild Klodnitz, where he had been until now.

"And did you see lots of soldiers in the streets?"

"Yes, lots and lots." Josel bent toward Heiko. "They're all flirting with our girls," he whispered. And now he turned toward the others. "But have you seen the officers out there in the lobby? They've got those red stripes on their uniforms. This must be where the General Staff is quartered."

Heiko brushed the remark aside. That did not interest him. "They're not from my company, they've got nothing to do with me."

The waiter came up and led Josel to the end of the table. Andreas was sitting there in a *salonik* (where had he gotten that dark suit, and he was actually wearing tassels at his neck, gray and blue, they looked good on him, he had to admit) and Ulla, wearing a green dress familiar to him, only the white stole around her shoulders was new to him. Ulla was holding a glass in her hand and talking animatedly to Andreas. It was Andreas who saw Josel first: "So there you are, finally," and he stood up to greet Josel formally, as if they had not seen each other for days.

Josel was displeased that Andreas had dressed up like a *fircyk*. Ulla remained seated and made her Martha Eggerth gesture, smiling at Josel with half-lowered eyelids, and Josel kissed her on the shoulder, like Jan Kiepura. They both had to laugh.

The waiter brought a chair for Josel, next to Ulla, and asked, "Will you have red or white?"

"What?" Josel's eyes widened in surprise. "Oh, you mean wine, no, I don't drink wine." Josel was proud of having worked this out right away. After all, the Hotel Upper Silesia was known far and wide as the most elegant in the entire region, so naturally at dinner you had a choice of red wine or white. But he did not like the taste of wine, he had tried it once.

The waiter: "I meant red or white *grape juice*. For children." He corrected himself with conspicuous emphasis: "We are allowed to serve only grape juice to minors."

"Well, I'd like a beer tonight!" Josel looked at Ulla and Andreas, and at their glasses; she had something red in hers, and he had something white. "Waiter, waiter!" He spoke as sternly as he could. "I would like a beer." He did not want to begin again on his being the brother of the bride and therefore enjoying certain privileges here. But if the waiter made difficulties about the beer, he would just have to. Ever since his ride here he had been looking forward to a beer.

The waiter set Josel's place with silverware and napkin, saying nothing. His face was as decisively disapproving as before.

So Josel had to. He began very slowly. "I'm a member of the family holding the reception here, and there, the woman next to the bride, she's my Mamuscha, she happens to be paying for everything, please go over and ask her whether I, Josel Piontek, at the *pierunnisch* age of sixteen, might somehow have a beer at the wedding of my sister."

The waiter shuffled away, slightly intimidated in spite of the many years of service that were marked on his forehead like rings on a tree. Ulla giggled. Then she looked at Josel and began: "Wherbsen Erbsen Rerbsen Erbsen kiks Herbsen Arbsen Verbsen Erbsen kiks Yerbsen Orbsen Urbsen kiks Berbsen Erbsen Erbsen Nerbsen?" And at a tempo that made Andreas stare at her wide-eyed.

Josel answered just as rapidly: "Irbsen Nerbsen kiks Therbsen Erbsen kiks Jerbsen Orbsen Herbsen Nerbsen." And only now did Andreas realize that he could not understand a word they were saying.

Ulla had just begun to describe a visit to the Admiral's Palace in Hindenburg where Bernhard Eté had played and Rosita Serrano had sung—and now it was spoiled; she was talking with Josel in this idiotic . . . gibberish. He downed his white grape juice as if it were schnapps, grimacing as he did so.

Josel: "Werbsen Arbsen Serbsen kiks Werbsen Irbsen Therbsen kiks Therbsen Erbsen kiks Serbsen Orbsen Lerbsen Derbsen Irbsen Erbsen Rerbsen Serbsen kiks Berbsen Orbsen Urbsen Gherbsen Terbsen kiks Scherbsen Nerbsen Arbsen Perbsen Perbsen Serbsen kiks Ferbsen Orbsen Rerbsen kiks Therbsen Erbsen Merbsen kiks. Werbsen Irbsen Lerbsen Lerbsen kiks

Serbsen Orbsen Orbsen Nerbsen kiks Herbsen Arbsen Verbsen Erbsen kiks Arbsen Lerbsen Lerbsen kiks Therbsen Erbsen kiks Merbsen Orbsen Nerbsen Erbsen Yerbsen kiks Ferbsen Orbsen Rerbsen kiks Werbsen Arbsen Rerbsen Serbsen Arbsen Werbsen kiks."

He smiled at Ulla. Andreas looked away.

"Don't you understand us, Andreas?" Josel asked facetiously.

No, Andreas did not understand. And besides, he was offended. He just shrugged his shoulders. That really set the two laughing.

The waiter came up with a glass of beer and a plate of soup. "*Fantastichnek,*" Josel said. And to the waiter: "Thank you." He spooned his soup. "It's quite simple, as a matter of fact," he said between spoonfuls. "Ulla will teach you how some day, won't you, Ulla?"

Andreas looked at Ulla; she had the same serious face as before, and that calmed him.

"Don't you know the Erbsen language?" Ulla would rather have asked something else. "It's very simple . . ." She wanted to get the explanation over with quickly, for in fact she thought the Erbsen language was foolish.

"No, don't explain it now," Josel interrupted her. "Let's let him dangle a while. What kind of secret languages do you have — in Breslau?"

Andreas did not know what to say. He had never come across any. In school they had written once with oak-apple ink, which only became visible a few hours later. Then there was mirror writing, but that was easy to decipher. But he knew nothing about any secret *language.*

"As a matter of fact, how do you like my cousin?" Josel poked Ulla in the ribs. "Well, what did you do for fun?"

"Oh," Andreas stared at the tablecloth, "we listened to a record by Gieseking. Chopin."

Ulla thought of that afternoon and the time in the drainage pipe, and she could not keep from blushing, redder and redder, even when she hung her head, lower and lower.

Josel was spooning his soup, not looking at her, thank God.

"Good," Ulla said, and left the word suspended in the air. At the moment she could think of nothing else. She swallowed some of her grape juice. She wished she had wine in her glass, then she could blame her flushed face on that.

"The soup could have been more filling," Josel said, and pushed the plate away. Then he reached for his glass of beer, on which the foam had settled by now. He stuck his nose deep into the glass like an old miner, and smelled it, then he took a long swallow. "What do you think, is Mamuscha watching or could I get a schnapps as well?"

"Sure, sure," Andreas said quickly. "But no schnapps for me. I'd like to try some wine, just to see what it tastes like. I had some once when we were on a trip, it tasted like pickle juice, I tell you, but it was simply cheap wine, there are supposed to be sweet ones too, but they're much more expensive. The best wines come from Italy." He grew animated. Maybe the others were forgetting about their Erbsen language now.

"How do you know that?" Josel was impressed. He did not know much about wine, though a little more about schnapps. The best was the Zubrowka from Poland, Uncle Wondrak occasionally brought some with him from Cracow, and he had sneaked a drink of it from his uncle now and then.

"A glass of wine? Well, I'll organize it for you, maybe even Italian wine," Josel said confidently.

Ulla had recovered enough to be able to talk again: "Andreas is a *pierunnik,* he's not like the others who come from the Reich . . . He could be one of us."

The waiter brought prunes with smoked meat for Josel.

"He's getting along so well that we'll soon have him rolling his *r*'s like us."

"This tastes *fantastichnek,*" Josel interjected, with his mouth full. "Mmm. Would you like to try it?"

"Soon he'll be able to say *pjä-rrunn-je* right." Ulla was beginning to gush.

Josel looked up from his plate. *Pierunje,* that was just about the finest compliment you could pay a newcomer. He considered how he could best talk to Andreas alone; maybe he could persuade him to ride out to the shed with him. It was important to find out how he would react. If he liked the scheme, then he could cut him in on it. Josel looked over at the other tables; a few of the older girls, who had strewn the flowers, were still sitting around Water Milka in white dresses. But for them it'll soon be time to go home, Josel thought; his two or three years' advantage made him feel more grown up.

Andreas to Ulla: "Should we tell him what happened at the transmitter?"

The music had stopped. The three had hardly noticed, only the voices of those across from them had grown louder.

"Well, I'm not criticizing, no, it's none of our business, whatever they're doing up there must be all right, I mean, it's *świnstwo,* a filthy mess, they send our boys to the western border, where they'll be corrupted by those loose morals, that's for sure."

"Oh, stop talking about politics," Frau Bortel said, beaming at the others. "These men, they've got nothing in their heads but politics and the price of schnapps," she said, and edged inconspicuously a little closer to the man.

Andreas was annoyed that he had listened to the conversation for a moment, and quickly said to Josel, "There was a raid there!"

"What's for dessert?" Josel asked, and shoved his half-empty plate aside. "I don't have any appetite tonight. But I'd still like something to nibble on."

"We saw it, Josel, just imagine . . . the raid on the transmitter." Ulla's voice rose sharply. She could not conceive why the news of the raid on the transmitter did not make Josel excited or at least curious.

He only asked skeptically: "What kind of raid? A real one? And what were you doing at the transmitter?"

"We were just passing by," Ulla said.

"Well, this is how it was," Andreas began rather circumspectly in a calm voice, reducing Ulla to silence. It was his habit to play down exciting news. "You remember, don't you, you were supposed to ride out to Frau Zoppas's and invite her to the reception, but you had to go to your HY, and so we went instead. On the way back we were somewhat delayed . . ."

"Yes, just think," Ulla interjected in an artificial tone, "she was

about to become engaged to a soldier, our young widow Zoppas." She wanted to laugh, but she fell silent.

"Well, on the way back we came past the radio transmitter, it
was already dark . . ." Andreas continued.

From the other side the voice of the Sergeant interrupted him:
"But that calls for a celebration, madame, don't you agree!"

Fräulein Willimczyk, the bookseller, trilled: "Oh, you're from
the Rhineland, they say it's beautiful there . . . the scenery!" She
regarded the sweating Sergeant with a mixture of hero worship
and fear. He took her hand and brought it to his lips, and sang
out, spluttering: "I kiss your foot, madame."

"Well, go on, tell the whole story now," Josel said, edging
closer to Ulla. Andreas began his account, although the story he
told was incomplete. Ulla looked into her glass or at the tablecloth, she accompanied his sentences occasionally with small
gestures and muffled sounds. She said nothing. She opened her
mouth once, when Andreas mentioned the drainage pipe, but not
an indiscreet word escaped her, only something resembling a sigh.

By the time Andreas finished his account, they had not only
been interrupted five times by the "cabaret program," they had
emptied their glasses in little sips.

First interruption: Fräulein Kunewicz, sales clerk at DEFAKA,
who was an alternate in the light-opera chorus, and was therefore introduced as "a regular at the Gleiwitz Municipal Opera"—
they had established, mostly by imagination, that she was a
distant relative, so they could invite her but would not have to
pay her for performing—sang and danced "Juliska Juliska from
Budabudapest."

Second interruption: Great-aunt Lucie (Lanolin) and her blind
son Bert from Kalinowitz near Gross-Strehlitz sang and mimed
the sad ballad of Edward and Cunegonde.

Third interruption: Charlie Chaplin, in the person of Mining
Engineer Rudnitzki, sang: "Chez Maxim at any rate, we'll be oh
so in-ti-mate . . ." and clicked out a dance routine in his tap shoes,
like Fred Astaire in the American films, which for some time now
they had no longer been showing at the movie house.

Fourth interruption: Charlie Chaplin again, or rather Mining

Engineer Rudnitzki, gave a speech. And at the end of the speech he said, "*Voilà!* There she is! Our Zarah Oleander!" He took the bowler from his head. And ceased to resemble Charlie. The mining engineer was nothing more than a rather comically disguised mining engineer. Which he always was.

Yes, and there she was climbing to the stage with slow, undulating steps, she drew her train aside a little too carefully and draped it about her feet, her hands and arms enveloped in long black gloves almost to the shoulders, atop her curly locks a black hat with an openwork veil pulled completely over her face, and over her shoulders a bell-shaped black cape made of crêpe paper and covered with glitter; Josel saw it all clearly. She shushed the applause teasingly, and when the band struck up she quickly extended one foot a bit more — that made her shorter — then began in a smoky baritone: "The wind sa-a-ang me a so-o-ong . . ."

"Hey, that's Uncle Wondrak!" Andreas nudged the others.

A few in the audience chortled. Water Milka fidgeted restlessly in her chair, still talking at Aunt Lucie (Lanolin), who, charmed, was stretching her face with its thick glasses toward the little stage.

Into the rippling applause the Sergeant barked, "To be sung on the can after bean soup . . ." And since no one around him laughed, he laughed for them, in spite of the slightly offended look of Fräulein Willimczyk.

Everyone had long since recognized Willi Wondrak, the lawyer, as the vamp up there, but when the "songstress" tore the veil from her face with a jerk, they all went "Aaaaahhhh" in simulated astonishment as if by secret agreement and clapped even more vigorously. Willi Wondrak, as Zarah Oleander, exited to the rear. The band blared a chord after him and then went into a slow foxtrot.

"So, kids," Josel was almost singing, "now I'll organize a *Bimber* for us! And then we'll tie one on!" The Sergeant, on the other side, yelled: "Here, a soup kettle full of schnapps for us!" Josel looked at Ulla and Andreas, who were sitting in their chairs with serious faces. "Then you'll have to finish telling me about it! Enjoy yourselves, *chłopcy!*"

Josel produced a not quite full wine bottle, passing it around to let them admire the label; it read SONNTHALER PARADIES

GRÜNBERG, and as the others looked at him nonplussed, he just grinned and put his index finger to his lips. Then he took back the bottle, pulled out the cork and sniffed at it. "The finest of the fine," he said, and let the others smell too. "That's not wine at all, you see, that's home-distilled *schnapsik* — I swapped for it!"

He poured some for each.

"Not so much!"

"Oh yes, a full glass, it has to look as though it's wine! Or water! Come on."

Ulla waved the glass back and forth under her nose and went "mhmh," as if the mere smell were making her drunk. Andreas resisted at first, for he had set his heart on drinking wine tonight; a red wine, sweet, and from Italy, one you just don't get every day, one that was good enough for a wedding reception. But Josel said, "A good *schnapsik* for starters, the wine comes later!" He poured some for the Sergeant too, who had slumped forward onto the table, knocking over two glasses, nearly causing a commotion, which Josel could do without. And Fräulein Willimczyk, the bookseller, first sighed, "Oh Lord, but that's forbidden," before she let him pour her a glass, and Count Poremba, who could smell schnapps from far away, and home-distilled from even farther, marched up with his glass from the other end of the long table and said, "Oh, just a drop, my friends," and held out his glass the longest.

When Andreas had reached the end of his story, the "second and serious part of the cabaret program, with *tableaux vivants* by Valeska Piontek" was just being announced.

"And you didn't go on into the radio station, I mean, after the cars drove away?" Josel asked.

"*Piernika,*" Ulla answered for Andreas, feeling a chill creep up her spine, "try to imagine it, it was like . . . like a ghost story, well, I was afraid, *bien sûr*, wasn't I, Andreas?"

Andreas had the feeling that he had talked enough. He remained silent now. But Josel dug deeper: "And you say it was a raid, a real raid?"

"It was a raid all right!" And turning to Ulla: "Or what would you call it?" All at once he was not sure of himself.

"Well, you couldn't call it anything else. Yes, it was a raid, of course." Ulla said that too clearly for her uncertainty to escape attention. She squinted toward the door where a group of guests had just gathered to greet Archpriest Pattas.

"We should listen to the news on the radio!" Josel said.

"You mean . . ." (Andreas hesitated) "they'll mention it on the news, this . . . Gleiwitz? I don't think so." He was more than a little startled now by what he had apparently witnessed.

"Why on earth not?" Josel said. "We're right on the border here, and why do you think so many soldiers have been here for days? We're sitting on a powder keg."

Ulla looked toward the door through narrowed eyes, to her the people there became revolving shadows, and when she shut her eyes, it didn't stop them, the shadows continued to spin inside her head, behind her eyelids. "Maybe it wasn't a raid," she whispered, "maybe it was only our imagination."

Andreas was seething. Less than two hours ago he had been lying with Ulla in the drainage pipe, and the damp dirt inside had penetrated through his clothing to his skin.

"But that's nonsense! That's the way it was!" he burst out. "We went through it!"

"Hurrah for nonsense!" the Sergeant yelled. He leaned sideways across the table, tipping over another glass, and demanded another schnapps. Josel showed him the empty bottle. Fräulein Willimczyk took this opportunity to edge her chair back even farther, for while engaging her in conversation, the Sergeant had moved closer and closer to her and seemingly by coincidence, but in reality quite on purpose, had bumped her shoe with his boot, touched her knee with his, her hands with his. He turned his reddening drunkard's face toward her now, and tried to take hold of the Fräulein, who was slowly edging away.

Ulla must have watched the others for too long (and certainly she had drunk too much schnapps), for suddenly everything was revolving. "All right, it was all the way you said, Andreas," she said slowly. "It was real. Only—the blue light, I keep thinking of that blue light, what did the blue light mean, it was there, *bien sûr,* wasn't it?"

A fanfare. And Charlie Chaplin, in the person of Mining

Engineer Rudnitzki, spoke out over their heads: "As the first of the *tableaux vivants* this evening, you will see *The Angelus,* by Millet, depicted by piano teacher Frau Valeska Piontek and her brother, lawyer Willi Wondrak.

Josel knew he had to get dressed as a Volga boatman right away for the second *tableau vivant.* He just wanted to have a look at the beginning. One of the musicians pushed a wheelbarrow onto the stage, placed a basket next to it, and stuck a pitchfork into a wooden block standing farther to the left. Mamuscha appeared in a heavy, full peasant skirt, with a white apron over it, a kerchief on her head tied at the nape of the neck; in passing she plucked at the stuffed potato sack on the wheelbarrow, which had collapsed in the meantime, set down a basket between herself and the wheelbarrow, stretched her head forward and bowed it halfway; she folded her hands and assumed the purest and most pensive expression that Josel had ever seen on his mother. Uncle Wondrak, who had come from the other side in heavy clogs that clattered loudly, almost tripped on the stage (somebody at the table began to giggle, he must have still been thinking of Willi Wondrak as Zarah Oleander, but stifled it immediately, as if someone had poked him). He positioned himself next to the pitchfork, took his hat from his head and held it in front of his belly, looking more at the rim of the hat than at the floor. Only the background with the fields was lacking in this picture, otherwise it was astoundingly similar to the one hanging at home in the music room.

Josel left the hall quietly.

Mamuscha loved these *tableaux vivants,* they were supposed to have been the fashion when she was a child, she always told them that; later they had gradually been forgotten. Fairly recently she had read in the newspaper that some *tableaux vivants* had been performed at a theater in Warsaw, so she began doing them again. At Christmas the neighbors came from all over and marveled at them, even the local Party leader, Hanke, put in an appearance; he reacted enthusiastically and tried to talk Mamuscha into performing *The Three Peasant Women* by Leibl or something or other from the illustrated *Manessa Manuscript.* But Mamuscha's ambition was fixed on doing Rembrandt's *The Night Watch,* she had already begun to devise the first costumes of crêpe paper, but when she realized that she could never commandeer so many men in the neighborhood—perhaps only with the help of the district leader, who could compel his Party comrades to help her—she gave it up instead. But Josel was sure she would have another try this Christmas.

20

Aɪʀᴇᴀᴅʏ ᴄᴏɴᴄᴇɴᴛʀᴀᴛɪɴɢ ᴏɴ the *tableau vivant,* Valeska
stepped into the hall, her hands folded, her head half bowed, her
shoulders sloping gently forward. She shuffled along in her clogs,
which made an awful noise on the parquet floor, though it was
quieter than if she had clomped in on them. That caused a hollow,
wooden explosion with each step; she had tried it out earlier in
the hallway. Just as she was about to position herself next to the
wheelbarrow, she discovered that the potato sack had collapsed;
she fluffed it up again as she passed, and then she stepped onto the
spot marked with white chalk. At the same time her brother
stumbled onto the little stage from the other side and took up his
position next to the pitchfork. The voices of the guests, which had
remained at the same level as they entered, now slowly died down,
but not completely, and somewhere a gurgling laugh could be
heard. For an instant Valeska considered raising her head
and glancing over there, but then the picture would have been
crooked, so to speak, so she stood there motionless, waiting for
silence gradually to fall . . .

She always loved the shifting of sounds into perfect quietness.
As a little girl she had often walked through a blossoming summer
meadow into the woods, first into green, then dark, then into the
blackness of the firs, and she could have listed the individual
sounds that fell silent with every step: the buzzing of insects, the
chirping of crickets, the crackling of the sun in the twigs, the
vibrating of the air, the whispering of the wind in blades of grass;
and in the dense black forest, where the sun fell only as darting
rays of light, it was so quiet you could hear your own breathing
and the breathing of nature.

All at once she realized that the musicians had forgotten to
sound the bell as agreed, without which the picture was incomprehensible; in any case she always chose *tableaux vivants* in which

acoustical effects contributed to the intensity, as a medium to aid concentration, and perhaps that is why she had difficulties with Rembrandt's *The Night Watch,* because she did not know what music would be appropriate to it. At first she had thought of a glockenspiel like the ones known from descriptions of the city of Amsterdam, but Handel's *Largo,* which could be played on a phonograph, would surely be more impressive. As the bell still did not sound and the buzzing of voices did not cease, Valeska looked over at the musicians after all, with a helpless but also tortured expression on her face. She gestured with her hand. And immediately, as if they had only been waiting for this signal, the bell began to sound from the far end of the hall. A good idea of the musicians, Valeska thought, since it heightened the impression that the little church was far away. This quick, impatient, admonishing bell, brightly ringing at an unvarying pitch, finally silenced even the last voices in the room; it became quiet, very quiet, so quiet that when the Sergeant clutched at Fräulein Willimczyk's waist and a seam burst, even that could be heard. The quick, impatient, admonishing ringing strained everyone's nerves, not just Valeska's and Willi's on stage presenting the picture, but those of the guests as well, who were affected, perhaps even upset by it in a very strange way. And the first hesitant, faint, almost intimidated applause might have been only an expression of uncertainty, or a repression, an exorcism of the screaming bell, and when the others joined in the applause, perhaps they wanted only to drown out and smother the admonishing bell.

Valeska stood there and did not move. With a certain satisfaction she measured the applause, which was swelling into a tribute now. She had known she would have a hard time with the *tableaux vivants,* particularly if they came after the "amusing" part of the cabaret program. Earlier she and her brother had discussed at length whether they should be placed at the beginning, to set the mood, but had finally decided in favor of the finale. This was mainly because Archpriest Pattas had consented to come, but only later, at about half past nine; by then, so she thought, the silliness of the cabaret would be over, and the Archpriest would be there for the more contemplative part of the evening. This didn't mean that the Archpriest would not have enjoyed what Valeska considered the coarse, if not vulgar, numbers of the cabaret program; he was a native of Lublinitz and had been ministering in Upper Silesia for thirty years. He loved a strong word now and then. In his sermons he was not above a suggestive joke (which elsewhere might have occasioned a reprimand from the bishop), and when calling on his parishioners he never refused a liqueur. Some families kept a bottle of blackberry cordial in the pantry especially for Father Pattas, and during *Kollende* house-blessing time it was not unusual for the choirmaster to have to help the Archpriest home.

Valeska herself did not mind when parties got loud and a bit crude; for this reason she had chosen the *tableau* of *The Volga Boatmen* to close the program. It would cheer people up, and besides, everyone could sing along with the "pretty little tune," as she called it. But what her brother Willi characterized and even praised as his "cabaret numbers" would probably be too much for the Archpriest to cope with, especially since, though Valeska had scheduled Irma's church wedding for Sunday, the event was not yet certain. Valeska's relationship with Archpriest Pattas was based on a pious trust in him which she had retained since her girlhood. She had attended his rosary devotions when he was still a curate at St. Stephen's, and later he had married her and baptized both her children. Sometimes she had mistaken him for the Church, and vice versa, and when he celebrated the high mass at Whitsuntide in a red robe with a silver dove embroidered on it, his voice resounding through the church like an organ until the windowpanes rattled, she even marveled at him. But ever since the incident occurred with the Polish doctor up in the Beskids, she had stopped going to him for confession.

They had never talked about it, but he gave the impression of knowing everything. During mass he could spot her in the twelfth row of pews—and she had to avert her eyes. Since then she had gone to All Saints or the Church of the Holy Cross for confession; the curates changed often there, and the friendly priest to whom she confessed her transgression in a shaky voice accepted it as a serious but nonetheless common sin, and relieved her of it through the penance of saying five Our Fathers and one Apostles' Creed.

And she had recited the five Our Fathers and two Apostles' Creeds for good measure, but she did not feel relieved, and sometimes she asked herself, at least in the period just afterward, whether she would ever be able to wash her soul clean of it, whatever the penance. Especially since she faced a similar situation many years later. Leo Maria had by then been incapacitated for a long time, and the man who came to the house selling magazine subscriptions had simply touched her in a way no one else had ever done, in a way that made sparks fly, and she thought: Five Our Fathers and an Apostles' Creed, I'll do fifty, it's worth it! And it was. They did it in the hall, standing up, because she wanted to be able to hear if a door opened downstairs and one of the children came home from school, or if Leo Maria called her. She took a subscription to *Westermann's Monthly* and then recited fifty Our Fathers and ten Apostles' Creeds (but the feeling of guilt was not expunged); that first sensation in the dark hall could not be erased, when the stranger had pressed her against the wall and raised her skirt and she had clung to his large, thick, wet mouth with her thin, bitter lips. Every time *Westermann's Monthly* came, she remembered the episode, so she had Halina take it to the attic at once, so that it would not be lying around to remind her. She had written to the publisher three times to cancel it, but for an entire year she had to endure the ever-renewed evidence of her emotional confusion—for she never actually used the word "infidelity."

The applause swelled. Perhaps it was not as loud and spontaneous as before, with the earlier numbers, but it was more intense and sincere, at least so it sounded to her. Now was the time to make their exit before the applause grew ragged; she simply left the *tableau,* her skirt slightly raised, without glancing at the guests or even bowing. And her brother followed her, the pitchfork in his hand; the bell kept ringing in its impatient way until they had both left the hall and the door had shut behind them. Willi went at once into the hotel cloakroom, where the others were getting dressed for the *tableau* of *The Volga Boatmen;* she went into the powder room.

She had insisted on changing in the ladies' room, as there was only one cloakroom on this floor; the men could change there, since there were seven of them. The upper floors, where there would have been plenty of space, had been closed off by the army.

She was just about to undo her heavy French peasant's skirt when she bumped her elbow against the door handle and felt a tingling jolt. She grimaced in pain. The air in the narrow stall was stale and suffocating; it smelled of chlorine and rotting leaves, and she did not know whether the stench came from the white toilet bowl in front of her or from the heavy calico.

Halina had discovered the material in the attic; it had been damp and needed first to be dried in the sun. Valeska refused to go to the attic herself to look around, having once seen a dead bride sitting there, bald-headed and in a white dress. She had been so frightened by this apparition that she began to scream, until the people in the house ran upstairs and found that the ghostly bride was a mannequin Josel had dragged in from the dump and wrapped in a kind of bridal gown made out of an old curtain. He had played "getting married" with her up there, above the others' heads, until he grew tired of the game and the silent wooden mannequin and forgot her. Josel, who since then had become a "grownup," or at least so he felt, did not like to be reminded of it, indeed, he was embarrassed by this childish marriage game up there in the attic, and it was some time before he admitted to it.

All the secrets Halina brought down to her piece by piece from the attic — old newspapers, musty-smelling fabrics, broken toys, or simply an empty cardboard carton or a wooden orange crate from Africa with brown branding on the sides — merely confused and irritated her, like the heavy skirt she was busy folding, which, as she noticed now, was worn in many places and would soon fall apart.

Someone went into the next stall to relieve herself. It was the wife of Neumann, owner of the printing plant, Valeska could tell by the short, groaning sounds reaching her ears. Valeska squeezed herself back into her black-beaded dress and put on her shoes. Only now did she discover the writing on the door: DOWN WITH HITLER! LONG LIVE THE KAISER! This puzzled Valeska. Lower down someone had written in red: THÄLMANN LIVES, and beneath that a hammer and sickle were drawn. She jerked the door open and not until she reached the lounge did she take her first deep breath of air. She put the folded-up clothing on a stool next to the wash basin, where a can for tips stood, and in front of the mirror she took off the kerchief and combed her hair into place; once again she saw herself as she was in reality, and was happy.

In the stall the groaning was drowned out first by a damp splashing, then by a dry metallic sound, and finally by an ever-mounting rush of water that sounded as if the toilet, the stall, the ladies' room, the hallway, indeed the hotel itself were being flushed away. Valeska picked up the folded bundle, dropped a ten-pfennig piece into the can, and fled through the door. She put the bundle of clothes down outside the cloakroom, from which loud voices were coming. Someone must have told a joke, for laughter was pressing against the door, which was suddenly flung open, and the many-throated laughter burst out. "*Ey uchnyem,*" somebody yelled, and the others joined in, "*E-ey, uch-nyemmmm,*" sounding so boisterous that Valeska braced herself for the task of re-establishing the appropriate seriousness.

The first Volga boatmen came out wearing characteristic Cossack caps made of rabbit fur or lambskin or simply of wool. The wide coats they were wearing were of various colors and lengths, most of them reaching well below the knee; only her brother Willi had real boots, and in them he marched back into the ballroom at their head, Josel bringing up the rear, with his coat brushing the floor but concealing his shoes. Valeska slipped in through the other door up front, went around the band and positioned herself inconspicuously next to the little stage on which a Volga boat of cardboard had been set up in the meantime, and she watched the Volga boatmen lay hempen ropes over their shoulders and take up the poses in which she had coached them yesterday, modeled on Ilja Repin's painting, *The Volga Boatmen*. The murmuring had begun again, there was even less silence among the guests than with the *Angelus tableau*. Valeska gave the signal agreed upon to the accordion player, the band struck up—the trumpeter a little too soon—the Volga boatmen moved in place, choreographically bending their backs and straightening up, and chanting in a slow, persistent, monotonous rhythm which reverberated dully: "*Ey uchnyem . . . ey uchnyem . . .*" and Valeska sat there watching, not stirring.

Josel bent under the yoke of the towline and sang, "*Ey uchnyem, ey uchnyem.*" He looked over to Mamuscha, who had sat down and now was leaning back in her chair with her eyes closed. Josel had the impression that a candle's gleaming light was being reflected from her face.

But he could not locate the candle.

21

Until the moment when the little band on the platform began to play dance music, Valeska had heard, wherever she went, only conversations about the war or about peace, but mostly about the war. She herself was not talking much this evening, and it seemed as if her guests, who had long known of her husband's illness, respected her silence. She sat down among them and let herself be enveloped by their voices, and waited for the icy coldness she had brought with her to descend upon them too. But hardly had she moved on when the conversations grew more lively and cheerful, indeed even animated. By now half her guests were enjoying themselves on the dance floor, and the others sat in clusters around the tables, their faces sweating from good spirits, beer, and ordinary bliss, laughter now and then floating up from them. Water Milka walked about distributing home-made cigars from her worn leather case, and when the case was empty, more cigars would appear in it as if by magic. Countess Poremba had put the silver fox around her shoulders again, it was the most precious thing she had to display, even if it was a warm August evening. She might have to pawn it as early as next week, for the Count had reported to the army as a reserve officer but had been turned down, and so their only hope was war.

The Count had asked Schachtner, the owner of the delicatessen, to join them at their table; he felt particularly honored by this and introduced his two daughters effusively. He had four of them, but the other two were still too young to attend such a party, the sole purpose of which was to meet a future husband. He sent all four of his daughters to Valeska Piontek for piano lessons, and it was only because of this that the Schachtner family (whose real name was Szachniczek) had been invited. None of the four daughters was gifted, and they would not learn more from Valeska than

Viennese waltzes and Christmas carols for household use. However, that was enough for the delicatessen owner, who considered musical training a part of their dowry. He yearned to marry off at least one of his daughters to an aristocrat, perhaps he could get closer to such circles through Count Poremba. He would send a hamper of wines and delicacies to the Count's hotel the next day; whether or not a bill would follow depended on the subsequent behavior of Count Poremba. At the moment, he was showing positive signs of at least delaying the bill.

"We could drive out together some time to visit our closest friend, Countess von Krappitz, at Krappitz Castle," said the Count. "Unfortunately, they've already commandeered our automobile, but you'll . . ."

"Yes," the delicatessen owner beamed, "my Opel is at your disposal, of course . . . it's classified as a supply vehicle." And he laughed as if at a joke, but his daughters pressed their backs against the wall and did not. He had enjoined them earlier: "You must make a good impression, sit up straight and stretch your necks so people won't see how short you are — and always be serious! Only geese giggle, and nowadays men want serious wives and not poultry."

The younger daughter was about to burst, though, because of the funny Countess, who kept plucking nervously at her fluffed-up silver fox, and who obviously suffered from a palsy in the vertebrae of her neck, for she was constantly twisting her head to the left in an irritating rhythm. And that was supposed to be a countess . . .

On the table next to the beer glasses, Josel saw still other, smaller glasses with a clear liquid in them. He sniffed at them, and they smelled like homemade schnapps. He tried a different glass, it too smelled of *schnapsik,* and he walked along the table down to the middle, where a group had formed around the wedding couple; there too he saw the same clear liquid in ordinary water glasses on the table next to the stale, pale yellow beer. Even in Mamuscha's glass.

Schnapsik. But he could not spot a liquor bottle, either on the table or underneath it. There were only beer bottles standing about, Schultheiss-Patzenhofer. Might they be pouring the stuff from . . . ? He resolved to examine the bottles when he got a chance, for *schnapsik*. Someone, he guessed, must have organized that with real style; it might be Mamuscha herself, who did not want to pay the expensive liquor prices at the Hotel Upper Silesia. It was surely Mamuscha. The more he thought about it, the more certain he became.

"It's beyond me," Chief Inspector of Mines Kotulla said. "First we're a frontier zone and a combat area, then we're a frontier zone and a corridor, and now we're a frontier zone and a combat area again . . ."

"Oh, stop that!" fat Polensky said, reeling by in search of a partner to dance with. He despised Szachniczek for having changed his name to Schachtner and for having hung a huge enamel sign above his shop in Lindenstrasse: FINE FOODS, which meant nothing more than that his prices were on an average a "fine" 20 per cent higher (but people today don't want to buy in an ordinary grocery store any more, so they look for FINE FOODS AND DELICATESSEN), and he had no intention of dancing with one of the daughters, who were gazing at him now, pale and with eyes full of devotion.

"What's your opinion, Herr Magistrate?" Chief Inspector of Mines Kotulla turned now to the County Magistrate (retired), who had been sitting in deep silence. Montag had grown accustomed to speaking only when spoken to. Now he was being addressed directly. "That about a corridor," he said, "that began with the non-aggression pact which Hitler himself signed with Piłsudski. What a pretty trick to play on our pre-emptive strikers . . ."

"Yes, you're right there. But now he's gone back on it. Does that mean . . . ?" The chief inspector did not say it in so many words. No one needed to.

"But we have to get our colonies back," said Count Poremba, who had come up unnoticed. Either he had smelled the *schnapsik* or was actually interested in stating his views, which always reached a climax in the sentence "We-have-to-get-our-colonies-back." Count Poremba reached for a glass and took a cautious sip, as if fearing that it might be water after all.

The new director of the municipal library, Dr. Kamenz, was arguing with Fräulein Willimczyk the bookseller; she was for August Scholtis, he was for Arnolt Bronnen.

Dr. Kamenz was almost the only Party member at the reception, and Valeska had invited him mainly to bring him and the County Magistrate together, hoping he might make an exception and allow Montag to borrow books in Polish, which had not been permitted for some time now.

"Do you know," Dr. Kamenz said, turning away from Fräulein Willimczyk to Valeska Piontek, indeed perhaps toward a larger audience. "Upper Silesia is a border area, and the literature that originates here must look that way too, engaged, polemical, aggressive. We, the guardians and defenders, but also the shock troops and chosen custodians, we must preserve our ethnic diversity and richness, the uniqueness of our folkways, in relation to German culture and to the general Silesian background as well. In this lies the organic integrity of our border literature and its particular mission . . . And I haven't seen much of that in Scholtis up to now, at any rate."

Valeska moved on, and Fräulein Willimczyk was taking pains to get away from Dr. Kamenz too.

Water Milka startled the others with the news that big tobacco fields were being planted at Peiskretscham because it was predicted that no more tobacco could be imported from the outside, and she prophesied tobacco rationing in the immediate future. Count Poremba was depressed but indifferent; as for the others, Schachtner, the delicatessen owner, was disappointed, the head of the municipal library indignant, but perhaps only because not even Fräulein Willimczyk, the bookseller, was prepared to listen to his pronouncements on Upper Silesian literature. Yet these were notes for a speech he was going to give at the library on Harvest Day, and as a bookseller, Fräulein Willimczyk really would have to attend. The bookshop in which she worked was, in general, just too Catholic for him, and he was considering not placing any orders with it in the coming fiscal year.

In the rationing booklets, Dr. Kamenz was getting excited, received by all German citizens (he emphasized this) there were no coupons for cigarettes or tobacco, thus it followed that tobacco would not be rationed. To believe otherwise was to spread gloom and defeatism, if not worse.

Water Milka astounded the others not just because she was the only woman who smoked cigars (that was known, but still irritating), but above all because of the beautiful smoke rings she sent floating up to hover magically over the room; she could blow two or three side by side or even one above another. Best of all, she could poke her finger through the middle of one of them and move along with it, or set a ring above someone's head like a halo.

Now she puffed three smoke rings into the air and turned slowly, looking at the others: "I'll drink to that, how about a gentle white Polish vodka!"

Valeska was about to signal the waiter, but Fräulein Lucie (Widera), who preferred to stick with the sweet blackberry cordial, pushed her glass of schnapps over to Water Milka.

Perhaps Water Milka should not have mentioned the Polish vodka. For Dr. Kamenz, who had the feeling that he was wasting his talents in this provincial town anyway, started in again. He could not believe that in this renowned establishment, so close to the border, which was in itself a national issue, Polish liquor was being served. He was already thrusting his arm into the air to call for the waiter. The combined efforts of the Porembas barely managed to prevent him; they were afraid the liquor would dry up, for they had just begun to empty the odd glass into a medicine bottle they had sequestered under the table to provision themselves for the difficult days ahead.

By this time Water Milka had declared triumphantly that tobacco and clothing rationing cards would be issued within the next few days — they were already printed and she had seen them: brown tobacco cards and yellow clothing cards, in various denominations. One would get five cigarettes a day to start with.

"What? Only five cigarettes a day?" fussed the president of the waterworks. This news interested even non-smokers like Wondrak and Archpriest Pattas.

"If the Lord of the Library can get by with five cigarettes a day," Water Milka said sarcastically, "then everything must be in order."

"In wartime one must do without," spoke up the Sergeant in a voice that showed he was hoping for the opposite from the war.

"What's at issue here?" asked Aunt Lucie (Lanolin), with her blind son in tow.

"And what's at issue in the whole world?" Count Poremba asked. "Our colonies." He was already drunk, you could tell by his voice.

The delicatessen owner fetched a bottle from underneath the table and filled his glass and those of the others with a clear white liquid. Josel too reached quickly for a glass and held it beneath the beer bottle, then he sniffed it and tried a sip: yes, it really was *schnapsik,* of the same quality he'd gotten before at Polensky's for two marks.

Valeska, who had missed none of this conversation, thought of Hedwig Solanke's wedding a year ago, where the conversation, along with births and deaths, had centered mainly on the latest fashions and the designs by Bleyle, and perhaps on the new hair-styles, as was usual—things were different now.

Valeska gestured to Andreas. When he came up she laid her hand on his shoulder and said loudly to the table: "Andreas asks me why our Emilia is called 'Water Milka'; wouldn't you like to tell him how you came by the name?"

Water Milka was unwilling, but the others wanted to know too. A lively discussion ensued, and Valeska was glad to have succeeded in changing the subject, at least for a moment. She drew Dr. Kamenz aside discreetly, she wanted to introduce him to the County Magistrate.

"What a mad name, Water Milka," said the president of the waterworks.

"Because she walks in the water," said Lucie (Widera).

"She can predict floods," claimed Frau Kulka.

"She walks in the water the way we walk on a road," said Inspector of Mines Kotulla.

"She reads the water like other people read the Bible," Fräulein Willimczyk the bookseller said.

Andreas stood there feeling left alone with a question he had never asked.

"I just know the Klodnitz's ways," said Water Milka, in a voice that came from somewhere else and would suffer no other voices near it. "I grew up on the river and I've been watching it for years. All rivers are alike. I understand their language a little, the coloring of the water, the flow, that's all . . . No secret there. So, enough of that, *ludzie*." She put down her cigar.

"Emilia Piontek, known as Water Milka, wants to dance now." She pointed to Andreas. "Can you dance, Andreas? Well then, let's dance! You aren't afraid of me, are you?"

"Of course not," Andreas hastened to say. "Why should I be?"

But he would much rather have danced with Ulla.

"How old are you? Oh, fifteen. And you say you come from Breslau, yes? A beautiful city, Breslau, isn't it? And a fine river, the Oder, yes, at Breslau the Oder is a river to be reckoned with. I've seen it," Milka said softly.

Andreas understood every word. At last, someone who did not laugh at his feeling for Breslau. He would tell Josel and Ulla that too. Oh, he could take Water Milka with him and show her all the secrets of the water, upriver, far outside the city.

It was a slow dance. But perhaps only Water Milka was dancing it as slowly as this. Andreas hung in her arms, and the smell of tobacco and river mud almost suffocated him.

She would have told him the story, him alone.

"Yes, it's true, I love this river, this dirty, filthy, brackish, sluggish river, my Klodka, the quiet, peacefully flowing water in the summer, that whispers with the willows and combs the river grass, sometimes you have to get very close to it to tell which direction the water is moving. No, it's not powerful, this river, you can throw a stone from one bank to the other and in the dry season you can roll up your trousers and wade across it without swimming. But in rainy weather or in early spring when the snow melts, the river is transformed, it rears up, rises high, tears itself loose from its tame bed, then you wouldn't believe it's the same river, it pours out over the pastures, over the fields, sluices away the soil and the newly sown crops, sometimes garden fences too, houses, and livestock, and it makes blocks of ice rear up against each other, crushes boats along the shore and even shatters bridges.

"I know when the water is coming. Even in the evening the water says nothing, just the wind blowing from the southeast, and far away in the Beskids the lightning flashes, but already I can hear the water singing, I tell the people, *'Ludzie,'* I say, 'the river's coming, the Klodka's getting angry,' but they don't believe me, they laugh, 'Just let the river come,' they say, 'we're having a bad dry spell this year and a little water wouldn't hurt the fields.' By the next morning the water has already reached the pastures along the bank, and by noon the gardens, and a cloudburst has begun that doesn't let through a glimmer of light or hope, and the bushes, the shrubs, and the trees are under water, the chickens flutter to the rooftops, and the dead mice and rats float between the fence pickets, and the water breaks in the windows . . . And then finally they believe me.

"No, I don't pray to a water saint, not even to St. Nepomuk, I don't know any spells and don't carve any secret signs on the poplars along the river, but I walk barefoot through the flood to the river bed and feel the power of the water, I observe the currents and the moon, then it's not hard to work out whether the water will rise or recede.

"And I went to the people once and said, 'Have no fear, *ludzie,* tonight the water will rise one more time, one of you stand watch outside, so that no one suffers damage, but early in the morning the waters will recede, in the High Tatra it hasn't rained for days, no more is coming.' And that's what happened, too, and the people brought their livestock down from the rooftops, and strewed sand on their floors, and kissed my hands.

"Yet it's really a simple thing, and I don't like it when people try to make magic out of it.

"And much later I heard people say : 'Look, here comes Water Milka!' And then some of them crossed themselves. So I went to them and said, *'Ludzie,* I just like being by the river, I grew up there, and that's why I know it so well, I simply understand its sounds, its currents and its colors, like other people understand the wind or the forest. That's all, there's nothing more. Got it?

"So, that's the way it is."

Now the dance could have ended. But the two danced on,

probably because the music played on. There was no other reason. And to step out of the music would have required an effort of which neither was capable.

Up front at the wedding party's table, Mining Engineer Rud-nitzki began to sing:

> The Saar wherever
> Is German forever

"Yes, let's sing a song," shouted Heiko from the other side. He didn't know that one. He would rather have sung "Hail Duke Widukind's Clan!" But the others knew the song, which was sung to the melody of the miners' song "Good Luck," and a few of them joined in:

> And German is my river's shore
> And German my homeland forevermore.

They had sung the song when the Saar was still occupied by the French, they had sung it when it became German again and oaths of loyalty were sworn, they still sang it now, although more rarely. They had lots in common, the two provinces, not just coal and the border, but mainly those.

"How about our Korfanty song?" Josel called out.

And Uncle Wondrak was already beginning to strike up the melody, *pom-pom-pom*. And Aunt Lucie (Lanolin) was going *tam-taramtamtam*. "Now, everybody sing," Uncle Wondrak called out, and with his left hand gave the beat:

> Korfanty came a-riding
> upon a billy goat
> the Polacks thought it was
> our own dear God himself
> they kneeled right down before him
> and worshiped in his band
> though it was just Korfanty
> the hurdy-gurdy man.

Everybody nearby sang along, so loudly that the band could not be heard.

"Fine, and now the second verse," Josel called boldly to them all. And he began:

> Korfanty came a-flying
> upon a bottle of gas
> the Frenchmen thought it was
> a blimp up high did pass
> they brought out all their cannons
> and loaded them en masse
> they aimed them at Korfanty
> and shot him in the ass.

There were not so many who knew this verse, mainly the younger people, but when they finished it, the others applauded and there was general laughter. More and more couples stopped dancing and came over, Water Milka and Andreas among them.

"Come on, more, who knows the third verse?" Willi Wondrak egged them on. After a pause someone in the background suddenly began to sing:

> Korfanty came from Oppeln
> without a single dollar
> and then all he could double
> was just our debts and squalor.

The rest was drowned in loud laughter. The music stopped playing.

At the end of the table a man whom Josel did not know stood up, raised his glass and yelled: "*Prost,* Korfanty! Quarter past eleven!" And then his knees gave way and he collapsed as if in slow motion. Willi Wondrak and Inspector of Mines Kotulla ran over to him, set him on a chair with his arms over the sides, and pulled it up to the wall; now he could not fall over again, or get to the schnapps either.

"Does anyone know another verse?" Willi Wondrak called out into the slowly ebbing noise. But no one knew any more verses.

"Then the first one over again!" he cried, and it was as if that had opened the floodgates. They were singing so loudly now that the noise penetrated the doors and reached the lobby, and two officers stuck their heads through the doorway.

County Magistrate Montag had stood up, he was making his way slowly to the exit. The song hurt his ears. If he left now, he could still catch a streetcar. But there was Valeska coming up to him. "Oh, but you can't leave yet, please, Herr Magistrate, just stay another half an hour!" She slipped her arm under his and simply led him back.

> . . . though it was just Korfanty
> the hurdy-gurdy man.

22

ALTHOUGH THEY CAME together slowly and by design, in the end they collided like two planets anyway. Automatically, Valeska anchored her bun more firmly. Finally she had Water Milka alone. She only hoped now that no one would come along to disturb them for the next few minutes. "You're doing well, Milka!" Valeska pitched her voice so that Milka could hear it was useless to evade her.

But since the question was not a question, Milka saw no reason to answer it. She sensed what was coming; lawyer Wondrak's secretary had been dropping some hints earlier. She hoped that her sister-in-law Valeska would come to the point quickly, then they could get it over with. She exhaled smoke, simply now.

"I saw you dancing earlier with Andreas, you're like a young bird, yes, did you know that? . . . Slim, trim, elegant . . . I hardly recognized you." Valeska forced the artificial tone still higher so that Milka could not miss it.

"People change," Milka said vaguely.

Valeska accepted this help thankfully. "Yes," she said, "don't you ever think about changing? I mean, you can't keep on living out there in that hut forever?"

"Why not?"

"There might be some greater opportunities — for you, and for us too."

Milka put her cigar on a plate and adjusted her blouse. "I have always taken advantage of my opportunities, no matter what other people thought, and that suits me very well. I dance, I enjoy myself, I laugh . . . By the way, the idea of the *tableaux vivants,* amazing . . ."

"*Tableaux vivants* are coming back into fashion. They used to be the custom only with really wealthy people . . ." Valeska stopped short. That was not the point now. "Well, Milka," she said, collecting herself, "there has been some friction between us now and then, I mean, you've always done what you wanted to, and that was right of you, just not always so easy for us to understand . . . Actually" — her voice was charged with energy now, and perhaps what she was about to say constituted her only sincere words that evening — "I've envied you from the very beginning, and Leo Maria has too, yes, he has."

Milka looked up in surprise. There was a note in Valeska's voice that belied her usual pretense, and for her Valeska Piontek was a woman who masked her entire existence in pretense. It would not have mattered to her, either, if Valeska and her brother had not tried to get her committed to the insane asylum in Tost that time.

"You were the only one of us with the courage to arrange your life the way you wanted it, and you made reality out of something we had never more than dreamed of." Valeska plucked up all her courage, hoping that other people forgot more easily than she did, and went on: "But we're none of us as young as we used to be, and you, don't you think about security sometimes too? Don't you want to move in with us? Now that Irma's leaving, there's room for you. Willi wants to open an estate agency, and we'd like you to come in with us . . . What do you think, wouldn't you like that?"

Milka stubbed out her cigar in the plate. So that was it. She had to admit it, these strange siblings were not only ready to invest ingenuity in prying her loose from the hut on the Klodnitz, they were willing to invest money as well. And she could tell from Valeska's tortured expression that they were serious about it.

Milka launched into her cigar ritual. Not that she meant to leave Valeska on tenterhooks, not in the least, but for her it was time for one last cigar, and she prepared it now with ritual care. True, she had nothing against having an audience while doing so; Valeska's upset and somewhat perplexed gaze would suffice for a start. And Valeska tried to cast herself in a role she would probably have to play often enough in the future. She could not gauge whether or not she was playing it well, but if one could inhale patience through the nose, then she was doing so. She could imagine that she might even try a cigar herself one day, just *try* one — if Emilia were living in the house and the walls, furniture, and curtains took on her smell, then she would probably get used to cigars too.

"You're too late," Milka said, after blowing out the first smoke in dense clouds; she was fascinated by the sight. "I made a different decision yesterday. Very different." Her face was glowing, but you couldn't tell whether it was because of the cigar or because of her "different" decision.

She had knocked the wind out of Valeska, who was firmly convinced she had made her sister-in-law the best proposal of her entire life while underplaying her own interests. And since that did not happen often, she was all the more helpless now.

"Dear Valeska, I'm convinced that you all want the very best for me." And for the first time she probably was. But she could not help adding a small dig: "Today, anyway! — But you said yourself that I've always done what I feel like. And you see, sometimes I feel like doing something very *different*. You think it was fun rolling cigars out of this grubby stinking tobacco? Take a look at my hands, all stained with the tobacco juice, chapped, ruined . . . But who wanted anything to do with me back then? Not you and not your brother, so I got into it myself and I made my own fun, nothing else. And now I want to get away from here. The Countess Hohenlohe-Langwitz advertised in the personal column of the *Upper Silesian Voice* for a lady to be her traveling companion. Yesterday I was at the Langwitz estate — the Countess engaged my services. We leave for Karlsbad the day after tomorrow."

Fräulein Willimczyk and Archpriest Pattas sauntered up as if by coincidence.

"You've been hiding from us. My, it's a real *tête-à-tête*," the bookseller clucked. "Come, come, my cardinal-to-be, let's listen to what our girls have to say."

"Is that your last word?" Valeska hastened to ask. "I mean, is your mind made up?" She still had Leo Maria and his illness as a card to play. But she was no longer as confident as she had been two hours ago that it would make an impression on Milka.

"You know, Valeska, I don't intend to change anything about it. I've always sought out *my* opportunities, so now I'll be reading

Fontane, Hamsun, and Hans Christoph Kaergel—not to mention the local news in the *Upper Silesian Voice*—to an old, rich, and very dignified lady, yes, that's what she is."

That gave Fräulein Willimczyk her cue. "Father," she screeched, "Father, listen," and everyone heard her, not just the Archpriest. "Hans Christoph Kaergel, a writer . . ." She spoke as if the very mention made her want to spit, as one does when the word *djobok* is uttered . . . "Oh well, I don't have anything to say about that, nowadays it would just cause trouble."

But since she did not see Dr. Kamenz around, she kept talking: "Kaergel is required reading for the HY, our shop is mobbed by those boys, you wouldn't think we were a Catholic bookshop." You could tell by her eyes how hard it was for her to accept this, even now. She would have liked to describe to the Archpriest some of her attempts to steer the boys in the HY shirts away from Kaergel and on to Scholtis, Wiessalla, or at least Gerhart Hauptmann. But since it had all been in vain at the bookshop, it seemed even more pointless to her here.

The Archpriest would have liked to move in closer to the two women, but Fräulein Willimczyk was still blocking his way with her words and her body. She had set up a name in front of her like a fence, but nobody much wanted to climb over it.

"Don't you simply want to get me away from the river, Valeska?" Water Milka said softly. And after a while, almost pleadingly: "Leave me by the river, I need it."

Valeska could feel that it no longer made any sense to play her trump card, Leo Maria. Slowly she began to freeze over. It all fitted Milka: singer at the Zoppot Outdoor Opera, mistress of a visiting tenor, usherette at a movie, cigarmaker in a refugee hut on the Klodnitz River, and now: lady's companion! Reading Fontane to a half-deaf countess, promenading at spas, taking little sips of water containing iodine or iron or something. She knew it would not be easy to free Milka from this magic net, and just now it was impossible.

She looked around for her brother Willi. Would he like to give it one more try? On the other hand, she did not want to admit defeat, at least not yet.

Both women felt very strongly that they did not belong together. So Valeska, resigned, kissed Milka on the cheek.

Willi Wondrak observed this with satisfaction: the two women must have reached an agreement, then. He looked a little sweaty, he had removed his tie, which was hanging half out of his jacket pocket, his shirt was open down to where the black curly hair began on his chest. He was smiling as if he had just danced the most beautiful dance of his life. Whereas he had only taken the Wild Monk, who obviously had no tolerance for alcohol since his imprisonment and had fallen over after only a few glasses of *schnapsik,* into the cloakroom of the hotel, where he could sleep it off in peace. For no one knew where he was living now, and Willi Wondrak, who tried to rouse him at least temporarily with a few slaps on the face, got nothing out of him either. He had improvised a resting place for him in the cloakroom amidst cases, trunks and rolled-up costumes, with a satchel under his head for a pillow. Just as Wondrak was about to leave, the monk took from beneath his cassock a little wooden cross he had carved himself and gave it to him.

Wondrak took it and kissed it, before hiding it in a pocket. Nevertheless, he did not forget to lock the cloakroom behind him.

"You see, that's the way our sinful world is," Archpriest Pattas said loftily. He was looking at the dancers and holding a glass of schnapps in his hand.

Valeska hastened to put on a smile, and held up her glass as well: "To the true world!"

"And what would the true world be without the sinful world?" trumpeted Polensky, on whose arm one of the delicatessen daughters was now hanging, and his glass sailed upward.

Willi Wondrak watched in astonishment, then he did something very bold for a man in his position. He took a little liquor glass from the table, said *Prost* to Valeska and to Water Milka, downed the schnapps and, when he saw their frozen faces, pitched the glass behind him in a high arc. "*Chłopcy,*" he shouted, to drown out the sound of the glass exploding, "how about a rrrrreal polkaaaaa!"

The Sergeant came panting back from the dance floor with Lucie

(Widera). The band was playing a tango, which was too strenuous for him, and besides, he had already drunk too much for that. He pushed Lucie along in front of him, pressing his hand against her back and sometimes rubbing it along her blouse. "Look, there's Father Pattas!" he announced from a distance. He let his hand drop, for sitting next to the priest he saw Fräulein Willimczyk, who had just lifted her schnapps glass, saying: "I'd like to drink to that — Father, how does the Bible put it so beautifully? — that the cup of war may pass us by."

Milka was still preoccupied. "That I may some day see the place in which all rivers merge into a single river. Some day I'll travel there, to the Mississippi," she whispered.

"Father," the Sergeant said in his cold, foreign voice, "it's a strange world. Help me! I'm dancing with a girl, she's from Biskupitz. From Biskupitz!" He tugged Lucie (Widera) over to him and displayed her like a circus barker showing off a freak: the girl with two heads. "From Biskupitz," he repeated, "have you ever heard such a name before . . . ? Biskupitz! I dance with a different one, she's from Schi . . . Schi . . . she's from . . . well, Schimischow, I dance with a woman who is from Ujest . . ." By now he was talking past the priest to all the others: "Have you ever heard a word like that? *Ujest,* it sounds like someone sliding down the drain, doesn't it?" He began to laugh, and looked around him, but, as so often, he was the only one laughing.

Fräulein Willimczyk strafed him with her gaze, less for poking fun at the name Biskupitz than for caressing Lucie (Widera)'s back. The Sergeant thought: Well, next time I'll dance with the bookseller.

"You just have to get used to it," the president of the water-works interjected. "I've been here a year, and still have some difficulty. Well, there's a set of locks in the new Adolf Hitler Canal at . . . hm, what's the name, at . . . Sla-wen-tzitz, yes, that's it, Slawentzitz, and now they're building another at Nies-dro-witz, but there's an even worse one, I can't even pronounce it myself . . . Luise!" he called to his wife. "Oh yes, it's called Wy-dzi-erow." Now he too began to laugh: "Wydzierow!"

"Recently I went on an inspection tour to a little place called Krzidlowitz, and once I was in Kottkrzidlowitz, no, Kottlischowitz," Inspector of Mines Kotulla bleated.

And finally Dr. Kamenz added his two cents' worth. He came from Upper Silesia, but from the left bank of the Oder, the better side, because serfdom was abolished thirty years earlier there. "You are right, gentlemen, but all that will change, the towns are getting German names now, Przeschlebie, for example, is now called Sandwiesen, Niesdrowitz is Niethammer . . . I sit on the committee that determines the new names."

The others were still laughing. Lucie (Widera) disengaged herself from the Sergeant's arm, she wanted to leave the table, she did not like it when anybody laughed at her country or her language.

"I've been in places like Nie-wod-nik, or Plaw-ni-o-witz, right on the border," the director of the municipal library went on. "They wanted a branch library, as if anybody there could read German . . ." The director spluttered.

The rest at the table did not laugh. They let their glasses drop, but held on to them, as if they were the only things around worth holding on to. They stared into their beer or their schnapps, and some of them tried to down their anger and rage — or simply their bitterness — with their schnapps.

Count Poremba was insulted. Twenty-five years ago, he thought, I would have shot these gentlemen in the head, in a clearing at dawn. But now he preferred to remain silent.

Valeska wondered whether she should refuse to give the son of the inspector of mines piano lessons in the future. To hear him talking like that! He was an Upper Silesian himself, after all.

Water Milka wished for a flood that would sweep away the Sergeant and all the other foreigners.

"Sit down, Sergeant," the Archpriest said in a voice that was unusually sharp. (The Sergeant thought he had heard a command, and he sat down briskly, which he barely managed.) "And listen to me! You too, gentlemen, and you, and you, and you!" He looked about him. "You have not understood this country and you will not understand it, and the time is coming soon, pardon me for saying so, for you to leave this country."

He stood up. Not because he wanted to preach. No, his voice was implacable.

Suddenly it became very quiet. Even the Sergeant, who had gotten hold of himself and was about to launch into another joke, was stopped short by the Archpriest's abrupt gesture. The music sounded louder now, even the shuffling of shoes on the parquet could be heard. It seemed to Valeska as if something were ticking inside the glasses. Something or other. Some kind of a curse.

"You laugh at the names of a few towns and villages," the priest continued, "because your awkward tongues handle them so clumsily. But, gentlemen, remember, this is a region which has grown up historically between Teutons and Slavs, Germans and Poles, and each of those names bears witness to this . . . For someone who has grown up here and who must live here, and who likes living here—you won't be able to grasp this—the names are like music. I have thirty years of ministering behind me, all in this land, Upper Silesia, I have been everywhere, and everywhere I found the same love and faith in our homeland and in our holy Mother Mary. Shall I tell you all the places I've been? Oh yes, listen to the music of these words: I have been in Budtkowitz, in Jellowa, in Knurow and in Laurahütte, in Malapane, in Gogolin, Zaborze, Miechowitz and Groschowitz, in Maltschaw and in Leobschütz, in Deschowitz and in Krappitz, in Bobrek-Karf, in Potempa, in Kulisch, in Pitschen, in Bielitz . . . Let me think of some more, in Straduna, Rybnik, Niewodnik, in Leschnitz, Patschkau, Peiskretscham, in Zernitz, Jasten, Korkwitz, in Ostrosnitz, Nieborowitz, Wischnitz, in Zawada. These are just at random, as they occur to me, but listen to the music . . . the music in these words . . . Kottlischowitz and Schelitz, Collonowska and Tillowitz, Brolawitz and Poppelau, Markowitz and Tropplowitz, Schammerwitz and Steugerwitz, also Steuberwitz, Miedar, Brynnek, Hanussek . . . Tworog, Piltsch, Botzanowitz . . ."

"Those are not names, you don't write them with letters, you write them with notes, and you have to sing them," Valeska interposed. In her thoughts she was already sitting at the piano, striking the keys. "Yes, this language must be sung!"

The Archpriest nodded to her. "And then there's Golkowitz

and Kranowitz, there's Katscher and Bleischwitz, then there's Rosenkrantz and Guttentag, Gwosdzian and Cziasnau, Alt-Schodnia and Tworkau, Skrzidlowitz and Karchowitz, Rudzinitz and Blechhammer and Turawa and Zabrze, yes, that's what Hindenburg used to be called, what a beautiful soft satiny sound ... Yes, those are the ones that just come to mind, but I could recite names to you for half an hour more. None of these names is accidental, each one has a long history of its own.

"You would be surprised, Herr Direktor"—the priest's voice returned to normal—"how often these names even have a patriotic, a German patriotic history, which does honor to our state of Prussia. Yes, Sergeant, one must love this land, this language ... these people, in order to understand all that."

Valeska looked at the Archpriest and her eyes gleamed feverishly. Perhaps it was faith, perhaps only the schnapps.

Milka remembered that she still held the glass in her hand she had been going to toast with earlier. She said, "To the Mississippi!" But only hesitantly did she raise her glass.

"To the Mississippi!" said Heiko, who was just coming up, and took in the word like a hovering, echoing puzzle.

Fräulein Willimczyk pressed all her boldness together so sharply that her vision blurred: "To our *Pfarrosch,* to our Silesian word-music!" she cried.

Willi Wondrak moved around the table to clink glasses with Valeska: "To our small, narrow world, and may a little piece of it belong to us!" He displayed an enigmatic smile that only his sister was able to decipher.

"To my red raspberry world," Josel said, but no one was listening to him. And so he added something that seemed more important to him anyway: "To my shed." He raised his glass too.

"To this goddamned thundering flooded collapsing bullet-riddled world!" yelled the president of the waterworks, waving the only wine glass.

The County Magistrate remained silent. To the world of lies, he said to himself, to the world of Satan that awaits us! Down with it! Curses upon it and on all of us as well. He toasted with the rest, but in his stony face nothing changed.

The Sergeant held his glass between his legs. What the priest had said made him thoughtful. Now he saw the upstretched hands and the glasses, he stood up and yelled: "To this stinking world! To this stinking world! To this stinking world!" Fortunately he grew quieter with each repetition. In his condition it was quite probable that nothing much more would happen to him tonight. By now he had leaned over onto Fräulein Willimczyk and was propping himself up on her, and with his right hand he gestured so vigorously toward the other glasses that finally he was left staring stupidly into his empty glass.

They were all waving their glasses. High, higher, highest.

"Emperor, king, nobleman. Peasant, miner, beggarman."

Only now did old Krupniok come over to them. "Praise the Lord!" He said it quite softly, almost offhandedly.

But even that resulted in an explosion. The Sergeant threw his glass into the air, others followed suit. Polensky and Willi Wondrak dropped theirs on the floor and trod on the crunching splinters. Others simply flung their glasses on the table after they had emptied them. But later they regretted having done so.

The band was playing a polka.

Ulla and Andreas inclined their heads to one side and leaped across the ballroom with a long, sliding, shoveling motion. They did not know how to polka, they simply watched the others and tried to imitate their movements. It was the first polka of their lives.

The County Magistrate wanted to leave, unnoticed by anyone, unnoticed even by Valeska Piontek, he still wanted to work some more. But if he got up now, they'd all look over at him and not let him go. Perhaps he should go on and tell the story that had occurred to him so suddenly yesterday. He began:

"I'll tell you a story, my friends and . . ."—he hesitated, but after exchanging glances with the Archpriest, he said it—"and my enemies, which will make this country more comprehensible. None of those stupid stories with *pierunnje,* not a dreary joke in dialect, the kind you like so much to laugh about, but a fine, simple old tale."

He paused.

"In our town there are three bridges over the Klodnitz River, everyone knows them. When you climb up into the tower of All Saints Church, where the mighty bell of St. Hedwig rings out over the town, you can see all three of them at once, green the first, white the second, black the third.

"A time will come when one bridge will collapse, the second will be blown up, and the third one, the green one of wood, will burn down. So then someone will come and build a bridge of paper over the Klodnitz, and those who have doubts about this bridge will sink beneath the raging waters when the river rises, but those who believe in the bridge and cross over it will reach the other, the safe side . . ."

"What's he talkin' about?" belched the Sergeant to no one in particular.

"What colossal nonsense that is," the president of the water-works called out. "I'm beginning to control the Klodnitz right now, so nothing is going to collapse any more, no matter how great the flood."

"That's an Israelite! Whoever talks like that is a Jew!" shouted Dr. Kamenz hysterically.

"Yes, that's true . . ." In her mind's eye Water Milka was testing the safety of all the bridges in town. "We do have three bridges in our town, a wooden one, a stone one, a steel one . . . Lord, it'll cause a disaster!"

"That about the paper bridge, it's an old Christian legend," the Archpriest said with elaborate forbearance toward Dr. Kamenz. It seemed more and more uncanny to Valeska. And when she saw the retired County Magistrate standing there withdrawn into himself, as if listening to the bridges crash, all at once she cried out: "Music! Music! Come, we'll dance, Herr Magistrate!"

And as if it had only been waiting for this cue, the band suddenly blared out and with a stamping rhythm drowned any possible continuation of their talk. Valeska drew the County Magistrate away from the others and onto the dance floor; she tried to get into the swing, she hoped that with time she would be able to adapt to the new, strange rhythm. She determined to ask the County Magistrate later why he had told that story.

She was out of breath. She would have preferred slower music. Perhaps "I'll Dance With You in Heaven" . . . That was one of the new songs she had liked.

23

AFTER THE MUSIC and the noise in there in the ballroom, the silence out here in the hotel lobby now seemed almost frightening to Josel. As far as he could tell, there was no one left in the lobby; the soldiers who earlier had been standing around in clusters or running back and forth had vanished; only the smoky, bluish air in which the wall lamps floated reminded him of their being here. Josel took a few more steps, inaudible on the soft carpet, keeping an eye out for the desk clerk; he did not want to bump into him. Beside the revolving door he discovered a man in a hotel uniform with his back turned to him, immobile, as if he were staring out through the door, just like the bellboy Josel had seen this morning from the other side. But it was not the boy. From his height and his bulk it had to be an older man. Maybe he could get past him, but if the clerk spotted him from his desk, he would surely never let him go upstairs. And he did not have the nerve to use the elevator. Cautiously, but no longer protected by any pillars, Josel went a few steps farther. He thought over what he could say to the clerk. Maybe: Oh, I just want to have a look at the rooms my mother reserved on the third floor. Or better: I have an appointment with someone. (With whom he would rather not say.) Or better yet: The General sent for me. Then he decided on the most banal excuse of all: I was looking for the men's room. If the clerk stopped him, he would not get upstairs anyway, so what mattered was a quick and not too embarrassing retreat.

Josel heard the music start up again, muffled, in the Mint Room. He decided to risk it. Cautiously, he crept down the two steps to the lobby and crossed it at its narrowest point. He darted a quick glance at the desk. A man was sitting there bent over a table writing, another man with his back to him was filing something. Josel slipped past the sign NO ADMISSION TO CIVILIANS and then — this was the hardest part — up the stairs to the right,

and he was out of sight of the desk! He stood still for a moment
and listened. He heard nothing from the lobby, not even a few
words between the two night clerks; they seemed not to have
noticed him.

Josel took the remaining steps two at a time, until he had
reached the upstairs passage. He smoothed out his long trousers,
which he was not quite used to yet, and leaned against the banister. Although he saw nothing but a long, empty corridor with
closed doors on the left and right, he knew that he was inside a
secret, exclusive, forbidden world, and that left him somewhat
breathless. No, it was not fear, but perhaps the expectation that
one of those many doors might open at any minute and something quite unexpected, indeed wonderful, might happen. But
maybe it was only because he had run up the stairs so fast.

Nothing happened.

Josel walked along the entire corridor and counted the numbers
on the doors. In some film or other he had seen people in hotels
leaving their shoes outside their doors in the evening, but here he
did not see any shoes at all, not even the soldiers' boots. He did
not hear sounds behind any of the doors either, and when he
twice bent over to look through the keyholes, there was nothing
there but darkness.

He had imagined it otherwise: a long corridor, certainly, with
many doors numbered from 1 to 50, even numbers on the right
and odd on the left—except for 13, yes, the 13 was missing here
too. But it isn't a real hotel unless you know what's going on
behind those doors. An opera star is staying here, and a confidence man there, a count over there, and there a sales representative, the owner of a mine or a forest, a gambler there, a suicide
there . . . and waiters and bellboys hurry through the corridors
bringing coffee and flowers and letters . . . At least that's the way it
is in the movies. And here nothing but locked doors on a long,
sober corridor, and the longer you stayed in it the more it swallowed you up with its silence, its diffuse light, its yawning, and
revealed nothing of the secrets which must be concealed behind
the doors. Josel did not even hear his own steps on the soft carpet,
he heard only his own breathing and the pounding of his heart.

He stuck his hands in his pockets and felt his thighs through the cloth; he could feel that he was there, yes, that he was there. And even if, as in a fairy tale, everyone had gone from the ballroom, the corridors, the hotel lobby, the houses, the streets, indeed the whole town: he was here. Josel reached for a doorknob, he felt the round, smooth wood, he leaned against the wall: he was here!

He went up the stairs to the next floor.

Before him in the silence boots suddenly appeared through the banister, and above them two soldiers, and before he could decide whether it might be better to turn back after all, one of the soldiers grabbed him by the arm, pulled him up to him, and asked in a voice that sounded less threatening than puzzled: "What are you doing here?"

Josel scanned both sides of the corridor while searching for an answer. There was no one in sight but the two soldiers, who seemed to be standing guard to the right and left of the stairs. At the end of the corridor two doors opposite each other were open; light shone from them, and a muffled clatter of machines could be heard. "I'm looking for someone," Josel said.

"Who are you looking for here?" asked the soldier, who was still holding on to him.

Another soldier, a long piece of paper in his hand, came out of the open room in the distance and went into the room opposite. The machines clattered on.

"No civilians allowed here! Didn't you see the sign downstairs?"

"I'm looking for the General," Josel said boldly.

"The General?" the other soldier queried. "The Major-General?"

"Yes," Josel said in a somewhat firmer voice now that he had succeeded in freeing himself from the soldier's grasp. "The Major and General!"

"Well, who are you? And how did you get in here, anyway?"

It was clear to Josel that he might have gone too far. He thought it over. If he simply ran back down the stairs, taking two or three steps at a time, he couldn't hope to get farther than the lobby—they might even shoot at him, both of them had pistols in their belts. After all, they were on the Polish border here and mobilization was under way. Even though Uncle Wondrak said there are always two possibilities, he knew that now there was only one left for him, to keep on bluffing, whatever happened. So he said, "I'm Josel Piontek, I'm the brother of the bride whose reception is being held down in the Mint Room, and I have to, or rather, I'm supposed to speak to the Major and General."

"But what've you got to tell him? We can't let you in just like that," one of the soldiers said.

"Have you . . . have you some identification, perhaps?" the other asked.

Josel thought fast. "My mother sent me, she's a piano teacher and gives lessons to Count Ballestrem's children, everybody knows her here . . . and what I have to discuss with the Major and General I'm allowed to discuss only with the Major and General."

One of the soldiers laughed: "Yes, but does your mommy know the Major-General?"

Josel made one last try. "My mother, Valeska Piontek, has a message for the Major and General concerning the Poles that could have something to do with the war . . . And if I can't give it directly to the Major and General, then I'll just have to leave." If only they would refuse to let him through to the General, he could simply vanish.

Behind them, at the end of the corridor, the soldier with the long sheet of paper went back into the room from which he had come.

"Well, I'll report this, then," one of the soldiers said, and left. Meanwhile, the other soldier searched Josel, shoulders, chest, pockets, and pants legs down to his shoes. Josel thought that was funny, and he almost laughed, because it tickled when the soldier brushed his hand over his crotch.

Then someone called out, "Have the youngster come in!"

"I'm Josel Piontek," he said energetically, "and not a youngster." What would the Major and General think of that?

The two soldiers laughed. "Oh, go on in," one of them said, and opened the door of room 314, planting himself in the doorway and clicking his heels.

Josel entered. Immediately he recognized the soldier he had seen in the lobby earlier in the evening and had taken to be a general. To be sure, he was sitting on the bed now in his shirt, collar open and sleeves rolled up; at his neck and on his forearms was conspicuous, matted gray hair. The eiderdown, pushed back behind him, was puffed up high.

Josel saw a young soldier standing to the left of the bed, who was reflected three times in the folding shaving mirror behind him. "Good evening, Major and General," Josel said, looking at the soldier in the mirror. He could not tear his eyes away. After the door was closed, the soldier sat down on a footstool, which made his reflection even larger. He wore his uniform properly, buttoned to the neck, and on his shoulder straps were two stars, more than a lieutenant then, Josel thought. His face seemed rather young, he would have guessed his age to be about the same as his brother-in-law, Heiko. This lieutenant, or maybe first lieutenant, looked as elegant in his uniform as the men in the movies, which did not remind him of war at all, but rather of great celebrations and ceremonies. Maybe he'd be able to ask him to attend the reception, he might even dance once with Irma—or with Ulla, or with Mamuscha, that would be *fantastichnek*. If only the photographer is still there!

"So, you have a message for me?" asked the General. Photographs and handwritten letters were spread out on his bed.

"Pardon me, Major and General, sir," Josel said (and now turned directly toward the general), "my sister Irma is celebrating her marriage, down in the hotel, to Corporal and Artillery Officer Candidate Heiko Birkner from Dings . . . burg, who's been quartered with us for the past two weeks, and my mother wants to know when the war is going to begin." As soon as he had got the question out, Josel noticed that it was not particularly well put, he was too excited. So he tried to improve it at once and said, "My cousin Andreas was there, as a matter of fact, when the transmitter was raided."

The general on the bed and the lieutenant in front of the mirror exchanged looks; their smiles had disappeared.

"What do you mean by that?" The general reached for a glass on the nightstand, there was water in it or some other clear liquid; he took a sip and shuddered.

Surely the general doesn't have *schnapsik* in there too, Josel thought.

"Go ahead, talk," the general said. "So your cousin was there when they raided the transmitter this evening?"

Josel said, "Yes, he told me about it earlier. He was with Ulla, she's a friend of ours — still just a child," he added, " — in Zernik, they were riding back on their bikes just before eight, and they went past the transmitter just when it was happening . . ."

"All right, what was happening?"

"Well, some men in civilian clothes drove up in two cars and stormed the transmitter building."

"Take notes, Werner," the general said to the man in front of the mirror. He continued his questioning: "Were there officers among them?"

"What?" Josel remembered only that Andreas had said the men were in civilian clothes. "What do you mean by that? Pardon me, sir," Josel said, as he looked at the perplexed face of the general. "They were civilians . . . They were in civilian clothes."

"Your cousin said . . . ?"

"Yes, he said so."

And the general said to the lieutenant, or first lieutenant, "Give me the teletype on that, please."

The lieutenant searched through a folder and pulled out a long sheet of paper, like the ones carried back and forth across the hall. He gave it to the general, who scanned it again. "It says here that they were Polish guerrillas." And to Josel: "What's your name?"

Josel told him his name.

"All right. Your cousin, he was there, and you think he's telling the truth? How old is he? And isn't he maybe half Polack?"

Josel felt his face flush at the word. He hadn't yet been called a Polack, nor had Papusch, or Mamuscha, Water Milka or Ulla, or anyone else in his family either. He knew instinctively that the word "Polack," uttered by someone who hadn't grown up here, was the greatest insult, one which could not be left unpunished. But what could you do to a general, a real live general?

Josel stammered out his answer: "My cousin Andreas Pilgrim is from Breslau, he attends the St. Matthew Gymnasium there, he's only been visiting us since yesterday. But please allow me to say, sir, that all of us here are Germans, and the Poles are on the other side of the border — and the Polacks are over by the Russian border."

The young officer in front of the mirror replied, "It wasn't meant like that . . . Do you think your cousin is still downstairs at the reception? And can you bring him up here?"

"Yes, of course he's still down there. He's as old as I am, fifteen, and he's dancing for the first time in his life there . . . but that about the Pol . . ."

"Well," said the lieutenant in front of the mirror, "we're sorry about that." He stood up. "But go downstairs now and get your cousin . . . a soldier will go with you." He went to the door and called one of the sentries over. Accompanied by the soldier, Josel walked first past the sign NO ADMISSION TO CIVILIANS and then past the two night clerks, proudly and purposefully, more slowly than before, and he would have loved to climb the stairs again and again, with Andreas, with Ulla, with anybody else, so many times, in fact, that the night clerk's eyes would bulge.

After Josel had found Andreas on the dance floor and taken him from Ulla's circle, he confirmed before the Major-General what Josel had said earlier. And although initially he was somewhat excited, he related the details matter-of-factly.

The young officer left and came back bringing more long sheets of paper. The Major-General skimmed through them. He said, mostly to himself, "A curious affair. A very curious affair!"

And then he gave a sheet to the young officer: "Read that, please." While he was reading, the Major-General continued: "At 1500 hours the security personnel were withdrawn from the transmitter, on explicit instructions from Oppeln. And the transmitter chief was called to Oppeln for a meeting, that's all very strange. And I'm rather inclined to believe these boys here . . ."

"May I take the liberty of speculating that it might be a provocation," the young lieutenant said, raising his arms, and in the mirror six arms rose up.

"Rubbish!" said the general, and drained the rest of his glass. "What puzzles me is that no further news has arrived, they're busy playing it down, which I don't understand. When it would be the best possible pretext," the general said. "Spectacular, spectacular."

"Spectacular," the young officer repeated. "Shall I radio that to the General Staff in Neisse?"

The Major-General shook his head. "No, no, it's too late for that anyway." And turning to the two boys, who were standing rather uncertainly in the doorway: "Thank you for your information. You may go now."

The young officer led them out, and when they were already in the corridor, being accompanied to the stairs by one of the sentries, the Major-General came out once again and called Josel back. "You asked me something," said the Major-General, taking a pile of papers from another soldier. "Didn't you want to know whether there'd be war?" He glanced fleetingly through the papers. "Yes, there will be war, and very soon!" And when Josel in awe said nothing, but stared dumbly at the papers that were beginning to flutter beneath the general's hands, the young officer said, "But keep it to yourself, that's a command from the Major-General! Is that clear?"

"Yes," Josel said, timid for the first time since coming up here, "no one will learn anything from me. *Naturalnie.*" He thought of his shed, and as if by lightning it was illuminated in his mind, with the trees encircling it and the river nearby. He wouldn't have to close the shed. More soldiers would come, the war would begin, very soon, as the general had said, but surely it wouldn't end "very soon," that's the way it had always been, anyway; wars don't end so very soon, he knew that from school.

"There you are," he said, as he came up to Andreas, who was still waiting in the corridor. All the doors were shut, only the last two wide open as before, and the clattering of the machines was audible at this distance. Josel was not certain whether some such thing as a General Staff was quartered there, and whether he had spoken with a real general. In any case there had been some twenty or thirty soldiers and officers in the lobby that evening, but up here he had seen not more than seven, and only empty, quiet, forbidding corridors and silent, locked doors—and no secrets. Indeed, he hadn't even caught sight of a bellboy. This hotel, it seemed, would yield no more secrets. They went down-stairs to the lobby.

Then Andreas tugged at his jacket. He gestured for Josel to stop. He himself went a few steps further, in the direction of the night clerk's desk. Two men were standing there, bent halfway over the counter, conferring with the clerk. One man's face seemed familiar to Andreas, and he remembered immediately where he had seen him before. He must have been one of the men, yes, the longer he looked at him from the side, the more certain he was that he must have been there at the transmitter during the raid; that was the very man who had directed the others, yes, he was the one. Andreas whispered this excitedly to Josel.

" . . . So we would need two," the man was saying to the clerk. "Better send them right up to our rooms." He pressed something into the clerk's hand. The other one also slipped the clerk something discreetly, indiscreetly. "We've had a rough day today, and tomorrow won't be any picnic either . . . Nothing wrong with a little fun," he leered.

The clerk dialed a telephone number and said, "Why don't you go into the bar, gentlemen? I'll send two ladies in to you and then you can decide."

"They're clean, aren't they, the . . . ladies?" asked the one whom Andreas thought he had recognized.

"Well, young man?" the night clerk asked warily and reprovingly as he caught sight of Andreas.

"We just wanted to . . ." Andreas said, fixing the man's face in his mind again. Yes, he was the one. He could go back upstairs to the general and tell him. Only this man spoke fluent German, as he had just heard. Why should he attack a German transmitter? It confused him. "We just wanted to have a look," he said.

Josel had come up. "It's our first time here in this hotel, you see. It's really *fantastichnek!*" he said approvingly, and looked around the lobby. He really meant it.

The call had gone through. The clerk said something into the receiver: " . . . right, two then, yes . . . ten *emmchen,* naturally for each, of course."

The two boys wanted to go on to the ballroom. Andreas was

dying to tell Ulla that he had just seen one of the men who had taken part in the raid on the transmitter; it may even have been the leader.

The officer's interrogation had excited Andreas more than he wanted to admit. If nothing else, it was the first time he had faced a real general, close up. And even if this one had only been sitting on the edge of his bed in his shirtsleeves and without dozens of other officers standing around him, as he had imagined it, the situation had still been something very unusual for him, and it seemed to him now that he had perhaps responded to his questions too briefly and coolly. He did not know whether he should go back upstairs to the General and Major and say: "One of the men who took part in the raid is downstairs, you'd better speak to him yourself." That would take a lot of courage, and he could not muster it just now. So he scraped together what courage he had left into a single sentence: "Have you heard anything about . . . the raid on the transmitter yet? I was there when it happened!" He said it loudly, looking at the two men by the desk. But they had just turned away and were sauntering off toward the bar. "I saw it!" Andreas said, as loudly as he could, but the two did not turn around. "I was there, by chance!" The two were deep in conversation. Maybe I was mistaken after all, Andreas thought.

"What kind of raid?" The other night clerk had come up.

"Why, the one on our Gleiwitz transmitter. Haven't you heard about it? There was even shooting."

"And just how did you happen to be there?" The night clerk injected as much skepticism into the question as he could produce after thirty years' experience in hotels.

"Purely by chance," Andreas answered indifferently. He was not interested in telling the night clerks about it. Since the two men had disappeared into the bar, he saw no reason to share his secret with anybody else. "You'll hear about it on the radio," he said, and thought: If it was a raid, then it'll be in the papers tomorrow.

"Oh, please," Josel said, giving Andreas a little poke, "please, where is the bellboy?"

"Which one do you mean? Klaus? Or Hottek?" The clerk's

voice was gentler and friendlier now, since he had seen Josel walk by with the soldier.

Josel hissed at Andreas: "I'll be right there, you go ahead!" And to the clerk he said, "I mean Hottek." He did not know any of them by name, but the name Hottek seemed more familiar to him.

Andreas went up to the ballroom.

The clerk wiped the counter with his sleeve, although no dust could be seen. "Hottek," he said, "has the early shift, he has to be on call by six; he's sleeping now, if he's lucky."

"Well then—" Just in time, Josel suppressed the "too bad" he had been about to add. Now he didn't feel safe asking about the other one, Klaus.

But the clerk spared him the question. He said, "And today is Klaus's day off."

"Do you have only those two?" Josel asked, somewhat dubiously. Uncle Wondrak had always claimed that big hotels have swarms of bellboys, after all, they cost practically nothing . . .

The other clerk, who had a head like a tadpole's, came even closer. "You're a very inquisitive boy," he said, and acknowledgment was mixed with disapproval in his voice.

"I'm only asking," he said, "because my friend might want to become a bellboy." Andreas was gone, thank God.

"Oh, the boy who was with you?" The clerk straightened up the brochures and restacked the newspapers that were lying there in a pile. "How is old is he, then?"

"Fourteen," Josel answered. He wanted to go now.

"Have him come talk to us! With the war coming, we can always use somebody . . . We give free room and board." The telephone rang. "And pocket money." He lifted the receiver.

Josel thought, now is my chance to leave. But the other clerk, with the tadpole face, leaned over toward him. "What were you doing upstairs at the command post . . . with those officers?"

There was an impatience lurking in the question which Josel recognized from his mother and could not stand. "That I won't tell you!"

"Top secret!" Josel added. He was enjoying the clerk's irritation. He turned and left. The lamps in the lobby were still floating in blue smoke, and the floor seemed as soft as cotton to him now. The muted music from the ballroom penetrated as far as the main staircase. Josel felt superior. He had found out not only that a command post of the Wehrmacht had been installed upstairs in the hotel, and maybe even a branch of the General Staff, but also that the war would start soon, very soon at that; and that one and maybe two of the men who had been in the raid on the radio transmitter on the Tarnowitz road that evening were staying here at this hotel, unless Andreas had been mistaken about their faces; and he had also solved the puzzle of why, on this very evening, he had been unable to find a single bellboy in the Hotel Upper Silesia. He wished he had a few more puzzles.

24

I T   S U R P R I S E D   M O N T A G how easy it was for him to walk, he
did not feel that his body was moving forward now, but rather as
if the pavement, the façades of the houses, and the trees lining the
street were approaching him, as if they were all flowing past him.
He experienced this with a gentle amazement and an easy happiness. It wouldn't take him long to get home this way. He had not
drunk much at the reception, he had taken only little sips when
Frau Valeska raised her glass to him from across the table, or
Water Milka or lawyer Wondrak. Only with Krawutschke did he
have to drain a whole glass of *kartoffka,* the local potato schnapps;
he insisted on telling him the story of Hanotschka, who had run
away with the owner of the merry-go-round, a story which Krawutschke repeated often that evening, in the hope that it might
somehow dissolve into unreality. After the *tableau vivant* of *The
Angelus,* Krawutschke quietly laid his head on the tablecloth,
directly across from Montag, and out of his rabbity red eyes
squeezed two thick tears, as clear as the *kartoffka* in which he had
so liberally indulged.

Montag had not been on Wilhelmstrasse for a long time, at least
not at this hour of the night. He was slow at recognizing everything: the low iron fence in front of the hotel, the paving stones,
the house fronts, the blue-dark shop windows, the bridge, the
linden trees growing out of the pavement which he touched in
passing. And yet everything seemed strange to him today. It was
not just the emptiness of the street—on his way here this evening
it had been crowded with people whom curiosity, restlessness,
and the expectation that something was going to happen, something quite unusual, had driven from their homes, driven together
outside. It was not the soldiers patrolling Gleiwitz as if it were an
occupied town, nor was it the muffled, buzzing sound that floated
on the air and hardly changed. A motorcycle with a sidecar came

down slowly from the railroad station, the soldiers were wearing their steel helmets and had metal chains hung across their chests. They drove quite close to the curb, as if checking on the late passersby.

Montag leaned over the railing of the bridge. The stone had absorbed the heat of the day, and now released it again in bursts, like breath. The river below was a black mirror flashing and flowing on. It was a small, dirty river, but he loved it more than the mighty rivers he had seen in his lifetime. The old Klodka was simply itself, dirty and patient, sometimes wild too (in early spring when the snow melted), and turbulent, like the people who had settled all around it. He took a *tschinker* from his pocket and threw it into the water; the coin flashed a few times before silently sinking.

And only now did he see what was different: the street lights had been painted over with blue, and their tinted light cast a blue glaze over the landscape.

Montag walked on, away from the main street into the dark. In Niederwallstrasse a convoy approached him, the vehicles with headlights dimmed, the soldiers on top sitting silent and immobile as dolls. The smell of sweat and gasoline trailing after them was so sharp that Montag stood looking after them until the noise of their engines that echoed from the walls began to dissipate; he saw the black pieces of artillery obscenely erected, watching them until they were swallowed up by a curve.

The square next to the little allotment gardens, where only this afternoon he had seen tents and anti-aircraft guns, was empty. That was such a surprise to Montag that at first he thought he had made a mistake. But it was the same square. Tin cans left behind, empty beer bottles and paper, testified to the fact even in the dark. He must stop deluding himself.

He strode more rapidly now. The sky was wrapped in gray-white foil that hid the moon. Perhaps it would rain tomorrow. On the horizon he could make out the Laband Woods, and in front, in the fields, scarecrows that had not yet been taken down.

It was shortly after midnight when he reached home. The Pionteks' house was dark; only from the window of Leo Maria's room did a little light escape to the outside through chinks in the black-out curtains. He went into his kitchen, washed his hands under the tap, splashed a little cologne on his fingertips and then massaged his temples with it. That refreshed him. Now he no longer felt so tired, and he decided to do some work.

He took a few loose sheets from the drawer, then went into the pantry and returned with two thick folders full of handwritten pages. He sat down and took a look at the mountain of manuscript. If he had been able to see his face in the mirror then, he would certainly have been surprised at his expression of self-satisfaction, an expression that seldom appeared on his face. He was aware of the imperfections in what he had written down over these many nights, but the evidence of time spent, quite a lot of time taken up over these pages, that pleased him. He opened the first folder and stacked the pages neatly so that they looked like a fat white block; in so doing he had to straighten this sheet or that and his eye would catch on a flourished G or a T which had turned out too large or too bold, or on a passage where much had been crossed out. Perhaps he only did this to feel so many pages covered with writing between his fingers.

Montag read the closing of the seventh chapter:

In the 1928 elections for the Silesian Sejm, the battle against Germanization was openly adopted as the ruling party's political platform, and all government bureaus supported it in this. Korfanty had been forced so far into opposition that he again used the German language some of the time in his campaign. Terrorism before the election was so scandalous that on 8 February 1928 Korfanty took the rostrum in the Silesian Sejm to demand an accounting from the Upper Silesian government. He protested against the undermining of freedom of thought, freedom of assembly, free elections, against the pressure exerted by the central government on the officials. He accused the wojewoda *of financing, out of the local government budget, a band of common criminals who were committing robberies and murders under the guise of Polish patriotism, he accused them of making contributions to certain malicious newspapers such as* Polska Zachodnia *(Western Poland), which were the veritable instigators of civil war.*

"The voting rolls are forged," Korfanty continued, "civil servants,

*teachers for example, are appointed for the sake of the lowest political
motives. The taking of bribes is in full sway, the talk is all of champagne banquets, extortion of money for political purposes, misuse of
official power. Our government bureaus are filled with ignoramuses
and jackasses, and this despite the fact that Upper Silesia is not Asia!
Our country is being disgraced, Poland is being disgraced!"*

*Following this speech, the Sejm passed an emergency resolution,
unanimously except for one dissenting vote, in which the* wojewoda
*was called on to cease all activity on behalf of any party before the
elections, to prohibit officials from abusing their office, and to punish
those guilty of such offenses.*

*Grażyński responded by banning the distribution of Korfanty's
speech of 8 February 1928, and closing down all newspapers that printed
it. The rebel organization circulated a demand for Korfanty's removal
that was couched in characteristically brutal terms:*

*"We must expunge this criminal from public life, this criminal whose
hands are stained with the blood of the Rebels, and who for thirty pieces
of silver has amassed an immense fortune at a time when Upper Silesian workers and peasants have had to suffer the direst poverty. It is
time to finish with this rubbish in Silesia and put it behind bars where
it belongs. Down with this disturber of the peace, this ally of the
Silesian Hakatists!"*

Grażyński, the wojewoda, *was also implicated in this appeal; he
allowed the publication of the smear in a newspaper that was a government organ.*

In an anniversary issue of the Kattowitz newspaper, Polska Zachodnia, *on 11 November 1928, E. Krzemień wrote an article, "From
the Time of Tumult in Silesia," making a clear thrust at Korfanty:
"The rebel organization is fighting as hard as it can against subversive
separatist tendencies, which have nothing to do with Polishness."
Krzemień went so far as to demand that Korfanty be boycotted mor-
ally, since he was still serving the Germans, and was harming Polish
interests outside the country by publishing false reports in his newspaper*
Polonia *about conditions in Silesia.*

*In 1928 the political conflict between Korfanty and his opponents was
carried into the League of Polish Women's Organizations. A schism
resulted in the League, to which 110 groups with 10,000 members*

belonged. The majority of the groups followed representative Szym-
kowiak, the rest, Korfanty's wife.

Reading it over again at night, Montag was sure. He had begun
work on K's biography because he wanted to write the life of an
unscrupulous, demagogic, ambitious, nationalistic politician, but
the more he steeped himself in the material, the more he wrote,
the more he saw a real human being behind the historical facts,
and discovered his empathy with him. But the last sentences
probably went too far. He crossed them out again. Besides, they
were not factual enough for him.

He went into the pantry again to get a bottle of beer. When he
opened it, the beer foamed up, and he was just able to rescue his
spread-out pages. While pouring the beer slowly into his glass, he
thought of the canning jars he had seen on the pantry shelf.

Among the papers he found a list of words he had collected,
Upper Silesian expressions, slang, mostly from Water-Polish:

Bieda — poverty, lack of money
Bloblik — little boy
Dupa — stupid, clumsy person, also ass
duppen, dupsen — to fuck
kascheln — to walk on thin ice, slip
Karbidka — miner's carbide lamp
Klapidudek — Mr. Whosis, what's-his-name
Krupniok — fresh blood sausage
Labánder — big, tall person
Lusche — puddle of water
Mohbabe — slow, sluggish girl
Potschen, Papuschen — slippers
Pierunie or *Pierunje* — an almost affectionate curse; only
    someone who was born and grew up in Upper Silesia can
    pronounce this correctly
Pinjunse, Pinunze — money
Pitwok — pocket knife
Poler — a Pole
Polack — derogatory term for an Upper Silesian who feels
    Polish

Polackei — contemptuous term for the country of Poland
Poschundek — orderliness
Pressufka — cheap plug tobacco
Skarbnik — mountain spirit
Tepschlag — lout
Tuleja — dumbbell, idiot
Schur — a thick soup with fried onions, smoked bacon and sausage, served with mashed potatoes. National dish of Upper Silesia, what *soupe à l'oignon* is to a Parisian
Gruchlik — loudmouth, a noisy person
Metzka, Kaja — cap
Frela — young lady, miss
Staro frela — old maid
Tschutschmok — a shy person
Schlimok — an awkward person
Galoty — trousers
Kapisder — hat
Pschinzo or *Pschintzo* — nothing
Strach — fear, ghost
Kapusta — sauerkraut
Guwno — shit
Pullok or *Tschul, Tschulik* — cock, penis
pullen, sechen — to urinate
Ujek — uncle
Kartotschki — potatoes
Klacken — carrots
Kapudrok — jacket
Salonik — Sunday suit
Hadra — a cloth, rags
Haderlok — ragpicker

He had written them down a few years ago. He thought about occupying himself more systematically with that in the future. He had to smile at the word *Tuleja*. It pleased him particularly. He repeated it to himself, aloud: "*Tuleja*." He wrote it down again: TULEJA. He thought a poem or a book should be written, just to hide this one word within it.

Montag put down his pen and leaned back in his chair, taking a deep breath. The handwritten pages, a moment ago quite close to his glasses, had all at once moved away from him, and the longer he observed them from this distance, the stranger they seemed to him, as if they had been lying on the kitchen table for a long time, untouched.

For days, perhaps weeks, he had been sensing this growing process of alienation. Once written down, his own sentences moved away from him, seemed quite impersonal to him; he read them again and again, but had to listen deep inside himself in order to recognize them by their echo as his own. Sometimes he did not even read through what he had written down; hardly had he ended a sentence and begun a new page when his interest vanished.

Not only the sentences, but things too were moving away from him. When he reached for his shaving brush lying on the shelf in front of the mirror, he had to move a step or two closer before he could touch it. Sometimes he had to grope twice or even three times for the light switch; it seemed as if the wall was receding from him in the darkness. If he wanted to go to the pantry to prepare himself something to eat, sometimes he had to make several attempts. A button that fell from his hands and rolled under the cabinet all at once seemed so far away that he did not even bother to bend down for it.

K, too, was moving further away.

If he shut his eyes, he was no longer able to place K in the precise situation in which he wanted to describe him. There was too much darkness around K now, and sometimes he couldn't distinguish K's outlines in the darkness.

He began to take less interest in K's triumphs, and hardly any in his defeats, but was concerned more with the peripheral episodes. For instance, he would like to have known what kind of books K read. Did he like music and, if so, what kind? From Sanicki he learned that he particularly loved the overture to Glinka's *Ruslan and Ludmilla*. Had anyone ever seen him drunk? "Girlie parties" at the Hotel Lomnitz in Beuthen (during the preparations for the plebiscite) were the invention of the opposition press, mainly of the German-language satirical paper *The Pieron*. Was he camera-shy? Considering the degree of his fame and popularity, there were relatively few photos of him.

He would have liked to know what had become of Walerus, to whom the rebel Polish officers (during the third revolt) had given the assignment of arresting K. When K learned of this, he drove out to meet Walerus, and in a private conversation dissuaded him from the task. Walerus did not arrest K. On the contrary, he and his men finally broke out in cheers for K. (Later K saw to it that Walerus was given the lucrative liquor concession at the railroad station in Kattowitz.)

Wosniak had given him access to a journal by Judge S, who had been a judge of the civil court in Kattowitz before the World War, in which he had read the following:

Accused persons with names beginning with K, among others, came under my jurisdiction. Thus Korfanty appeared before my bench several times as a defendant. It was a matter of small debts. He was regularly convicted too, except in only one instance where the suit hinged on his personal oath. This was the case: Korfanty, who was the editor (and I believe also the co-owner) of several newspapers, had commissioned a Polish-Jewish student to translate (into Polish) a pulp novel, *The Love of a Negress,* for a fee of twenty marks. The student delivered the translation and claimed not to have received the money, which Korfanty, who appeared in person, asserted he had paid. The student firmly maintained he had never received a penny. In response to my inquiry, Korfanty had to concede that he possessed no receipt for the disbursed twenty marks. In an excess of trust, he had not asked for one. Since he had no other proof of payment, I informed him that he could require the student to swear an oath of non-receipt of the money. Whereupon he did so. But the student belonged to that group of pious Jews who consider it a sin to swear an oath. So Korfanty was made to swear, and he did so in this form: "I swear by God the Omnipotent and Omniscient that I paid twenty marks for *The Love of a Negress,* so help me God." I could not help feeling that Korfanty had sworn falsely, but the trial law obtaining gave me no basis for implementing my judicial conviction in the decision. The oath constituted irrefutable evidence. I therefore had to turn away the plaintiff with his charge.

While investigating the role of Nowina-Doliwa, the Polish military commander in the third uprising, whom Korfanty opposed vigorously, he found out that hidden behind this strange-sounding name was none other than Count Matthias Mielżiński, who had taken part in the revolt in Posen and was among those Pan-Polish aristocrats who received Paderewski at the Hotel Bazar and thus laid the foundations for the new Polish republic. A year before the war, the Count had been sentenced to a long prison term after a sensational trial for the shooting of his wife, *née* Countess Potocka, and his nephew, whom he had caught committing adultery.

He was now interested not in the historically significant quarrels between Nowina-Doliwa and K, between the military and the civilian leader in eastern Upper Silesia at the time of the plebiscite, but rather in the harsh light cast by the Count's action on a certain stratum of pre-war society. Montag remembered it, for at the time he had been a young lawyer in Lauban. The trial was played up in all the newspapers and was discussed spiritedly in legal circles as well as in cafés and in the street. At that time he had known nothing about K.

He liked to lose himself in details and trivia now.

A speech by K with which he campaigned throughout the towns and villages of Upper Silesia in 1903 (on that occasion he had been elected on the first ballot as the first Polish national delegate to the Prussian Landtag) began like this: "Praised be Christ Jesus! With this greeting of our fathers we come to you, dear brothers and sisters, to join battle with you for our most precious treasures, for our faith and our heritage!" Montag had found this speech in an old issue of *Polak,* and the first sentence pleased him so much that he read it several times, and at once committed it to memory. It was a sentence that displayed K's insight, his intelligence, his demagogic skills, his political consciousness more than many later, frequently reprinted speeches he had made in the Sejm.

Montag went to the window and peeked through the curtain. The Pionteks' house was still dark; it seemed they had not yet returned from the wedding reception. He fetched two tall fruit jars from the pantry, placed them on the table with a clink, selected a few pages from his mountain of manuscript, and stuffed them into one of the jars. He put the lid on. Montag's hand lay calmly on the table. He was still hesitating. Perhaps he should wait for the news. But his resolve no longer had anything to do with the political situation, no matter what turn it might have taken by this time. It was *his* situation. His very private one.

Carefully, he rolled up the sheets in the first folder and stuffed them into the jar, then proceeded in the same way with the sheets from the second folder. The pages of the eleventh chapter, on which he was working at present, he left out. He took two rubber rings and placed them in their grooves, then he placed the lids on top and sealed them with the metal clamps. He had closed them so tightly that not even air could penetrate them.

With the two jars under his arm he went to the door. He extinguished all the lights. Outside, he double-checked to make sure that all was still quiet at the Pionteks'. He stood in the doorway until shapes became clearly discernible. The air was gray-black, and his vision was still rather blurry. He left the door half open and went way back to the gooseberry bushes; there he set the fruit jars on the ground temporarily, his eyes having grown used to the dark. He walked with firm steps to the shed which stood next to a wire fence, precisely midway between the garden cottage and the Pionteks' house, and found a spade. He began to dig between the gooseberry bushes. He thought of the children outside his window that morning burying a dead bird while declaiming an invented litany of lament. He too could have sung a litany of mourning while lowering the jars into the hole he had made. Somehow it amused him that he, the County Magistrate, retired, or better, superannuated, was burying a manuscript beneath the gooseberry bushes in his own garden, fragments of a biography for which nobody had any use.

He scooped the loose dirt over the jars and tamped it down with his shoes, then he made the sign of the cross, quickly and almost furtively. No one could see him, but still he did it secretly. He trampled on the dirt, his trousers snagged on the prickly branches of the bushes, dirt stuck to his shoes. A sudden euphoria overcame him, he would have liked to go on stamping on the dirt because the stamping had ceased to be merely functional. He might even have whistled a tune, except that he could not whistle, he had never been able to learn, his friends had teased him about it as a boy. No matter how he puckered his lips, the noise that came out was more like a hiss than a whistle. He trudged back to the cottage, took his shoes off outside, and placed them in the entryway beside the door. Still fully dressed, he lay down on his bed. He was not yet tired enough to fall asleep, but he did not feel like reading any more either. On the nightstand Bergengruen's *The Tyrant and the Law* lay open.

The air in Montag's room felt heavy and close; he had passed by the roses and had brought some of their fragrance in on his clothing. He thought of Myslowitz, where he had grown up, and of girls in white dresses and boys in black suits preceding the wedding couple on their way to the church, strewing a carpet of blossoms from little baskets. Once he had gone along with them; he had picked out the biggest basket and heaped it full of rose petals, and now and then on the way he would stick his face deep into the petals, and the scent rose within him and almost made him reel — until someone came over to him and said, "You've no right to be here, you don't even know how to make the sign of the cross," and took the basket away from him. And he had made the sign of the cross, three times in a row, from left to right, and finally did get the basket back. "I'm too old for that now," he had told his mother the next year when she had wanted to send him along at Corpus Christi. He had gone without a basket and watched the others from a distance.

His grandfather had known the reason. "That's not for you! That's for the others." And when everyone else was out of the house one day he showed him how the white silken scarf is placed around the shoulders and the black straps tied around the arm, and he demonstrated to him how to read from a silken scroll while singing and swaying back and forth from the waist. At first he had laughed, but when his grandfather would not stop and he saw in the old man's eyes that the singing and swaying had placed him in a different world, he fell silent. He had watched him in silence. Initially he had retained nothing of what his grandfather sang for him; only later, on another occasion, did a line lodge in his memory, *Shma yisrael adonai elohenu adonai echad,* or something like that, it was the only thing he had retained, but he did not know what the line signified, he remembered it as a melody, as notes, not words, and the melody had pleased him, he could still sing the line even now: *shma yisrael adonai elohenu adonai echad.*

Recently, Montag had caught himself slipping back into memories of childhood more and more often. Sometimes he just lay there staring at the white ceiling, and saw himself as a child of three or four: chickens gathered around him and pecked out of his hand; he saw a brightly lit castle in a dark forest in front of which he and his parents were standing; he saw himself beside a young white goat; he saw himself in a clown costume with a pointed hat on his head beneath a blossoming apple tree. These images were of a peculiar rigidity, they had no continuation, no history, they did not move, they were only reflections, as if he were remembering not his childhood but snapshots from his childhood which he must have seen at some later time. He was remembering them because he had remembered them before. The pictures in his memory did not begin to move until he was in Breslau and at school there.

Now, when he wanted to imagine the little town where he was born and had spent his first four years, it was never anything more than a postcard with a panorama of the town which his father had once received from his brother and which had remained on the dresser, leaning against a pewter pitcher, for a long time. So it must have been in that town that his grandfather had locked him in the cellar with the goat and given him strict instructions to stay there quietly and see to it that the goat made no noise when the soldiers came. He had waited a long time in the dark with the goat, and while the soldiers were making a racket upstairs, he had lain down over the goat so that her bleating could not be heard. Thus the animal was saved, but he could not get the smell out of his clothes, no matter how often they were washed. Had it really happened in that town, or had he only kept it in his memory because his grandfather told him about it?

You could see on the postcard the marketplace of the little town, the town hall, two churches, a fountain. He would like to know — now — whether there had been a synagogue as well. He could still remember the *cheder*; his grandfather had taken him there once, there were many children bigger than he, who were bent over books reading something aloud while others were conversing in a foreign language quite incomprehensible to him, which sounded like a rather complicated sing-song. When his father found out about it, a bitter argument ensued, and he was not permitted to go there again.

But perhaps those were nothing but images he had pieced together from stories told later.

Quite a different town was coming toward him now, different streets, different people, or was it a dream creeping up on old Montag in his bed . . . There is a church which he and other people are streaming into, and he merges with those who are kneeling before an icon in a side aisle, and the priest, in a gleaming white robe, raises his voice loudly: "And Jesus falls for the third time beneath the cross." The others repeat it more softly, he too recites it, only now does he notice the words are not in the language he is used to, and he has some trouble with them.

When his eyes get used to the dim light of the church and he looks into the faces of the worshipers, it seems to him that he has seen all of them sometime, somewhere, before; and really, that woman up front, kneeling next to the pillar, isn't that Hanna Dombrowska from Trynnek and next to her Wladi Waroschek, the schnapps merchant from Hüttenstrasse; and there, the cripple with one arm, isn't that Meier from the Huldschinsky estate, who along with his wife collected door to door for the Third Order, and Herr Fensterkreuz, the librarian at the municipal library, whom they fired back in '33; and there the Lustigs, the whole family, with five daughters and two sons, who gave the best children's parties every year in the villa in the forest; and Herr Kosinski, who campaigned for the Communists in 1932 but was not elected. And up front, that could be Father Nemeczek, to whom he had confessed a few times, whom they had come for one day, it was hardly two years ago, and locked up because he was supposed to have hidden someone, but somehow the Church had gotten him out of the Gestapo's clutches and smuggled him across the border into Poland, at least that was the story told at the time. They were all faces which had faded from his field of vision in the last few years; a few of them, he had heard, had moved to Poland to live with relatives, others had emigrated far away, to Palestine or to the United States of North America.

Montag lay on his bed. He had reached a state in which he could no longer differentiate between dream and memory, between a remembered and what an imagined reality. He was alone and accountable to no one.

Montag toyed with the idea, as he had done once or twice before, of crossing the border to Kattowitz, where surely he could still find somebody or other who was related to him. He knew the time was growing short for him to do so. They had not come for him yet! Yes, he did know ways to get across the border, at Sosnitza, for example, which they now call Öhringen, along the Klodnitz, or through the great, dense forests behind Rauden, or near the Scharley mine. Or he could simply take the streetcar as far as Beuthen . . . Perhaps it would be best to go by train, with one suitcase in the baggage net, coat and hat on his knees, and a rosary in his hands, just as one travels to Poland . . .

"And Jesus dies on the cross," the priest cries, and the shuffling of the faithful moving on to the next Station of the Cross is so loud that Montag is tempted to hold his hands over his ears — actually it was the sound of a car driving up.

Montag got up and switched off the light in his room, and with this motion he wiped away the faces and the memory as well. Voices could be heard outside, and laughter; a car door slammed, then voices again, calling. It was the Pionteks. All at once, quite close to him, a splattering sound and groaning, as if someone were heeding a call of nature in the garden. Montag listened intently and for a moment he considered going outside to see who it was; he did not do so. Not because he was afraid; it was not fear — at that moment he would even have thought fear to be logical — it was something else: it was simply indifference. Suddenly he was not interested in what was going on outside; he felt no desire to find out what was taking place there, outside of his house, in the garden, in the night, in the house in front, in the street, in the town. He had buried those handwritten pages of his. Only what was really around him remained around him now.

He accepted the sounds. But that was all. This, here, was his world now; it was here inside, in this garden cottage which he had selected, on fifty square meters.

K was dead. The manuscript hidden. The work of the past few years preserved and buried. His ideas locked away. And, what he always thought about, his daughter: she was in safety.

He decided not to leave the house any more.

At least he would try it. It struck him that he had not switched on the crystal set to listen to the news; he had forgotten to, but perhaps it was more than forgetfulness. Perhaps it was just the fear of hearing what he did not want to hear, something that had been forcing itself upon him more and more ever since he had seen the soldiers heading off in the direction of Plesser Strasse. In any case, he felt that he was on the right road, on the way to being self-sufficient.

Even yesterday he could not have conceived of living without his newspapers, but now, having buried the manuscript, he knew that nothing would make any difference at all.

He got up and shut all the books that were lying around and put them neatly back in the bookcases. He moved the table aside, pushed the cabinet further toward the north wall, and arranged the chairs so as to provide a long, broad corridor across the room; when he opened the door to the entryway, it was lengthened a few steps more. Now he could take his walks indoors too.

Montag inhaled deeply, he snorted. The light was growing slowly thinner, a black, grainy gloom came toward him; if he had not held fast to the table and leaned forward over it, he would have fallen to the floor.

When the light flowed back, he was reassured that it had been only a brief spell of faintness. He would have forgotten it immediately, if the twitching of an eyelid at intervals had not kept reminding him of it for a time. It could be that he had drunk too much at the reception after all, more than his old body could take, anyway, or perhaps he had dug too quickly in the garden; maybe moving the furniture had overtaxed him. In any case, he blamed it solely on his body, which had failed him. His reason had not lapsed for even a second. That calmed him, above all for what was still to come.

Montag was already deep in sleep when the sound of a car door slamming and the roar of an engine starting up and driving away intruded into his dream.

25

W HEN JOSEL ENTERED the ballroom, the air hit him like hot steam. He saw the people sitting at tables, addressing one another with broad gestures, and further back, as if behind a veil, the dancers stamping back and forth to the beat of the music. Suddenly Josel wanted to dance, with a desire that he had not felt the whole evening. And even before walking over to Mamuscha, he looked around for Ulla, with whom he wanted to attempt the next dance. He went past the man who earlier had said "A quarter past eleven" and who had then fallen over; he was still hanging motionless in his chair, and no one was paying any attention to him. Josel said loudly, "A quarter to twelve," as if that had as much magic in it as a quarter past eleven, but the man did not stir. Josel discovered that they had tied him to the chair with his suspenders so he could not fall out of it.

The man stank, he stank so badly that Josel, looking at him, was more and more revolted; he stank of schnapps, of beer, of tobacco, of urine, and a puddle had formed at his feet. Josel was alone with him here in the corner; he took a glass from the table and, positioning himself so that if anyone looked this way only his back would be visible, he raised the glass and doused the man's face with schnapps. With a satisfaction new to him he watched the schnapps run down the man's face, over the closed eyelids, the nose, past the mouth to the chin. Josel backed away slowly, looking at the coarse pores of the man's face, watching the schnapps drip from his chin onto his neck and his shirt collar, and he asked himself whether he would have done that if he had known the man.

The music stopped and most of the dancing couples returned to their seats. Only a few diehards remained standing on the dance floor, their arms hanging down, waiting for the band to strike up again. Uncle Wondrak had a jaunty paper hat on his head and was tugging Mamuscha along after him; laughing, they both fell into their chairs.

"Mamuscha," Josel said. He still felt a flush of excitement, which could be heard in his voice. "I need to tell you something!"

Valeska straightened up and let go of Willi Wondrak's hand. She pressed the bun into place at the back of her head, as she usually did when she was embarrassed.

For the first time that evening she had been thinking of nothing but what was happening at the moment: how the Sergeant had come up to her and practically dragged her off to the dance floor; how she had signaled to her brother Willi Wondrak behind the Sergeant's back; how he finally caught on and cut in during the dance; how she then danced with her brother until the piece came to an end; how it had pleased her to be held tight by him and spun in a circle, so that she had not thought of it ending at all; and how they had both looked at each other and had broken into laughter about how they had gotten rid of the Sergeant.

"Come, Josel, sit down with us," said Valeska, whose face was glowing. "I'm sorry, but your Uncle Willi Wondrak has just rescued me from the Sergeant." She fanned her face with her handkerchief. "And as long as I live . . ."

"Mamuscha," Josel said insistently, "there's going to be a war, the General told me so."

Valeska held her temples with both hands. Her head was pounding. "Son," she said, "you've had too much to drink."

"But if the Major and General said so himself," Josel persisted.

"Yes, of course there's going to be a war," Uncle Wondrak interjected in a gently placating voice. "Generals and—what did you call him?—Majors, they have to predict that, it's their profession." His voice changed: "Feeling better now, Valeska? What on earth shall we do with the Sergeant? He's tight, tight as a drum, totally smashed, we've got to keep an eye on him. He mustn't drive the car home. If they pick him up, he won't get to the war on time."

And to Josel again: "All that's nothing but propaganda, understand? Let's ask the County Magistrate, he reads four German newspapers and three Polish ones, you know, nowadays you

hardly dare say it out loud — " (he looked around) "but he's the
only one of us who understands these things, believe me, Josel."

"Oh," Valeska said, "it's getting late, it's almost midnight. We
should be thinking about leaving. The youngest, at any rate" —
she looked at Josel — "and the oldest!" She clapped her hand to
her heart.

Josel gave up. Anyway, nobody would believe he had spoken
with a real live general, just a few minutes ago, though Andreas
could back him up, if he were here. And it wasn't just any old
general and any old war, it was the general who was quartered
here in the Hotel Upper Silesia and in command of the forces in
Gleiwitz, and it was the war against Poland. But he stopped trying, because even Uncle Wondrak, who usually treated him like a
grownup, was using that irritatingly patient tone of voice he
otherwise reserved for his more dim-witted clients. And what
if Mamuscha weren't joking, she might take him home and he
wouldn't be able to dance with Ulla even once.

"It's about time for us to look in on Papusch," Valeska said. She
was still quite out of breath.

"*Pschinzo*," Josel said. "I haven't danced a single time yet tonight, I'd like to dance at least once, please, Mamuscha."

The two let him go, though only after making him promise he'd
be back shortly after midnight, and that he would bring Ulla and
Andreas with him. Valeska tried to think how to get her hands on
the Sergeant's car keys. He had to be prevented from driving at
any cost. The best thing would be for her brother Willi to take
charge and begin by driving the Sergeant and the children home.
Then he could come back with the car for the others, that would
save them the taxi fare. Willi was the only one who knew how to
handle a car. After he lost the spectacular case of the Proppitz
peasants v. Schaffgotsch on the second appeal, he bought a speedy
used BMW 328 in Oppeln (he said it was so that he could reach his
clients in the countryside faster, but in town there were persistent
rumors that he had taken a fat bribe from Schaffgotsch, because
the land in question had been bought soon after by the waterworks at forty times its original valuation!) and drove to Cracow
or Breslau in it on weekends, and on holidays as far as Marienbad

or Prague. But after the soldiers came to Gleiwitz, he had put it up on blocks in a shed and taken off the wheels. He sent a message to the district leader, who had inquired several times about the car, saying that the engine was burnt out.

Josel was searching for Ulla. He came past the drunk again, between whose fingers someone had placed a burning cigarette. The smoke curled upward. The schnapps had dried on his face, which gleamed like a full moon.

Josel considered asking Hedel Zock to dance. True, she wasn't much older than he, three years at the most, but ever since he had kicked her in the shins on field day at school, she hadn't wanted to have anything to do with him. At the moment, however, she was busy with skinny Michalek. And beside those two, in fact, he saw Ulla with Andreas; they were turning in a circle in time with the music, but with different steps, it was as if they were moving in time with a quite different melody which only they could hear. Their faces were very close together and they seemed to notice nothing of what was going on around them.

He spotted Hanna Borowtschik in conversation with Curate Mikas. He knew it might seem funny if he asked Hanna to dance, but why shouldn't he? She would probably be grateful to him for the rest of her life for rescuing her from the Curate, and he could prove that he wasn't afraid of her. The Borowtschiks, you see, had come from the Kattowitz area only a year ago. The story was that the father had taken the Polish miners' side during a strike — and that he had more than once argued in favor of the annexation of eastern Upper Silesia by the German Reich. Anyway, he had been deported. The Borowtschiks moved to Strachwitzstrasse and shortly afterward began calling themselves Baron (accent on the first syllable); that was the time when people began changing their names. Even though Baron, the mining engineer, had never been seen in a Party uniform, rumor had it that he was a party big shot. So everyone shunned the family, and Hanna too, who attended the private school in Teuchertstrasse, got the cold shoulder from her contemporaries, both girls and boys. Not until the mining engineer appeared in the news sheet *The Gleiwitz Mine,* because he had reportedly spoken out at a workers' meeting for German–Polish reconciliation, did the people in the Trinnek district realize they had been misinformed. Valeska Piontek was the first to invite Frau Baron to her home, and afterward she let the neighbors know that she found her delightful. "Oh, she's so very *tolerant*," she said everywhere, again and again, for "tolerant" was an expression in vogue, and anyone who mattered was *tolerant*.

Josel thought: If I dance with Hanna, it might make Ulla angry, well, not angry, but at least remind her that she's not the only pretty girl in the district. So he walked up to Hanna and, after executing a rather exaggerated bow, said, with an intonation acquired from dancing lessons: "Fräulein Borowtschik, may I have this dance?" But he could not prevent a sudden attack of nerves that she might turn him down; for one thing (*pierunje!*) he had called her "Borowtschik" and not "Baron," and for another, though he had passed her a few times earlier in the evening, he hadn't greeted her formally.

But Fräulein Borowtschik took no offense, she blushed just as in the serial stories he had read in the *Upper Silesian Voice,* inclined her head slightly, revealing a large yellow ribbon at the back of her head, then she gave him her arm, somewhat surprised but willing. The sentence the Curate had begun was left hanging in the air, but he was not in the least indignant or disappointed or insulted; his watery blue eyes were already directed toward another victim — Franzek Fieber, who was Lutheran, to be sure, but who for some time now had been training with the Don Bosco Catholic swimming club for the junior district meet in Kraulen, so it was probably just a matter of time . . .

Josel steered Fräulein Borowtschik straight toward Ulla and Andreas, but it was difficult to manage; couple after couple worked their way in between them. Fräulein Baron could not have been more than twenty-five years old, but she definitely had something of the *staro frela* about her already. No, she was not an old maid in the usual sense, she was too well-dressed for that, her movements too quick and her voice too serious. But maybe that was it: everything about her was just a shade too much! Her dress a little too tight, her earrings a bit too showy, the clip in her hair larger than usual, it too not quite suitable to her age. And the rouge on her cheeks was too thick: it had been applied with the same brush she had used on her lips, and the wart to the right of her nostril had been all too clearly darkened with eyebrow pencil. From this wart sprouted three coarse black bristles, standing erect, and Josel was worried that they might tickle him when he got closer to her while dancing—he could not take his eyes off them. They called that a beauty spot now, ever since La Jana had appeared in a film with one of them. It always amazed Josel how girls were somehow able to turn something ugly to advantage.

"These new-style dances," Fräulein Baron said, "I love them, but they're not exactly easy, are they?" She was trying hard not to step on Josel's feet with every beat. "They're nice dances, don't you think?" she added.

Josel mumbled something, and kept dancing on his heels to keep the toes of his shoes from being so badly scuffed. "How do you like the band?" he asked, out of embarrassment.

"I find them very good. Did you notice, earlier they played a Lambeth Walk, that's the latest dance from America, but it's not allowed here, I think."

"I beg your pardon?" said Josel.

"A Lambeth Walk. You know . . ." Fräulein Baron put her hand on the back of Josel's damp neck and let it slide downward, making a slurping noise; didn't sound nice, Josel thought, but it did feel good. "It came to Kattowitz when we were still living across the border. I can't really do it, but I have seen it being danced, really wild, legs all over the place . . . You have to admit, these old slow numbers are pretty boring."

Josel agreed with this as well. Though he was glad not to have to dance the *lämbes wook* with Fräulein Baron, at least not now, for it was all he could do to keep his feet out of harm's way during this old slow number.

"Oh, you know," Josel said, "I like to dance a slow one now and then." When he had a chance to dance at all! he thought. He had not danced more than six times in his life, and four of those times on the sly, where it had to be kept secret. Still, it was pleasant being pushed back and forth by Fräulein Baron. He slowly began to grow angry that Andreas had spent the whole evening with Ulla. It was his own fault, of course, for sending the two of them to Zernik this afternoon because he had wanted to go to his shed.

It was nothing but his own *pierunnisch* egotism, and he only wanted to make the money to go to Warsaw with Ulla.

Ulla and Andreas danced past, and he could see they were doing better than he and Fräulein Baron. Typical of a Breslau boy, he thought, he's been here exactly twenty hours, makes eyes at Fräulein Ulla Ossadnik, and already the girl's glued to him. Not that he was jealous; he would leave that (and a few more traits, too) to the grownups, at least that was his intention. Apart from kissing Ulla once underwater when they were swimming (he was still proud of having convinced her that only fish, not people, could kiss underwater—until she tried it with him), nothing had ever happened between them. They were simply close friends, weren't they, otherwise: *Pschinzo!* Yet as Josel watched Ulla's head bob up now and then among the dancing couples, he thought that all the same, when you had been "close friends" with someone for that long, there ought to be something more to it. Maybe it's true that he wouldn't have begun to think about it except for Andreas. He wondered how he could get that across to Ulla without her laughing at him.

Fräulein Baron was still stumbling around, hanging heavily in his arms, but Josel thought that she smelled *pierunnisch* good. Her perfume must have come from abroad, from Poland—no, from much farther, from France; even girls in primary school used Polish perfume. He sniffed at her dress and said: "What did you say the name of that dance was again, *lämbes wook?*"

"Oh, the old dances," Fräulein Baron said, "they're just as nice today, when they're danced young . . . a waltz, a polka, a polonaise . . ."

A Gleiwitz proverb, You dance differently in the morning than in the evening, occurred to Josel. A polka and a polonaise, he had never danced those, and waltzes were not for him, you had to spin so fast that it scrambled your brains. He was more for American dances.

By now Josel had worked his way over quite close to Ulla and Andreas, and was looking directly into the girl's face, with its veiled expression; yes, it really was like that, and she had to open the curtain in front of her (inner) face before discovering Josel next to her. Then she began to laugh, and Andreas released her from his arms and joined in the laughter, and their faces were so open that Josel buried any suspicion deep within himself. Josel laughed too. Only Fräulein Baron was not laughing, because Josel was dancing in place now, which ruined her laboriously devised dance patterns. She looked down at her feet, and that only made things worse.

"Mamuscha wants to drag us home from here in a minute," Josel shouted across to Ulla and Andreas. He was not quite sure whether the two had understood him.

After the next turn, when they were together again, he said, "Our time is running out, Mamuscha wants to drive us home, in the Sergeant's car."

"Right now, when it's so much fun?" Ulla yelled back.

"When it's so much fun," Andreas echoed, whirling Ulla around.

Josel inquired about the Sergeant. Andreas had last seen him in the men's lavatory, where he was alternately puking and sobbing, and Fräulein Willimczyk was pacing up and down outside in the corridor, handing everyone who entered the men's room something for her Sergeant: a handkerchief, a serviette drenched in cologne, a digestive pill. She did not dare go in herself.

"The next one'll be a polka," Andreas said, and stamped his foot. And Ulla: "Yes, skinny Michalek bought a round of drinks for the band, I saw him."

Josel was suddenly afraid that the polka music would find him still saddled with Fräulein Baron. He had never before danced a polka. "When are *we* going to dance together, Ulla?" he called, mentally snatching at a lifeline.

Andreas swung Ulla around directly into Josel's arms. "Dance on, you two!" he said. And turning to Fräulein Baron: "May I have the pleasure, Mademoiselle?"

Fräulein Baron, charmed by the young man and his refined manner of speech, was glad to make the switch. And before Josel knew what was happening, Ulla's hands were resting on his shoulders and they were trying out the first steps, jostled by fat Polensky, who charged by at that moment with Helga Honisch. Josel could have cheered; ten minutes ago he would not have believed that he could be whirling across the dance floor with Ulla in his arms, and without any complications. Oh, if only Mamuscha could see them, and Ulla's father too. This dance might make it easier for him tomorrow when he formally requested Ulla's hand. Yes, he was firmly determined to do so. At fifteen he was still too young, perhaps, and if you wanted to be literal about it, he was really only fourteen and a half; but Irma at nineteen and three-quarters was also too young, and she had managed it. Even though Mamuscha had been crying her eyes out for the past few days.

Andreas's cheerful face and Fräulein Baron's eagerly studious one revolved around him while he held on to Ulla's body where it was narrowest; he wanted to leave his hands there as long as he could. And he was ashamed of himself for having harbored even the slightest suspicion of Andreas earlier.

The music was over.

"Did you find out anything?" Ulla asked curiously.

Josel did not understand. Inwardly he had been concentrating entirely on the polka. At the summer festival he had seen the dancers leaping across the hall; it must have given them great pleasure, for they emitted small, sharp cries from time to time. Josel said, "I've never danced a polka before; you know I can only do the simple dances."

"Is there going to be war? You and Andreas were upstairs with those officers, weren't you? What did they have to say?" Ulla seemed to be interested in other things besides playing the piano, dancing and music.

At that instant the band struck up a furious polka rhythm, and as if shot out of a cannon, the singer from the municipal opera stormed onto the still empty dance floor with her fiancé Werner Schalcha (that was his name, wasn't it?), heads and hands inclined downward, and only when they had reached the other side and were starting back, did they jerk their heads and hands upward triumphantly. No one followed them; the picture looked so perfect that no one dared spoil it.

Josel had resolved not to repeat to anyone what he had heard from the General . . . But now he wanted to more than ever. Yes, it was a raid on the transmitter, you were right about that, we can expect the very worst now, and that means war, maybe even within the next twenty-four hours—that was what he really should have told Ulla.

But now he wanted to dance with her, to dance with Ulla Ossadnik, in the Mint Room of the Hotel Upper Silesia in Gleiwitz, and if it's a polka, well, then a polka!

"Later," said Josel nonchalantly. "Shall we?"

And Ulla echoed him, but brighter, almost singing: "Shall we?"

And now other couples stormed the parquet, even Andreas and Fräulein Baron, their heads bent very low, swept past them, Fräulein Baron's little red mouth drawn into a pout, and who knows, maybe the little shrieks that gradually filled the ballroom came from it.

Josel and Ulla twined their fingers together, dipped their heads toward each other, their faces almost touching. At first Josel had to hop from one foot to the other, but they were both surprised at how fast they were mastering the polka steps; it was quite simple, you just had to give yourself completely to the beat. Ulla's and Josel's gaze met, and the smile of each drifted into the face of the other and lingered there for a long time. Josel had forgotten Andreas, Fräulein Baron, the General, and Mamuscha, even the shed on the Klodnitz.

So he was all the more surprised when a uniform materialized in front of him and removed Ulla from his arms. "Just once around with you, little Fräulein!" It was the reedy voice of the Sergeant, who then absconded with Ulla in sprawling leaps to a distant corner of the parquet. And Josel, half numbed, withdrew a step, to the edge. Other dancers brushed past him.

Ulla let the Sergeant slide her across the parquet. For hours now she had done nothing more than react to others. Only now for the first time did she feel a resistance growing in her body, but this was happening so slowly that it would probably be quite some time before she had the strength to free herself from her partner; she was dancing with movements that were strange to her and she was hearing music that came from very far away.

Meanwhile, Fräulein Willimczyk was standing at the edge of the dance floor, her face distorted with anger. She had a wet handkerchief stretched between her hands, and every time she spotted the uniform of the Sergeant in the throng of dancers, she cracked it like a whip.

Then Andreas leaped up and, with the element of surprise on his side, spun Ulla right out of the Sergeant's grasp, and now he was romping with her across the dance floor to the rhythm of the polka. Josel watched them shocked, with relief, with triumphant joy, these emotions scudding across his face as rapidly as clouds before a summer storm.

Alone on the dance floor, the Sergeant began to reel, and Josel thought, now he's going to have a fit, something he had long wanted to see. But the soldier only fell into the outstretched arms of the bookseller, who then placed her wet handkerchief on his face and began to wipe it, as the Sergeant tumbled to his knees with the sound of a whole pigsty and danced on that way amidst the other couples, until he got his hands on the handkerchief and shoved it between the legs of the screeching Fräulein Willimczyk, and kept pushing on it while she screamed and beat on his head with both fists.

With this scream the polka ended. Andreas and Ulla hopped over to Josel, they were quite out of breath. "The first polka!" Andreas said, without letting go of Ulla. "My first polka," Ulla whispered, and in her thoughts she was already practicing it on the piano. "Wild," Josel said, and it was not clear whether he meant the music or the Sergeant, who was still scrambling around on the dance floor and had now begun to unbutton the jacket of his uniform.

Meanwhile, the humiliated Fräulein Willimczyk had run into the kitchen, where she grabbed at the first object she saw—a pair of poultry shears—and was actually intending to cut off her nipples with them. She began silently doing so, and the cooks, who saw the blood trickling down, ran over and tried to stem the flow by placing water-soaked rolls on the wounds.

26

THE TOWN WAS full of soldiers, heavy artillery and tanks, air raid drills were being carried out, and in the border areas a blackout was in effect. Everywhere you went the talk was about war and the enemy, and earlier in the evening, Valeska could not remember how or when, the rumor had gone around that Polish forces had attempted to occupy the radio station on the Tarnowitz road—yet in a strange way all this seemed remote. There would be war, somewhere and sometime, but no one was prepared to admit the truth—Valeska was not—that the war would have to begin here, a few kilometers from this hotel. Valeska remembered a film she had seen long ago; there was dancing upstairs in a ship's ballroom, while down below water was already flooding the engine room, and a similar feeling crept over her now as she watched the dancers in the Mint Room. She waved again to Josel and Ulla, energetically now, for the time was coming to drive home. Her brother Willi came up, not with the Sergeant but with the manager of the hotel, who was obliged to inform her, in a conscientious and rather long-winded manner, that the music must stop at one o'clock, it was a directive from the local command post with which they simply had to comply, since a group attached to the General Staff was quartered upstairs in closest proximity. "You do understand." Then he produced a garland of apologies, but Valeska was no longer listening; fine with her, it meant the guests would go home earlier. She wanted to make a start now anyway, with Josel and Ulla and Andreas, and the drunken Sergeant of course, and perhaps with Aunt Lucie (Lanolin) and her blind son, and old Krupniok, if there was room. Throughout the reception she had seen her brother only fleetingly, flickering about like a will-o'-the-wisp in his blue silk suit. He took care of all the details, discussed the program with the band, speedily and inconspicuously replenished the *schnapsik,* and brought the crumbling and

bickering groups back together. He had rescued Countess Poremba's silver fox, settled on the construction of a new water tower
in Gleiwitz-Petersdorf with the president of the waterworks (on
property belonging to Valeska), bedded down the Wild Monk,
who was reeling after only four glasses of *schnapsik,* in the cloakroom of the hotel, and he was just coming back from the hospital
where he had deposited Fräulein Willimczyk. Fat Polensky had
stayed behind to complete the official report. Willi was glad nothing about this had yet reached the ballroom from the kitchen, he
did not want his sister to be upset. They both set out now to
locate the Sergeant; she went to the left, while he would search to
the right.

Count Poremba sprang up as Valeska passed him; he readied
himself to ask her to dance, but she cut short his preliminary
choreography by stretching out both hands to placate him, and
hurried past. She was thinking of Leo Maria as she bowed to the
president of the waterworks, she was thinking of the music room
as she kissed the ruby of Archpriest Pattas, she was thinking of
Halina as she pressed her way through the dancers, she was thinking of Irma and Heiko, who had already retired to their room in
the hotel without taking leave of her, as she looked for Ulla and
Josel, she was thinking of the old brickyard she had sold. On the
far side of the room she joined up again with Willi Wondrak.

He shrugged his shoulders. She raised hers. They said nothing,
the music was too loud.

They moved further away from the band. Willi Wondrak discovered a few blood spots on one of his shirt cuffs and quickly
drew the sleeve of his jacket down over it. "What'll we do?" he
asked Valeska. He saw her eyes growing sleepy. He would have
liked best to drive her home now.

"*Muj Bosche,* I have to go to Leo Maria, it's late," she said. "I'm
worried!" And with the memory of Leo Maria's sick body her face
was slowly creased by the furrows that had so mysteriously disappeared after the *tableaux vivants.*

"Yes, you're right," Willi Wondrak said. "First thing to do is
drive you home now." He took her by the hand with such protec-
tiveness that it reminded her of her childhood, when he had led

her across makeshift wooden bridges over brooks and ditches along the road.

"But the children? They have to come home!"

"I've only seen Andreas, his face was very pale, he's probably had too much to drink too," said Willi Wondrak.

"Where did you see him?" Valeska wanted to go to him right away. "Maybe Josel and Ulla are there too? They were dancing just now, but they've just disappeared all of a sudden."

"It was in the men's room. Stay here, I'll go and get Andreas first." Willi Wondrak worked his way through the dancing couples. He liked watching the others dance, but he did not care to dance himself.

Valeska rummaged in her purse for the little bottle of cologne, dampened her handkerchief, and patted her face with it. Behind her a dispute broke out as to whether the *Krakowiak* could still be danced. Valeska did not dare turn around, because she was afraid of getting involved, maybe even being forced to arbitrate. A voice (it was Kotulla's) asserted: "*Krakowiak,* brothers, that's a Russian dance, of course, and now, since the non-aggression pact . . . eh, with Russia, a *Krakowiak* now!" The other voice (Valeska could not tell whose it was): "That's a Polish dance, I saw it myself, in Kattowitz, back in the days of the plebiscite, that's when they came, Korfanty's people, with music and songs and the *Krakowiak,* so that we'd vote for the Poles." And Verena's voice: "So much Tchaikovsky on the radio, as if we didn't have Brahms." Valeska heard something like a grunt and off to one side saw someone sitting on a chair, snoring, with a napkin over his face. *Muj Bosche,* that's all I need. Valeska went over and lifted the cloth a little, it was Wons, the veterinarian, whom they had tied to the chair and propped against the wall so he would not tip over. A taxi should take him home immediately! Valeska was indignant that no one had paid any attention to him; the others were sitting only a few steps away heatedly discussing the *Krakowiak*. She dabbed again at her forehead with her handkerchief, the cologne had long since evaporated, and she felt nervous tension growing in her fingers and climbing up her arms. If she started to search for Willi Wondrak now, they would probably miss each other completely as they had already done, so she decided to stay put. Directly in front of her, Count Poremba and Dr. Kamenz collided with each other, but before there could be further complications Valeska spotted her brother, who had Andreas by the hand, and rushed to them. "Let's go!" In her haste she even forgot the snoring veterinarian, Wons, on the chair, but she did not forget to run into the kitchen, where a small casserole filled with a few leftovers had been made ready for her, she wanted to take it home for Leo Maria and Halina. And when she finally climbed into the front seat of the car, Willi Wondrak was stowing Aunt Lucie (Lanolin), with her son Albert, old Krupniok, and Andreas in the back seat.

Andreas felt miserable. He kept trying to swallow the saliva collecting in his mouth because he was afraid he would have to vomit. Nevertheless, he would have liked to get out and dance with Ulla again. He was not sure whether the spinning in his head when he closed his eyes—and indeed the spinning only began when they were shut—came from the *schnapsik* or the dancing. He leaned against the woman with the thick glasses whom they called AuntLucieinparenthesesLanolin (funny, isn't it), and the many folds of her dress were warm on his knees.

Valeska was about to toss a joking comment to the others packed together in the back, who virtually squeezed into each other at every turn in the road, but perhaps she only wanted to cheer herself up, for her worries had come back along with the furrows in her face, and she reproached herself for having left Leo Maria alone so long. Who knows what state she would find him in now—and would she get any rest at all until Josel had come home, and until she had found out why, for example, the County Magistrate had left so early?—but she would probably have to wait until late in the morning to ask him about it . . . If she could see some light from the garden cottage, even a ray, and she would have to notice it in spite of the careful blackout the County Magistrate always observed, that would set her mind at rest. But she would prefer to put off everything, she still felt caught up, the music whirred in her head and the light still warmed her skin, the scent of the ballroom streamed from her dress . . . Valeska placed the casserole between her feet and tossed her hands jauntily in the air and behind her, and the others sitting there leaned forward as if they had only been waiting for this signal, as if they could break out of their little, narrow, gloomy space this way, into the light, into the music, to the shining faces they had just left. It was all Willi could do to find his way in the dark with his lights dimmed. The others pressed their lips together in the attempt to hold fast to what was increasingly crumbling away as they drove into the darkness, and with faint amazement, perplexed admiration, and a slowly growing displeasure they looked back on the wedding reception in the ballroom of the Hotel Upper Silesia. Each of them was thinking of something else.

"But there, just look there!" Valeska almost knocked over her casserole and rubbed her eyes like a child when a magician has made a rabbit disappear. She tugged at Willi's arm and pointed off to the right: "There's nothing there, nobody and nothing," she said, full of amazement and fright. "Just this noon, the entire square was full of soldiers, artillery, tents, and horses under the trees, don't you remember . . . Or is this a different square?" Suddenly she was unsure; in the darkness and after this celebration everything looked different, less real.

"Yes, they've marched away," Willi shouted to her. In spite of the darkness, he had recognized the square as the one Valeska meant, but he did not want to think just now why the soldiers had disappeared.

Valeska leaned over to him and whispered, "War! Willi, that means war!"

Willi Wondrak did not answer. The others remained silent too until the car stopped. Perhaps it was because they were afraid of re-entering the dull humdrum of their everyday lives that they stood in front of the house for a while, watching with eyes wide as Wondrak doubled back across the street, sidewalk, and the edge of a field, to drive back to the reception.

"Goodnight," said old Krupniok. He went behind the house and relieved himself. Aunt Lucie (Lanolin) sighed, shaking her feet, which had fallen asleep in the car: "What a night!" And she breathed in deeply. "Can you smell the delightful fragrance of the lavender? What a night!" She went up to the lavender bushes, and only her sighs could be heard, and then she came out, balancing some blossoms in her hands, which she crushed, in order to hold her fragrant hands under the nose of her blind son. "What a scent, isn't it, what a scent . . . Our country, really, only our country has this scent," she said. Andreas noticed that it was characteristic of this woman to say everything she said twice.

In the distance the sounds of the switching yard could be heard, the squealing of the wheels, the colliding of couplings, the short, vigorous blasts of the steam engines.

In the darkness you could not see far, but as far as Valeska could see, everything here belonged to her, the house, the garden, and even behind it a piece of a field.

"Fantastic," Valeska said.

"*Fantastichnek*," Andreas said, who had heard Josel say it that way. The word pleased him. He thought of Josel and Ulla, and the rest of the way to the house struck him as quite unreal; he would have liked to dance another polka, with Aunt Valeska, with Aunt LucieinparenthesesWidera, or with Fräulein Borowtschik or Baron, it didn't matter which. The music was still vibrating in his limbs, and he danced one, two, three, four steps along the garden path; his feet scuffed on the ground and the others laughed, but to him it wasn't funny at all. He would be very happy to wait here outside until Josel and Ulla and Irma and Heiko arrived. He would have liked to see Ulla one more time to tell her something, or perhaps not say anything to her, just look at her. For today that would be enough, and tomorrow, yes, tomorrow, he didn't know what tomorrow might bring; he only knew that in the few hours he had spent in Gleiwitz he had learned more about life than in all the time up to then, and that he had found a true friend in Josel, whom he trusted, and he wished for some situation in which he could prove this to Josel. And as for Ulla, yes, he was head over heels . . . He was not sure whether you could call it love exactly, things had gone too fast for that, but it was what he used to imagine love would be like. No matter, he had a secret with Ulla, so big that it must reach from here to the sky, it added up to the same thing as love, maybe more. He resolved to stay up until Josel came home, and tell him about it.

The silence of the night embraced them all before they went

their separate ways, embraced them so closely that Valeska thought she would suffocate; no one spoke another word, they stood before the steps to the house and listened to the silence. That now and then a shot resounded close by or farther off changed nothing; rather it reinforced the silence, for ever since the soldiers had come from the Reich, those hollow, bursting sounds had been part of it.

Valeska opened the door, and a blue light from the entryway fell across her. It puzzled her that Halina was not already coming down the stairs; she hadn't fallen asleep, by chance? She drew Andreas into the house. For the boy, such a day must have been confusing; she stroked his hair, simply feeling too exhausted to untangle the conflicting emotions which she thought she perceived on the boy's pensive face. She let her hand rest on his hair for a moment, hoping that it would calm him, as her father's hand had once imbued her with confidence and peace and courage. Strangely enough, her mother's hand had never done so—rather it would have repelled her. Andreas withdrew from her touch. Valeska knew that they would not be able to solve the riddle tonight either.

The others went to their rooms, Valeska accompanied Andreas to his. It occurred to her that she had left the casserole sitting on the bottom step out front, and she hadn't checked to see whether there was still a light on at the County Magistrate's. She wanted to lean forward and give Andreas a kiss on the cheek, a fleeting breath of a kiss, but then she hesitated. It was Andreas who wrenched her from her thoughts. "Thank you, Aunt Valeska, it was a terrific party . . . for me," he said. "Really *fantastichnek!*" (All right, so Josel could still make it sound better.) "And tomorrow I will see Uncle Leo, won't I?"

"Yes," Valeska said absently, for she was more and more puzzled that Halina had not heard them, "tomorrow you can visit Uncle Leo. Sleep now, Josel will be coming soon . . . you don't have to wait for him."

Already on her way to Leo Maria, Valeska assembled all the polished, sparkling, and affectionate sentences that she hoped would make him happy. From below, the sounds of the others reached her; from above nothing could be heard, not even Leo Maria's coughing. She had been gone for seven hours, and she realized that much could have happened in that time. A disaster, even. She started. But she did not run fearfully up the stairs; she stood still as if petrified. She sensed that she was only imagining her fear. It took other things to frighten her, but she did not stop now to consider what kind of things; for years nothing had frightened her, her fear was always artificial, put on, she used it for effect. She could not have said when was the last time she had been really frightened, frightened to death. Valeska had never been frightened to death, or if so it must have been long ago. Perhaps that time when they fished her sister out of the river, her body swollen; or after the war, when the rebels were shooting near the railroad station; or the time when she was lying in the grass with Erich, on the banks of the Klodnitz. He had kissed her while pulling her skirt up, higher and higher, and then he began to tug at her slip, and then he had stuck something into her, something cold, wet, slippery; she had grabbed at it, it was a live fish that was quivering inside her. And she had screamed, screamed silently. That time she had believed she would turn to stone and never be freed from it again. Erich had lain next to her, laughing, and then taken the fish and stuck it in his jacket pocket, where it flopped about a while longer.

Valeska did not know why she had remembered that just now. Having reached the upstairs hall, she decided to call Halina. She did so twice, the second time so loudly that she was afraid of waking Leo Maria. She sat down on a chair and pushed off one shoe with the other, and then the second with her bare toes. Free of their tight covering, she felt her feet growing. Then a door banged, Halina was on her way, on her way to her, and the two women met in the blue light of the hall. Halina still had sleep in her eyes, and her movements, enmeshed in dream, were slower than usual.

"*Proszę,*" Halina said, and set the casserole on the windowsill.

"Thank you," said Valeska. She rubbed her heavy feet against each other. "How is my husband? Is he sleeping?" And before Halina could reply: "Did the telephone ring?"

"*Tak, telefon już trzy razy dzwonił, ale ile razy biegłam do aparatu, nikt się nie odzywał, tylko ti-ti-ti-ti-ti.*" (Yes, the telephone rang three times, but each time I went up to it, no one was there, nothing but this ti-ti-ti-ti-ti.)

Actually, Halina was afraid of the black appliance, which had been installed in the house fairly recently. Halina had been in the house for three years, and was afraid of nothing except the *Pan*'s fits of delirium, when he hurled everything he could get his hands on at the door; she kept to her room then until things quieted down. Later they all knelt on the floor together and cried and cleaned up the mess. But this black instrument that screeched at the most inconvenient times was too strange for her.

"Oh, won't you ever understand?" Valeska sighed, "you have to lift the receiver right away, at the first ring, and then you just say the *Pani* is not at home, please call again later."

"*Pan* much cough this night, oh, verry bad . . . I have fear because always spit much blood, I want going to doctor, but *Pan* holding me back, by *ręka* . . . until he fall asleep . . ."

The *Pan* had indeed suffered two fits of coughing that night, the first shortly after the *Pani* had gone. Something or other must have happened on the radio and he had called, but she didn't hear him because she was busy in the kitchen washing the dishes, and he had begun throwing things at the door again. So she ran upstairs, and the *Pan* was very excited about whatever was on the radio; the program had suddenly been interrupted, and he had heard Polish being spoken on the air. "Just listen," he had said, "just listen, there's nothing on the air, just crackling, buzzing, I didn't touch the dial." They had both sat there and listened for a while, and then the *Pan* turned the dial and tuned in to another station, you could hear merry music, and on another, someone was talking about art. Then he tuned in to Gleiwitz again, and it was still silent, and suddenly his coughing started. She had lit his incense sticks and waved them in front of his face; there was nothing more she could do, and when he sucked in the air with a whistling sound, the air which was insufficient for his skinny body, a vise clamped around her head and squeezed it tighter and tigher. The *Pan* had sent her to the County Magistrate, to ask him

whether he too had heard that on the radio, and she had gone out
to the garden cottage and knocked on the window, but no one
had opened the door. She had drummed on the windowpane
again, because she thought she spied a glimmer of light behind
the curtains. But the silence was unbroken, and suddenly she was
afraid of the night, of the hunchbacked house, of the County
Magistrate, even of herself. She ran back as fast as she could. If it
really had been the way the *Pan* said, that they had been talking
Polish on the radio and singing the Polish national anthem, then
maybe war had broken out and the Poles had already crossed the
border, and in a situation like that it might better for her to be at
home in Chlodno and to hide in some shed there, there were
many sheds along the river that were slowly disintegrating, where
gypsy families had once lived and then tramps, never more than
for a few days, she could hide there and wait until everything was
over, and then maybe people would talk to her again, now that it
was all so long ago, and she considered whether she should go get
the doctor for the *Pan* and his coughing and then not come back
again; the border had been closed for days, but she would manage
to find a path through the woods. The *Pan* would not let her go
for the doctor, and when the second coughing fit came, he did as
before, held firmly to her hand until his body quieted and the
whistling when he inhaled grew fainter and then stopped altogether, the vise around her head loosened, and when she thought
now about why she had really wanted to leave, not a reason
occurred to her.

"Yes, I must go up to him," Valeska said, but instead of going
to the door, she slumped into an armchair. She pressed the hairpins even more firmly into the tight bun of her hair, she undid the
button at the nape of her neck, as she had already done earlier, she
scratched at her armpits, although nothing there itched, she bent
forward and began to massage her feet, while considering what
else she could do to stretch out the time down here. She feared the
walk upstairs.

"*Pan* now sleep solid, since an hour . . . I make always little fires,
new fires, whole room full of green smoke . . . and *Pan* fall asleep,
solid . . ."

"Yes," Valeska said wearily. But her weariness was nothing physical, it came wholly from within.

Halina wondered whether she should tell her the story about the radio, but it was better if the *Pan* told it to her himself. "*Czy była fajna uczta?*" (Was it a nice party?) she asked softly.

"*Muj Bosche,*" Valeska said, "I nearly forgot. That, in the dish there, that's for you." And after a pause she added, "Yes, it was a nice party, and it would have turned out to be the nicest party of my life, yes, Halina, I really mean it, if only Leo Maria could have been there, and you too . . ." Her voice broke slightly with emotion. She herself was not sure whether the emotion was genuine or only a matter of words. Maybe she should have taken Halina along to the reception, at least for an hour or two. And Leo Maria, in a wheelchair.

Halina took a folded-up piece of paper from her skirt pocket. "I found this in garden . . ." She unfolded it and showed it to Valeska. It was a handbill, the words on it looking as if they had been rubber-stamped:

CATHOLICS! GERMANS AND POLES OF UPPER SILESIA! DO NOT LET YOURSELVES BE GOADED INTO A WAR AGAINST EACH OTHER. THE ENEMY IS NOT ON THE OTHER SIDE OF A BORDER. IT IS ATHEISM.

"In our garden, you say." Valeska asked. "And many! *Muj Bosche!* Just burn it, right away. Otherwise we'll have trouble with the Party." She tore the handbill into little bits, but slowly, as if she wanted only to tear up the paper and not what was on it.

"Oh, Halina," she said, "so many things will change." She looked into the girl's face; it was the face of a young girl which had been turned too quickly into that of an aging woman. Valeska admitted to herself that she was now noticing Halina's face with genuine interest for probably only the second time. The first time had been about three years ago when Halina had rung the doorbell. It was the hair that had struck her first, she could still remember the flaxen, almost platinum blonde hair, a color not seen in this region, which fell straight onto her shoulders. It had grown darker now, and Halina wore it short, with three curls on her forehead which she set every morning with a curling iron. Her eyes were a deep, dark brown. Aunt Jadwiga had sent her; she needed to get out of the little village on the Birawka, because she had been involved with a *Grubjosch,* a miner who was an ethnic German, who had made her pregnant. And even though her belly grew rounder and rounder, she had gone to bathe every day in the Birawka, even in November, until she had a miscarriage. The village constable had come and interrogated her at length, but before a detailed investigation could begin, Aunt Jadwiga put her fledgling on the train to Gleiwitz with two and a half złotys and half a German mark in silver in her pocket, along with a letter to Valeska Piontek.

Valeska had taken her in immediately. Halina never talked about what had happened in the village, and Valeska, who learned the story from Jadwiga's letter, did everything she could to keep her from being reminded of the past. Only Josel sometimes asked about her origins, but she never talked about anything except the Birawka, on the banks of which she had grown up, and the little village, where the women worked on the estate of Hrabia Kotucil, who had been a Count Kottusch, and the men dug coal in the Święta Barbara, which had been called the Barbara mine. Now there is water up to the knees in the tunnels. Sometimes Josel went down to the Klodnitz with Halina, and they sat in a field rather far from the bank, while Halina showed him how to weave eel baskets from the long green reeds, but she never went along when Josel put the baskets in the water, she watched from afar; perhaps she was afraid she might discover one day the head of her *Grubjosch* in the rushes or among the crests of foam, green and waxen and rigid. It seemed to Valeska that in the years before she had seen only a mask, and that now for the first time she was seeing Halina's true face. Was there not perhaps a certain resemblance to her own face, maybe even to Irma's? "You look pale, *moje dziecko,*" she said. "Wait! Sit down here!"

She pressed the surprised Halina into the chair, went into the bathroom in her stocking feet, and came back with a drawer from the wall cabinet in which she kept her makeup. She seldom used makeup except on special occasions, like tonight, and even then, when she touched up her lips with rouge, it was hardly noticeable. To darken her eyelashes, as was becoming fashionable among young girls, would have seemed to her a sin. The only thing she did daily was to rub a little rouge onto her cheeks, because she had a feeling that she didn't get enough fresh air, and was therefore always pale. This feeling had persisted ever since her childhood. For a time she was called "pale Vally" at school, so she took to eating rose hips and ribwort and rowan berries, which she picked on her way to school. ("They have lots of iron in them, and iron strengthens the blood," her grandmother had said.) A teacher had advised her to drink cocoa, but there was no cocoa at home, it was too expensive, just cocoa bean shells; she boiled them three times but nothing helped. When she was sixteen, she was allowed to buy makeup: rouge from Mouson. Even today she still said *ruusch von Musonk.*

Now she dusted Halina's alarmed face with a powder puff, and on her cheeks, which were reddening somewhat with surprise, she rubbed some of the rouge which she applied heavily to her lips; with a black pencil she darkened her eyebrows. Valeska ran out again and brought back a white blouse with frills at the neck. "*Wdzij to!* Yes, slip it on, it's just right for you." She slipped Halina's gray knitted jumper off her, as the girl sat numbly on the chair, and began to undo the buttons of her old black blouse. "When Irma and Heiko come, they're going to see you beautiful," Valeska said.

Then Halina, who until that moment had been the quiet servant, returned from her Birawka past and accepted the white blouse like a flag, drew the white, cologne-scented linen over her body, and when her head emerged and her arms were down again and the collar was smoothed into place, she looked more beautiful than Valeska had ever seen her. And Valeska took off her amber necklace and put it on Halina, to make the girl resemble her even more. Perhaps she only wanted to embellish herself with the blouse, the necklace, the powder, and the rouge.

Then Halina groped in the pocket of her jumper, found two balls of wax, popped them into her mouth, distributed them to

left and right with her tongue, and beamed at Valeska. Valeska
had watched at first with some incredulity, but when Halina's
cheeks taughtened and bulged, she began to laugh. "*Fantastichnek,* Halina," she said (she actually said *fantastichnek!*), and for
the first time it occurred to her that she had to do something to
find a husband for Halina.

Valeska approached Halina and put her arms around her; she
drew her closer until she felt her body and her slight resistance
too, the gentle resistance of Halina's body, and the smell of her
skin rose to her, the smell of her hair, of her breath, and slowly the
other body slumped toward her. Halina succumbed quite slowly,
she was overwhelmed as they embraced, a tremor crossed her
cheeks and tears welled up in her eyes, and the trembling spread
to the rest of her body and made Valeska's body tremble too.

For two days Valeska had wanted from Irma this embrace that
was more than an embrace, in which one human takes leave of
another, and this evening, before the reception, Valeska had tried
again, one last time; but Irma had recoiled and pushed her away,
her entire body had rejected her in advance, and Valeska had felt
that something was lost that could never be regained; nor could it
from this embrace, which she had not intended, which had simply
taken her by surprise, and she remembered how it had been that
other time when she too had recoiled . . .

Yes, it had been at her own wedding, they were gathered in the
living room around the piano which stood in the middle of the
room like a black catafalque, no one saying a word, only the sighs
of the women hanging in the air and a Polish litany her grandmother was whispering to herself; and then Leo Maria had come,
along with his cousin Ernst, who was both the best man and a
witness. They looked almost alike in their stiff, black, formal
attire, except that Leo Maria had sprigs of myrtle stitched to the
collar and cuffs of his suit; she herself wore a wreath of myrtle
over her veil, and she had pinned a little wreath she had woven
herself to the bosom of her dress. After the wedding she had put
this wreath and two sprigs of Leo Maria's into an empty tea
canister, where they would always stay green, as the saying goes,
until one of the partners was unfaithful. Before Leo Maria led her

from the house, her mother had to take leave of her. She had approached her, and Valeska was—afraid? Apprehensive? Irritated? Perhaps all three at once. She retreated from her and only in the kitchen, where Leo Maria could no longer see them, did she allow herself to be embraced: for the last time she belonged to her mother.

Now Valeska pressed Halina to her, the newly discovered Halina, as if she were her own daughter and as if she had to take leave now, this very minute, of her body and her youth. In more than one way Valeska tried to delude herself, but she had taken leave of her daughter long ago, and each time the delusion had grown a bit more obvious. She would have preferred it if there had been a clean break between them, some incident or other, a situation that would have made the change unmistakable; but they had drifted apart slowly, and she had been so busy she had not even noticed. The ritual gained in meaning; it sealed a loss, made it final.

The two women released each other from their embrace and sank into their chairs, exhausted, bewildered, and transformed; they were silent and avoided each other's eyes. Perhaps that was the price of the instant in which they had been joined; from now on they would be strangers even more than before.

Valeska sat there motionless, even the sound of the car for which she had been waiting so long failed to reach her. Instead she caught the scent of incense trickling down from Leo Maria's room; in general the air was growing heavier, for at night the swamp vapors began to rise. Valeska could have sat like that for a long time, letting the night roll over her and recede. She did not notice that she was beset with sighs and objects she had (once) purchased and then put on a shelf and forgotten, with mirrors and yearnings that would have frightened her if they had ever appeared before her as apparitions, by the stones of her memory, which she piled laboriously one upon the other, and which always collapsed again. If she had looked, she would have seen that the things around her already had fractures and lesions, faint blemishes almost imperceptible to the naked eye—a warning that could no longer be ignored.

What more would it take to shatter everything? An old Gleiwitz proverb had it that true catastrophes are heralded by the call of a jay, and hadn't she heard a jay that noon, on her way back from the Archpriest?

"I'm going upstairs to Leo Maria," Valeska said dully. She rose from her chair and, rowing against the tide of her past and her future, struggled up the stairs. And dreamily Halina, embarrassed or somnambulant, put back the drawer with the cosmetics, put away her old clothes, and more than that, in this moment she put away forever the remnants of all the people she had ever encountered.

27

WHEN VALESKA CAREFULLY opened the door to Leo Maria's room, she saw him behind a curtain of green smoke, propped up high against a heap of green pillows. It was as if he had not changed position at all since she left him earlier that evening. Nothing in the regularity of his breathing suggested that a little while ago the coughing had exploded in his chest and that he had been waging a skillful, though wearisome and constantly more hopeless campaign against his body. Valeska was not sure whether he had just at that moment been wakened by the sounds she had brought with her from downstairs, or whether he had not even been asleep. Indeed, for a fraction of a second it shot through her mind that those eyes might never close again, unless green myrtle were placed upon them. Quickly she said, "How are you?" and made an effort not to cough as the green smoke entered her half-open mouth.

"Thanks," Leo Maria said, in the listless voice she had been familiar with for years; he didn't move. "I'm feeling better now."

"I'm glad you're feeling better." Valeska was still not quite there. She bent forward slightly. "Oh, Leo Maria," she said, "it was a beautiful party. Maybe we should have taken you along after all and put you in an easy chair, wrapped up in blankets, for an hour or two . . ."

Leo Maria drew one hand from beneath the covers, but only to indicate his disagreement.

"They all asked about you, and they sent their regards, everyone." And she made the word "everyone" reverberate as if it might still catch up with the others, on their way somewhere, so they could confirm it. "I brought you some flowers, a whole armful, Halina will bring them up right away," she lied.

The hand came out again.

"Yes, I know, you're only supposed to look at them . . ." She

256

sighed. She sat down on the chair, and no one in the world, herself included, could have said from what depths that half-suppressed sigh had risen—from the depths of fear or of satisfaction. Valeska lifted Leo Maria's almost lifeless hand and, bringing it to her lips, held it there until the flickering pulse told her of a night of the fear of death, a longing for death, a dream of death.

"Tell me about the party," Leo Maria said.

Valeska spoke hesitantly at first because she did not know how to begin. She knew only that she could not tell the important things right at the beginning.

Leo Maria liked listening to her—not to what she was saying, somehow he had already heard all that, no, he wasn't interested in that now, but simply to her voice. It was always hard for him to answer her routine question, "How are you?" and everything within him still resisted answering at all. She never stopped asking the question, sometimes twenty times a day, and its meaning must have escaped her long ago; it had become habitual, like a characteristic but unconscious gesture of the hand. But then one day, suspicious or perhaps only worried, she asked, "Don't you feel *any* better?" She had spooned a new medicine into him which had an even more disgusting taste than usual, one she had had concocted by an herbalist in Ratibor, and it had made him dizzy; it did in fact keep him from coughing for a while, but he had the feeling it would paralyze not only his lungs but all his limbs. And she asked again: "Really, don't you feel better? You have to feel better sometime!" So he had answered her, "Yes, I'm feeling *better*!" Valeska's face had brightened, and a note of optimism sounded in her voice as she said, "From now on you'll feel better and better, I've found the remedy!" And Leo Maria had grown used to saying, "I feel better!" even though it was not the correct remedy this time.

Why did she really want to know how he was feeling? Not even the doctor wanted to know, at least not any more, now that he had withstood this illness longer than any doctor could have predicted. Essentially all they wanted to know was whether he was still alive or fading into death, Valeska was no exception in that. To him, at least, it did not seem very likely that he would ever leave this room again, unless it was feet first, but he could not talk about such a clear and simple matter with anyone, least of all Valeska. Sometimes he thought how it would be if he were simply to slip away, while Valeska was sitting beside him reporting on her day's activities in a cascade of words, or reading aloud to him from the newspaper, sitting beside him but not really there at all. He would not betray himself, however; when the time came he would send her out of the room on one pretext or another, for he wanted to prevent her from witnessing it at all costs; no one must be permitted to, he would simply take all the sticks of incense in his nightstand, light them, and croak behind a thick green cloud.

Valeska had finished reciting the list of people who had come to the reception in the ballroom of the Hotel Upper Silesia: "I promise you, when you're well once more, I'll rent the ballroom again, even if it costs me my last *tscheski,* and the lights will all be blazing, right out into the street, the blackout will be over by then — and not that little band either, I'll get Bernhard Etté with his entire orchestra, and then the two of us will dance, all alone, on the parquet, yes, Leo Maria, we will."

She put as much sincerity as she could muster into the words, but she had to admit to herself that it wasn't much.

"I'm looking forward to it already," she said. "And you . . . ?"

"Yes, Valeska," said Leo Maria, "I'd enjoy doing that once more." And by embellishing the lie with a somewhat stronger smile he tried to make it sound true.

"And all of them danced," Valeska said, "including your son Josel, just imagine!" She said nothing about having danced herself, with Count Poremba and with the Sergeant, and with her brother Willi.

There was no way Leo Maria could imagine how his son Josel had danced.

Valeska pressed Leo Maria's hand. "The others will be here right away!" She did not know what others those were, because she did not know whom Willi Wondrak had persuaded to go home. Most of them, it seemed, had wanted to stay on until the lights were turned off and they were thrown out of the hall . . .

Josel, of course, would surely be coming soon, God knows it was past time for him.

"Willi, you know, is driving them back in the Sergeant's car, he drove us too." A little laugh began to tumble out and she held her hand before her mouth. "The Sergeant . . . he was so drunk, so soused that finally all he could do was lurch around the dance floor on his knees." She laughed louder then, thinking of how the Sergeant had danced a set with her and pinched her breast once.

"Willi took his car keys away from him so he couldn't get into the car, he would have driven into the first tree, and the war would have been over for him before it even started." She was still laughing.

Leo Maria could not join in her laughter, he had to be careful that his even breathing was not disturbed, otherwise the coughing would start again and that might bring on another attack. And besides, the Sergeant did not interest him much. He had seen him only twice, and his blustering manner had not pleased him; also it annoyed him that he was always whistling a tune wherever he went.

Valeska thought of what she had agreed with Heiko. "Heiko has learned the Our Father by heart," she said, still somewhat baffled that anyone not from this region could do it. She paused, her voice grew energetic: "I talked Heiko into it, letting the Archpriest marry them on Sunday. He promised me."

"Really!" marveled Leo Maria. "And what does Irma think about that?" He would have liked to see his daughter Irma in a white dress, that was always beautiful, a bride in white with a veil; but those in charge now would not let them go on much longer, church weddings, he was sure of that, and young people had their own ideas anyway. For him there were three occasions in life for which you should be clothed in white or black, as an indication of their importance: first communion, marriage, and death.

Valeska did not reply. She did not want to discuss it any more with Irma, she would do whatever Heiko felt was right. And Heiko had probably only been afraid it might hinder his promotion if he were married in a Catholic ceremony. She'd better discuss it with Heiko once more, tomorrow would do, when she went to pick them up at the hotel. He might have forgotten his promise by then. Young people were so unreliable nowadays, especially when they came from the Reich.

"I'm going to pick up Irma and Heiko at the hotel tomorrow morning, that is *today,* at eleven o'clock. I'm to have breakfast with them there, they said, and then I'll bring them here to you. We'll have a little celebration here especially for you! Ulla Ossadnik is coming to play Chopin's Second Scherzo. By now she can play it better than I can. And Milka is coming too."

Now it was out.

Leo Maria propped himself up a bit and asked her to wedge the pillows in against his back. He seemed revivified.

"Be careful, you'll start coughing again! Should I light some incense?"

"No, not now, later, for going to sleep."

And Valeska told him how Water Milka had appeared in a man's suit (just imagine!), with long trousers, and smoking cigars, all that was missing was a monocle, and wearing the badge of the NS Women's Corps on her lapel (just imagine!), and how everywhere Milka had gone she had spread cheer with the cigars she handed out and with her stories, which she told again and again.

They had gotten into a conversation quite spontaneously, and thank God there had been no mention of the sanatorium at Tost, and the incident in Flusskretscham wasn't discussed either. "She's absolutely *tolerant.* And just think of it, she turned us down! She's beginning tomorrow as companion to the Countess Hohenlohe-Something-or-other, do you hear: as the lady's companion! *Pttt!*"

Only now did she become aware of what that meant: companion. Milka couldn't even play the piano, and it was doubtful whether she could read well either, with the proper inflections.

"Anyway, she's not moving in here," Valeska said hoarsely. "She turned me down! Simply turned me down! I offered to double her salary, Leo Maria, just imagine! And she turned me down! She has enough money, she claims, and now she wants to travel and see the world. Yes, just imagine, she's traveling companion, that is, social *and* traveling companion to Countess Hohenlohe-Something-or-other, but this Countess has to sell a few pastures or a chunk of forest every year just to travel to Karlsbad, well, the field mice are already squeaking the news to each other.

"Milka, so I heard from Mainkas, has bought the river pasturage on the Klausbach, and now she wants to raise tobacco there, not much is being imported from abroad because of the exchange rate; and she acquired the acreage around the water tower for a song, since no construction is allowed there, but now the *Reichsautobahn* is supposed to go through there . . . She doesn't need our money any more, *naturalnie*."

She could hear the amazement creeping into her own voice. She had heard rumors to this effect before, but had only half believed them. The thing about planting tobacco she had heard from Milka herself. Perhaps one day the property could all be joined together, that is, what she owned herself and what belonged to her brother Willi Wondrak; with Milka Piontek's holdings thrown in it would amount to something really substantial. That would give some people quite a jolt. Valeska herself was dazzled by the prospect.

"I'm glad," Leo Maria said, "that the quarrel between the two of you is over. It always hurt me very much, you know, that Milka came to visit me only when you weren't at home."

"I'm very glad too," Valeska said. And she did not mind telling another fib. "She even embraced me, your sister, when we were saying goodbye!"

"Thanks!" Leo Maria said, and pressed her hand again. Since the funeral of their mother, Leo Maria and Milka had seen each other only rarely. The death of their mother was not the only reason, it was also due to Milka having given up her well-paid position managing the estate of Count Ballestrem and starting to earn money at home rolling cigars for Weiss & Co. Not even Leo Maria had been able to worm out of her the reason for this decision. She had moved into one of the refugee huts on the Klodnitz, and sometimes could be seen sitting on the river bank at work with her boards and tobacco leaves. Her brother, Leo Maria, in an affectionate way, thought this slightly crazy, but his wife Valeska thought it incomprehensible and scandalous, and Willi Wondrak even considered it bad for business and his profession.

Leo Maria was a respected photographer in the town, even though he had not been active for some time. Valeska had been "officially accredited" as a piano teacher, though she had only a limited number of pupils, and her brother Willi was one of the most prominent lawyers in Gleiwitz—it seemed more or less reprehensible to them that Emilia Piontek supported herself by rolling cigars, of all things.

For Valeska, such an activity was second only to prostitution. Together with her brother she had tried everything (it was better if Leo Maria kept out of this) to talk Milka into getting a different job or entering a convent, for since age thirty-seven she was still unmarried, she could have become a nun.

Milka had refused, and rejected anyone's prying into her way of life, and Valeska was surprised by the confidence and independence with which Milka defended her meager design for living. Her brother Willi Wondrak had nevertheless managed to have her sent to the insane asylum at Tost for a compulsory examination, after which she was released, though not until six days later. After that she had broken off all contact with her sister-in-law Valeska Piontek and with Willi Wondrak, and she had only gone to Strachwitzstrasse to see her brother when Valeska was not at home.

Ever since Valeska had found out that Milka was buying up pieces of land here and there with her inheritance and her earnings from Weiss & Co., now and then reselling one of them in exchange for something larger, she had been hoping to effect a reconciliation with the help of her husband. Perhaps that way she could be gotten out of the refugee huts; she could move into the house with them and take over the management of the real estate, which by this time had grown into a full-time job. Besides that, her brother Willi Wondrak had thought of buying Milka a bicycle, so she could ride to the river when she felt like it.

Valeska wondered why her brother had not yet returned in the car. Could she have failed to hear him? Was Josel perhaps in his room already? And the drunken Sergeant too? She looked at the window, it was open, with the blackout curtain Josel had installed on Sunday hanging down over it because a dim light burned in this room all night long. No, she could not have missed the sound of the car. She listened. It was quiet outside. More precisely, there was a carpet of softly exploding sounds, but woven so evenly that it became a different kind of silence. Now and then, louder, the dry metallic sound of the couplings banging together in the distant switching yard. And in here Leo Maria's rattling inhalation.

Maybe it was too quiet for Valeska, or she was not yet tired enough.

"Anything in particular on the news?" she asked, as if she really were hoping for nothing in particular. Then she remembered hearing about the transmitter. "Oh," she said, "there was something on the radio, Polish voices, they say they were singing *Jeszcze Polska nie zginęła.*"

He had wanted to tell her about the radio as soon as she walked in. "Yes," he said, "I was going to tell you about it right away. Something must have happened at the Gleiwitz transmitter. What do you know about it?"

Valeska suppressed any hint of impatience. She said, "Somebody or other passed along the rumor that the Poles were trying to capture the transmitter, the new one, in Zernik, but nobody believed that. The place is crawling with soldiers, how could they ever get across the border? That's all I heard."

"Let me tell you what was on the radio," Leo Maria said, and he was aware that it had excited him more than he wanted to admit, maybe because it reminded him of the time of the plebiscite. "I was lying here drinking the tea that Halina brought me. On the Breslau station there was some chatter about new books, I wasn't really listening, I was just waiting for the eight o'clock news, after that I wanted to switch to the Deutschland station, they broadcast the sound portrait on Thursday nights, and you know how I love those sound portraits, that series ... that series *The Great Germans,* this time on 'Tilman Riemenschneider — Woodcarver and Rebel.' I underlined it in the listing ..." He paused in order to restore the regularity of his breathing.

"Well, it must have been about ten to eight, yes, about then, when suddenly there was a crackling in the radio, and after that the sound cut out, a real interruption, and the crackling kept coming during the break. Suddenly there was a Polish voice, louder than usual, as if someone was shouting into the microphone . . . I can still remember the beginning exactly, because it was so quiet beforehand, for quite a while, and you know how they always make some announcement, like 'Please pardon the interruption,' but there was none, and it was weird then suddenly to hear that excited voice."

Leo Maria was gasping for air.

"The voice said quite clearly: 'Attention, attention, this is Gleiwitz. This transmitter is in Polish hands.' I yelled for Halina right away. And then it went on: 'Upper Silesian rebels have seized the initiative in self-defense, because . . . because we do not want war with Poland, which the National Socialists of the Reich are plotting against our brothers . . . Don't let yourselves be drawn into it.' "

"Oh," cried Valeska. Only now did she realize that there must have been something true in what she had heard, and that the marriage of her daughter Irma was one side of it, and the war the other.

"Well, something like that," Leo Maria said. "It went so fast, half German, half Polish, I wasn't able to catch everything, but 'Upper Silesian rebels' and 'we do not want war with Poland' were part of it, and I did hear shots too . . . At the end a voice shouted, 'Long live Poland!' I heard that clearly. And then crackling again. After that it was quiet, just a buzzing in the radio. So, nobody sang the Polish national anthem . . ." He paused.

"When Halina finally got here, it was all over. But she had realized that there was some interruption on the radio. Then I twiddled with the dials, the news broadcast from Breslau was on the Troppau wavelength, but they said nothing about Gleiwitz, indeed how could they, it had only just happened . . . I sent Halina to the County Magistrate, it was time for the news, after all, and he must have heard it too, but Halina came back and said that the Magistrate didn't come to the door."

Leo Maria had so strained himself by talking that his breath was coming faster and the whistling sounds were louder. Valeska was already fearful of a renewed coughing attack. She tried to coax him to breathe more slowly by laying a calming hand on his chest—though she didn't really want to interrupt him.

"Then I played with the dial again, there was folk music coming from Breslau and Troppau and the sound portrait was on the Deutschland station, and not until half-past nine, I think, did the Gleiwitz station come back on the air. But they didn't say anything about it or explain."

"And on the news . . . ?"

"Yes, listen," Leo Maria continued, "I listened to the news at half-past ten and at midnight. Nothing about it, nothing."

"Maybe it was only a . . ." (Valeska did not know how to express it) "some broadcasting trouble, that is, some interference?" She did not believe it herself but perhaps it would calm Leo Maria down.

But Leo Maria did not want to be calmed. He had found it all very exciting, even if the coughing attack that followed almost tore out his lungs. He liked the sound portraits more than that silly music, he never missed a single Thursday night sound portrait. And now there had been a sound portrait from real life!

"I tuned in Kattowitz later, nothing was said about it there either. But the news always comes at the same time and maybe it was already over by the time I switched stations, I don't know . . ."

A thought occurred to Valeska. "After all, we do have a telephone," she said. "What if I just ring up the police station and ask what's going on?"

Leo Maria had suppressed his coughing for a long time, but now it began afresh, he sat up straight and attempted to keep the paroxysms under control.

Valeska watched him. She took the saucer with the sticks of incense on it from the nightstand. "Shall I light one for you?" she asked.

Leo Maria relaxed. He shook his head. "No," he said in a faint voice, "maybe later. In case it gets worse." By now he felt exhausted.

"Shall I ring the police?" Valeska repeated.

"Now, at this time of the night?" Leo Maria asked incredulously. He imagined the telephone in his own house ringing at two in the morning, it would upset everyone, no, then the telephone would have to be taken out. He said, "We can't use the telephone this late!"

Valeska was stubborn. "But I could say that my friend Tina Zoppas lives very close to the transmitter, and we were afraid that something might have happened to her. Then somehow they would have to . . . let us know."

"Let me try the news one more time. In ten minutes it'll be two o'clock, the Deutschland station broadcasts the news one last time."

Leo Maria asked Valeska for the crystal set that was gathering dust on the shelf; since Valeska had given him the Saba radio he seldom used it, except when he wanted to hear something on short wave from very far away, like the boxing match in America that time between Max Schmeling and Joe Louis, or the talk in German from London after the *Kristallnacht,* or the commentary in Polish after the invasion of Prague.

He put on the headphones and slowly manipulated the dial. The disadvantage of the crystal set was that the sound came and went with the ether waves, and only fragments could be heard.

Valeska watched him: a spidery man, white against the white pillows, inhaling the air with a whistle and exhaling it with a rattle, with round black headphones on his ears, staring at a cylindrical glass in which, when you looked closely, a fine, filigree wire moved across a small, shiny crystal. What did all this have to do with her? Shouldn't she go downstairs to Josel's room and see if he was already in bed? Shouldn't she finally retire to her own room next door and sink into her own bed and her own self-imposed loneliness?

Valeska leaned back in her chair. She could stay here, too, and wait until everything was over. Only she didn't know *what* would be over. The news wouldn't tell them anything new. For days they had been waiting for the war, which was being talked about everywhere, at eight every evening they gathered to learn once and for all that it had started, and at midnight there were still a few who assembled to hear the last broadcast. They fought off their sleepiness or set the alarm or splashed cold water on their faces to stay awake for ten minutes, so as not to miss the war, it could break out, you see, and they might not notice it at all or only too late, and so they stood listening to the strange voice from the radio and afterward softly went their separate ways. There was no exuberance as in August 1914, there was no fear as during the plebiscite in May 1921; there was something, though, more like indifference and fatalism. Even ten years ago people on the Reichspräsidenten-platz could be made to shout: "Kattowitz will remain German!" Today they didn't give a damn, they simply felt: We're not going to be asked what should belong to us this time, and the Poles won't be asked either; it won't be decided by either of us. This time it's something that will sweep right over all our heads.

Valeska was annoyed that she was pursuing such thoughts at all. That was something that occupied the County Magistrate, he subscribed to five newspapers because of it, he knew more than all of them, knew so much that for some time he had no longer been talking about it.

Leo Maria tucked the covers up higher, as if he had a chill. He kept twisting the dial, and his face showed that he had not yet found anything.

Outside a shell exploded, rather far away, only a dry, hollow bang could be heard, but the noise was louder than everything else. There were sounds like that during the day too, but then they blended with other sounds. That sound, Valeska thought, has nothing frightful about it, rather something unreal, as if you had your ear right next to a rosebud that was just bursting open. An enormous weariness overcame her; it seemed as if the green smoke, which had disappeared entirely by now, had penetrated her body and was numbing it now from within. She felt that she would not have the strength to get up and go to Josel's room to check whether he had come in, not even to go into the next room. She prepared herself to spend the night here in the chair next to Leo Maria. She had loosened her dress and taken off her shoes, now she undid her hair and the braid fell down her back, long and thick. It freed her from something or other, only she did not yet know exactly what. That the long braid told her age would not have occurred to her.

To judge by the dancing of Leo Maria's left hand on the blanket, he must be hearing something important through his black earphones. He turned one of them outward and indicated that she could listen too, but she made no move to. He would let her know what was most important. Except in these days, political news did not interest her much; it was enough for her to look at the headlines in the morning *Voice of Upper Silesia,* then she scanned the local news, and on the third page a review of a première at the municipal theater or a piano concert—*Boschedank,* they were always short, there was not much space for them, so she could read through them quickly before bringing Leo Maria his breakfast. For what she did not read then was lost; she never found time later to look at the paper again. And at night before going to sleep, there were only two books for her, the Bible and *Lives of the Saints,* she took turns reading them. The Bible lay on her nightstand, *Lives of the Saints* she had wrapped in newspaper and hidden in the linen closet. Since she was usually tired and fell asleep right away, she seldom got through more than two pages, so she would never read either book to the end. Also there were interesting illustrated magazines in the house which Leo Maria received every week from his reading circle, his fellow members in the Joseph Club had given him a year's subscription, but she never even glanced at them. The crossword puzzles were already solved, many pictures and the installment of the serial were cut out, and there were rips everywhere, not to mention the grease spots and coffee stains. Leo Maria, you see, was the last to receive them, because of his "lung disease"; by now they were already eight weeks old.

Valeska was on her way into darkness or sleep; her eyelids drooped.

Leo Maria removed the headphones. Listening to the scratchy voice that kept fading out, to the yowling and buzzing and whistling, had left him wider awake than ever. "Perhaps there won't be a war. Are you listening, Vally? They may reach an agreement yet."

Valeska was listening, but she was incapable of opening her eyes (and had no desire to). Now, at this hour, it would take some greater excitement. She only nodded.

"Well, negotiations were still going on in Berlin today. On the Polish radio they said that England and France had both reaffirmed their mutual assistance pact with Poland, an attack on Poland would mean war with England and France too." Leo Maria thought it over. He said loudly: "They won't dare!"

He put the headset and the crystal set on the nightstand, which was already cluttered with other objects that he had to push aside to make room.

"But listen, on the Deutschland station they did mention Gleiwitz. Wait, let's see if I can piece it together." He pondered, trying to reassemble from the chaos of voices and noises he had heard the one sentence that mattered. "Well, then: Polish border provocations have not diminished, this evening Polish . . ." He searched for a word.

Valeska interjected, "Insurgents," because she still remembered that.

Leo Maria looked at the instrument as if he would find the missing word there. It was a different word! "Yes, now I've got it: guerrillas . . . Polish guerrillas have carried out a raid on the Gleiwitz transmitter, all . . . were captured, one killed . . . Nothing about a proclamation, nothing."

Without opening her eyes, Valeska said—and her voice wavered almost as much as the voice on the crystal set—"I still don't understand how they got across the border, it's just crawling with soldiers . . ."

"Maybe they were dressed as civilians?"

"But you said they called them Polish soldiers!" Valeska persisted.

"No, I didn't say anything about soldiers, I said 'insurgents,' no, it was that funny word: 'guerrillas.' Yes, they could have been dressed as civilians."

"But how would they have gotten across?" Valeska resigned herself to opening her eyes and sitting up in her chair. She could not get it into her head. There were soldiers everywhere, wherever you looked, how could the Poles have penetrated that far in spite of them, far enough to blow up the transmitter or at least try to, and maybe the gas and water works, anything could have happened. She had spoken with a soldier outside that noon, and he had said it could break out any day, maybe even tonight. "We'll beat the hell out of the Polacks," he said. They come from all over, only none of them from our region; the ones called up here they send right away into the Reich, or even farther to the west, even though it would have been better to leave them here close to the border, at least they speak Polish.

She would almost prefer it to begin soon, a little farther along the border, that would calm them all. Not that she was afraid the town would be occupied by the Poles, even for a short time, nobody here believed that was possible, and even Herr Koschniczek, who had been a Socialist and even a Communist earlier, and had voted in the plebiscite for a free Upper Silesia, said: "The government of the Reich will see to it that no Frogs get into the Ruhr and no Polacks into Upper Silesia. Remember, we are Germany's arsenal."

She was curious. She said, "If the Sergeant is sober, I'll have him drive me to Tina Zoppas's tomorrow morning. I'm sure she'll know more than we do, don't you think so?"

"Don't forget the Gleiwitz proverb: The closer you are to the grain, the less you know how it's growing," Leo Maria said. He knew very well that that was no answer. The whole thing was probably of no great importance. No more than a sentence on the news, and by tomorrow it would be forgotten. It might not even get into the newspapers, at any rate not into those in the capital, and no war would break out over it.

It seemed to Valeska that she heard the door of the garden cottage creak. So the old County Magistrate was still awake. She would drop in on him tomorrow and take him some of the casserole, yes, she had thought of him too when she was collecting the leftovers. Had he been working this late, perhaps on his biography? Since that night in November he had not spoken to her about it, and once when she asked him about it directly, he evaded the question. Since then he no longer talked about politics at all, even when sitting in Leo Maria's sickroom, he spoke only about his daughter in Paris and how she would be visiting him in the near future. But he had been saying that for over a year, and she had not come. His visits too were growing less and less frequent.

The last time, yes, it was March that he had come into their house. Now she saw him only when he went to the garden gate to pick up his newspapers, and she had to arrange it so that she came along "by chance" if she wanted to talk to him. And yesterday when she had invited him to Irma's reception, he had come up with every possible excuse, from illness to the lack of a black suit, but she had brushed them all aside; she had even offered to send a taxi for him, but he had rejected that, it seemed even to upset him. Suddenly he had accepted her invitation after all, and had indeed come, but she had not found time to talk with him. He must have left rather early, too, after telling the story of the three bridges. A beautiful legend, yes, but it had left her in an odd mood. Valeska attempted to reconcile this memory with the sounds outside, but did not succeed.

Perhaps it is true that one's clearest thoughts come when one is between waking and sleeping, when one's body is no longer one's own, and the mind is already on its way to other deeper, less conscious levels, there to experience adventures from which only a few banal, superficial visual symbols remain, which we then call a dream when we awake. Valeska was just setting out on this path.

She might have laughed about it yesterday, but today it was all clear to her. She now realized in all clarity how isolated Leo Maria had been in his world of photographs, and that nothing had remained for him but to make his loneliness even more intense in illness. And Irma, who lived her life as children do, naïve and confused and benumbed, and who in her nineteenth year had suddenly decided to marry a soldier who had been in the house for five days, and nothing could alter her resolve. And Josel, still a child, who had been isolated through the incessant lying of others, and yet hoped to escape it through bigger lies of his own. And she herself, sitting here at Leo Maria's bedside, very close to him yet far away—were not such lies no more than flights from isolation, flights that became longer and longer because the loneliness around her kept growing more immense?

She had been trying to escape it throughout her life. She had had playmates as a child, as a young girl, but essentially even then she was considered a "loner," as her teacher, Fräulein Ruthenbeck, said (she said "lone wolf," but since she mumbled and no one was listening anyway, the others made "loner" out of it), and she wished for nothing more. It made her break out in a sweat of discomfort if a schoolmate, or a friend doing needlework with her, came up to her and touched her, or when one went so far as to begin describing a first love affair. Erich had driven her even further into herself when he stuck the fish in her. The only one with whom she had wanted a deep and genuine relationship, and who she hoped would relieve her loneliness, was Leo Maria, that is true, and nothing could dissuade her from that, no matter how many fleeting and quickly forgotten dreams tried to tell her otherwise. But before their relationship could be seriously tested, it was over. Leo Maria had retreated into illness and she into her real estate speculations, perhaps because she had never found the courage to talk to Leo Maria about this. Sometimes she sat at his bedside, as now, looking into his green face and seeing right through him. She pondered how it could happen that an apparently healthy person could from one day to the next be afflicted with asthma, and later paralysis of the legs. And she remembered that once, quite suddenly, she had discovered red spots on her body, on both breasts, and was so frightened that she could speak to no one about it, not even to a doctor. She wished, indeed she prayed, for the spots to go away—and in a day and a half they had actually vanished, all by themselves. Why couldn't people get rid of other, even worse illnesses the same way? She had been lucky, because she had resisted the illness, with all her might. That was it, then: Leo Maria did not have the strength to resist.

She had longed to bear children, and to experience another kind of time through her swelling and receding body, and had succeeded twice; after that had followed one stillbirth, and she would wrest no more from Leo Maria's body.

Irma had turned out so different from her, yet always until tonight, until the wedding reception, she had looked for herself in Irma—in the color of her eyes, in a curl, in a defiant gesture, or at least in the way she pursed her lips when speaking. But in fact Irma was like Leo Maria in every respect, and had remained as alien to her as had Leo Maria, to this very moment, and maybe that was why Irma evaded that one ritual embrace again and again, indeed rejected it, because she did not want to be taken into the body out of which she had been cast twenty years before. Josel had seemed alien to her at the very beginning, even in her belly, it had taken her almost ten months to bear him, and in those days when she was waiting anxiously for him finally to free himself from her womb, she could not get rid of the absurd notion that the baby did not want to go out into what people call life, and when the bleeding persisted, the fear struck her that this lump of flesh wanted to drag her along with it into the darkness. But later she discovered more of herself in Josel than in Irma, in a hidden smile, in many of his movements, his energy in asserting himself, in his zeal at telling lies, in the way he hid his feelings, and she watched him as he, still a child, tried out deceptions and came to terms with loneliness. Once she noticed him masturbating in the laundry-drying room upstairs: she was looking in through an open door, and felt herself being overcome by a slow paralysis— she neither wanted to stop him nor could she take her eyes from the child's tortured, twitching body. But since then she had felt guilty, in some inexplicable way, in his presence.

It must have been about that time that Leo Maria discovered she had married him only because another man had left her— Erich Stroheim, whose parents had owned a hat shop in Bahnhofstrasse and had later moved to Vienna, and who was spending the summer here with his grandparents. She had never spoken to Leo Maria about it, but it was clear to her that he had only two alternatives once he found out: either to leave her or to bind her to him even more closely. He had smashed his camera in a fit of rage, had run away, and had come back home again three days later with pneumonia. Ever since then he had refused to leave his bed.

28

THE SILENCE THAT had settled in embraced them both. He could imagine a time when there would be nothing but silence around him—an immeasurably long time, without questions, without answers, without stories, and without the banging of a piano, only a soft, dim condition in which he would drift along, the outline of the other only barely perceptible. Around him would float vague, cloudlike, transparent islands of things past and also to come. Indeed that was what was special about it, that in such a state one's memory was not just one's own, but was mixed with the memory of everyone, and that the past itself forced something new into being. It was somewhat like dreaming, yet quite different, for it happened before one fell asleep, before real dreams came, it was much less specific, less graphic, and nothing remained of it afterward except a few beads of sweat on the skin. None of the others had the patience to sit and wait for this state to set in, maybe you had to be ill, or ill for as long as he had been, maybe you first had to learn it too—at any rate, he had always been on the way there alone, and he had not yet really arrived, so how could he have taken Valeska with him, or Irma, or Josel?

He was thankful that Valeska had not gone. From behind his closed eyelids he perceived her outline, a black rectangle that gave off a smell of sweat, stale party, and exhaustion, and he knew that this image would remain with him even when she was tossing in her bed in the next room, or kneeling at the house altar to whisper her prayers, or descending the stairs in the morning. He had loved her, perhaps he still loved her, and he regretted now that he hadn't told her so more often. Yet he *had* said it often: when she reprimanded a pupil and then led him to the door with a few words of warning at the end of a lesson, he sometimes stood by the door and told her, quite softly, before she raised the piano stool higher for the next pupil; or when she showed him a deed for a field she had purchased over near the water tower (although she showed him only every third or fourth acquisition, he knew that), he pressed her hand and whispered it; or on Saturday evening when she put on her best dress and went with him to the movie at the Arena, or to the New World, or to the municipal theater, he repeated it. And when she came to his studio and looked at his new photographs and even praised him, he thought it.

There were so many opportunities to say this simple, beautiful, banal sentence to her, and he did not let them go by, but perhaps each time he meant only: "You're a marvel, Valeska!" She had shrugged it off, sometimes smiling, sometimes grateful, sometimes gracious, sometimes irritated, sometimes arrogant, sometimes peevish, sometimes she had simply brushed the sentence away. Later on he no longer had the courage to say it, and attempted to express it in other ways, for example, in the pauses which he now inserted into many sentences, in a gesture he prolonged, in a fit of coughing he repeated — but she did not understand this, from the very beginning she was caught up in trying to fill in the pauses in her own life, and the pauses in others' as well. She was so practical, so sensible, everything she turned her hand to had to turn out well, including marriage. He had to give up his job in the Ballestrem laboratory, and immediately after their marriage she fixed up a room for him as a photography studio and posted a sign outside:

ATELIER FOR

PHOTOGRAPHY

L. M. PIONTEK

She showed him off everywhere, for he had done well for her even if the business was poor to begin with. There were already enough photographers in town, and ever since the new Photomatons began making passport photos, the only photographs to be taken were of children at their first communion, once a year on the Sunday after Easter; a marriage now and then, a baby picture, a soldier newly called up, and busywork from his brother-in-law, the lawyer. Valeska made money from her piano lessons and some real estate deals about which she seldom enlightened him, and because he was bored staying indoors in the room so grandiosely called his "atelier," he began to take photographs outside: fortifications, ruins and towers, the towers of the town, of the outlying area, the towers of Oppeln, Beuthen, Ratibor, all of Upper Silesia, for many of these towers, especially in the countryside, had been left to decay, and in a few years or a few decades they would exist only in his photographs. The newspapers began to be interested in them, the *Voice of Upper Silesia* printed one tower photo by him each week, with a description of the site, the location, its condition. His work was praised by Karl Szodrok in the *Silesian Monthly,* and the Neumann printers even wanted to make a book out of it.

For this reason he was sometimes on the road for days, sometimes weeks, and once when he came home he discovered that in his absence Valeska had photographed the wedding couples, the children, and all the people who had come while he was away, and since she could not develop the plates herself, she had sent Josel with them to a photographer in Hindenburg who did not know her. When he saw that Valeska wanted to take his photographing away from him too, he had smashed the camera and locked himself in his "atelier" for three days. That was when his asthma began, and it grew worse and worse; it was later that his legs went bad.

He had long since stopped hating Valeska for this; he had been completely at fault, and she had simply not wanted to lose the customers. Later she bought him a new camera, which was still set up in the locked "atelier," obsolete and gathering dust. Once he had dragged himself on his knees to the "atelier" and imagined how he would photograph with it: yes, from now on he would photograph only outdoors, in nature, by natural light, the wedding couples too, the communion children and naturally all the towers, the castle towers and the church towers, the towers of the town and the water towers, the cooling towers and the pithead towers, the towers of the fortifications and the light towers, the control towers and the observation towers, the border towers and the watchtowers . . . Yet he had positioned himself in front of the camera and, setting the automatic shutter release, photographed himself again and again, for days, nothing but himself in the ridiculous hope of learning more about himself from these photos . . .

He pondered whether he should take up photography again. They could push him to his "atelier" in a wheelchair; he could continue to make notes on the towers; Josel could go with him and help him, at least during vacations. Things would go a little slower, but he could try it; he would just have to make Valeska understand.

He opened his eyes and regarded the unchanged image before him, somewhat flattened in the diffuse light: Valeska in her chair, leaning back, her head half bowed, her hands crossed in her lap, her body unmoving, frozen, as if it were not she, Valeska, and not this room, but only a photograph.

"You've fallen asleep, Valeska," Leo Maria said softly.

"Yes," Valeska said, this time after a long pause.

In the photograph nothing changed.

29

Even before Montag was fully awake, he had the feeling that someone was prowling around the garden cottage. The many nights he had spent in this room over the past months had made all its sounds familiar to him, so that any new, strange, or unfamiliar noise caught his ear at once. Above all when it was close by. Sounds from close by made him suspicious unless he had made them himself. But it was not yet clear to him what kind of a sound it was that had wakened him. It might have been only a gust of wind hitting the old pear tree and pressing a few branches against the house; that evening he had already sensed that there would be a change in the weather.

Montag lay on his bed, still in his dressing gown, listening toward the outside, waiting for the sounds and their repetitions. Now he clearly heard a rubbing along the house wall and a scratching at the door. Then the glass began to vibrate. So he knew that someone was touching the window.

Sounds of knocking. Sounds of dripping. The knocking grew more urgent but no louder; it sounded as if someone outside were tapping the windowpane with a fingertip, slowly and softly, as if to transmit secret signals.

"Herr Montag! Herr Montag!" he suddenly heard now. "Herr Montag, please, open the door!"

Montag recognized the voice, it belonged to Josel. It seemed to come from far away. At first he did not know whether it was because he was still half asleep that reality seemed at a distance, or whether his decision to respond from now on only to his inner world had put him at a distance from the sounds outside.

"It's me, Herr Montag, Josel Piontek!"

Montag could not tell whether it was the thick curtains that distorted the boy's voice, or whether it was so laden with fear that it produced hissing sounds: Ish me, Shoshel Pshonshek, at least that's what it sounded like.

Now he got up and groped his way to the window in the dark. He pushed the velvet curtain aside a little, he wanted to make sure that Josel was alone. It was dark outside, so dark that he could not make out anyone, only a black, vibrating spot. That might be him, Montag thought.

"I'm coming," he said softly, without considering whether the boy outside could even hear him. Montag pressed the switch of the table lamp, and the light leaped into the room so milky-white that at first he had to shade his eyes. Dazed, he turned and went to the entryway. As he turned the key in the lock, something occurred to him. He asked, "Are you alone, Josel?" And when he heard a sound from outside, so blurred and soft that he was not certain whether or not it was an affirmative reply, he turned the key a second time and opened the door. For him it was reassurance enough that he had answered at all.

Josel stumbled inside. He leaned against the wall of the entryway exhausted, as if he hadn't the strength to stand by himself. But perhaps there would not have been room in the narrow entryway to pass the old man. "Thank you," he said.

Montag locked the door again carefully. In the half-dark of the entryway—he had purposely left the light off—he looked into the boy's face, and the anguished expression he perceived even in the shadows kept him from asking any questions. He grasped Josel by the arm and drew him into the room, feeling how the boy was trembling underneath his jacket.

"Come in, Josel," he said, and tried to put as much trust and gentleness into his voice as his surprise and weariness would permit. "Come in and sit down. You're trembling, my boy." Montag led the boy, who seemed blinded by the lamp, to the green armchair and sat him down. He sat across from him on the edge of the bed and took a closer look. In his dark suit he was almost swallowed up by the dark green of the armchair, his huddled position intensifying the impression. Josel had turned his head aside because the light hurt his eyes, but perhaps also because he was afraid that what he had just done showed all too clearly on his face. Montag took a white cloth and hung it over the lampshade; the light bathed everything in a soft, silky glow which comforted them both.

They looked at each other now, silently, and felt their fear receding.

Josel, who only a few minutes before had believed he could not live through the night if he did not talk to someone about what had just happened to him—best of all to Montag, the old County Magistrate—all at once could not utter a single word. Not because he was so exhausted, he simply did not know how to explain everything or how to begin. And he may have hoped too that what had happened would turn out—in the presence of the old man, in the growing familiarity of the objects around him, in the slowly turning light and the exchange of their glances—to be nothing more than a heavy, deep, and ugly dream.

The silence seemed oppressive to Montag. And at the sight of the boy sitting there before him, his hair sweaty and untidy, his shirt open and the collar crumpled, deep fear on his face, he felt a wave of shared fear and sympathy break over him. And he knew he would never succeed in withdrawing entirely into his inner world.

As long as anyone asked a question, he would reply. So his first thought must be to forestall the questions. It was not enough to withhold himself from the world outside, he had to withstand its ever-renewed temptations. The boy had been no more than a temptation, and even this first one had been enough to destroy his laboriously constructed defenses. Maybe he had been sent as a test. He could go over to Josel now, take him by the hand, and lead him out. And he did step up to Josel and brush the matted hair with his hand, but then let it rest on his shoulder.

"Tell me about it, my boy. Can I help you?" He bent down to him. The smell of vomit was so strong that he went to the washstand, dampened a washcloth, and splashed some cologne on it. "Here," he said, "wipe your face."

The boy rubbed his face with the cloth, then his neck and hair; that refreshed him. And the pleasant smell reminded him that he was no longer at the square with the merry-go-round and no longer on the run. He gave the washcloth back to the old man, and when he felt his hand, he drew it quickly to his lips and kissed it.

Montag, confused by the boy's surge of emotion, quickly withdrew his hand. He went to the washstand, poured water into the basin, and put the washcloth in it. Then he massaged his own temples with cologne. He felt a burning on his hand.

"I killed someone," the boy said.

Montag turned around. He had already braced himself for something unpleasant, the outward signs pointed to it. But *that* he had not expected. The outside world had forced its way in to him, with all its complications. Everything else was illusion.

"I killed someone," the boy repeated defiantly, but softly. He was not certain what reaction to expect from others: amazement, a scream of horror, or silence.

"Does anyone know you're here?" Montag asked. He went to the cabinet, opened a drawer, and took out a pipe and a tobacco pouch. He had stopped smoking months ago.

"No," the boy said.

What Montag did now—open the pouch studiously and pack the pipe with care—was only an empty ritual with which he hoped to stave off the future. For if the three words Josel had hurled at him were actually true, he would have to wait and let the boy talk until he had come to the end of his story. Any question would only alter it.

He hummed a bit while lighting his pipe; the boy might take that as an expression of contentment, of disbelief, or as encouragement to keep talking.

The boy waited until the pipe was burning evenly (he too had been caught up in the lengthy ritual), then he slid forward to the very edge of his seat.

"I really did kill someone. I just smashed him over the head with a bottle, and he didn't move any more. My God, I didn't mean to do it." Josel looked into the old man's face, which was tinged by the yellow light and blue smoke. Since he could see no change in it, he continued to speak. "He was lying there, breathing hard, and then a shiver went through his whole body and he collapsed. The blood was running onto the ground from the back of his head. So I turned him over, his body was as heavy as a wet sandbag, I just wanted to turn his head around to see his face, but I couldn't, I would have twisted his head off, so I heaved his whole body over on its side, and I saw the blood running over his whole face. Only the whites of his eyes were showing."

Josel began to shiver, he could feel it in his neck and shoulders. His chin was trembling too, he had to clench his teeth. Yet it was quite stuffy in the room, almost hot. On this warm night the old man had not opened a single window.

At this moment Josel wanted most to break down and cry.

"Who was it?" Montag asked.

"Oh, the Sergeant." He said it as if it were common knowledge. Then he added, "Sergeant Metzmacher, who's quartered with us. You knew him, didn't you?" Montag struck another match and tried to relight his cold pipe; perhaps he had forgotten how to pack a pipe correctly, or the tobacco had become too damp in the cabinet. He only hoped his surprise had not been too obvious to the boy.

"I can tell you how it all happened." Josel said it not as a question, but as an introduction.

"Tell me about it, my boy, go ahead and tell me. Perhaps I can help you." Montag was ashamed of himself for saying such a stupid thing. It amounted to an admission of disbelief that this boy, yes, this fourteen-year-old, could have committed a murder, for how could he help him if he had?

The boy swallowed. "I'm telling this only to you, understand? Just you." His voice grew shrill. "I have to tell someone, you know . . . And then I'm getting out, *abtrimoo* . . . They'll never catch me, I'll just disappear from this *pierunje* place and never come back, never . . . to this cursed corner of the world . . ." And now the boy did begin to sob.

Montag slid his chair up closer to Josel. He laid one hand on his knee, and when the boy did not stop crying, he drew him to him and held him close until he had quieted down. Then he sent him to the wash basin. When the boy took off his jacket, he saw several blood spots on his right shirtsleeve.

"Take off your shirt," Montag said.

The boy hastened to do so. The old man's voice had never before been so stern.

Montag took the shirt and felt the spots. The blood had dried, but its color was still fresh. Montag sniffed it. It smelled sour. He dropped the shirt. It was as if only now, touching the soft red-black stains, had he grasped the meaning of the words Josel had uttered and repeated a little earlier.

"And you won't tell Mamuscha . . . that *afterwards*" (and he dwelled on the "afterwards," as if this really was the turning point of his life) "I came to you?"

"And if they catch you?"

"They won't get anything out of me," Josel said. His voice was firmer. He felt better now that he had taken off his shirt. He had been sick earlier, vomited up all that *schnapsik* and everything he had eaten that evening, and because he had no handkerchief with him, he had wiped his face with his shirt. Maybe it was that smell that had made him so weak and miserable, and soft.

"They won't get anything out of me, either!" Montag went to the cupboard and took out a shirt, and as if in confirmation of his words, gave it to the boy.

"Here, put this on. It'll be a little too big for you, you'll have to tuck it down into your trousers. With your jacket over it, no one will notice."

Both of them felt they were in the process of acquiring gestures and looks which were standard between fathers and sons.

"There, now sit down and begin at the very beginning." Montag said it matter-of-factly, as if he were asking what the boy had done at school that day.

And Josel forgot that he had to tell him about a murder he had committed only an hour ago.

"Could I have some more of that perfume?"

He liked the smell of it. You should always have something like that in your pocket, he thought.

Montag nodded. "Do you want a cigarette?" he asked. He had let his pipe go out. It hadn't tasted good. But if the boy had committed a . . . murder, then he could smoke a cigarette. Perhaps it would calm him. "Shall I roll you one?"

Montag took some cigarette papers out of a drawer and placed the little white sheet in the groove between his two fingers. He nodded encouragingly at Josel.

And the boy said, "I saw you in the hotel, at the reception. You were talking the whole time with Krawutschke. You left quite early, didn't you? . . . One man was so drunk that they tied him to a chair with his own suspenders, so he wouldn't fall over, he slept in a corner until they shoved him under a table . . . And Mamuscha wanted to take us home with her at twelve, but we wanted to dance another polka, Ulla and I, and Andreas as well . . ." He repeated the name again, as if wanting to call to mind a person he had known once, whom he had met a long time ago. "But Mamuscha nabbed Andreas and took him along. So I danced with Ulla until it was time for us to go too, but we didn't want to leave with the others; everyone was hoping one last thing would happen, an adventure or something. There wouldn't be any in the car, with Uncle Willi driving, we knew that. So Ulla and I went on foot, and in Bahnhofstrasse, not far from the hotel, we caught up with the Sergeant. Well, he was so drunk he could barely stand up."

Montag had rolled two cigarettes; he lit both and handed one to the boy. Josel took it and puffed on it; heat and a biting sharpness gathered in his mouth.

"So the three of us walked toward home together. The Sergeant was really staggering, then he braced himself and puked, just puked all over the place. We left him standing there, but then we went back after all, and held him on either side, we couldn't just leave him standing there, he would have collapsed in a heap somewhere and just lain there. Finally we came past the square where the merry-go-round is. The soldiers had gone, it was deserted, only the merry-go-round stood there at the edge, with its white horses, and a gypsy wagon . . ."

Josel swallowed some smoke and had to cough. He thought of Papusch and saw in his mind's eye how he raised himself up in bed, his face reddening, and Mamuscha waving the green sticks of incense in front of him . . . He put down the cigarette on a plate on the table. Suddenly he no longer knew why he was telling this story in such detail. After all, it had nothing to do with him any more. He had killed someone and had to get away from here, that was it. He said, "That's all, *wszystko jedno*: I killed him."

Montag interrupted: "No, you must be more precise — if you want me to help you!"

"Well, we each took one of the Sergeant's arms, Ulla and I," Josel continued, "and he was supporting himself on our shoulders. Naturally, we couldn't drag him all the way home like that. They sat down on the steps of the merry-go-round then, Ulla and the Sergeant, and he gave me his cap and said he had a burning thirst which he had to quench now, right now, and I was to go inside and get him some water, then he'd be all right and we could go on. The gypsy wagon next to the merry-go-round was dark, so I couldn't knock; I had to go over to the little allotment gardens on the other side, there were water pipes in the plots. Ulla told me to go ahead and do it. So I ran off with the cap in my hand, leaving the two of them sitting on the wooden steps.

"Here it comes, Herr Montag. When I came back holding the capful of water, being careful not to spill any, I saw them there, lying in the grass next to the merry-go-round. I was so scared I dropped the cap: the Sergeant was lying on top of Ulla, he had one hand clamped over her mouth, and down below he had torn everything off her. I think I said something then, I don't remember what, but it was pretty loud, maybe I even screamed . . . but the Sergeant didn't hear me, and Ulla didn't either. Then I saw a bottle lying in the gutter, so I picked it up and smashed the drunken swine over the head with it."

He paused.

And Montag said musingly, out of the blue: "A stone, a leaf, an unfound door."

These words seemed to settle like balm on the boy's excitement. Josel paused and then went on: "Well, I hit him over the head with it, and he slumped. Ulla crawled out from under him, she pushed his body away, but not even enough to tip his face on its side. Ulla didn't say anything. She wasn't screaming, she didn't even look at his head, where the blood was running down."

They had both stood there as if petrified, they did not have the courage to touch each other, they waited for something to happen, anything: for the Sergeant to roll over and stand up and walk away, for somebody or other to come over to them from the street and start screaming terribly, for the lights of the merry-go-round to come on all at once, yes, even for it to start turning, faster and faster and faster, to the tooting of the old calliope, but nothing happened.

"And you know what she said then, Herr Montag? She said: 'Run for it, run for home. If they find out, you've had it— a sergeant, that's no joke these days.' That's what she said! Everything began to spin inside my head, up here, like the horses on the merry-go-round. Do you understand, Herr Magistrate, he was trying to do something to her, the Sergeant, and I, I saved her, and then she said *that* to me! I think she didn't understand at all what was going on! Suddenly a light came from somewhere, probably from the gypsy wagon on the square, and Ulla ran away. I turned the Sergeant over then, because I wanted to see his face. And I've already told you how the whites of his eyes frightened me. Then I thought: Go, get out of here! I ran after Ulla, but it was as if the night had swallowed her up, I looked for her, I went past her house, it was all dark . . . And now I keep thinking that when they find him, the Sergeant, they'll come here, after all, there are fingerprints on the pieces of the bottle, so I'm trapped . . ."

A mild excitement came over Montag. He knew the whole story now, and he did not doubt that it had been told exactly as it happened. He would have liked to interrupt a few times during the account, but he knew that, although he could interrupt the story, he could not interrupt reality. "Nonsense," he said. "You're talking through your hat! How old are you, Josel?"

"Fifteen," Josel said.

"So you're still a child! A fifteen-year-old child doesn't kill a grown man by hitting him with a bottle. You *tuleja!*"

"But I did!" the boy insisted.

"I don't believe the Sergeant is dead. He was so drunk he simply couldn't get up again; maybe he has a concussion, that's all."

He knew how feeble these sentences sounded. But he could not tell the boy what was already going through his head: what extenuating circumstances might be brought forth in the case.

"Herr Montag!" Josel stood up. "You haven't taken in what I've been telling you. I didn't make it up out of thin air. A murder has taken place. It's only a coincidence that I was involved in it. But I was. That's why I'm getting out of here."

Montag realized he would have to change his tactics. He looked at the boy, who was now leaning against the table, and saw how good-looking he was. His face had grown no older, but perhaps a little harder, firmer, more masculine; it no longer showed any fear or any confusion, as it had before when he began his story.

"I do not believe that the Sergeant is dead. But all right, Josel, let's not belabor the point. No one will hit upon the possibility of it having been you. Besides, you didn't pass anyone on the way home, or did you? And Ulla won't breathe a word . . . You say he's lying on the square where the merry-go-round is. Anyone could have killed him there."

While saying this, Montag felt himself being entangled in a false and unworthy chain of reasoning. He stopped. He fell silent.

"That's another reason I came to you, Herr Montag. If they suspect one of the people at the merry-go-round, then you have to go to them and tell them it was me . . . I'll be gone by then anyway."

Montag felt himself put to shame. He should have known that the boy could only react in that way. The best thing would be for both of them to go to the square and take a look at the Sergeant, in case he was still there; maybe he wasn't dead at all. We can't just leave him lying there. But he did not dare utter the thought, for that would not only mean new complications with the outside world, but would put both the boy and himself in jeopardy. Only now had he become aware that with every sentence he was sinking deeper and deeper into complicity.

"Perhaps there will be a war soon, anyway, everybody's talking about it," said the boy. He tugged at the collar of his shirt, which was too big and had slid beneath his jacket collar.

Montag moved to the table, beside the boy. "Get away from the war," he said. "Go to Breslau or to Berlin, go to the West." And in a different, reproving voice, the artificiality of which was immediately evident, he said, "What in the world will I tell your mother, when she comes here and asks about you? — and she'll go to every-one and ask about you! It'll be easy enough for the others to comfort her, for they don't know anything, but what will I say to her? You just want to leave here, you don't realize that it could mean the death of your father who is so ill . . ."

That was Montag's final verbal offering. He did not want to have to reproach himself later on for having failed to mention this.

But Josel did not let it sway him. It seemed as if the boy had considered all that on the way home from the merry-go-round.

"You don't need to tell Papusch anything about it, yes, I'm even asking you to keep quiet. Nobody will find out that I've been here. I'll simply be gone. Gone. I'll write sometime or other along the way, naturally. After all, they just want to know that I'm alive. Mamuscha has so much to do with her piano lessons and her property that she won't miss me at all."

His child's face seemed much older to Montag now.

"Do you have any money?" he asked.

The boy shook his head.

Montag opened another drawer and fished around for a bill: "Take that. Get on a train. That will take you as far as Breslau. Or Berlin. There are so many people there, no one will ask any ques-tions. Get some kind of job, you won't attract attention. And then write home, understand!"

Montag pushed the money across the table toward the boy; he was averse to putting it directly into his hand. Suddenly he felt a painful pounding in his temples, and he had the sensation of losing a part of his strength with each blow. The light began to revolve slowly. He wished that Josel was already out of the house.

Josel put the money in his pocket. "You're a good man, Herr Montag." And he wanted to take his hand again and kiss it, but Montag had already stuck both his hands in the pockets of his dressing gown.

"And you're not a Jew either, are you?" Josel asked.

Montag felt a blow on the head. The light was turning faster now. He held fast to the edge of the table with both hands. It was some time before he could speak, longer before he could move his hands, his head, his limbs, even longer before he could manage a painful smile.

"What makes you ask that?" he asked the boy.

"I've always said, old Montag is no Jew. Ulla heard it somewhere or other, I don't know where. She said that's why you sent your daughter to Paris and hid here in the garden cottage." He looked at the old man, who had squeezed his eyes shut in a grimace.

"When Mamuscha heard her she got really angry and said we mustn't talk about it and that none of it was true, and that she'd known the County Magistrate for many years . . ."

Josel bent down and picked up his soiled shirt. He rolled it up.

"Well, I knew it wasn't true. Thank you for the money. I'll pay you back."

It was time for him to go.

Now they both fell silent.

The old man, because he was still quite numb.

The boy, because he was listening for sounds outside.

A shot exploded far away in this silence.

I haven't told him everything, the boy thought.

I should tell him everything now, the old man thought.

Neither said anything.

I wish I were already out of the region, the boy thought.

I shouldn't have let him in, the old man thought.

Passing the house once more, that's the hardest part. I'd better cut across the stubble field in the back. I'll go first and get the money I hid in the flowerpot.

When he's gone, I'll nail shut the windows and the door from the inside, the old man thought.

"I think I'll be going now," the boy said. He went to the window, pushed aside the curtain, and pressed his face against the pane. It was still dark outside. It would soon be dawn, but he wanted to be at the railroad station by then.

"Yes," Montag said.

"I'll take the shirt with me, I'll throw it into the Klodka on the way," the boy said, but he still did not turn to go. When the door shuts behind me, the boy thought, something will have disappeared, gone forever. Something or other, he knew, would be over when he left the room here, the house, the garden. "And when you see Ulla . . ." he paused, and in this pause he took his first step toward the door — "tell her I'll go to Warsaw some day and touch Chopin's heart . . . Oh, it's better not to tell her anything at all."

They went through the passage, past so much stone and dried-up expectations. As Montag was reaching for the door handle, he hesitated once more. He heard his own voice say: "Come, let's pray for you!" He placed his hand on the boy's hair and said, "A stone, a leaf, an unfound door." Then he turned the key twice.

The old man and the boy were standing close together in the passage, each of their movements resulted in physical contact in the narrow space, the sounds they made were amazingly loud. Josel took out of his pocket a small white ball he had carried around with him all day, and had actually wanted to give to Ulla. "Here, take this," he whispered. "It's a Japanese paper flower, if you put it in water, it will open like magic . . . When I'm in Breslau or Berlin, I'll send you another by mail, as a sign that everything is *poschundek.*"

Josel opened the door himself and went out, without looking back again. He went a step farther, then was swallowed in darkness.

He had grown older that night, but not yet old enough. Suddenly he knew that he had left his childhood behind him, and he turned around quickly, as if he could sum it all up in one glance and take leave of it, but it had disintegrated into a thousand particles of mourning, melancholy, pain, and gloom. He climbed the fence and walked across the harvested wheat field, the stubble crunching under his shoes.

Montag stood in the doorway, listening into the night. The monotonous sound of a motor could be heard in the distance, otherwise nothing. He stepped outside. Far off in the Polish sky it looked as if someone were beginning to paint gray lines on the dark horizon with a broad brush. From there soft detonations could be heard; it was like a gentle thunder, rolling along on quiet wheels.

Montag went back into the house and locked the door with two turns of the key. He felt the paper flower in his hand. A stone, a leaf, an unfound door; of a stone, a leaf, a door.

30

OUTSIDE SOMEONE WAS drumming on the front door. The photograph was destroyed. Valeska and Leo Maria started. "Open up! Military police! Open up!" A strange, sharp voice from below. Valeska jumped up from her chair, rushed to the window, and jerked down the blackout curtain: Who's there? The door is open, our door is always open, why all this racket in the middle of the night? But she said all that only to herself, she sat there in her chair and did not move, the sharp voice from outside hurt her ears. "Military police! Open up!"

Then a shot rang out on the other side, in the garden, a dry bang, entirely without echo. In that instant a scream broke out which had been locked in Valeska's throat since the first loud noise. She left the door open and ran down the stairs, and as she ran, she screamed: "Don't shoot! *Bosche kochane!* Don't shoot! What's the matter?" Until she reached the bottom and tore open the front door.

A soldier stood before her, she could make out in the gray dawn a gray German Wehrmacht uniform, on which nothing caught the eye but the broad, gleaming, gray metal chain across the chest. He lowered his pistol.

"Are a Sergeant Metzmacher and a Private Birkner quartered in your house?" asked the soldier, and his voice was perfectly calm. Outside, noises were coming from the back of the garden; they sounded like the blows of an axe.

"What's going on?" Valeska asked, and she felt her excitement growing, it was mixed with fear too, but she would not admit that. She wanted to go out into the garden, but the man in the uniform blocked her way.

"Don't be afraid," the soldier said. "Sergeant Metzmacher and Private Birkner did not report to their units by midnight. We've been detailed to bring them in." And as Valeska stared at him dumbfounded, still not grasping any of this and only registering the sound in the garden, he added: "That is all."

"But why this racket in the middle of the night? My husband is gravely ill upstairs!" Valeska felt how powerless her voice was, not only because the sky was pouring out a gray, mollusk-colored light (they had not even noticed upstairs, behind the blackout curtain, that the night was drawing to a close), but also because she was still standing there, before the door of her own house, while noises were coming from her garden that frightened her. It sounded as if someone were trying to break into the garden cottage by force. "The Sergeant is quartered here, that's correct," she said, in a voice that was not so sure of the assertion.

"Take me to him!" the soldier barked, stern now, and the tone of his voice made it unmistakably clear to Valeska that this was an order. She resisted, if only feebly: "What's going on? That's my garden cottage!" she said.

"Later!" said the soldier. As tersely as that.

Valeska went up the stairs slowly, not so slowly as to attract attention. In her head she prepared a few sentences to say to the soldier if the Sergeant did not happen to be in his room, which she already anticipated. "Private Birkner," she said, "you must surely have known" (she looked around), "married my daughter Irma yesterday, and had three days' special leave because of it." She turned around and stopped on the stairs. "Surely you must have known that!"

To judge by the sounds reaching her, someone was now breaking into the garden cottage.

Valeska went on: "And the Sergeant was there, at the wedding reception, he was even a witness to the marriage ... But I don't know when he got back, I left earlier, I have a husband who's ill." Valeska spoke loudly, perhaps because all the sounds were so loud now, or because she wanted the whole house, everybody in their rooms, behind their doors, to hear her, perhaps also because she wanted to show that she was not afraid.

Frau Hupka stood at the door to her room listening, her children were sound asleep; since she could not find a key to lock herself in her room, she pushed the door handle upward, determined to let no one into the room. Lucie (Lanolin) clutched her blind son to her; no matter what happened, she would let no one separate them. Halina crept even further under the covers, she would not come out unless the *Pani* called her. Andreas was less surprised by the noise that had wakened him than by the fact that Josel's bed was still empty. He got up, pulled on his pants, and carefully stuck his head into the hall.

Valeska knocked at the Sergeant's door but did not wait for an answer; she turned the handle at once and switched on the light inside. Even before the light flared on, she could tell by the smell that the Sergeant's bed was empty. At that instant the thought struck her like a blow that Josel's bed might be empty too. She leaned against the door jamb and let the soldier past. "He's not there," she said. She meant Josel.

She crossed to the other side of the hall, where Andreas was peeking out, and asked in a voice that immediately betrayed her suppressed skepticism: "Is Josel there?" She did not wait for an answer, the "No" was written too plainly on Andreas's face. Valeska went back.

"Well, where did you say the Sergeant and the Private were supposed to have been?" The soldier spoke in the same calm voice as before.

"At the Hotel Upper Silesia, that's the biggest hotel in town, right on the main street, I could take you there . . . We celebrated the wedding there, the whole night in the big ballroom . . . Only I left earlier because of my husband." Valeska was stuttering, but only because a question kept intruding stubbornly into her thoughts which no one could answer now: Where is Josel? She went down the stairs with the soldier, out the door, around the house, into the garden.

"Heiko got special leave for the wedding, three days, he said so, and for a wedding they do give you special leave, don't they?" she asked along the way. "You don't think he'd . . ." Valeska left it unsaid. And the soldier did not say what he thought.

They were standing in front of the garden cottage, the door of which was broken open; the yellow light from the passage fell outside at a slant. The pigeons, which had flown up before when they heard the shot, were coming back, cooing excitedly. The trees were filling with gray light and edging closer. Two soldiers stepped out the door of the garden cottage, each of them— Valeska noticed it at once—wearing a gray metal chain on his uniform; they whispered to each other. A dreadful suspicion arose in Valeska's mind: that shot earlier, that was the soldiers, they've killed him, the County Magistrate. She wanted to go into the garden cottage through the shattered door, but the two men in uniform blocked her way.

"You knew that man?" the soldier asked.

Valeska moved back a step. Now she knew for certain they had killed him. "Why did you do it?" she asked.

The soldiers exchanged glances. "The man shot himself," one soldier said quietly. "We heard a shot when we were knocking at your front door, then we came back here." And the other soldier said, "Look, we didn't know there was a garden cottage here."

"No, no, no, no," Valeska stammered. "Let me in there." And when none of them budged: "Please, let me go in! I just want to see him. Is he really dead?"

"Yes, he's dead," the soldier said. "Who was this man?"

"He was my tenant, County Magistrate Montag, retired," Valeska said. "Everyone around here knew him, a harmless old pensioner . . . But why did you do it?" It was not a conscious refusal to believe in his suicide; such an act was so far beyond her grasp that she wouldn't have believed it if she had seen it happen.

One of the soldiers was getting angry. He grabbed Valeska's arm roughly and shoved her through the door. "Here, see for yourself," he said. He pushed her through the passage into the room, but did not let go of her.

Valeska did not scream, she did not tremble, nor was she any longer afraid. Real death left her numb and helpless . . . The body of the Magistrate, in a brown dressing gown, lay stretched out between the table laden with books and papers and the window. She saw a ripped-open, bloody head without a face, the hand next to it holding a pistol. His glasses were lying on the table, intact, as if he had taken them off first. Valeska did not even bend forward, although the light sketched this scene quite dimly; she could stand there that way for a long time, for a very long time, and she would not move so much as a centimeter. Was it from a wish to be dead herself and lying there like him?

They led Valeska back out of the garden cottage. "Thank you," she said, "I'll be all right." She returned to her house more slowly than anyone could have walked.

The soldier she had first seen called after her that no one was to leave the house or to enter the cottage until the police arrived, but she was scarcely listening.

"My son Josel," Valeska said tonelessly, "hasn't come home from the wedding reception . . . He's just fifteen."

"We're driving to the hotel now," one of the soldiers said, and jammed one of the ripped-out boards into the doorway. "If the Sergeant or the Private come here, they are to report to their units immediately, tell them that's an order!"

"Take me with you," Valeska said. "Maybe they're all still at the hotel, maybe they're still dancing . . ." She said it very softly because she knew very well that this hope too would be shattered with the rising sun.

"We haven't got room." The soldiers laughed, they climbed onto a motorcycle that had been parked, hidden, down the street, gunned the motor and rode away, waving. If it had not been for the smashed-in door of the garden cottage and this unfamiliar, blunt, watery light, she might have believed that nothing had happened; she had just come home late, very late, from the reception. But there was this crazy light. She could not remember since her childhood having been outside under the sky so early in the morning.

She walked into the house and went up the stairs, slowly. Every step took a piece of life from her, and she was afraid that her store of life would be exhausted before she reached Leo Maria's room. She sat down on a step and took Andreas, who had come from his room and silently pressed against her, into her arms, clutching at him as if she wanted to hold tight to something which had been lost to her today.

"Joselek, my Joselek," Valeska whispered.

And after an endless interval: "Joselek, my Joselek."

31

LEO MARIA'S COUGHING suddenly rang through the entire house. Valeska pushed away Andreas's arms and stood up. It was good that something had reminded her of her duty, or even simply that other people were living on behind their doors. The light from outside penetrated all the cracks and painted odd geometric figures on the walls. Only now did Valeska realize how poorly the windows had been blacked out. She raised the curtains and was glad to see the light tumbling in and filling the space, objects regaining their plasticity, colors their luminosity, and when she went up the stairs, she could hold on to the steady railing, which before had seemed as two-dimensional as a drawing.

In her haste she had left Leo Maria's door half open. She could see him now from the hall, sitting upright in bed, the pillow stuffed behind his back and the coughing quaking inside his body. First Valeska let the light in here too, to rinse away what had accumulated in the room from the night and from themselves. Then she went in to Leo Maria and laid her hand on his forehead to check his fever (he had none), but also to give him an illusion of warmth and composure. She let her hand rest on his forehead until she felt sweat beneath it. A few times the sick man could get no air, and his body was convulsed, his face growing red and distorted; she could already tell he was suffering a particularly severe coughing attack. In his hand he was holding a glass into which he spat whenever the coughing eased. Valeska saw a layer of red foam on top; so he was spitting blood again. She took some gauze from the nightstand and wiped his sweaty face with it. She closed the window, took the copper saucer from the nightstand, and lit a stick of green incense. She added three more to it, placing them so close together that they would ignite each other after a while; she sprinkled a few grains of incense on them and watched the smoke curl slowly up. She did all this with such care and concentration that it might have been the only thing in the world that mattered to her. She herself had become unimportant, as had the dead Herr Montag, Josel was the only one who mattered— but where was Josel?

Valeska waved the saucer in front of Leo Maria's face, blowing on it to make the smoke thicker. Leo Maria inhaled with a strange whistle, and every exhalation was accompanied by a light groan. She had the feeling that underneath it all a new attack of coughing was building up, and she wondered whether she should call the doctor, perhaps even the Archpriest.

Leo Maria slid deeper into the pillows; exhausted, he handed her his glass of sputum. His breathing grew calmer, his body relaxed, his face smoothed out slowly beneath the veil of green smoke, his eyes grew larger and regained some of their deep brownness. Perhaps they would soon fill with green smoke.

Leo Maria was breathing heavily as if there were not enough air in the room, and he was holding on to Valeska's hand so tightly that his warmth was transmitted to her.

"Are you feeling better?" Valeska asked anxiously.

"Yes, I'm feeling better." He spoke softly, but his voice sounded different, as if from now on he would never be able to speak loudly again.

Halina was standing in the doorway, her sleepy eyes still half-closed; since she had not combed her hair, she had simply put on a white kerchief. She leaned against the door jamb, as if needing it for support.

"Oh, Halina," Valeska said, "you're up already. *Bosche,* what time is it?" No one gave her an answer. "Well, take this glass away, and this time put in two spoonfuls of that disinfectant stuff." Valeska thought of getting up and pulling down the blackout curtain, to keep the light from intruding. Maybe the harsh light was to blame for her headache.

"What was going on out there?" Leo Maria asked.

Valeska wafted the saucer back and forth in front of his face, as if that might prevent him from asking about the shot. "Some soldiers came," she said. "They were looking for the Sergeant because he didn't report to his unit last night. It's probably regulations."

"What did they do with him?" Leo Maria always tried to slip his words between two breaths, then they cost him practically no air.

"Nothing. He hasn't come back yet from the reception. They're looking for him at the hotel now."

Halina brought back the glass.

"Come, help me change his things," Valeska said. She put the incense burner on the nightstand and took a fresh shirt from the cupboard. Then the two women began to rub down the sweaty, emaciated white body with towels.

Leo Maria was visibly better. With his body toweled dry, covered in a fresh nightshirt still smelling of starch and eau de Cologne, he was calmer, his lungs growing more and more numb from the green smoke. Now he might be interested again in the shot, and the violent events in the garden cottage. He had heard the sounds from up here, even though his window faced the other side, the street side.

"Halina, go and see what time it is," Valeska said. "It's quite light outside, but *muj Bosche,* I don't know when it gets light this time of year." She did not want to go to the window and look out to see whether the sun had risen, she was afraid of the broad white horizon. She would rather sit here in the room and let the green smoke spin a cocoon around her. Valeska sprinkled some more grains of incense onto the saucer.

"Maybe they came because it's about to break out," Leo Maria said.

"What's about to break out?" Valeska asked.

"The war," Leo Maria said.

Valeska had stopped thinking about the war, at the moment she had no clear notion of what a war could be. Now she would have to tell Leo Maria that the County Magistrate was lying stretched out on the floor of the garden cottage, between the table and the window, without any face. In his silk dressing gown, which he always wore while sitting at the table and writing. So he must have been writing something beforehand, perhaps a will or a note of farewell, yes, he would certainly have done that, he was always so *precise.*

Valeska thought of removing the board from the door and going into the cottage; who would be able to tell whether anyone had been in there in the meantime? She could look around on the table where so many papers, newspapers, and books had been lying, along with his glasses. To be sure, she would never muster the courage to enter the cottage alone; no one likes being alone with the dead. But she would go in with her brother, yes, she could call him, he would find a taxi somehow, or perhaps he was still driving around in the Sergeant's car. At about six o'clock she could call him, or half-past six, if the police hadn't come by then.

Yes, and that Josel hadn't come home yet, she would have to tell Leo Maria that too, unless Josel suddenly came storming up the stairs.

"I wonder what's keeping Halina?" Valeska said.

It was now fully light in the room. Valeska switched off the lamp on the nightstand, in whose pale light the drifts of green smoke had collected.

"I'll see where Halina is," Valeska said. "I'll be right back. Maybe you should try to go to sleep now." She put her hand on his forehead; it felt quite hot now.

Valeska wanted to go find Halina, and Josel too; she wanted to see whether the Sergeant was there, or the police, whom the soldiers were going to send. She found Halina by the clock in the living room, between the works of the clock and the open glass door, turning the hands. And every time the bell would have to sound, at the hour or the half-hour, she held on to the pendulum so that the strokes would not chime throughout the house. Halina jumped when Valeska's reflection appeared in the glass; she did not turn around. "The clock stopped," she said.

"Isn't Josel back yet?" Valeska asked.

"No," Halina said. *"Andrzej mówi, że nie może zasnąć, nie chce być sam w pokoju."* (Andreas says he can't fall asleep, he doesn't want to be alone in the room.)

"Maybe I should go into town and look for Josel, what do you think, Halina?"

Halina knew that this was an invitation for her to go into town and look for Josel. *"Dobra,"* she said, *"wyciągnę rower i jadę do hotelu."* (Good, I'll take the bicycle and ride to the hotel.)

Valeska shook her head. She would have liked to send Halina

into town, but if anyone stopped her, with her poor German she might even be suspected of being Polish, or of being a spy, there was talk about spying everywhere. No, she would telephone, later. Valeska studied her image in the clock glass, and she thought that the braid hanging over her shoulder made her look funny, even grotesque. She had never seen herself before in this way. It did not matter that the braid made her look older, she didn't mind; it made a laughingstock of her. Valeska dashed into the washroom and there, in front of the mirror, simply cut off the braid, just at the nape of her neck, and combed the short hair into place with her fingertips.

"It's already half-past four," Valeska said as she cast a passing glance at the clock Halina was still winding. Tomorrow she would go to the hairdresser, who would cut her hair more carefully and might even wave it with a curling iron, as was the fashion nowadays. Why shouldn't she do it, Hanna Sedlaczek had appeared with a permanent wave recently, and she had six children! Her children had demanded it of her, she said, you just have to keep up with the times. By now Valeska no longer knew why she had cut off the braid, but she had done it, and so it must have been the right thing to do.

Halina shut the door of the clock again and watched the golden pendulum swing back and forth, quite regularly, from left to right. The ticking followed Valeska on her way to Leo Maria's room, and it could still be heard there, so that Valeska asked herself whether it would not have been better for Halina to have left the clock unwound.

"It's half-past four, Leo Maria, you should try to get some sleep," Valeska said in an empty, expressionless voice.

Leo Maria nodded slowly; he was glad enough that she hadn't asked him again whether he was feeling better. He took her hand and held it tightly in his own, and he knew that it was not just her hand that belonged to him, Valeska belonged to him, as much as any human being could belong to another. This feeling relieved his coughing a little, indeed, he could probably not have endured the sickbed and the frequent attacks of asthma if he had not remained aware that they served to bind Valeska still more firmly to him. His skin tightened; he shivered. He pulled the blanket up to his chin without letting go of her hand.

In his thoughts, Leo Maria traversed the old paths, the path to school along Hüttenstrasse, the path to the Concordia mine, the path to Przeschlebie to the artificial lakes, or the path down to the river. He had traveled these paths a thousand times, he knew where the holes and the puddles were, the stones and the cracks, where the tar first melted in the sun; he had learned it all through the soles of his feet, for from early spring to late autumn he had walked them barefoot. He could still remember in exactly which streets there were cherry trees, or apple or pear or rowan-berry trees. He liked best the path down to the river, which was neither tarred nor paved, on which water stood in the early spring and dust crunched under his feet in summer. There were still many roads then that were nothing more than a set of ruts worn over the centuries by peasant carts. Only later did the roadbuilders come from the Reich and enjoy their gold rush with Prussian state funds, for after the Kaiser got stuck in the mud on his way to visit Prince von Pless, a large sum in the Prussian budget was allotted to roadbuilding in Upper Silesia. At the same time there was a new Prussian regulation to the effect that fruit trees must be planted along the new roads, perhaps to provide the poor and somewhat undernourished populace with fruit. But since no one tended or fertilized these trees, they produced scant fruit, and it did not pay to pick it since the peasants could not sell it in the market, and anyway, the poor people stole fruit from the less accessible orchards of the big estates, where the takings were far more rewarding.

This path to the river was lined with old linden trees, which (according to the Prussian regulation) were quite useless; they only exuded a fragrance that was so sweet, so strong, so sensuous, so seductive, that Leo Maria sometimes climbed up to the top of a tree and let himself be enveloped and overcome by the fragrance. On the road to Myslowitz there was a flaming sea of poppies, there were apple trees on the Kattowitz road, and on the road to Königshütte was the sparkling golden flax on the left and the green storm of spring barley on the right. He loved these paths of his childhood, and still knew his way among them better than he knew the faces of his own children.

So they had danced, they had even danced the polka, that had been the right thing to do, even if Josel was still a little young; who knows how long they will be able to dance. In the newspaper today he had read that in view of the grave situation the government was considering prohibiting all "amusements," at least for the time being. It was good that Irma had pushed so hard for the marriage; if she had listened to Valeska, it might have been too late. Why hadn't he gone along to the reception, nothing worse could have happened to him than the coughing attack he'd had earlier, and he could have watched the others one more time, dancing and having fun!

He put his hand on his chest and poked at it, he felt a prickling there and was afraid the urge to cough would begin anew and bring on another attack, and perhaps he only did so to prove to himself that having fun was not what mattered now. In fact, no one had wanted him there, he was only a burden in his precarious state; Valeska had not wanted him there, even though she talked about it, she knew it would be too tiring and too much bother. From his side of the family they had invited only his sister Rosalka and her husband, who lived in the Ruhr, and his sister Milka, and her only because he had been able to convince Valeska that this would be the best possible time to effect a reconciliation. Rosalka had not come. She had sent a telegram that afternoon from Berlin, so they had gotten that far, but it had seemed hopeless to try to reach Gleiwitz in time; all the trains were delayed and many were being canceled because of troop movements, and the farther east they came, the worse things got.

Valeska had invited the people in whose circles she moved now. The president of the waterworks, who, as he learned from Milka, was not the president at all but simply an ordinary director transferred here from the Reich, and not even Catholic; and Count Poremba, who was involved in questionable compensation cases, and gossip had it that he was neither a count nor had he owned property across the border; and Nowak from the roadbuilding firm; and Polensky of Polensky & Michalek; and the Archpriest and Przygoda the property owner, with whom her brother had business dealings which she had her finger in too. It was probably better that he had not been there. She had always made decisions for him and had gradually robbed him of all volition, but perhaps it had always been that way, and she had only done something that in essence he expected her to do.

In his family the women had always decided what was to be done. His mother had borne five daughters, and the sixth child was Leo Maria, the only son. After that she wanted no more children. With these five daughters she oppressed her husband and her growing son, and all the money was spent on the girls. Leo Maria had to wear his father's shirts and suits, shortened and taken in for him; his mother would have even liked to dress him in girls' things, to keep from buying him any new clothes. They could all *wish* for a present at Christmas or on their birthday, but she determined what useful things he and his father needed. He was sent to secondary school when he did not want to go at all, and then taken out when the money grew short, just as he had come to like it and wanted to work toward a certificate. Then he wanted to learn photography, but his mother had placed him as an apprentice in Ballestrem's laboratory; that was a career with a future, she had said, since so many products were being made from coal now. And then, when he married Valeska, he all at once had to be a photographer, because he had always wanted that for himself. He admired his sister Milka; she had always done whatever she wanted. She went to the conservatory to study voice, and when her voice gave out, she became the mistress of a singer, and later an usherette in a movie theater in Neisse, and after that she rolled cigars. At least those were always her own decisions, while he was constantly being pressured into things. His father had been no different. As long as he could remember, his father had talked to him about his plan of leaving the "whole hen house," as he called it, and traveling with only him to the West—to the Ruhr, where his sister and brother-in-law had settled, where people earn more money, the cities are bigger, the churches taller, and the winters warmer—but something or other had always interfered. And finally his mother fell ill, she had cancer, and his father

knew that she would die soon. So he went into the forest with his
son one day,

    where we were completely alone, and he showed me
the money he had saved secretly, sewn into the lining of his jacket,
it would be just enough for two tickets to Cologne, one full and
one half fare; he had checked on the fares at the station. He would
cut my hair short, and I was not to stand up during the journey,
that would fool the conductors, a trip to Cologne for each of us,
only one way, for it was clear he would never return, and we could
walk the rest of the way to Bottrop, where his brother-in-law
lived, it wasn't that far. His mother was tortured by illness for two
more years, but one day she sent the doctor away, got out of bed,
and began working in the kitchen and the garden, she read the
newspapers and was interested again in what was going on in the
world, she was happy that young Korfanty had won the election
and would become a member of the German Reichstag, which
was a much talked-about sensation — not an aristocrat, no, he was
the son of a poor cottager from Zawadze near Königshütte, practically next door, who had been elected by his own Upper Silesians in his first campaign, by a large majority. Mama went to
church and had a mass said for a free Upper Silesia, and his father
was in despair, because he had voted against Korfanty, and on
Sunday, he said, he would go to the railroad station with me and
simply get on a train, go first to Kattowitz and then farther,
anywhere. But before that, Mama went back to bed and said quite
simply to send for the *Pfarrosch,* she was ready to die now; there
was no one at home except father and me, I had just come home
from school, and my father said to me, "Sit still there and don't
cry," and I listened to her breathing and thought, as long as she is
breathing, she can't be dead, but I no longer know whether it was
her breathing, or my breathing, or my father's breathing that I
was hearing.

  My father stood up, took a hand mirror from his jacket pocket,
and held it in front of my mother's mouth. He bent down, a faint
sigh could be heard. "Lord, Thy will be done," my father said, "I
think the priest is too late." I knew then that something terrible
had happened, I tried to keep it away from me, I played dead.

Then my father went to the window, parted the curtains and opened them, then he draped a sheet over the wall mirror and stopped the pendulum of the clock. He did all this very slowly, as if there were some impediment between the commands of his brain and their execution by his limbs. Mama was dead. She had simply stopped breathing and was dead. I couldn't grasp it, I had imagined it so differently, much louder, more agitated, more dramatic; there was no screaming, no groaning, no whispering, there were no last words, not even a sigh—that had come from him. She was his wife, after all. And I had come in from outside, the sun still in my face, and the smell of wild barley on my skin.

The light flooded in and drowned everything in a diffuse gray-white light, without contours; only her head stood out waxen and vivid on the pillow. Father broke a few green sprigs from the myrtle in the window box and scattered them on her relaxed, bony yellow face. "Come, Leo," he said to me, "place this on her eyes," and I closed her eyelids and filled the hollows with evergreen myrtle. "Look at her once more, your mother! Let us treasure this picture." From the pillow he took the handkerchief she must have used to wipe the sweat from her face for the last time, and laid it over her face.

My father looked at me. "It's good that you've cured yourself early of crying, you see, I'm not crying either! Otherwise, in this region you'd always be crying. Crying is something for women. Wait here in the kitchen," my father said, and packed a loaf of bread in the white tin box. "The priest will be here any minute. I have to hurry, a quarter of an hour late and the last car will already be gone down the shaft, they'll dock me for the shift, and we really need the money now." As soon as he had gone, I heard the tinkling of the little bell which the acolyte swings constantly when he is on the way with the priest to perform the last rites for someone dying. The bell came closer and closer, and now I did begin to cry . . .

The next day my father took his jacket from the cupboard and slit a seam of the lining with a razor blade. With the money he bought the cheapest coffin he could, but he had mountains of gladiola heaped upon it, the salmon-colored gladiola she had loved, and at her head pale violet ones, it was August when she died, and gladiola were blooming in gardens everywhere and were not expensive. She had been well liked, Frau Piontek, and people came from all over, they had to be served a schnapps, at least, and some food as well, and both men cried at the grave, one of them because he had lost his mother, the other because all the money was spent and he knew he would never again scrape together that much money, enough to travel to the West with his son. Yet for ten years he had lived and worked for nothing else. After that he went with his son to the station a few more times and they took the narrow-gauge to Kattowitz, and there, at the big station, they studied the signs on the trains, Warszawa, Berlin, Kraków, Łódź, Praha, Breslau, Brześć n. B., Poznań, but nowhere did they see a train to Cologne, it must be very far away.

The dream that his father had implanted in him faded, but he had never forgotten it entirely. Leo Maria tried to make a reality of it in a different way. After he had found work at Ballestrem's he had himself transferred, first to Beuthen, then to Gleiwitz, and he had hoped in time to get to Oppeln or Breslau, or perhaps even to Berlin — Ballestrem's was everywhere. But then Valeska Piontek had married him and made a photographer out of him, and now he hoped that his son, that Josel would perhaps one day make the dream a reality, but before he got married. For it was the women of this black earth who coaxed potatoes and turnips from even the most clay-filled soil, who bathed in the dirtiest rivers, who with their prayers transformed the ugliest churches into cathedrals, and blessed the black earth that enslaved their men: *Darz Panboczek tej czarnej ziemi!* or: *Gegenwart sei diese Erde!* They could say it in both languages. He hated this land, yes, he hated it, and he was glad that it would soon receive his cadaver, it was good for nothing else. The poor people dug their corpses into it and the rich dug coal and ore out of it, that's the way it was, yes, it was.

32

VALESKA CAREFULLY WITHDREW her hand from Leo Maria's hot, sweat-dampened one and put it in her lap. She yearned for something, but was still searching for what it could be, perhaps something as simple as sleep, perhaps something dangerous, like a dream, perhaps just the closeness of another human being, though not of that man whose skin she had just touched. She rubbed her hands together, and it sounded to her like paper rustling. She sensed that he sucked in strength from everything he touched; perhaps, after lying in bed for three years, he could only survive by holding them tight and using up their energy, hers and Irma's, Josel's and Halina's, and his sister Milka's too. He lay there like an octopus, his chest swelled up and sank down again, and his tentacles groped around in all directions under the covers, and although she was afraid he might ask about Josel, it puzzled her that he had not already done so. He was busy readying himself for his new victims, Milka and Willi, or the new *Pfarrosch,* who had already visited him twice and had first anointed him with oil and then predicted a rather long life for him. Valeska could not imagine how she would manage without him, but perhaps he could be persuaded to get up and be carried to his studio; now that so many men were being called up, they'd be looking for a photographer, and now that the County Magistrate was dead, she could have the garden cottage remodeled; he could continue his photographic experiments there. She regretted what she had done to his photos that time, but every time she began to talk to him about it, he faked a coughing attack, and now, she thought, was probably not the right moment either.

He had been on the way then, as so often, to photograph his towers, and she had been photographing some people in the studio when she discovered the enlarged photos behind the canvas, bigger than any she had ever seen. In all the photos there was nothing but himself, Leo Maria. Valeska herded everyone out, they did not have to pay, she herded them out and locked herself in, and examined the photos again and again. Only Leo Maria, always and everywhere, his face thirty, forty, fifty times, each in different light, in various closeups; now just the eyes, then just one of them, then his nose, his mouth, once the little wart to the left of his chin, and then his body, in numerous positions, different each time: a closeup of his shoulders, his chest, navel, knees, his feet, his back, his sex. Again and again she tried to imagine why he had done it. Why hadn't he photographed her, or one of the children, or a dead bird, a mounted butterfly, a flower — why never anything but himself? She could not understand it, she could not fathom it, her imagination was not rich enough to do so. Imagination was something for rich or for very poor people; throughout her whole life she had always had to think of the next step, she would have made no progress otherwise.

Valeska sat there with the photographs strewn about her, her emotions reeling between fascination, shame, excitement, terror, delight, shock, anger, curiosity, disappointment, despair. She did not know why he had done it, but now she knew that she had never possessed this body. She had gotten a sharp knife from the kitchen and stabbed into each photo, slicing them up or shredding them, and she wondered why she had not finally stabbed herself,

when Leo Maria came home, I hid. I waited until he had gone into his studio, I went into the next room, held a cup against the wall and listened. It was very quiet in the room, he didn't call out to me, he didn't pray, he didn't cry, he didn't scream. After a while, he began to smash the camera, I could tell at once by the sounds he was making, but I didn't know how to stop him. Perhaps I didn't want to stop him. Only later, but not until much later, did I go to him in the studio when it was quiet again in there, I wanted to ask him, "Why did you do that?" very calmly, in a superior way without showing my feelings, but instead he asked *me,* in his calm, cold, neutral voice: "Why did you do that?" and he added just as matter-of-factly: "You did not comprehend, there was no reason . . . You didn't understand me . . ."

He walked past me, he didn't strike me, although I had expected him to, indeed hoped he would, maybe that would have saved us, but he didn't do it, he simply walked past me, without saying a word. After that he never set foot in the studio; later he went to bed and simply never got up again, he made me feel that I had grasped *nothing* about him.

Maybe he was right. Valeska went to Archpriest Pattas and confessed to him, and the Archpriest told her to recite ten Our Fathers. She did so, but she had never before been so much aware that there were things even in her own life which could not be expunged from her memory by confession, or penance, or remorse.

33

Valeska and Leo Maria fell back into a dream in which they collided and then rebounded, as if each were possibly on a different planet, when the white sky exploded. A few shots had rung out before, short and crisp, as if to make the stillness even more intense, but then the noise of the artillery broke out, muffled, ponderous explosions, which reverberated for a long time, until they were relieved by fresh ones; in between was the short, metallic barking of the flak. Valeska threw open the window; the white sky was spread out uninjured. She was not afraid, the sounds came from far away, as if through cotton. There were no birdcalls from the trees in front of the house today.

"That's the war," Leo Maria said.

Valeska stared out, she wanted to discover fire or smoke or solace somewhere, but she saw nothing. This war had arrived with sounds.

"To judge by the noise, there's shooting along the entire border," Valeska said.

"Is that the Poles?" Leo Maria asked.

"What do you mean? That's our side." She said it almost with pride in her voice.

"Is everyone in the house?" Leo Maria asked. He was not so sure whether it was only "our side"; for the time being, perhaps, but it could soon be different, after all the two sides were only a few kilometers apart from each other. "Shut the window now," he said to Valeska. "I have to be careful, with my cough." Perhaps he just wanted to shut out the sounds in that way, or to push them further away from him.

Valeska listened to the artillery fire. "So that's why they came to get the Sergeant," she said. "They already knew the war would be starting."

She said nothing about Josel. She was counting on him turning up at any moment, she had been counting on that for quite some time. But now that it was light outside and the war was beginning, he would have to come home. She wondered whether she should begin saying a rosary for Josel anyway, secretly, of course. Or for the County Magistrate. She would rather not talk about what had happened to the County Magistrate. She had already devised a response if Leo Maria should ask. One day, very soon, she would tell him: He moved away. To Zernik. Or to Sosnitza. Or to Ratibor.

There was a knock at the door, and Halina came in. Her headscarf had slipped off, her stringy hair hung down on both sides, her whole body was trembling, and she pressed herself against Valeska. "*Wojna,*" she said, "*mój Boże, to jest wojna. Oni się powyrzynają. Zdrowaś Maryja, Matko Boża, módl się za nami, grzesznymi, teraz i w godzinie śmierci naszej. Amen.*" (War, my God, it's the war. They'll wipe each other out. Holy Mary, Mother of God, pray for us now and in the hour of our death. Amen.)

"Come, let us pray, for everyone," Valeska said, and went with Halina into her bedroom. There the two women knelt before the house altar with the Black Madonna on it. "Let us pray for all those who will lose their lives in this war," Valeska said loudly, so that Leo Maria could hear her through the wall.

Halina cupped her hands and held them before her face. "*Oszczędz, o Panie, naszą wieś Chlodno w tej wojnie, zachowaj nas wszystkich!*" (Oh Lord, spare my village, Chlodno, in this war, spare us all!)

Valeska thought of Josel, she thought of the County Magistrate, she thought of Irma, she thought of Heiko, she thought of her brother. And what she had to say to her God now, she preferred to say so softly that no one could understand.

Through the wall she heard a barking, waxing and waning cough. She made the sign of the cross from left to right and arose, leaving Halina alone at her devotions. Actually, she wanted to change her clothes, but postponed that until later. Passing his room, she saw Leo Maria through the open door, he was leaning halfway out of bed, his head hanging over the bowl. Andreas was kneeling at the foot of the bed, his face pressed into the covers as if to keep all noises away, those in the room and those outside. Andreas must have told him that Josel hasn't come home, she thought immediately. After all, he couldn't have known that she had kept it from Leo Maria. *Muj Bosche,* she didn't know how she would reply if he asked her about it. For a moment she considered simply leaving the house and going to search for Josel, and it occurred to her that she had thought of doing so more than ten times that night, but she probably would not be able to muster the strength now to go alone. Maybe she could go with her brother Willi. Valeska went to the stairs and then down them, and a strange music accompanied her on the way to the music room.

She would have prayed for Leo Maria too just now, except that she had not thought of it. But instead of calling on Him, it was better that she call on the doctor and perhaps the Archpriest too; everyone in town was awake now anyway.

By now all the other guests in the house had gathered in the music room. When Valeska entered, they leaped to their feet, crowded around her, and bombarded her with questions. When they realized that Valeska's answers could not dispel their worries, they returned to their seats and their fears. Lucie (Lanolin) sank back into the big armchair and comforted her blind son, Frau Hupka sat down stiffly on the couch, her children clambered up beside her and froze into porcelain figurines, old Krupniok remained propped against the wall. As they listened to the explosions, they wanted to be prisoners in a dream called war, and only gradually could they concede that the dream had become a reality.

Valeska went to the telephone and lifted the receiver. She hesitated for a moment, it seemed to her that she would damage this web of artificial sounds by speaking loudly and in a natural voice into the device. She opened the door to the terrace to let in the sounds from outside.

Valeska called her brother first. She let the phone ring a long time, for she was determined now not to spare anyone, but there was no answer. She didn't know whether to be reassured or upset. At the Hotel Upper Silesia they told her that, due to the situation . . . no information could be given on the telephone, none whatsoever. This reply made Valeska rack her brain: could the

Poles have penetrated into the town? She could not believe it. Besides, the Führer had always said that no enemy soldier would ever set foot on German soil. She grew hot nevertheless. But perhaps only because all the others were staring at her.

Valeska dialed the doctor's number. She let his phone ring a long time, longer than her brother's; a doctor, after all, *has* to be at home. She waited until a sleepy voice answered. Valeska was surprised by this, she could not imagine that the doctor had not yet noticed that a war was going on. So she began, somewhat confused, by excusing herself, but the voice interrupted her and explained that the doctor no longer practiced; now a sales representative, the former Doctor Sedlaczek was out of town. Valeska thanked the person and hung up. It was striking how many people were out of town these days, or had sent their children away. Count Ballestrem had sent his wife and children to a spa, Bad Reinerz, almost as soon as they had returned from the Baltic. And the Thonks, whom she had invited to the reception, had just set out on a "cultural trip" to Saxony, which they claimed to have been planning for four years — now, of all times.

Valeska decided to call the rectory. There too it took a while before anyone came to the phone. Finally the assistant priest, Jarosch, answered and inquired assiduously about her husband's symptoms. But Valeska was not to be deterred. She expected something other than medical support from the Church, it must not depend on whether he was spitting blood now and how much. And again she was surprised when Jarosch informed her that he did not want to disturb Archpriest Pattas at such an ungodly hour.

Valeska could not imagine that a single person anywhere in town remained undisturbed, not even the Archpriest of the congregation of Peter and Paul. Therefore she demanded a visit for her fatally ill husband, Leo Maria. She caught herself dramatizing his illness in ever more agitated words, and when the assistant, thus swayed, finally promised her that the Archpriest would come, the feeling came over her all at once that she did not care whether Archpriest Pattas, Assistant Priest Jarosch, or Curate Mikas came. She hung up.

Valeska went upstairs.

34

In the meantime Halina had taken her place again at Leo Maria's bedside. She was trying her best to light a stick of incense with first one match, then another, until it began to glow. Halina pursed her lips and blew at the smoldering dot, straining her eyes to watch the green smoke curl up. She did all this with a care and devotion which indicated to Valeska that lighting the incense was not the only thing that mattered to her.

Leo Maria propped himself up and patted the sweat from his face with a towel. The coughing spasm eased a bit.

Valeska had stopped in the doorway. "He'll be here right away," she said. She said it so softly that no one heard her. Besides, she did not know herself who would come first, the doctor or the priest. Perhaps both were needed. She watched Leo Maria take a bottle from the nightstand, unscrew the cap, and hold the bottle to his nose. He sucked in the smelling salts, first through his left nostril, holding the right one shut, then through the other. Now Leo Maria lay back, peaceful, tired from his struggle; he breathed deeply, and his lungs filled with air and with green smoke. And Halina adjusted her breathing so that it merged with the rhythm of Leo Maria's.

Valeska was too tired for this game. Still standing in the doorway, she asked, "When did it begin? I mean, the war."

Only after a while did Halina answer. "It was ten to five. I know exactly, I was looking at the clock."

"Downstairs everybody is awake," Valeska said. "They're gathered in the music room. Maybe you should make them some tea. Two heaping spoonfuls. And rinse the teapot first with boiling water." Oh, maybe she should do it herself, nobody in this house knew how to make tea as well as she did.

Halina knew that this was only a pretext to oust her from the place to which she had more right by now than the other woman.

She would have liked to stay there a while longer, maybe even to the end. At the very least she wanted to stay until her inner protest against this command had faded. Then without uttering a word she relinquished this preferred spot.

Halina keeps getting stranger, Valeska thought. And she asked Leo Maria, "Are you feeling better?"

Leo Maria lay there, his breathing labored, but he was calmer now.

"Where is Josel?" he asked.

Valeska had been expecting the question; earlier, on her way upstairs, she had devised an answer.

"He's at my brother's," Valeska lied, stroking Andreas's hair. He was still sitting there at the foot of the bed. Valeska expanded her reply: "I called Willi, I was simply too anxious. They left so late that he took Josel home with him."

Leo Maria was not pious, he was Catholic, and he believed her. But it annoyed him that his brother-in-law Willi was involved in this too. "When will he be here?"

"As soon as things quiet down out there, I think," Valeska said. She picked up the incense burner and blew on it. But she may have done this only because she did not want to look at Leo Maria.

"Why not turn on the radio, there might be a news broadcast, maybe something's happening."

Andreas jumped up and switched on the People's Receiver. At first a buzzing could be heard, then a crackling, then music, a march. "Leave it on," Leo Maria said to Andreas, "just turn the volume down; there may be special bulletins." He paused. "Well, there must be something special happening, otherwise they wouldn't be playing marches at this time of day."

Without wanting to, they listened for a while to a kind of music that did not correspond to their mood.

"We don't know anything at all," Valeska said, this time with the deepest conviction. "They've been shooting for a quarter of an hour, it must be war. Which is what everybody was waiting for, a real war, that's what it must be . . ."

Her face showed how disappointed she would be if the shooting did not develop into a genuine war.

For weeks the radio station and the newspapers had been whipping the people into a frenzy in which everyone hoped to find the solutions to his own problems. And everyone thought, this is a war that will only affect the others.

"I listened to the Polish news last night," Leo Maria said. "They've concentrated all their troops in the area around Posen; from there it's only 240 kilometers to Berlin... Maybe they're going to let our troops cross here and set a trap for us..." He spoke disjointedly. He felt very weak, too, and was beginning to sweat again.

Valeska said, "Our side started it, we have the upper hand. It's always that way." This seemed as simple to her as two plus two.

Airplanes roared by, low over the house, the windows rattled and the noise broke against the walls. The sick man's chin jerked upward, as if someone had punched him. The racket was both thunderous and stirring, it was enough to scare anybody—but the noise soon ebbed away. By the time Andreas opened the window and looked out, only tiny silver birds could still be seen over the Tarnowitz Woods.

"They're already over the border..." Valeska's musings followed the sounds ebbing away into Poland. "Our troops must have marched to the border at midnight. I saw it myself when we were driving back, the square was completely empty, you remember, Andreas, where the anti-aircraft guns were with the camouflage nets, and the tents, and the field kitchens, they were gone, all gone."

"Shouldn't we go down in the air-raid shelter?" Andreas asked suddenly. "We did air-raid drills just before I left Breslau."

Valeska remembered now. They had stacked sandbags against the cellar windows and painted a big white S outside; they had wrapped rags around the ends of broomsticks, fastened them with wire, and placed one of these fire-fighting implements on each floor; they had filled an old tin tub with water in the laundry room and put a box of sand next to it; they had stored a metal box containing gauze bandages, adhesive tape, and iodine at the bottom of the stairwell, and painted a big red cross on it. That was all far in the past, or so it seemed to her. "Not until we hear the sirens," Valeska said. She was glad to have found an excuse.

"I was thinking of Aunt Wera in Königshütte," said Leo Maria. He was not afraid. He would not let them carry him to the air-raid shelter. But he was thinking of the fear Wera and her family were going through now as the planes thundered over them; after all, Königshütte was not far off. Wera was his mother's sister, and he was acquainted with her children, even though they no longer spoke German; he had visited them a few times in Königshütte, and his cousin Tadeusz had come to stay one summer during the school vacation.

"As soon as peace comes, we'll go there for a visit," Valeska said. "It's not so far. Can you remember when the streetcar still went all the way to Königshütte?"

She had uttered the word. Yes, she herself would have liked to know what peace was. "At the reception," she said, "there was talk about what would happen to people who were moving away from here. You know, don't you, Father Nemeczek, for example, the one who preached against the Party and was locked up afterward? The Archpriest told me once that they found a parish for him in Kattowitz. The Church takes care of its own. And the Lustigs, they didn't go to America like the others. You remember Eva Lustig always said that the Führer and all that wouldn't last long, and they wouldn't leave Upper Silesia and home, but would just go across the border, so they would be close by when it's over . . . We've never heard from them since, have we?" Valeska wanted to be reassured that it was not so bad not to have thought about the Lustigs in such a long time. There were things which, in her overtired state, she would do better not to think about too deeply.

"It's a cursed corner of the earth . . . Oh, a cursed earth," Leo Maria swore softly but vehemently. "Will it ever stop, people killing each other on account of this cursed earth? The poor put the seed into this hard, dry Upper Silesian earth, nurture it with their sweat, and the rich take its fruit. The poor go underground and dig in the earth of the Lord, they shovel out coal with methane in their lungs, and the rich sell it. And the poor bash each other's heads in from across a river or across a road or from one forest to another, and the rich divide up the rivers and roads and forests among themselves and sit at the same table. And now the poor are plowing the earth of the Lord to bits with the cannon of the rich . . ."

Valeska reached for the rosary in her pocket. She had never heard Leo Maria talk this way, *muj Bosche,* she was rather shocked. But the words pleased her, even though she had not understood it all; it sounded very biblical to her.

She laid her hand upon his, perhaps that would calm him.

Leo Maria propped himself up on his elbows and continued to speak: "And nevertheless — don't we love this land, this raw, fallow, bludgeoned land, the dirty rivers and the clear brooks, the gloomy green forests and the ugly, filthy, stinking, sad towns, the hot, withering, moaning summers and the cold frost-rattling winters, and in early spring the wild deluge and the salty, icy, clattering wind that comes from Russia, and the waters cascading from the Beskids, the Tatra, and the Altvater with its white, gleaming, endless birch forests; this land with its old fortresses and coarse-timbered churches, with its pilgrims' sites, paths and processions to Calvary, where a Golgotha is made of every hill, looming in the shadow of death . . ."

Oh, that's it then, Valeska thought, he's quoting from the Bible, and that calmed her, otherwise she would have had to assume that he had gone mad. Andreas stared at his uncle; a feverish gaze grew in his eyes.

And Leo Maria lapsed more and more into the tone of an Upper Silesian country priest, no longer knowing what was arising from his memory and what were sentences he had put together more recently: "Land of my Klodnitz, land of my Oder, always we looked toward the West with yearning, that is true, but our soul, O Lord, our soul has remained deep in the East . . ."

Leo Maria was aware that what he was saying must seem quite artificial to Valeska, and if someone else had shouted it, his reaction would have been the same. For him now it was an initially hesitant, then natural, and finally organic progression, the origin and impulse for which lay deep within him, close to his childhood, when as an acolyte he had gone from house to house during *Kollende* with the curate and the sacristan and had given the response: O thou thrice-blessed earth!

"Thou thrice-cursed earth!"

Leo Maria coughed. Valeska shook the incense burner to knock away the ash, and the green smoke intensified and thickened. Only someone in a fever could talk like that. She placed her hand on his forehead, it was burning hot. Sweat was running down his neck. Valeska waited for him to calm down.

"I'm going for the doctor now," she said. It was the only thing she could think of. But she did not get up and leave the room. Perhaps it would have been better after all for Halina to be sitting here in her place. All at once she felt utterly helpless, lost, and superfluous.

Irma was far away, during this night she had removed herself a hundred years from her; she could no longer imagine that she had once been her child. Everything they had lived through together was summed up in two or three anecdotes which she would rather not think about. Only Josel was still important to her. And perhaps her brother Willi.

"Give me the stone," Leo Maria said to Valeska after a while, in a changed voice. She glanced up, startled. She had no longer expected so much sternness from him, not from his voice.

Andreas interrupted them: "Hey, someone's talking on the radio. Shall I turn it up?" He did not even wait for an answer, just increased the volume. A tinny voice came from the speaker:

"The General Staff of the Wehrmacht announces: By order of the Führer and Supreme Commander, the Wehrmacht has taken over the active protection of the Reich. In fulfillment of its mission to crush Polish aggression, German army troops assembled early this morning on the Polish border to launch a counteroffensive. At the same time, squadrons of the Luftwaffe were sent to subdue military targets in Poland. The navy has begun the task of protecting the Baltic Sea. The battle for the rights and freedom of our German brothers outside our borders, which was forced upon the Reich, has now begun. The Polish border provocations will be rapidly crushed. The German offensive will be borne forward into enemy territory along the entire Polish border . . ."

"Give me the stone," Leo Maria repeated.

"The Führer and Chancellor of the Reich, Adolf Hitler, will

address the German people from the Reichstag today at 10 A.M. The speech will be broadcast live by all German stations . . ."

Leo Maria himself switched off the radio.

Valeska dried the sweat from him. She knew nothing about a stone.

He shoved her hand away, harder than he had actually intended.

"The stone there, in the drawer." He pointed to the nightstand.

Valeska's hand trembled a little as she pulled open the drawer.

"No, not the top one, it's in the very bottom drawer," Leo Maria said.

Valeska opened the bottom drawer, which, as she knew, contained only cotton.

"Behind it," said Leo Maria impatiently.

Valeska pushed the cotton forward, and for the first time discovered something else in the nightstand drawer — marbles and dried roots, letters addressed but unsent, dried green myrtle, a child's blue ribbon, a few colorfully painted tin soldiers, many rubber alphabet stamps and, under them, slips of paper stamped in violet:

WE PRAY TO THE SAME GOD
BUT WHOM DO THE NAZIS WORSHIP
CATHOLICS, DON'T LET YOURSELVES
BE ROUSED AGAINST YOUR BROTHERS

"At the back!" Leo Maria said in a hoarse voice.

Valeska was bewildered. She had not expected this. Quickly she put the cotton back over the handbills. She dug around in the drawer nervously and blindly. She discovered a tear-shaped black stone, fist-sized, which looked like polished coal, but when she grasped it she could feel its weight. A cross had been scratched on the stone, somewhat clumsily. The stamps, the handbills — she could still not understand it all.

The sick man cupped his right hand, and she placed the black stone in it.

"I found that on the way to Königshütte, the cross was already scratched into it, I was ten years old at the time. I've kept it with me ever since, and it belongs to me alone, I've kept it hidden from everyone, from my mother, my father, my sisters. Even from you.

"Give it to Josel," he said.

And after a while: "I think I'm going to die soon." It was as though he had brought the sentence from a long way away and it was a great effort to deliver it here intact and intelligible. Leo Maria lay there, and little green bubbles formed on his lips.

Valeska recovered from the confusion into which a simple wooden drawer had thrown her. She steadied herself with the old words: "It'll get better, Leo Maria." This time she really did not know what else to say to him.

"Yes," Leo Maria said, "for months you've had nothing else to say to me. That's your only medicine! You've never understood my illness, you've always thought it was fake, something I was imagining, so you could keep busy with living . . . That's the only reason I went to bed . . ." He wanted to say something more, much more, but a new attack of coughing smothered his words.

Valeska held a fist in front of her open mouth. She watched the spasms seize the white, emaciated, alien body before her. She did not dare to touch him again.

Andreas sat on the floor, staring at the sick man. A kind of clarity entered his face, as if he finally knew why he had come to Gleiwitz; but that could also be an illusion.

Leo Maria spat blood into the bowl. He fell back. His breathing slowed somewhat. "My black stone," he rattled. "From this black earth."

The explosions outside did not stop. It seemed almost as if they were part of the silence they were waiting for now. Maybe they would never stop.

"I think I'll try to sleep for a while," Leo Maria said suddenly, as casually as he could manage. "Leave me alone now . . . Wake me when Josel comes . . . I'd like to hear the speech at ten . . . You would too, wouldn't you?"

Valeska took Andreas by the hand and left the room slowly. It was very simple. She did not even look back. She had thought it would be harder. She paused in the doorway, she was waiting for a signal, but none came, not a sound, not even a groan. She

should have stumbled now, or fainted, or screamed, to postpone
it a little. It was a consolation that he had sent her out. She would
go back in to see him soon, when the Archpriest came. It would
be good if he came soon.

Why did he never show me the black stone?

The old Upper Silesia
.... Border following the plebiscite of 1921

ABOUT THE AUTHOR

Horst Bienek was born in Gleiwitz, Upper Silesia in 1930. He began his literary career as a journalist in Berlin, where he studied with Bertolt Brecht at the Berliner Ensemble. Arrested on a political charge in 1951 in East Berlin and sentenced to twenty-five years' forced labor, he spent four years in the Vorkuta prison camp in the northern Urals before being freed by an amnesty. Since 1956 he has lived in West Germany and continued his career as a poet, essayist, and novelist as well as an accomplished filmmaker. His first two novels, *The Cell* and *Bakunin: An Invention,* and two volumes of poems have been published in English. He is the recipient of numerous literary prizes, among them three of Germany's most coveted: the Hermann Kesten Prize, 1975; the Wilhelm Raabe Prize, 1980; the Nelly Sachs Award, 1981. *The First Polka* is the first book of a tetralogy, the Gleiwitz Suite, which follows the Piontek family circle through World War II. The remaining titles: *September Light, Time Without Bells,* and *Earth and Fire,* will be published by Fjord Press.

ABOUT THE TRANSLATOR

Ralph R. Read is an Associate Professor of Germanic Languages at the University of Texas at Austin. He is a prolific translator specializing in contemporary German fiction. He is the translator of Bienek's second novel, *Bakunin: An Invention,* as well as the entire Gleiwitz Suite.

ACKNOWLEDGMENTS

For information, supplying material, and help on this book, the author wishes especially to thank: The Institute of Contemporary History, Munich; The Spiegel Archives, Hamburg; Tadeusz Nowakowski, Munich; Stanisław Sopicki, London; Alexander Rupp, Ottobrunn; Heinz Friedrichs, Munich; Luzie Gaida-Krolow, Darmstadt; Ludwig Schweda, Dortmund; Toni Weigand, Sommerhausen; Irmgard Wieczorck-Sabais, Darmstadt; and many others.

The italicized quotes from Korfanty are from E. Sontag, *Adalbert (Wojciech) Korfanty.* Supplement to the Königsberg Yearbook, Volume VII, 1954. With cordial permission of the "Göttinger Arbeitskreis."

Robert Lehmeyer translated the selections from Eichendorff's poetry.

The map on page 324 is by Dieter Höss, from *Oberschlesien in 144 Bildern,* Rautenberg Verlag, Leer.

The typefaces used in this book are Galliard Roman and Italic, a contemporary adaptation by Matthew Carter of Robert Granjon's dynamic 16th-century design.
Printed on acid-free paper and bound by Edwards Bros., Inc., Ann Arbor, Michigan.